LADIVINE

Also by Marie NDiaye in English translation

Three Strong Women (2012)

Marie NDiaye

□ ▪ ◉

LADIVINE

Translated from the French by
Jordan Stump

MACLEHOSE PRESS
QUERCUS · LONDON

First published in the French language as *Ladivine*
by Editions Gallimard in Paris, 2013

First published in Great Britain in 2016 by

MacLehose Press
An imprint of Quercus Publishing Ltd
Carmelite House
50 Victoria Embankment
London EC4Y 0DZ

An Hachette UK company

Copyright © Editions Gallimard, 2013
English translation copyright © 2015 by Jordan Stump
Copy-edited by Dominique Buchan

A CIP catalogue record for this book is available
from the British Library.

ISBN (TPB) 978 0 85705 335 0
ISBN (Ebook) 978 1 84866 603 0

2 4 6 8 10 9 7 5 3

Typeset in 12/16½pt Roos by Patty Rennie
Printed and bound in Great Britain by Clays Ltd, St Ives plc

LADIVINE

SHE WAS MALINKA AGAIN THE MOMENT SHE GOT ON THE train, and she found it neither a pleasure nor a burden, having long since stopped noticing.

But it happened, she could tell, for no more could she answer without a second thought to Clarisse when, rarely, someone she knew took that same train and called to or greeted her as Clarisse, only to see her stare back in puzzled surprise, a hesitant smile on her lips, creating a mutual discomfort that the slightly flustered Clarisse never thought to dispel by simply echoing that hello, that how are you, offhandedly as she could.

It was this, her inability to answer to Clarisse, that told her she was Malinka the moment she got on the train to Bordeaux.

Had that been the name she was hailed by, she knew, she would immediately turn her head — had someone spotted her face or recognised from afar her slender form, her always slightly unsteady walk, and called out: "Hey there, Malinka, hello."

Which couldn't possibly happen — but was she sure?

There was a time, now long gone, when, in another city, another part of France, girls and boys called her Malinka because they knew her by no other name, and she had yet to invent one.

It was not out of the question that a woman her age might one day accost her and ask in delighted surprise if she wasn't that Malinka from her past, from that school and that city whose name and look she, Clarisse, had forgotten.

And a smile would come to Clarisse's lips, not hesitant but bold and assured, and she would be neither puzzled nor surprised, though she would most certainly not recognise that woman who claimed to have known her when she was Malinka.

But she would recognise her own name, and the way the last syllable hung in the air, trailing a wake of promises, of happy anticipations and unspoiled youth, which is why, at first, she would think there was no reason to allow any awkwardness between her and this old schoolfriend she couldn't recall, and why she would do her best to match her joyful expression, until she remembered the danger that came with consenting to be Malinka again, if only now and again.

What she would have to do then, she didn't dare even think.

The brusquely turned back, the scowl of feigned incomprehension, these went far beyond the timid violations of civility and good manners that a resolutely inoffensive Clarisse Rivière could even consider.

She sat in the train, eyes fixed on the window, on the specks and tiny scratches she never saw past — such that she would have been hard put to describe this countryside she'd been travelling through for years, once a month, one way in the morning, the other in the evening — and trembled uneasily as she imagined having to hold herself back should someone call her Malinka.

Then her thoughts wandered, little by little she forgot why she was trembling, though her trembling went on and she couldn't think how to still it, in the end vaguely putting it down to the vibrations of the train, which, beneath her feet, in her muscles, in her weary head, chanted the name that she loved and despised, the name that filled her with both fear and compassion, Malinka, Malinka, Malinka.

It had not always been easy, when her daughter Ladivine was

small, to make this covert trip to Bordeaux, spend a part of the day there, then be home early enough to arouse no suspicion.

But she had always succeeded.

Of that she was neither proud nor ashamed.

She had done what she had to, and would go on doing it until one of them died, and for that she had dug deep into her reserves – meagre, she knew – of intelligence, ingenuity, strategy.

She sometimes thought she had none of those talents, or had lost them over the years, and yet somehow she drew on what she didn't have and came up with a workable system, perfectly suited to the situation.

But of that she was neither proud nor ashamed.

Like an animal, she did what she had to do.

She had no opinion on the matter, no emotion, only the stubborn, immovable, almost innate conviction that it was her twofold responsibility to act and to keep it a secret.

And when, arriving in Bordeaux, she set off on foot for the Sainte-Croix neighbourhood, always sticking to the same streets and the same sides of those streets, it was less the obligation of secrecy than her self-imposed duty never to weaken that kept her from taking a taxi, or later the tram, where some regular might someday spot her, speak to her, ask where she was headed, which Clarisse Rivière, who in this city was Malinka in spirit and incapable of falsehood, would have answered with nothing other than the truth.

"I'm going to see my mother," she would have said.

That she might have to speak such a sentence was unthinkable.

It would feel like a failure, in the one place where failure could never be forgiven or forgotten, or turned into a simple mistake: her very mission in life, which had no other purpose, she told herself, as resolute as she was evasive, than never to let it be known that Clarisse Rivière was Malinka, and that Malinka's mother was not dead.

She turned into the dark rue du Port, stopped at the house's sooty walls, used her key to get in, and there, in the damp entrance, opened the door to the flat.

Her mother, who knew she was coming, since Clarisse Rivière visited on the first Tuesday of each month, nonetheless always greeted her with the same cry of mock surprise, tinged with an unsubtle sarcasm:

"Well, what do you know, it's my daughter, at last!"

And this had long since stopped grating on Clarisse Rivière, who realised it was simply her wronged mother's way of expressing what, deep down, must nonetheless have been affection and even tenderness for her, for Malinka, who in another life bore another name, unknown to her mother.

Of Clarisse Rivière Malinka's mother knew nothing.

But she was not so ignorant as not to know she knew nothing. She pretended not to suspect that on the first Tuesday of each month her daughter Malinka came to her from an existence more structured and less lonely than the one she had sketchily described for her long before, in which she seemed to live and work only as a sideline, solely for the sake of coming to visit her mother each month.

Clarisse Rivière knew full well that, if her mother pretended to be taken in, if she never tried to learn more, if it sometimes even seemed that her mother wanted at all costs not to know, it was because she understood and accepted the reasons for her secrecy.

Understanding them was one thing, but how and why should she accept them?

Oh, for that, for her mother's mute submission to what should have enraged her, Clarisse Rivière would never, as long as she lived, have time enough to be grateful, with a gratitude dulled by resentment and despair, and to atone.

And yet what she had done was her duty.

It wasn't a thing to be justified or explained or excused.

Clarisse Rivière did not think it enough that her mother, having understood, and feeling the sorrow and sting of that understanding no-one could be told of, had become a difficult woman, petulant and volatile, often hurtful.

She wanted her more difficult still; she wanted her hateful and furious.

But the thing itself could not be spoken of.

It could only be expressed by irritability and antagonism, and even then only so long as these outbursts didn't bring them too near the words of the thing that could not be spoken of.

Clarisse Rivière sometimes thought that those words, were they spoken, would kill them both – her because what she had done, what she thought it her duty and obligation to do, could not be forgiven; her mother because to the humiliation of this treatment would be added the humiliation of having known and accepted it, albeit with anger and spite.

Those words would have killed them, Clarisse Rivière sometimes thought.

And if not, if they survived, they could still never see each other again.

That was Clarisse Rivière's greatest fear, having to give up her visits, even though they brought her only a mixed pleasure – moving, but heavy with frustration and sadness.

She entered the flat to find her mother standing near the window, where she had been watching for her to appear on the narrow pavement, and now her mother was no longer striving to put on a convincing display of surprise.

She simulated it in a lazy and half-hearted way, and perhaps, more generally, with a weariness of the very idea of performance, of the act in which they were both trapped for all time.

Clarisse Rivière would each time sense the depth of that weariness, and it would trouble her fleetingly.

Sometimes she thought they had finally burned through the many layers of silence and shame that did not so much separate as envelop them, and so had arrived at a sort of sincerity, assuming that sincerity can wear the costume of an actor.

It was, she sometimes thought, as if they could see each other perfectly through their masks, all the while knowing they would never lower them.

For the naked truth would not have allowed itself to be looked at.

"Well, what do you know, my daughter at last," Malinka's mother would sigh, and Clarisse Rivière no longer felt aggrieved, she smiled with a two-sided smile she never showed anywhere else, at once loving and circumspect, open and suddenly reserved.

She kissed her mother, who was short, thin, prettily built, who like her had slender bones, narrow shoulders, long, thin arms, and compact, unobtrusive features, perfectly attractive but discreet, almost invisible.

Where Malinka's mother was born, a place Clarisse Rivière had never gone and never would go – though she had, furtive and uneasy, looked at pictures of it on the Internet – everyone had those same delicate features, harmoniously placed on their faces as if with an eye for coherence, and those same long arms, nearly as slender at the shoulder as at the wrist.

And the fact that her mother had therefore inherited those traits from a long, extensive ancestry and then passed them on to her daughter (the features, the arms, the slender frame and, thank God, nothing more) once made Clarisse Rivière dizzy with anger, because how could you escape when you were marked in this way, how could you claim not to be what you did not want to be, what you nevertheless had every right not to be?

But anger too had abandoned her.

Never once, in all those many years, had Clarisse Rivière been exposed.

And so, as she aged, anger too had abandoned her.

For never had Malinka been flushed out from the cover of Clarisse.

Her mother lived in this single ground-floor room, paid for in part by Clarisse Rivière, its window barred to potential burglars by a black grate.

Meticulously maintained, dusted and cleaned every day with maniacal fervour and fussiness, the room was cluttered with dowdy furniture and gewgaws, unstylish and discordant, but, in their gaudy, varnished jumble, their outlandish accumulation in so confined a space, producing an effect of unintended but friendly peculiarity, something almost clownish, in which Clarisse Rivière somewhat queasily felt right at home.

She would sit down in a crushed velvet chair with tulle-draped arms while her mother stood close by in a pose of wary, defensive stiffness that no longer had any reason to be, a lingering trace of a stance from a time long before, when there was good cause for it, when Clarisse Rivière was trying to free herself of her duty, her mission – oh, she struggled to remember it, she had wanted to have nothing more to do with Malinka's mother, and that was very wrong.

Her mother knew there was no reason now to fear being abandoned or fled from, but in the first moments of Clarisse Rivière's visits she maintained a vigilant pose, pretending to stand guard over her daughter who might still make a run for it, and in reality watching over herself, in her stubborn, groundless refusal to let herself go, doing her best to incarnate for them both the dramatic figure of dignity irreparably wronged.

There was no need for that, Clarisse Rivière thought, and there never had been.

She knew, like her mother, that the wrong was there all around them, in the simple fact that Malinka was visiting her mother in secret because she had decided this was how it would be, and because once that scandalous decision was made there was no going back.

There was no forgetting the wrong, and no need to express it with scowls, with a special silence that, striving to be meaningful, freighted that wrong with a slightly embarrassing lyricism.

So thought Clarisse Rivière, who nonetheless felt her tenderness grow on seeing her mother so inept in her attempts to seem grander than she could ever be.

Because Clarisse Rivière's mother was only an ordinary woman who would have been perfectly happy with the little joys of a routine existence, who could scarcely be blamed for not always knowing what gestures to make on the stage that her daughter had forced her to tread.

She herself, Clarisse Rivière, sometimes stumbled.

Sometimes she began to weep in her armchair, sudden, violent sobs seemingly set off by some run-in with her mother, but which had no other cause than a brutal attack unleashed by her own conscience.

How can people live this way? she often wondered. Surely this was not how things were supposed to be?

But always, even through those tears, her fierce, stubborn, old resolve rose up to show her that things were just as they had to be, and so certain was that blind, stupid resolve, that savage determination from her youth, that Clarisse Rivière never feared she might abandon it in some moment of weakness.

Only in her actions did she falter.

She saw herself sobbing in the armchair, she thought herself mediocre, she thought herself an ordinary woman and a heavy-handed actress like her mother, except that for her there was no excuse.

Then it passed. That moment of weakness was quickly forgotten.

There remained only the slightly surprised memory of an awakening of the stubborn will that was her master, which she could not imagine defying. Why that power deep inside her had stirred she soon forgot.

Every first Tuesday of the month Malinka's mother was handed enough money to keep her in groceries until the next visit, and a little present as well, a bottle of eau de Cologne, a fragrance burner, a genuine linen dishtowel, because she also passionately loved things and surprises, and Clarisse Rivière, who took a great deal of trouble to come up with all this, could not bring herself to give her only a curt cash-filled envelope.

Then they would sit down in the tiny kitchen and eat the dish made by her mother the previous day, veal Marengo or shepherd's pie or cabbage stuffed with duck confit, and her mother alone spoke of her previous month's doings and the few people she had met at the local old ladies' club, and the fact that Clarisse Rivière could say nothing of her life, and that her mother could ask her no questions, no longer hung heavy between them.

There was a time when, on concluding her own account, Malinka's mother would fall silent and wait, discreetly desperate, mouth half-open, fixing her forlorn gaze, pleading but hopeless, resigned, on Clarisse Rivière's face, which turned so cold and so hard that her mother had to look away.

And a dense, painful silence settled in, until Malinka's mother went back to a story, any story at all, some trivial happening already recounted, and gradually Clarisse Rivière's face became itself again, the sweet, devoted, distant face that Malinka's mother knew and loved, so like her own.

Her mother no longer fell into those trances, no longer felt that pointless, misplaced anticipation.

Rarely now did she raise her eyes to Clarisse Rivière's delicate, almost unlined face, knowing she would find only the placid, remote, reserved benevolence that never appeared on her own clenched, tortured face.

She no longer asked for anything, hoped for anything.

Her turmoil itself was only a hold-over from times long gone by, when she still yearned to know of the life her daughter Malinka lived, despairing of ever finding out but not yet accepting that she never would.

Clarisse Rivière sensed that her mother had stopped wanting to know, that it was too late, that the equilibrium she had finally found in silence and uncertainty would have been upset with nothing much gained.

Because, unaware even of Richard's existence, or Ladivine's, what would she now get out of seeing their pictures, two adults, two strangers who knew nothing of her?

Would those smiling faces, those faces open to life, perfectly ignorant of Malinka's mother's existence, and happy in that un-awareness, would those faces not have seemed to her hostile, hurtful in their obvious contentment?

Her mother would pour the coffee, then say, "I'll get dressed," which meant she was going off to change from the jeans and sweat-shirt she wore at home to the beige polyester slacks and checked or floral blouse she wore only to go out, transforming the young woman she still seemed to be, her limbs straight and slender beneath the tight, faded cotton, into a homely, modest, proletarian lady of middle age.

And the more the years went by, it seemed, the deeper the gulf between her youthful appearance at home, which never changed, and the outmoded, humble look she put on as she readied herself to go out, as if the truth of age and anxiety had to come out somewhere, if not, thought Clarisse Rivière, the most essential truth, the truth of her very life.

Then they set out on a walk through the streets of Sainte-Croix, their itinerary always the same.

On running into an acquaintance, Malinka's mother would pause, slightly stiff, slightly solemn, like a very mildly put-upon queen, just long enough to swap a few inconsequential words with the other woman, who, though not unused to the sight, couldn't help casting furtive, curious glances at the cold, still Clarisse Rivière, that neighbour or belote partner knowing this was the daughter though she had never been introduced, and by instinct obeying the unspoken rule against asking questions, and even against visibly noting that standing by the mother was an unspeaking woman with a white face.

Malinka's mother thus led her daughter through the streets like the object of her dishonour, a dishonour too great even to be looked on, and Clarisse Rivière alone knew that, on the contrary, her mother had always taken an unstinting pride in her, and that it was she, Clarisse Rivière, who was walking arm-in-arm with the object of her shame.

They headed back to the little flat, already abandoned by the sunlight in mid-afternoon.

There Malinka's mother set about making some complicated treat, a pie, a batch of petits fours, sweets, impossible to finish before Clarisse Rivière had to be off, as she knew perfectly well, pretending to think that her daughter would be delighted to take that dessert with her, pretending to believe her daughter would like nothing more than to take it home, where there lived, in all likelihood (and her, the mother, no doubt guessing at this, because she knew nothing, because she had no idea who and how many shared her daughter's life), people who had no idea she existed, to whom her daughter would have to lie about the origin of the pastries and pretend to believe it.

Clarisse Rivière had long since stopped resisting.

She sat down in the velvet armchair and watched, quiet, indifferent, almost apathetic, as her mother fretfully bustled around her little kitchen, rummaging through the cabinets for dishes and ingredients.

And she, Clarisse Rivière, looked at her without seeing her, quiet, indifferent, sitting motionless in the velvet armchair as if she were the old woman here, and cold, impersonal thoughts fluttered through her untroubled mind.

She mused that she could easily bring home a cake made by her mother, for neither Richard nor Ladivine, not untrusting or curious by nature, would think anything of it.

But she never would, she thought.

She would sooner drop the cake into a bin at the station.

Malinka's mother was not to insert herself into Clarisse Rivière's life in any way, and she alone, Clarisse Rivière, was permitted to eat the food she prepared, the cake of tears, the anger-laced biscuits.

She alone, Clarisse Rivière, for the bitterness passed through her without swelling inside her.

And so she let her hard little thoughts wheel through her mind like shrieking birds, and her mother couldn't hear them. She was busy, and could not hear a sound.

Her mother would chatter on, commenting on what she was doing, and as the minutes went by and the time neared for her daughter to be going, she would launch mechanically into an unvarying speech whose purpose, long ago, was to inspire her daughter Malinka's pity for her lot, and the pity never came, but the words stayed the same, recited without passion or hope, as if out of fidelity to that long-ago woman, that Malinka's mother who thought herself capable of moving her daughter, and whose memory had to be preserved and respected.

Oh, but the pity did come, thought Clarisse Rivière, and it was still there, still throbbing and hurting the instant she saw her mother again.

But there was nothing that pity could do, because her will was stronger.

She would leap to her feet, making her mother start in surprise.

She would snatch up her bag and rush out as always, scarcely embracing her, leaving her mother there with her hands covered in butter or flour, and nothing could stop Clarisse Rivière from leaving, but she thoughtfully acted as if a surge of affection might still stop her, as if she had to fight back that surge, when in fact once out of that suffocating room she felt only relief, she felt almost happy, brought back to life by a rough, impatient pleasure.

The next visit, a month away, seemed so distant as to be hypothetical, and, although in reality never seeing her mother again would have tormented her cruelly, it was a delectable dream, and it filled her with a savage, dizzying joy.

Because she could easily choose never to come back, she could unburden her life of her mother's clandestine existence without anyone knowing or condemning her.

She fled down the street, half-running, giddy, she might almost have let out a whoop, and the blood pounded in her temples.

She felt as though she had eluded the threat, as though Clarisse Rivière had once again slipped free of Malinka's mother before she could change her role and, exploiting a lapse in her daughter's vigilance, turn into the mother of Clarisse Rivière.

But no, Malinka's mother was still just what she was supposed to be, and all was well.

She could forget that old woman, the Sainte-Croix neighbourhood, the dim ground-floor flat, oh she could forget that crazy old woman.

Once, lost in that bliss, she had fainted at the end of the street, one of her shoes coming off and tumbling into the wet, filthy gutter.

Someone helped her up and accompanied her to the nearest pharmacy.

And there, as they sat her down in a chair, pressed a damp cloth to her forehead and asked various questions concerning her health, her identity, as a gentle hand slipped her shoe back onto her foot and a shudder of disgust ran through her at the feel of the damp grit on her bare skin, she vowed never to let this happen again, so close by her mother's, strangers talking to Clarisse Rivière, trying to get something out of her, wanting to call someone to come and take her home, and her merely shaking her head in reply.

She had to overcome that frenzy she always fell into when she walked out on Malinka's mother, which, at its peak, could knock her unconscious.

She had deep, inexhaustible reserves of coldness inside her.

She would dig deep into those reserves as she walked out of the door, she told herself.

But her excitement always won out, and she couldn't help skipping like a child on the way to the station, her skin warming, flushed with the repressed fervour consuming her, the joy and the sorrow of freedom.

She vaguely remembered the days when her name was Malinka, a memory in black and white, with a fleeting impression of static faces, as if from some obscure old movie in which Malinka and her mother were not the leads but supporting actors for another, more interesting girl and her mother.

14

It seemed to her that she had known from the start, before she could even speak or understand, that Malinka and her mother meant nothing to anyone, that this was how it was and there were no grounds for complaint, that they were lowly flowers, their existence unjustified, lowly flowers.

Clarisse Rivière had forgotten the name of the town she grew up in, as she had forgotten virtually everything having to do with the life of that girl named Malinka.

She remembered only that it was outside Paris, and that at the far end of a cobblestoned courtyard near the railway line were two very clean little rooms, and one was hers, its window just above the ground, moss roses growing between the paving stones, and her mother slept in the other, on a fold-out couch crammed in next to the stove.

That girl Malinka had a room to herself, because she was a pathetic flower but also a sort of princess, oh, so alone, so unrecognised.

She was a princess to her mother, who often called her just that, Malinka's mother who was a queen to no-one but only a servant, and came to seem one in that girl Malinka's eyes.

"My princess," the servant called her, more than she did "My daughter," and in this that outwardly unremarkable Malinka surely found cause for vanity, thought Clarisse Rivière, although or because she was so very alone.

Her mother worked as a servant and cleaner in the city, in offices or spacious apartments, sometimes bringing Malinka with her, warning her not to touch anything, and she worked as a servant and cleaner at home, in those two rooms occupied by an unsung princess.

Her deep shyness vying with her self-importance, that girl Malinka followed the railway line to school, and nothing distinguished her from the children she joined in the playground, except that she had neither friends nor enemies and never spoke to the others.

She was better dressed than most, because her mother sometimes brought home beautiful skirts with scarcely a sign of wear or elegant little dresses given to her by the women who employed her.

Her mother, who was a servant, didn't look as if she should be her mother, she who was a princess.

And so one day, when her mother came to pick her up at school and one of the other girls, addressing her for the first time, asked with a frown of surprise and disgust who that woman might be, Malinka replied: "My servant," and felt she was speaking a very great truth.

All trace of repulsion vanished from the girl's face, and she let out a satisfied and admiring little "Oh!"

And Malinka realised that disgust would have spread to this girl's very body, she would have trembled and recoiled in a sort of horror, if Malinka had answered "My mother", and that would have been what's called a lie, since lies were ugly and repellent things.

Even alone, even colourless, a princess must never lie, Malinka must have thought.

That was how Clarisse Rivière imagined it.

Even as a child, that girl Malinka was already a lost cause.

But Clarisse Rivière also knew it was true, as Malinka had come to suspect early on, that their existence meant nothing to anyone in this world, not because those two, the servant and the beloved daughter, inspired any dislike, but simply because no bond linked them to anyone.

Malinka's mother had no parents or brothers or sisters, although she had never said so and never brought up the subject, although, Malinka later told herself, there might well be, in that hazy province she came from, people who claimed to be her parents, her brothers, her sisters.

But since Malinka's mother never spoke of them she and Malinka were embraced by no-one's affection and solicitude, and when the door of the tiny house at the far end of the courtyard closed behind them, after dark, with the rain pounding and rattling the windows, Malinka felt they were as alone as if the whole world around them was dead, since in that world there was no love sent their way, since no tender or anxious words were ever exchanged about them, the servant with her thin face and long, restless limbs, and the girl she called her daughter, all appearances to the contrary.

When she thought about it, which she rarely did, that was how Clarisse Rivière imagined it: no doubt that girl Malinka scarcely knew how to talk, words too rarely had a reason to come out of her mouth, and as if that were not enough she feared they might come out with the servant's slight accent, which she would have found mortifying.

And so she said nothing, or, now and then, answered her mother, who asked her about school only on principle and had no idea what kind of reply to expect, so foreign was that world to her.

Malinka's mother was a naturally, inexplicably cheerful woman, Clarisse Rivière remembered.

She used to come home weighed down with shopping bags, bedraggled by rain and exhaustion, then turn on the gas under a nice piece of meat, with a side dish of vegetables she'd peeled and diced before work that morning, and her cooking always filled the air with a gentle, healthy, delicious aroma, as cheery as she, Malinka's mother, who hummed, did a few little steps of a sliding dance on the tiled floor, never complained, never grumbled.

And so Malinka, unable to compare her life to other children's, never having been invited to anyone's house, long believed that her mother held no grudge against life or any living soul, not even the man whose face she looked for in crowds, whose figure or walk she relentlessly sought to find in every man she saw, but that irrational hope lay hidden behind words of lucidity and patience and so never appeared as what it was.

"Your father's got to be somewhere," Malinka's mother would say in her calm, melodious voice. "We'll run into him someday."

And this seemed so indisputable that Malinka never waited for her mother to come home without thinking she might appear on the arm of the man who had been waiting close by, calm and patient as she, waiting for her to find him at last, and that man, with a musical voice and no trace of an accent, that man who could not show himself until his face had been spotted in the street, would be her father, her glorious father.

He was the only person Malinka's mother ever spoke of, and she did so profusely, worshipfully, even if, Malinka came to realise, her descriptions were never particularly precise, and she seemed to know little of this eminent man's life, past or present.

And so Malinka never felt his good will watching over them.

Unlike the naive servant, she knew that the man's thoughts never turned to the two of them, that he might well know nothing of their existence, for they were only two lowly flowers.

"Your father's a fine man," Malinka's mother often told her. "You know, he's really, really nice. He has beautiful chestnut hair, and always wears it neatly combed back. He has a car. He might have a new one by now. I'll bet he's found a terrific job, too."

Malinka felt no contempt for those hopes.

She felt no contempt for the servant, her peculiar mother.

But she could not help believing that her mother might indeed one day come home with her grocery bags, her rain-soaked overcoat and the lush-haired man who had jubilantly allowed her to see his face in the street.

And were that man ever to come to pick her up at school, she knew, she would not be afraid to call him her father.

No disbelief or disgust would curl the other girls' lips on hearing that truth or that lie, she wasn't sure which, but maybe if it was a lie her own lips would stay pressed tight in a bitter crease.

Her face would be like her father's, that man who until now had let his love rain down on heads other than hers, leaving her and her mother in their vulnerable aloneness.

But, she understood, her face would be like her father's.

And another realisation hit her at the same time, with the violence of a thing long known but never quite grasped, now abruptly revealed in all its simplicity: being that woman's daughter filled her with a horrible shame and fear.

Oh, she was also ashamed of her shame and her fear, particularly because she was painfully aware of her mother's fragility, she who had no protector to rely on and was nonetheless wary of no-one.

But stronger still was her repugnance at the thought of letting it be seen, even simply in the street, on the bus, before strangers, that she was the daughter of a woman of no consequence.

From her earliest childhood, Clarisse Rivière would realise, she had done nothing but spurn her mother, and her mother had pretended not to notice, and perhaps had not noticed, in a way, having found another explanation for her daughter's coldness than the simple scandal of her own appearance, her own face.

Because that was a truth Malinka's mother would never be able to bear.

And Malinka knew it, in her despairing, furious love, because she could read the servant's emotions better than the servant herself.

She pulled away from her mother, renounced her before the world, seeing no other way.

She always took care to walk at some distance from her, and she was delighted to see that the people around them never included them both in the same knowing glance, the impenetrable woman and the beautiful teenager with the thick, curly hair, inherited, the marvelling servant assured her, from her many-splendoured father.

At fifteen Malinka heightened the natural pallor of her face with wan make-up.

She felt a boundless, remorseful, stifling tenderness for the servant.

She secretly watched her in the evening, studying her face, looking for any flaw in her good cheer, any decline in her confidence that she would one day bring about the appearance of the man who, the servant was sure, had once loved her, and loved her still, but did not know where to find her.

It was up to her, Malinka's mother, not only to recognise him in the street, but also, in some mysterious way, to make him appear, and for that small miracle the force of her own assurance might be enough.

Her good cheer never faltered, but over time it turned slightly abstract, as if her habitual happiness and optimism were making her forget she had fewer reasons for those emotions than when, as a very young woman, newly arrived here with the child in her belly, she founded her hope and her joy on the enchanted sense that every single day this land worked miracles more unlikely than a longed-for face's sudden appearance in the midst of a crowd.

Her good cheer was waning and weakening, but not her will to be cheerful, and the servant's gaze turned a little unfocused, very discreetly unhinged.

She asked Malinka, then in senior school, the same question as when she was in primary school.

"Did you work hard today? Is your teacher happy with you?"

And then she broke into a smile, as if already sure of the answer, not even listening to whatever Malinka might say, not even noticing that sometimes Malinka said nothing at all, and Malinka never took this amiss, understanding that in order to keep a light heart her mother's contact with reality had to be cautious, buffered by distraction and a faint, unwavering rapture.

The women who employed Malinka's mother seemed to think highly of her.

She often brought home little presents, and once one of her employers came for coffee. Malinka and her mother made pound cake and fresh fruit salad for the occasion.

The woman ate happily, casting inquisitive but kindly glances at Malinka. She complimented her on her hair, her cool complexion.

"She has her father's hair," said Malinka's mother, mechanically, ardently, then drifted back into the self-satisfied, benevolent, misty, slightly dim look that left her ever more rarely.

The woman suggested that she and Malinka move into a flat she owned, three rooms on the ground floor of her building.

"You'll find it so much more comfortable," she said, glancing with dismay around the little room that served as both the kitchen and the servant's bedroom, "and, you know, I won't ask much."

Almost apologetically, she added:

"It would make me so happy to help you."

An odd agitation suddenly came over Malinka's mother.

She stood up a little too fast, bumped into the corner of the stove.

Upset and subtly furious, she seemed stunned that this woman had failed to see who she was, her, Malinka's mother, whose goals were plain, who had only one ambition.

"I can't leave," she finally mumbled. "I mean, really now, I can't leave."

She let out a scandalised, mystified little laugh, eyebrows raised, staring almost wild-eyed at the woman, who smiled uneasily and put on a waiting face.

The servant composed herself and sat down.

And she settled once more into a quiet beatitude, like easing back into a warm bath of delusion, thought Malinka, and this frightened and troubled her even more than the absurd indignation that had brought the servant to her feet.

"You understand," said the servant in an exaggeratedly reasonable tone, undermined by her suddenly stronger accent, "we're waiting for someone, and this address is his only way of finding us, so, you know, what's he supposed to do if we leave? It's simply out of the question."

For the first time a harsh, hostile anger rushed to Malinka's head. After the woman had gone, she cried out, astonished to find herself daring to talk to the servant this way, daring to bring up what she spoke of only by allusions:

"Well, what do you know! News to me! So now he has our address? He's known our address these past fifteen years, and you always said he had no way to know where we lived, and he's supposed to come looking for us when all this time he never bothered? And that's why we can't go and live in that woman's flat? That's why we're staying in these two miserable rooms?"

Still sitting, the servant looked utterly defeated, and Malinka wished she had kept her mouth shut.

Her anger drained away, she tried to put on a smile, horrified to think that her smile probably looked like her mother's, similarly impersonal, misplaced and maddening.

Malinka's mother began to wring her hands.

"I'm not sure anymore," she said hesitantly. "You're right, your father must not have our address, how could he? There was no way to tell him before I went away, I didn't know how to get hold of him, I thought I'd have no trouble finding him here, I thought it was big, but not that big. But if we move, then . . ."

"No, let's not move," Malinka murmured. "Things are fine right here, let's not move."

The servant genuinely seemed to believe, with that part of her reason Malinka could not fathom, as elusive as it was maddening, that a change as major as moving would be a betrayal of the faith that sustained her in her nebulous, desperate, but confident quest for one particular face among so many others, and what did she have to help her go on imperturbably hoping but that faith, with its rituals and commandments, the very first of which was the prohibition against making any change to the life that had seen her certainty sprout and flourish, what did she have but that absurd faith, thought Malinka, to make her seem grander in her own eyes?

Oh, maybe the servant's heart was not as unassuming as it seemed.

Her pale, smooth-skinned daughter Malinka hoped so. She fervently wanted arrogance, pride and self-indulgence to play some part in her mother's ridiculous optimism; she hoped she was just a little blinded by her vanity.

Because, while the servant was well thought-of and evidently even liked by the women who employed her, Malinka realised there were others who did not know her, who did not always treat her so well.

Malinka had never seen her mother insulted to her face, but couldn't help fearing, every day, that she might be.

Everything about her, her hopes, her fears, her embarrassments, was a betrayal of the servant.

And so she ardently hoped that a sheath of outrageous self-importance and even inflated, unwholesome pride shielded her mother's heart with its crystalline hardness, but she doubted it, so humble did the servant continually prove, and, when she wasn't talking about Malinka's father, so serene and so sensible.

She doubted it.

Rather, she assumed that her mother patiently endured every affront, and that only her placidity, her slight withdrawal from the world, her inexpressive smile, helped her dismiss such things as of no great importance.

When Malinka began to slip, in senior school, she effortlessly hid it from her mother, not fearing her anger but wanting to spare the servant any needless anxiety, because there was little her mother could do for her, and less in that realm than in any other.

She took to signing her school reports herself, never showing them to the servant, who seemed to forget there were such things as marks and school reports.

Clarisse Rivière would later recall that Malinka had struggled to keep up, that she had hung on as best she could, but her downhill slide, starting when she was eleven or twelve, and at first gradual, uncertain, soon took on the sudden brutality of a verdict handed down at last after a long wait.

She would remember that as a very young girl Malinka had ambitions, that she'd sensed doing well in school would bring her nearer her goals than her mother's ignorant, vague solicitude, that she'd conscientiously striven to be worthy and, in a sense, perfect.

But she attained only perfection's outer form, as if the great efforts she made had hidden from her the real reason for those labours.

And so she became a model of application and assiduity, a pupil so polite that her presence was often overlooked.

She turned in her homework on time, written in an elegant and readable hand, always a little longer than required so no-one would suspect her of slacking off, although before so serious, so painfully intent a young face not even the sternest teacher would ever think such a thing, and those scrupulous pages, reeking of labour and terror, always drew a regretful, understanding comment and a below-average mark, inflated a little all the same, out of indulgence, in recognition of everything that was sad and unfair in all this.

Malinka never quite seemed to grasp what was asked of her. She understood only the express or unspoken laws governing the relations between pupils and teachers, which she obeyed in a mix of keen pleasure and arduous rigour, and so literally that she could have vanished without anyone noticing, so absolute was her submission to the image of a pupil who was nothing more than a pure receptive mind.

But what they were trying to teach her never found its way into her head, or lingered only a moment, then quickly faded.

At home, she sat for long hours at her desk, slightly befogged, trying in vain to connect her memories of the class with the sentences written down in her impeccable notebook.

She vibrantly remembered every detail of the teacher's face, expression or dress, and she could picture herself, too, as clearly as if she were studying a photograph, and she deeply admired that girl looking up at the blackboard with her perfectly attentive face.

But what had been said in that classroom, what that exemplary girl had heard and thought she understood, she could not remember.

She read and reread what she had written, and it meant nothing to her, had nothing to do with anything she had managed to hold in her mind, itself nothing more than a magma of words and numbers, misshapen ideas, incoherent hypotheses, which she ended up laboriously dredging through in search of something she could use, almost anything, to fill up a page with her beautiful roundhand.

Sometimes she forgot she was writing sheer nonsense and abandoned herself to the pure pleasure of the presentation, she spent ages scripting the date, or marking off the margins, or crafting elaborate capital letters, all curlicues and meanders.

That lowly, solitary Malinka made what she called friends at school, but, looking back, Clarisse Rivière would understand that in truth it was only a little clan of two or three teenaged girls that Malinka had somehow slipped into, almost unnoticed, less in the hope of remedying her loneliness than in obedience to the rules of school life as, with her keenly observant instinct, she understood them.

She knew absolutely nothing about those girls, who never spoke of personal matters in her presence and seemed to tolerate her only out of curiosity, perhaps wondering at their own tolerance, their own curiosity.

Malinka wished she could learn everything about them, as if she might thereby understand her own existence.

But, although she was so discreet that gazes slid over her with nothing holding them back, those girls perhaps unconsciously limited their talk to everyday things whenever she came near, and it felt to Malinka as if a sudden pall had been cast by the vague mass of her body, like a grey cloud blotting out the sun.

But she grew used to that, since it was her place.

She must also have known that by abandoning all hope of closeness with these girls she could consider herself excused from having to invite them home, into the house of the servant.

Because that was out of the question.

The thought of her friends meeting her mother sent her into spasms of almost amused revolt, so laughable was the idea.

She was nothing short of speechless when a teacher one day asked to meet Malinka's mother, looking faintly uncomfortable, as if, she told herself, all the more perplexed in that he could easily have let the matter drop there, he already knew it would never happen, because it was absurd, absurd.

But she said nothing, only nodded with her usual gravity.

He brought it up once more, she nodded once more, and then never again did she look up at him with a face hungry for approval.

And she avenged herself for that teacher's blundering indelicacy by handing in work untouched by her ardent desire for majesty, assignments without ornament, no curlicues, no coloured underlining.

She turned sixteen during the summer holidays, and never went back to school.

Clarisse Rivière would always remember the time that followed with a mix of incomprehension and terror, for it seemed that chance alone, or obedience to the whims of circumstance, guided the life of that girl Malinka, that empty-headed girl, as she often heard people say at the time: she's a sweet girl, hardworking, but empty-headed.

The only fantasy she would gradually assemble involved the quarantining of her mother, the dismissal of the servant.

And since she could only subscribe to the judgement that she had nothing in her head, feeling that head fill with the one single preoccupation of expelling her mother would fill her with the idea that she, Malinka, was a despicable person, her mind closed to everything but disloyalty.

The servant accepted Malinka's decision to leave school without a word, perhaps because it seemed not a decision but a natural passage from one state to another, like a change of season.

One morning, as she was leaving for work later than usual and Malinka was still lying in bed, she observed in her calm, unsurprised voice:

"You're not getting ready for school."

"No," said Malinka, "I'm not going anymore."

And that was all. The servant nodded and went off to catch her bus.

The next day she told Malinka she had found her a job, babysitting for a family whose apartment she sometimes cleaned.

And Malinka went off to look after the children, and neither liked it nor didn't. Sometimes, coming home in the evening, she caught sight of her mother on the bus, and pretended not to have seen her.

The servant discreetly refrained from calling out.

Her face turned resolutely to the window, Malinka felt her mother's gentle, placid, ever-benevolent gaze on the back of her neck, and the furious pity she felt at this shook her like a first taste of strong drink, so numbed were her feelings, so dulled her thoughts.

She looked after the children all through the summer holidays, which they spent with their parents on the Bay of Arcachon.

This was her first time away from the suburbs of Paris, but standing by the ocean she felt as if she had seen all this before.

The following summer, back in Arcachon, she suddenly told herself that nothing was forcing her to go home to her mother.

This idea must have been inching along unbeknownst to her since the summer before, so indistinct that she never spotted it among the charmless, colourless thoughts peopling her mind, because she was not surprised to find that idea blossoming inside her, nor to know precisely what she would have to do, both to protect her independence and to put herself out of reach of her mother's love and attentions.

Nothing said she had to go on being the servant's daughter forever, she told herself.

A cold feeling filled her with this, but she knew that was more easily fought off than the desperate tenderness that coursed through her heart when she thought of her mother, even more utterly alone than she.

A few days after the children went home to Paris she handed in her notice and caught a train for Bordeaux, where she took a room in a modest hotel near the station.

She found work waitressing in a café. She wrote to her mother, telling her not to worry, and received no reply.

She now went by the name of Clarisse. There had been a Clarisse in her class at school, with long hair that fell down her back like a silky curtain.

"Hey Clarisse! Come here a sec, would you?"

"Be right there!" she answered in her happy, slightly muted voice, which she worked to make faintly breathless and interrogative, thinking people found this particularly attractive.

She always shivered in delighted surprise on hearing her new name, and although in the beginning she sometimes forgot to answer, that was all over now, and the person she had become, this Clarisse with the beautiful, iron-straightened chestnut hair, with the smooth, breezy, winningly confident face, could not hold back a twinge of refined, pitying contempt for the person she was just a few months before, that clod who called herself Malinka and did not know a thing about make-up, that clueless girl with the hunted look in her eyes, that lowly girl who called herself Malinka.

She stopped laying tables and hurried towards the kitchen, where her boss was calling for her.

"So annoying – your co-worker just phoned to say she won't be in for lunch, so you'll be all on your own," the woman said in an anxious tone, eyeing Clarisse's slight frame as if to measure that delicate body's endurance.

But she knew, because Clarisse had already shown her, just how sturdy and steadfast that frail girl truly was, and Clarisse knew that she knew, and her cheeks flushed with pride and excitement.

How she loved those days when the other waitress didn't come in, when the lunch shift was entrusted to her alone! She had to be even more efficient, resourceful and charming than usual, even livelier and friendlier, both to keep the customers happy, make them think they had not waited as long as their watches said, and to memorise the orders and never forget anything someone might ask for out of the blue.

Striding lithe and quick through the dining room, she felt triumphant, exceptional: not many waitresses could handle thirty-five customers without a single complaint, and never get the wrong order or table, nor come across as anything but visibly and sweetly unruffled.

Apart from the cook and her boss, no-one knew what a challenge that was, for the challenge was precisely never to let a customer see anything was amiss, and this made Clarisse, that clever girl, all the prouder – that clever girl that she had become! That important, irreplaceable girl!

The platefuls of grilled black sausage with mashed potatoes or roast chicken with chips she balanced on her forearms made her vaguely and constantly nauseous, and sometimes, as she strode over the tiled floor in her crêpe-soled slip-ons, her disgust brought gushes of burning acid up from her stomach, but she smiled and talked, greeted and thanked in her quavering, muffled voice, with her exquisite manners, making this Saint-Jean neighbourhood brasserie feel like an upscale restaurant, and everyone found her so delightful, so charming.

And the regulars knew her by name and casually called her Clarisse, as if there were nothing odd about a girl such as her bearing that marvellous name.

No-one ever guessed she had once been a lowly Malinka; no-one.

The customers loved Clarisse, so pretty, so good-humoured, so good at her job, they loved her youth, which was never arrogant but innocent and fresh, and Clarisse felt it, and strove to seem even more perfectly unaware of the privilege of being so young, so pretty, so perfectly healthy and trim.

And it was true, being young and beautiful meant nothing to her, in the end. She wanted only to be an irrefutable Clarisse, with her straightened hair, her pale eyes, her breathy voice rising at the end of each sentence.

When evening came, in the room down the street that she rented from her boss, she thought back over her day, pictured the moves she had made, the way she had stood, tried to find things that could still be improved on.

And whereas in school her fanatical urge for perfection had nothing to focus on but the protocols of existence and the parameters of her homework, here she could finally use her intelligence and acuity to the full, aiming to do her job in the most exemplary way, leaving, in her conduct as in her sensibilities, nothing to find fault with.

She paid vigilant attention to the tiniest details. Every morning she studied her face and hands, checked and rechecked her black skirt and beige blouse for spots, pulled her hair into a tight plait and coiled it around her head.

Then she powdered her face to give it an impersonal air, to ensure that it showed no sign of fatigue, and no emotion other than those – joy, pleasure, enthusiasm – she so wanted to display.

How she loved her face in the morning, powdered, serious and inanimate!

That was how Clarisse was meant to be in the eyes of the world, a wonderful girl whose good points were all you ever saw, because there were no bad ones. And how that Clarisse was loved!

*

That day, then, she handled the lunch shift alone, and as usual she never slipped up. And her name rang out from one end of the room to the other: Clarisse, when you get a moment! Hey, Clarisse, more bread! Bill, please, Clarisse!

All of which left her slightly dazed and, for the first time, wearily apprehensive at the thought that in just a few hours her evening shift would begin, that she would have to smile and be cheerful, and hear her name rebounding off the walls like a wild bouncing ball, the beguiling name that was now hers but which, when she was tired, she sometimes feared she might not recognise.

Now and then she was awoken by that nightmare: the restaurant was packed, the customers all calling at once for Clarisse, and she standing there dully, aware they meant her but unable to move her limbs because she wasn't hearing the magic word, and when finally someone began shouting "Malinka!" she went back to work, smiling and light-hearted, but by then the room had emptied, oh, how she dreaded that stupid dream.

But she could easily fight off exhaustion, bleariness, the weird feeling, disagreeable but short-lived, that she could half see the silver letters of her new name shooting through the room.

What she found infinitely harder, that day, as the lunch rush was winding down, was seeing her mother come in, the servant, just as she remembered her, her slim hips sheathed in a checked woollen skirt, her putty-coloured raincoat, the thick, woolly mass of her short hair, and her small-featured face, her distant, placid demeanour, the servant herself coming into the brasserie with the same steady, unhesitant gait as if she were entering her own flat, in the house at the far end of the courtyard.

Although she must surely have seen Clarisse just as Clarisse had seen her, their eyes did not meet.

Motionless behind the bar where she had just made a cup of

coffee, Clarisse watched as her mother looked around and finally chose a table near the window, indifferent or oblivious to the suddenly closed, dull, frowning face of the boss, who gave Malinka's mother an almost outraged stare, then lowered her eyes and carefully studied her watch, as if, looked at long enough, it would end up consenting to help her turn out that unwelcome customer, that lowly woman.

Lunch was nearly over, and yet, Clarisse noted, a torrent of reassuring thoughts rushing into her mind as she turned towards the big clock on the opposite wall and stared at it vacantly, it was only 1.30. Often they had customers coming in until two.

She felt her boss's gaze on her burning cheek.

"That coffee's getting cold."

The voice itself was cold, metallic, indignant. Slowly Clarisse turned to look at her, and her boss's wary, surprised eyes locked with hers, and what she saw in them, something Clarisse knew nothing of, made the woman strangely calm, though her mood was still as ugly as ever.

"You'll have to make another cup. And then you can deal with her over there," she said, nodding towards Malinka's mother.

Venomously, making sure Clarisse was still looking into her aggressive, suspicious eyes, she added:

"I hope she's not going to make a habit of coming here. That wouldn't be good for business."

Clarisse brought the customer his coffee. Then she ambled to the table where her mother sat quietly waiting, her hands lying flat in front of her, her face turned to the window and the grimy, sunlit avenue, which rumbled with every passing truck.

Clarisse was moved to recognise her mother's tiny, delicate ear, decorated with the little gilt ring she was never without.

She staggered under her anguish and sympathy.

She had written to the servant several times, less out of duty or compassion or in hopes of reassuring her than to safeguard her own freedom, fearing her worried mother might try to have her tracked down, although asking anyone for anything would not have been like the servant at all. She always signed her letters "Your daughter, M".

And now her mother was looking up at her with her stoical face, her lower lip quivering all the same, her two hands no longer flat on the table but turned palm up in an instinctual gesture of supplication, a plea for mercy.

We do not know what earned us this treatment, we don't understand it, those two calloused, tapering hands eloquently said, but what does that matter if it's enough to ask for forgiveness, we can do that and more, whatever it takes, nothing would be beyond us . . .

And Clarisse waited, deeply aware of her dead-eyed gaze, a stranger's gaze, strictly professional, but feeling her own lip tremble no matter how hard she tried to keep her mouth tightly, severely shut.

"I'd like, maybe, a sandwich?" the servant murmured questioningly.

"Yes?" Clarisse answered in the same tone, because she had adopted that style of seeming never quite convinced of what she was saying, viscerally grasping all the mystery and charm this created, especially combined with her hushed, artificially muffled voice.

But it was not right to be charming the servant, or seeming mysterious before her pleading eyes. Fleetingly, Clarisse was ashamed of her enticing voice, that display of something slightly seedy in the life she now lived.

"I'll bring you a ham sandwich," she whispered, and her mother nodded, lost, smiling her mirthless smile, wanting to add something to mark the occasion and then giving up, as if warned off by some internal adviser more reasonable than herself, as if cautioned that this Clarisse was not exactly her daughter Malinka, that what was happening here was less a reunion than a first meeting.

She looked away, docile and adrift, seeming suddenly intimidated.

Clarisse pivoted on her heels, finding a reflexive and habitual pleasure in the feel of her nylon-clad thighs rubbing together.

Her boss was watching, with her sharp, slightly sardonic, experienced gaze.

Realising the other customers had all gone on their way, Clarisse felt her face turn red, though she knew her mother had not spoken her old name, Malinka. It was almost two o'clock, the café was often deserted at this hour.

But her boss knew, she knew everything, and she looked at Clarisse without hostility, with a sort of hard sadness, as if Clarisse had betrayed her, but she understood why and accepted it, then her eyes once again swept over Clarisse's long legs, narrow hips and thin face, now probably not to measure that slender body's resilience but to gauge its likeness to that other body, the body of the black woman sitting up very straight in her chair near the window.

Once her mother had eaten her sandwich and paid her bill, Clarisse took her down the street to the little room where she lived.

She usually devoted these idle hours before the dinner shift to a nap, and she found herself longing to slip into her bed as usual, knowing her mother would think nothing of it, would simply settle into the room's only chair and wait in unbroken silence. But she felt too much on edge even to think of sleep. And the thought that she might nonetheless have managed to drift off, forgetting the servant's presence, and then waking with nothing resolved, to the revelation that her mother was there, patient, immovable, that thought humiliated and irritated her at the same time.

How she wished her mother could be happy far away, without her, how she wished that, wrapped up in her own happiness, she might lose all interest in her daughter Malinka, how she wished, even, that her mother's love were monopolised by other children! How the weight of that unused love exhausted her, that vast but humble, mute love, irreproachable! How her own sympathy weighed on her!

"You can take off your raincoat," she said, with some sharpness in her voice, seeing the servant meekly keeping it on out of politeness.

Her mother carefully folded the raincoat and laid it on the bed.

She stood there, her discreetly approving gaze surveying the neatly made bed, the clean linoleum, the white sheer curtains at the window, and although she said nothing her silence was neither heavy nor eloquent, it was the peaceful, homey silence that once reigned in their house, the foundation of their entente.

And now that strange silence was taking hold of the room, filling it with hominess and melancholy. Frightened by the dullness she felt coming over her, Clarisse rebelled. She sternly reminded herself that freedom was a duty, as was anger, even unjustified.

"So," she said in a voice without affection, "this is where I live now."

"Yes, it's nice. It's clean."

"You must have a train to catch."

Oh, that involuntary pleading tone in her voice, as if she had to feel endangered by any decision Malinka's mother might make!

She felt as though she were falling into a deep hole of clinging, entangling emotions, of limp devotion and degrading resentment, with her mother looking on from the edge, untouched, superior and pure in her unwavering love.

A hint of a sincere smile creased the servant's lips. Was there not, Clarisse thought in disbelief, a kind of triumph in that smile?

Nausea washed over her, so powerless, so mediocre did she feel.

And she knew what her mother was about to say before the words reached her ear. Living so far away, she thought herself out of range of the servant's limitless feelings, but now they were coming back at her, and a shadowy fear that had been vaguely blighting her happiness for months was beginning to come true.

"I have a little room of my own," her mother said serenely, still smiling that sincere smile, a smile not of triumph, Clarisse realised, but of perhaps childish pride.

"What room? Where?" She groaned in dismay, her dismay having already understood and anticipated the answer.

Her mother took a step away from her, no longer afraid or intimidated but suddenly exultant at this evocation of her boldness and ingenuity.

She gestured broadly towards the window.

"Over that way, by the docks. I had all our things brought down. The old house is empty, but I gave them notice, I won't pay for nothing."

"What about your job?" Clarisse almost shrieked.

"I'm not worried. I'll find something here."

The servant looked at Clarisse, and now there was no trace of a smile or sign of delight on her face, only an air of sad understanding and, just beneath it, a sort of passionate resolve, a broader stubbornness that, for a moment, was not even about Malinka, or love, or the miseries of absence. Caught off guard, Clarisse felt her agitation fade a little.

Painfully aware of her weakness and unworthiness, she nonetheless stammered:

"You always said you'd never leave, because he . . . because my father might come looking for you."

Her mother winced as if lashed by a blow mysteriously landing in a place she thought she could no longer feel. Distant and ethereal, her old smile came to her rescue.

"I'd rather be close to you," she said simply, with no great ardour, merely acknowledging a fact.

Digging into her bag, she took out a piece of paper with her address written on it and laid it on a corner of the bed.

When the time came for Clarisse to go back to work, the servant walked her to the brasserie's door, then gave her a quick kiss and strode off with her sprightly step, the step, thought Clarisse, sour and annoyed, of a person who would never want to intrude on anyone's life.

The decision that showed Clarisse she could be just as fanatically obstinate as her mother first took the form of a discreet coldness, little different from the coldness that filled the air when they lived together, two lowly flowers.

Then, with that decision carefully weighed and resolved, it struck Clarisse that there was no need for coldness, any more than distance or feigned dislike, that what was needed was in fact devotion and tenderness, as if to make up for the heartlessness of the decision.

This was a liberation for her, and a sincere relief, because she had no wish to be cruel.

Here, then, began a happy time for the servant.

Every two or three days Clarisse came for dinner in the little flat her mother had rented in an alley not far from the port, and she was cheerful and chatty as she'd never been before.

She talked about the brasserie – which she would soon leave, without telling the servant – and inflated the customers' fussiness to enliven her anecdotes. And the fact that she never spoke of herself, never told of her existence away from the brasserie, never mentioned a name, an address, her mother most probably didn't notice right away.

Only when a dubious feeling drove her to ask a few unobtrusive questions did she realise she would never get an answer, and that, in any case, Clarisse's vague, trivial words left no room for any specific enquiry.

Clarisse never pretended she hadn't heard or understood. Her self-respect recoiled at the thought of deliberate, shameful playacting. She stared at an invisible point slightly behind her mother and sat in silence with a pleasant, patient, vaguely apologetic look, letting a bubble of discomfort swell between them until the servant finally popped it with a forced chuckle or a remark on the colour of the sky, and the mounting disbelief and stinging affliction in that little laugh was not lost on Clarisse, who noted it with some sadness, the calm, immovable, self-satisfied sadness of an absolutist.

Because once her decision was made there was no going back.

Only within the four walls of this little flat did she consent to be the servant's daughter, that girl named Malinka.

And eventually her mother realised this and gloomily accepted it, even if it sometimes mystified her at first, as if she couldn't quite believe such a thing could be happening, that her daughter, whom she'd rejoined and reconquered, and who seemed so cordial, so present, was in fact turning away from her completely, or rejecting her even more violently than if she had pressed both hands to her chest and shoved her beneath the wheels of a passing car.

Sadness and incomprehension put a new, embittered crease on the servant's lips.

Sometimes, when they ran out of banalities and both sat in silence, she burst into a laugh, sarcastic or self-mocking. And Clarisse realised her mother could no longer take refuge in fantasy, in the vague and the impalpable.

She herself so suffered from the pain she inflicted on the servant, who had done nothing to merit this punishment, that a weight settled into her chest and never went away, an alloy of grief and guilt whose volume and mass she felt every minute of the day, crushing her, smothering her.

But once her decision was made there was no going back.

Very soon Malinka's mother took a job with a cleaning service. Her hapless, dreamy mother's longstanding gift for finding work wherever she wanted inspired a certain admiration in Clarisse Rivière, although she suspected that her mother's vacant, infinitely mild air worked against her even as it eased her way, giving the impression, which was in fact true, that she would make few demands as an employee. Her work now was cleaning public buildings, late at night and early in the morning.

"For the first time in my life, I have co-workers," she said, with that voice that gave no clue if she thought this a good thing or not.

Nevertheless, Clarisse had the feeling she wasn't unhappy about it.

"That's good," she was foolish enough to say. "This way you won't be so alone."

"I wouldn't feel alone at all if I had my daughter beside me," said the servant, the bitter crease on her lips.

And it was so clear to Clarisse that she meant "on my side" or "if my daughter weren't my enemy", that in a rare rush of emotion she clasped her mother's hands and pressed them to her face.

But such surges of tenderness and contrition, even the heavy burden of her guilty conscience weighing on her ribcage and forbidding her, wherever she was, to feel fully carefree, none of that could shake her faith in the necessity of her choice, which, when she offered it up to her own judgement in the starkest terms, was to have nothing to do, ever again, with Malinka's mother.

These visits were no more than a tactic for keeping her quiet.

But how she loved that woman, even more now that she was seeing her suffer! How vile, how convoluted she felt next to the servant, who was so light, so clear, so valiant in her attachment! Clarisse knew she'd doomed herself, knew she would one day be punished for abandoning the servant. She did not like that idea, but she was not afraid.

Because once her decision was made there was no disobeying it, even in her thoughts.

She gave up her job at the brasserie and her little room near the station for a job in a downtown café and a one-bedroom flat in Floirac. She couldn't imagine staying on, now that her boss had seen who her mother was, though she never mentioned it again. But above all it was vital that the servant should not know where she worked, not know the address where she slept, just as she had no idea that Malinka was now Clarisse, and that glorious girl, that lissom Clarisse in the clinging black skirt and tight white blouse she wore for her job, that dazzling, expertly made-up girl, always a little breathless, as if she'd been running, stuck close to the walls in the street and looked over her shoulder, again and again, to make absolutely sure that her mother was not walking behind her.

She could not believe it didn't show.

She moved her face still closer to the mirror and a smile came to her lips. So this was what he saw when she leaned in to pick up the menu or put down the silverware, these features, stiff beneath the make-up, these red lips reshaped with the pencil, and nothing more, surely, since she herself could see nothing. And she knew this was the face of a girl in love, and he did not.

How could he?

She smiled, beside herself with pride.

Or maybe he did, maybe he had guessed?

Maybe at this very moment he was pressing his face to a similar mirror, in the mysterious place where he lived, studying his features, the features of a boy in love, smiling as she was smiling, overjoyed, wondering if she'd seen anything?

Maybe at this very moment he was imagining her smiling at her reflection, at once amazed and flushed with pride at what she had become, a girl in love, as if up to now, loving no-one, never thinking of love, she'd been living with an illness, from which she had recovered by the sheer force of her wondrous vitality?

Because that's just what it was, it was a sickness to love only her mother, with an angry, exhausting, guilty love, so unlike her love for the boy, ardent but happy, bubbly and light.

She could almost feel her heart, heavy with the wrong she had done, throwing off that weight even now. So was being a girl in love also a good deed? Could she somehow make up for her cruelty to the servant by her scintillating love for a boy with sincere eyes, with a high, tremulous brow?

That boy was a proud horse, a gentle horse. His slightly damp cheeks twitched just a little, she'd seen it, when he called her over to take his order.

Oh no (she smiled in spite of herself), being in love gave her too much pleasure to be a good deed.

In the mirror she saw her eyes darken and her forehead crease, just as they always did when she thought of the servant's sorrow, but her lips went on smiling, her beautiful lips painted the violent red of an almost happy girl.

She went out into the warm street, tottering a little on the high heels she now wore, which made her legs so long, slender and shapely, and found to her delight that the sight of her reflection in a shop window took her breath away.

That perfectly beautiful girl bore the perfect name of Clarisse, and by a wonderful stroke of luck she was that girl, that Clarisse, whose previous life and old name no-one could guess, for, so smooth and so beautiful, she offered the world the very image of harmony and unity. How lucky to be that girl!

She took the bus, walked a little further on to the café, in the city's stony, proud centre, where the façades were less sooty, and the cobblestone pavements not so narrow, not so cluttered with rubbish bins.

Le Rainbow had broad, glinting windows by which the men in the street could see Clarisse striding through the restaurant on her high heels, a little unsteady but tall and straight, and often she turned towards the window and smiled at those stares, which to her unending amazement confirmed that the perfect girl people couldn't help admiring as they walked by was her.

Maybe, she mused, the boy she loved first came into the café because he had seen her from the street, maybe he'd fallen for her simply on glimpsing that girl whose harmoniousness, definition and serenity Clarisse hoped she expressed. How she would love it if he confessed that he'd fallen in love with her purity!

She began to wait for him as midday neared, unworried, knowing he would come.

And when he did, he found the courage to look her in the eye, which he had never done before, and she looked back, just as frank, just as direct, because ever since she'd fallen in love with that boy she'd lost all trace of coyness, every impulse to look away through lowered lashes.

He sat down at his usual table and she hurried over, indifferent to the other waitresses' arch little smiles.

"Your usual Perrier with a slice of lemon?"

Just four days he'd been coming here, and here she was talking to him like that!

She felt her whole face reaching out towards him in a shimmering of white teeth and sparkling pale eyes; she felt and saw her face giving itself to him like a magnificent lily proudly and trustingly presented, sure of the offering's value, and the flexible stem of her body also bent towards him, under the weight of that luxuriant flower.

Fleetingly, she thought of her mother – that lowly flower from the far end of the courtyard, the awful pity she felt for her.

She recovered her face as one recovers one's composure, she dimmed it, closed it, but not so completely that the shiver-skinned boy wouldn't see it still shining with love for him.

She sensed that he had something to tell her, and then that, lacking the nerve and being so young, he'd thought better of it for the moment.

And so, when she came back with his drink, she took her time at his table, aware of the perhaps excessive hopefulness she exuded, like her own scent, but powerless to stop it spreading around her and perhaps intimidating the boy. But, she wanted to cry out with a laugh, what more did she have to hope for? Just being a girl in love was so good in itself, shouldn't it be more than enough for even the most exorbitant hopefulness?

"I don't think I'll . . . Well, I mean I know I won't, obviously . . . be coming in tomorrow, or the day after, for that matter."

What on earth was he saying, compulsively stroking his bubbling glass, sometimes staring at her in despair, sometimes studying his hands clenched around his drink?

What he was saying she understood, but not quite what it meant.

Still as merry as if he had ventured some subtle joke and she was waiting to grasp it fully before bursting into a laugh, she breathed:

"Yes? So?"

"Well, I . . ."

Desperately, he plunged in:

"Would you like to come with me this afternoon? Because I'm going home, I have to go back home to Langon."

"You want to take me with you?"

He blushed violently, misreading her.

"Forgive me, maybe it's . . . I don't know . . . forward, but I'm not . . . it's just that the idea I might never see you again made me so miserable . . ."

And that teasing hopefulness dissipated at once, replaced by a joy so intense that for a moment it felt like the opposite, like the bleakest desolation, which she would have survived, so well did she know that feeling and its distinctive warmth, and so attached was she to it, as to a faithful companion. Then she realised it wasn't that at all, and she let joy bloom unconstrained in her mind, thrown slightly off balance though she was.

The boy was fingering his glass again, still not lifting it to his lips.

He seemed distraught at what he'd let himself say, and perhaps convinced all was lost.

She forced her face to mirror the happiness she was feeling, the radiant gratitude, forced it to drop its dramatic, dumbfounded look, which, although more eloquently expressive of the depth of her emotion, might give the boy the idea he had shocked and upset her.

"That's wonderful," she whispered. "I've never been to Langon, for one thing, and . . . yes, yes, I want to stay there with you, oh I do, oh yes."

He found the courage to raise his unbelieving eyes to hers, and now, from the serious, stunned, stupefied look on his face, it might just as well have been that she had given him some dire piece of news.

This is how we'll be at our wedding, this is how the mayor will see us when he marries us, so in love that we'll seem like absolute idiots, totally lost, she thought, in time with the familiar radiant carillon sounding noon from the church next door, her lips, finally unbound, stretching into a perfectly fulfilled smile.

Was it then, Clarisse Rivière would later wonder, that she'd first vowed forever to be good to Richard Rivière, a vow that would determine the whole of her life with him?

Because she must have realised, then or just a little later, that there was no other escape from what she had deliberately done to the servant, Malinka's mother, who was never to know of Clarisse Rivière, never to delight in anything good that happened to her daughter, never to broaden her narrow circle to include those her daughter loved most, on whom she herself might lavish her vast, unused love – no, no other escape from that violence, that shame, than the deepest, most indisputable goodness in every other way.

Claiming not to be feeling well, Clarisse punched out and went to join the boy who'd hurried off to get his car from down the street, now waiting for her before the café, engine running.

He took her to her flat in Floirac to pack a few things. Then, on the way to Langon, they spoke of this and that with a spontaneity and an animation that delighted them both, and sometimes made them look at each other, amused and proud and observing them-selves from a shared distance, like parents moved by their children's behaviour.

She stole a glance at him, that boy with the thick black hair, the dusky complexion, the sharp features, and that face, that body, at once slender and solid, seemed in no way removed from her own, seemed in no way to live and move in a space and a manner not yet known to her.

And so she found nothing intimidating in the boy's dense physical presence at her side. Impulsively running her fingers through his hair, she felt nothing new, as though she'd done just the same thing many times before. There was nothing foreign to her, she marvelled serenely, in the young man's physical being. She felt she knew the scent of his skin, the shape of his fingernails, the way his muscles flexed beneath the fabric of his trousers when he braked or accelerated, and she loved it all, she told herself, she loved every fragment of his carnal reality as surely as she knew and loved her own body.

He sold cars for a living, he told her, he worked at the new Alfa Romeo dealership in Langon, and they had sent him to Bordeaux for a four-day training seminar.

"I love cars," he said with a bashfulness she found adorable.

Clarisse was enchanted to find him already wanting to confess his weaknesses and hoping not to displease her too terribly should she happen to harbour some special contempt for car buffs.

He continued in the same vein, as if eager to make a clean breast of all his least charming features: his parents ran a stationery shop in Toulouse, he rarely saw them, they "didn't think the same way", his father was exceptionally prone to anger, it had become too much to take.

He glanced her way, and although trembling inside she gave him an encouraging smile — her turn was coming, and she'd have to lie, the lie to come was already parching her mouth, and what would become of her vow to be good and her promise of irreproachable love if she started out telling lies to the boy she was in love with, so deeply in love?

"You don't have to love your parents, right, if they don't deserve it?" he blurted out, with an emotion so ill-contained that she realised he was revealing a sentiment as difficult to feel as it was to express, and so offering her his absolute trust at its most tender and troubled, his heart laid bare in the cup of his outstretched, trembling hands.

"Of course you don't," she said with conviction.

But, she thought, her throat tightening, suppose your mother more than deserves your love and you don't let her have it, suppose you keep it all to yourself, what to think of a person like that? If you're ashamed of your mother and keep her as far out of your life as you can, what kind of person are you then?

She found herself envying his certainty that he did not have to love his parents, not to mention the fact that there were two of them, supporting each other in their meanness. She then had a vision so brief that she didn't have time to be outraged or aggrieved, but the feeling persisted darkly inside her after she'd forgotten where it came from: the vision of a Clarisse grown old, with no-one left to support her in her meanness, whose children never visited, all too aware of what she truly was.

"My parents are dead, and in any case my father never came forward," she answered in an ugly squawk that surprised and shocked even her.

He let out a sad little "oh", then briefly and tenderly put his hand on her thigh. His fingers were short, but it was a strong, well-shaped hand, and Clarisse gently clasped it and pressed it to her lips, feeling she'd known that hand for a very long time, and could at this very moment, without hesitation or effort, lick every one of its fingers, give them delicate little bites.

"Clarisse isn't exactly my real name, but that's what they call me," she managed to add.

He parked in a little street on the edge of Langon, before an old grey roughcast house, whose upper floor he rented.

The street lay empty and silent in the warm, bright afternoon sun.

Cats were sleeping in the shadowy corners of doorways, and suddenly Clarisse remembered the courtyard of her childhood, the cats much like these, scruffy and thankless, that sometimes came begging for food, and her mother's inexplicable fear of them, almost as deep as her fear of dogs, on the subject of which she'd one day let slip that beneath their skin they contained human beings stricken with a terrible curse. How could anyone believe such a thing? But Clarisse avoided them all the same, and that day she was vaguely unhappy to find a cat sleeping on the house's front step.

She took off her high heels and climbed the stairs barefoot before the boy. Already it felt just like coming home after a few days' holiday!

He had a big room at the top, just under the roof, tidy and white, with a waxed wooden floor. He took her to a window and pointed out the river, sparkling and very green between two houses, and the white sunlight, as if bleached, erased by its own brightness.

Then they stood face to face, not yet daring to embrace but knowing they would, and waiting for that moment with a fervent, solemn emotion, and a patient one as well, because, thought Clarisse evasively, they knew that moment was at hand, so close, and they were lost in proud surprise at what they had already done, running off together far from Bordeaux, and now knew they would soon take each other in their arms and pull each other close, and they waited, dazed with love, fear and joy.

How young they were! thought Clarisse, and she felt a reverence for their youthfulness.

A dim memory briefly came back to her, a night spent with a co-worker at Le Rainbow who took her to his place while his wife was away, with whom she'd made love for the first time, quietly aware that she wanted only to cast off her virginity, which she then saw, she no longer quite understood why, as a burden, and she'd set her sights on that friendly man on the theory that he'd know what to do. And it was fast, cold and conscientious, like an expertly performed operation. And now, before this boy she loved, she was happy to have it behind her.

She saw his high forehead, tanned beneath the luxuriance of his thick, straight hair, his brown eyes slightly veiled by uncertainty (maybe he's a virgin, she told herself in a flood of protective tenderness), she saw his dusky, just barely pink skin, his full lips, the vigorous health of a very young man in the springtime of his life, and she silently mused that she would never love another like him, and silently thought of her existence to come and imagined it wholly devoted to two commandments that were two aspects of one single charge, to renounce Malinka's mother and adore Richard Rivière, but never to fail in even her tiniest duty towards either.

Because, in all that time, she would never once skip her monthly visit to the servant, just as, she thought, she would never break her promise of absolute, passionate love for Richard Rivière.

They married three months later in Langon's town hall, on a Thursday, so it wouldn't seem like a special occasion.

The elder Rivières came from Toulouse for the day, and Clarisse, who hadn't yet met them, thought she could feel the mother's particularly dubious gaze studying her head to toe, with no attempt at discretion.

When their eyes met Clarisse had to look away. The mother paid Clarisse a dishonest compliment on her interesting hair. Asking her maiden name, and hearing Clarisse stammer out the name of the servant as flatly and neutrally as she could, she enquired where it came from.

"From the North," Clarisse mumbled.

And she knew Madame Rivière didn't believe her, and also that, in a spirit of something like tact, Madame Rivière would never speak of it to Richard.

Clarisse found a job as a salesgirl in a clothes shop, then quit it to sign on as a waitress in a newly opened pizzeria.

The work was harder, but she loved taking the stage amid that unvarying spectacle, hearing the furious little music of her heels tapping the tile floor, feeling her arm muscles tense and harden when she brought out the plates, her response perfectly calibrated to the demands of the task, just as she loved the feeling, at the end of a shift, as she sat with a cigarette in the now clean, empty room, of having once again successfully transmuted potential disarray, with the customers pouring in and all demanding quick service, into a smooth and efficient mechanism, so discreet as to seem effortless, of which, with her clacking heels, her youthful muscles, her quick thinking, she was at once the inventor and one of the gears.

She never told herself this in so many words, but she understood her new status made her love her work all the more.

Because she was now Clarisse Rivière, and that Clarisse Rivière had a husband who sometimes came to pick her up at the pizzeria, and everyone could see them together, affable and charming and wonderfully normal, and when they talked about her they would say: "You know, Clarisse Rivière?" never guessing that she might bear any other name or be anything other than she appeared, a simple and ordinary person.

And that awareness never left her as she strode briskly between the tables, the awareness that she was a married woman who would be named Clarisse Rivière until the end of her days, and never again, because now that was all over forever, a very young girl with no link to the world save the painful sense that she didn't legitimately belong to it.

How she loved her husband's gravity, his quiet but stubborn ambition, his uninquisitiveness! The few questions he had asked about her childhood in the suburbs of Paris she'd answered cheerfully and laconically, inventing an existence so peaceful and happy that there was nothing more to say of it. And was that not, in fact, the truth? she thought to herself. Her father was dead by that time, and then her mother died when Clarisse was . . . sixteen? seventeen? She couldn't quite recall.

Once, and the incident soon came to seem as unreal as a dream, she spoke the name Malinka in front of her husband. She might have said something like: "Malinka's mother once cleaned some famous people's apartment, and you can't imagine how filthy they were!" But it might have been another sentence entirely, because, as after a dream, she couldn't recapture it after she'd spoken it, or rather after Richard Rivière told her she'd spoken it.

He didn't bother to ask who Malinka might be, and Clarisse only gave a quiet little laugh.

Eyes flooding with tears, she stared at her husband's shoulder, reminding herself that she could press her face to it whenever she liked.

After many elaborate calculations, Richard Rivière decided they could safely take out a loan, and they bought an almost new house on the edge of Langon.

He never talked much about his work at Alfa-Romeo, but Clarisse understood that his devotion, his patience, the work and reading he did in the evening to learn everything he needed to know about the various finance plans he might offer the customers but also to work up a smooth and persuasive pitch, all these labours, she understood, were aimed at his goal of becoming a sales manager and even, one day, the general manager of his own dealership. He hintingly admitted as much, then never brought it up again.

That reserve was just fine with Clarisse, who took to visiting Malinka's mother the first Tuesday of each month, never saying so but never lying outright.

She simply announced that she would be going to Bordeaux the next day, and Richard Rivière never asked what she had planned, but only smiled in that way of his, which she loved more than anything else, at once tender and absent, as if nothing really interested him but what he had in his mind at that moment, something to do with his work, she imagined.

It did not escape Clarisse Rivière that she loved his sweetly inattentive smile because it proved that she lived not in the very heart of his thoughts but a little outside, in a warm place, perhaps veiled by a serene shadow.

But that was just where she wanted to be, the better to safeguard her secret, to uphold her responsibility to the servant, on whom she heaped ever more generous attentions.

Her love for her mother was a foul-tasting food, impossible to choke down. That food dissolved into bitter little crumbs in her mouth, then congealed, and this went on and on and had no end, the lump of fetid bread shifting from one cheek to the other, then the soft, stinking fragments that made of her mouth a deep pit of shame.

She began bringing a little gift each time she went to visit Malinka's mother.

She noted certain changes in her mother's personality and behaviour, that woman who, when they lived in the little house, never let any sorrow or displeasure trouble her eternal good humour or lessen the extent of her disengagement, and she was so aggrieved to see the servant turning suspicious and caustic, and sometimes even belligerent, that she longed to throw herself into the river, not to die but only to float, to drift towards the sea, towards the disappearance of all memory of her and the servant's existence, towards absolution for all the wrongs she had done her mother.

It was only her great debt to her mother that kept her from abandoning her anew in this way. But nothing shocked her more than to hear sarcasm and feeble little digs flowing from her mother's lips, that vile vermin being vomited up. She thought fate had mixed up her face with her mother's, that it was she who, her voice ever gentle and calm, was befouling the honour of precious stones, of diamonds, and the still greater dignity of self-mastery.

For even the servant didn't recognise herself.

She would snicker sardonically as Clarisse entered the flat, then interrupt herself, sorry and bewildered, and clap her hand to her mouth. She would mumble an excuse, and Clarisse realised she was afraid her daughter might stop coming to visit if she was mean to her (because that, oh, that was how the servant put it).

So this, Clarisse told herself, horrified, is what she'd done to her mother.

Sinking beneath even the wildest waves would never erase such a crime.

What bitterness, now, on the servant's perennially pinched lips, what hard mockery in her eyes!

She began to complain of fatigue and back pain. Vacuuming an office at dawn, she tripped on a chair and broke her two front teeth. She refused to have a bridge put in on the grounds that she could not afford it, even though Clarisse offered to help pay. But did she not find a sour pleasure in revealing, through the thin smile that was now hers, her gaping sorrow?

She did, thought Clarisse, seeing the hole in her mother's mouth and feeling the dough of contemptibility swelling inside hers. *Her* mouth was the putrid abyss, not the servant's.

Her love for her mother was poisoning her. On leaving the servant's, she wanted now to shriek, now to sink into the river's clement waters.

She did no such thing, though, no such thing.

But as for the edifice of her goodness to Richard Rivière and, beyond him, to everyone she met or worked with, she built it up bit by bit, never forgetting, never wearying, in a constant, tranquil labour that was nonetheless not untouched by doubt, concerning not the need for that endeavour but its sincerity.

Could what she practised, she sometimes wondered, really be called goodness, or, more simply, niceness and apparent submission?

And in any case, what sort of goodness was a goodness that was aware of itself?

She took care never to upset Richard Rivière, never to needle him, tease him, provoke him, and when, as he so rarely did, he lost his temper, to answer only with silence.

Now and then she saw a brief flash of surprise or unease on her husband's face, when she so visibly and insistently fended off some potential conflict and stared at him with her inward-looking eyes, open wide onto her own abnegation, careful to keep a grip on herself, utterly withdrawn into her vow of kindliness.

It seemed to her at such times that her eyes never blinked, she thought she could see their pale, fixed, absent reflection in Richard Rivière's dark, puzzled gaze.

"Come on, say something," he sometimes sighed. "You don't have to agree."

As if prodded into action, she tried to pull her gaze out of the pensive depths where it was contemplating Clarisse Rivière's sacrifice and haul it back to the surface, where Richard Rivière was awaiting some word, some answer, albeit with his increasingly frequent air of having already set down his attentiveness and wandered off somewhere else, someplace more interesting.

And so, after struggling to recall the question he had asked her, or the subject on which he'd tried to draw her into some sort of dispute, after desperately casting around in slightly nauseous panic for some more or less suitable answer, she realised he'd forgotten all about it, that she was now speaking only to Richard Rivière's frozen, mute, polite shadow as he fled into the distance, him and his beating heart, his untameable hair, his impatient muscles.

She took that shadow in her arms and pulled it to her. There was still a shoulder there to rest her forehead on, to cover her eyes.

Her love for Richard Rivière bathed her in sweetness and gentleness.

Was she perfectly, purely good to him? Probably not, since he was aware – his unease made it clear – of a strangeness about her, when he should have moved about in her goodness without even knowing it, should even have been able to attack and defy that goodness without seeing it, without Clarisse herself seeing it.

Her pregnancy showed so little that she thought it safe to go on visiting the servant up to the seventh month.

She was intrigued to find her belly's already modest bulge becoming even more discreet when she boarded the train for Bordeaux. And when she walked into her mother's flat and her hand moved reflexively to her stomach, she could feel only a hard knot beneath her loose-fitting sweater, such that she once thought she was simply waking from a dream in which she'd been pregnant.

She told the servant they'd have to go two and a half months without seeing each other.

"Fine," said the servant, her voice cold and indifferent.

Then for the first time she burst into tears, and Clarisse sat stunned and still, rubbing her chair's velvet arms with both hands, and thinking that her own narrow, sharp shoulder could at least have accommodated her mother's moist cheek, could have covered her eyes.

When the child was born, she named her Ladivine. That was the servant's first name.

Clarisse Rivière would remember the months after Ladivine's birth as a time when she went badly astray, when she lost sight of the point of her promise.

She would blame this confusion on her deep happiness, which grew from intense to excessive, finally becoming unrecognisable and sometimes indistinguishable from grief. She even let herself imagine taking the baby to Bordeaux, presenting her to the servant, saying "Here!" and then leaving her there, going home, having nothing more to do with the child or Malinka's mother, whose sadness at no longer seeing Clarisse would be eased by the presence of that marvellous baby.

Once she got hold of herself, the memory of that madness tormented her. Wherever she was, she dropped everything and ran to the baby, to make sure she was there and hold her close, knowing a torrent of love would then sweep over her, painful, impenetrable, and separate from herself, as if coming from some mysterious outside and not from her own being.

Sometimes she thought this vast love for the child a burden, and she longed to be rid of it, even if it meant ridding herself of the child as well. But she didn't know how to find pleasure in that love, nor even what exactly to do with it; she felt as though, yearning to deploy itself unconfined, it was trying to shove her consuming love for Richard Rivière to one side, along with her imperishable, wrenching love for Malinka's mother.

Whence, no doubt, the devotion, almost the euphoria, with which she saw to the little chores that came with the baby.

Washing the tiny clothes and hanging them on the line in the garden, mashing the vegetables for the baby's purée, the routine and utilitarian nature of those tasks held back the waves of invasive, boundless love, and although every move she made was for the sake of the child she could in a way put the child out of her mind.

It was when she inhaled the warm, musty smell of the child's head, when she felt that compact little body's warmth through her clothes, that she knew she was in danger. That overpowering love unsettled her, leaving her first wary of its demands, then rebellious.

I don't need this, she thought, feeling heavier than when she was pregnant, as if that immense love for the baby were overstuffing her already full heart.

Richard Rivière, for his part, had conceived a very simple passion for the child, and never tried to get out of caring for her.

No swollen, oversized love was trying to push him beyond his limits, or take anything away from him, or split open his chest.

The Rivière parents took a day to come and see the child, and the moment she opened the door Clarisse felt the strange magnetic force radiating from the father's big, solid body, a force to be struggled against, she immediately thought, because there was something unpleasant about it, but also, on first meeting, something intriguing.

He had a broad, full face with delicate features and mocking eyes that let it be known, with an aggressiveness scarcely veiled by false benevolence, that he was a man who put up with no nonsense. He had enormous hands, deformed by arthritis despite his young age. He stood with his forearms well away from his thighs, not so much to spare his ailing hands any painful contact, it seemed, as to show that he was unarmed, which might well be a lie, said his jeering eyes, because he had no fear of lies, and no sense of honour.

A large dog came in with the parents, a big, healthy, powerful beast. Clarisse backed away.

"Don't be afraid," said the father, "he's with us, he's very well behaved."

Richard had gone out to buy bread, and he came back just then. A surprised, vaguely irritated look crossed his face, as if he'd forgotten his parents were coming, which couldn't be true, thought Clarisse, since he'd gone out specially to buy bread for four. His suddenly unhappy face settled into a guarded expression, just this side of rude.

He murmured a greeting to his father, still keeping his distance.

Filled with a compassion she had never before felt for her husband, an almost disinterested sympathy, Clarisse sensed that he was shielding himself from the crushing physical authority, the simultaneously attractive and repellent omnipotence that had entered the house with his father. How strange to see Richard trembling, he who ordinarily showed no fear of anyone!

She went and stood at his side, their arms touching.

She could feel him quivering in turmoil and sterile distress, like a dog, she told herself. He seemed to be trying to fight off a will stronger than his own, and that will was serenely waiting for him to give in and bow down, and Richard was still clinging to his anger and pride, and the other will saw that and laughed, requiring neither anger nor pride to maintain itself.

So Richard Rivière's father laughed off his son, thought Clarisse, moved, because he knew Richard's frail crutches would soon break, that his anger would tire and his pride falter, no longer at all sure of its reason for being.

Stiff but trembling, Richard didn't say a word, as if the energy he was burning to stand up to his father and keep up his dignity forbade any further exertion.

Clarisse showed the parents into the sitting room, babbling, describing what they could plainly see, the simple, brightly coloured furniture she and Richard had picked out, the pale yellow wallpaper they'd had hung. The parents nodded, never offering a compliment, the mother dubious and reserved, the father snide and uninterested.

Richard stood off to one side, arms crossed, and Clarisse thought he looked exhausted and drained beneath his still fiercely tensed face, as if his sense of himself could not quite keep up with his real nature, which, weak and helpless before the father, was, unbeknownst to him, already showing itself in his vacillating gaze, in his mouth's drooping corners.

"Let's go and see the baby," said Clarisse, having heard a faint squeal.

She started down the passage, then stopped short at the room's open door. Her hands instinctively sprang out towards the two sides of the jamb, as if to prevent anyone entering.

The dog was lying on Ladivine's bed, a little crib whose bars were lowered on one side so the baby could be picked up more easily, and its outstretched head, lightly grazing the child's, had a deathly stillness about it.

Equally immobile, Clarisse saw in a single sweeping glance, were the baby's body, her colourless face, her wide eyes looking deep into the dog's staring gaze, as if she'd plunged into an abyss of sibylline knowledge and perhaps become lost.

Yet Clarisse had the strong sense of a bond not to be rashly broken, a secret union with no immediate danger for the child. Not for a moment did she doubt the dog's good intentions.

She heard a horrified cry behind her, and felt herself being violently shoved forward. Richard burst into the room, snatched up the baby, and clasped her to him, turning his back to the dog as a shield for the child.

"Get that thing out of here!" he screamed out at the passage, where his parents were standing.

He backed towards the wall, scarlet with fear and indignation.

The father calmly stepped in. Clarisse saw his eyes study the scene just as hers had a moment before, and, no less quick and assured, decide that the danger was not where it seemed. This troubled her. She felt at peace, nonetheless, and very comfortably pure, as if washed clean from within by an intuition higher and wiser than hers, which had chosen her.

"I never want to see that dog in this house again!" Richard shouted furiously.

Clarisse noted that he was taking care not to look at the dog still sprawled on the bed watching him, dark and serene, silent and proper.

Something struck her, clear as day: that well-behaved dog had the same eyes as Malinka's mother.

Richard's father began to stroke its flanks, speaking tenderly into its ear, not to placate it, Clarisse told herself, because he wasn't afraid of it, but to erase any offence.

The dog stretched its legs, yawned, deigned to get down from the bed.

The father gently grasped its collar, once again, thought Clarisse, not to control it but as if taking the arm of a dear friend, and the two of them left the room without a glance Richard's way. He sighed in ostentatious relief. He rocked and caressed the child, who had begun to cry.

"That was close," he said accusingly.

Did he mean to include her in this censure, because she had not rushed forward to snatch the baby away from the dog's maw?

Clarisse wasn't sure, but she preferred not to know.

Her certainty that the dog had come to the child's room not to harm her but to teach her was twisting and turning inside her, and it troubled her like an unwholesome temptation of disloyalty to Richard Rivière. Shouldn't she have told him of that certainty, wouldn't he have understood it, found reassurance in it? Oh no, he wouldn't have understood, and his inability would have made clear to Clarisse what she already knew, that no breath had come to him to show him the way into the dog's mysterious soul.

She couldn't help seeing it as a sign of Richard's weakness that this inspiration had steered clear of him, but had entered his father's heart.

Madame Rivière had not bothered to enter the bedroom. She had set the table in the kitchen, and the father was sitting and waiting before his plate with the impatient, wearied look of a man who wants to put the chore of the meal behind him and be off as quickly as possible.

Richard showed the baby to his mother, who, thought Clarisse, examined it guardedly, her eye full of an outraged scepticism, as if this might all be a cruel joke she'd have to thwart before they could laugh at her. She clumsily took the child in her arms, then handed her back almost at once, with a furious little giggle.

Later, as the meal was nearing its end and Ladivine was back asleep in her little bed, they heard crunching gravel on the patio. It was the dog, pacing back and forth in front of the house, beneath the kitchen windows.

Seething, Richard asked them:

"What's with you having that dog now? Since when are you animal lovers?"

"It's to guard the shop," said Madame Rivière. "You've got to protect yourself these days, you know."

"It's got nothing to do with the shop," the father said with deliberation.

He waved his fork towards the mother, not looking at her.

"That's what she'd like to think, but that's not it at all. Why would we have brought it here if it was supposed to be guarding the shop? Why do we take it with us wherever we go?"

"Yes, why?" asked the mother, suddenly afraid.

"Because we can't not, that's how it is. It's an order come to life. What do I care about dogs? It's true, I don't even like them that much. This one's different. I had no choice."

Richard let out a disdainful snicker. He was trying to add disdain to his hatred, Clarisse told herself, but it was beyond him, and disdain refused to take root in so pallid a heart. His gaze was dull, at once full of hate and struggling to summon up a bit of disdain with which to harden itself.

The dog began to yelp. It was jumping up and down on the patio so its head could be glimpsed through the window. It barked when its eyes met those of Clarisse or Richard's father, then whimpered when its paws hit the ground and it was once again out of sight.

Identical to the cries of Malinka's mother, its laments were more than Clarisse could bear.

She walked to the window and the dog hurried off around the house, glancing impatiently back at Clarisse again and again.

She suddenly realised it was headed for the child's room, whose window looked onto the garden on the opposite side of the house. She whirled around, raced through the kitchen, ran to Ladivine's room. She first saw the bounding dog's huge frantic head through the glass, then the baby's pale little face as she hiccupped and moaned in her own vomit.

She cried out, picked up the child, patted her back until she heard regular breathing and the faint beat of that soothed, very young heart.

"How did you know, you nice dog, how did you know?" she murmured, staring at the window, where the dog, now at peace, could no longer be seen.

Richard Rivière's father had just appeared in the doorway.

For the first time Clarisse glimpsed fear in his cold eyes, but it was a respectful fear, docile, a pious fear that in no way diminished him.

She went back to visiting Malinka's mother, leaving the child with a neighbour who would also look after her when Clarisse went back to work.

Sitting in the velvet armchair that had slowly become hers at the servant's, her gaze wandering over the trinkets her mother had begun to surround herself with, little porcelain elephants, handbells of various sizes, vases never filled with flowers but abundantly covered with fanciful floral motifs, she listened with one ear as the servant told her of bosses and co-workers, with the monotonous insistence, the maniacal, forced intensity Clarisse noticed she always fell into when she sensed her daughter's thoughts straying, and rather than try to lure them back she seemed to drive them insistently still further away with her mind-numbing monologues.

"What about you, how are you getting on?" she would ask at long last, her tone at once aggressive and imploring.

And Clarisse would smile and say nothing, evasive, but smiling lovingly and sincerely all the same.

But her heart was pounding, and, thinking about the baby, from whom she did not like to be separated for these few hours, she told herself how she wished she could give her mother the gift of that child. How happy the servant would be!

And undoubtedly, she would be breaking her vow never to link her existence to the servant's, but also acquitting herself of it by so great a sacrifice, and so her responsibility to those two, to her child and her mother, would, she thought, be behind her.

Because she would then flee far from both of them, far even from Richard Rivière, not yet realising what she owed him. And would she not suffer terribly, never again seeing those three she loved far more than life?

But in truth she did not mind suffering, if it was the sorrow of love, of not having those you love close beside you.

Far more painful for her was fidelity to her irreversible decision, which was destroying Malinka's mother over a slow flame, and her too, Clarisse Rivière, with a brighter flame, more violent, perhaps purifying, but she didn't yet know – she did not know, and simply went on hoping in fear.

As the years went by, and Ladivine became a sweet, even-tempered girl, and Richard Rivière's skilful salesmanship, tireless work and quiet, indestructible ambition brought him ever greater responsibilities at the dealership, Clarisse Rivière began to see that winning on one front could only mean losing on the other, that this was how it had to be, that it was a matter of her destiny.

But she led her life onward with an untrembling hand.

Apart from what they were not allowed to know, she believed she gave of herself completely to Richard and Ladivine.

Every moment of her life was infused with the certainty that it could be sacrificed to those two, that it belonged above all to them, that Clarisse Rivière was to make use of it only so long as they didn't need it. Before that man and that child who suspected nothing and enjoyed her generosity in naive good faith, she pictured herself as a slashed wineskin pouring out the very essence of joyful abnegation, of eager, almost greedy selflessness.

But that notion of her own success was undermined by the increasingly troublesome thought that her voluntary, permanent self-effacement had constructed a thin wall of ice all around her, that sometimes her daughter and husband could not understand, though they said nothing of it, perhaps knew nothing of it, why they could not reach the heart of her emotions.

And yet she must surely feel emotions, said their confused, anxious gaze, and emotions more varied than what she allowed them to see, that unending, inexorable deference, which they might well have suspected was not pure but the product of praiseworthy labour.

And might they not be tired of this, might they not be put off, perhaps, by the thought that they had to be grateful for it?

Might they not be tired and put off by such relentless generosity, the patient, unforthcoming man and the increasingly mysterious and obliging child, neither of whom, perhaps, wanted so much goodness, and wished she would let them know her in some other way too?

Clarisse Rivière felt the cold settling in, furtively filling the house, seeming to grip Richard Rivière and Ladivine, gradually encasing them too in the very delicate rime of a slightly stiff demeanour. But she didn't know what to do so that this would not be.

She often laughed, often joked with them merrily, and her laugh was like crystal, it was brief and uncontagious. The more she devoted herself to her husband and daughter, the more she could feel them taking their distance, without defiance or resentment, as people turn away in discomfort from an incomprehensible passion.

But how frigid was the breath she exhaled.

Sometimes this left her discouraged, defeated, knowing the invisible presence of Malinka's mother in her dark street kept her from giving her gestures and words the guilelessness that would warm them.

And she felt equally incapable of raising her daughter Ladivine by a common morality's well-defined precepts.

No sooner was she called on to offer an opinion of some deed, to judge the appropriateness of some attitude or simply to say what she thought, good or bad, of some situation, than the servant's silhouette appeared before her daunted eyes, seeming to defy her to judge anyone, she who had long since found herself guilty.

She fell into the habit of shrugging her shoulders, mute and distant, lips slightly pursed, when Ladivine told her of some clique that had offended another, and before the child's upturned, questioning eyes, before the child striving to understand what to make of all this, she smiled curtly, saying nothing, and thus seeming to express her disgust at the story itself. And so Ladivine finally stopped telling her what went on at school, and Clarisse forgot that things she should know about ever happened at school.

She would realise this, far too late.

Even before silence invaded their house, a polite, cosy, placid silence, she had already closed her ears to the things Richard Rivière and Ladivine said, though she pretended to listen, though her face and her gestures were the picture of careful attention – but only the commonplace words by which they ordered their day-to-day lives were allowed into her consciousness. The rest she was not to hear.

Because if she did she would not be able to speak without lying, and while she wasn't lying when she was giving the man and the child all she could give of herself, she would be lying if she talked about this or that like a free woman. And for that lie the accusing face of the servant, who knew just how faithless Clarisse Rivière was, how much she already had to make up for, would never have left her in peace.

And then what more could she do, she who was already giving all she could of herself?

She was doing everything she could.

But it tortured her that she couldn't hold back the numbness gradually overtaking her household, the cold torpor exuded in spite of her by her artificial, oblique self, until in the end she grew used to it, and came to believe this was how things were supposed to be in happy families.

She stared at her thin, mild face in the mirror, only faintly lined with delicate wrinkles at the corners of her eyelids. She couldn't believe nothing showed in the still water of her grey-green eyes or the even crease of her slightly upturned lips.

Her light-red dyed hair was pulled into a loose chignon, her brow was pale and smooth, and two pearls gleamed opaquely on her ears. Who would ever suspect she was a woman in despair?

Like the rest of the house, the bedroom was neat and impeccably clean, not one piece of clothing in sight, everything in its place in the big blond-wood drawers, the polished wardrobes, their doors set with hard, efficient mirrors.

Clarisse Rivière still scrupulously neatened and cleaned this house they'd bought some years before, in the centre of Langon, once they had sold their little house on the outskirts, but now she hated the house as she had never hated anyone in her life.

Because long before she did, that house had heard and understood what Richard Rivière said, and its old brick and stone walls would forever preserve the memory of those terrible words, unaffected, never once sighing in sympathy with her sadness.

She wanted the house to grieve and suffer as she did, she wished it would collapse and swallow them both, her who did not want to go on living, and him, Richard Rivière, who had spoken those strange, dangerous words she'd long before managed to stop hearing but which he had so often repeated that in the end she had to give in and understand them.

Did he say "I'm leaving this house, I'm going to live somewhere else", or "I can't go on living here, I'm leaving"?

That pretty house never reacted, as if indifferent to the insult or aware that none of this really concerned it, and neither did Clarisse Rivière, she only smiled vaguely, retied her blue dress's belt on her hip, started out of the room, but that was when Richard Rivière put his hand on her arm and, realising she had once again succeeded in not hearing or understanding him, once again found a way to close her ears, like turning off a hearing aid, or, who knows, to make an unintelligible hash of the very clear words he'd just spoken in his patient, firm, friendly voice, he held her back with one hand as she fled, she who had sensed the threat in the air, her skin already prickling and shivering, and again he spoke those words that the house had already heard, that it had already absorbed in its thick walls, that had left it unmoved: "I'm going away, I'm leaving this house."

Clarisse Rivière did not collapse, any more than the walls did.

But the words and their cruel meaning had pierced her defenceless skin, the delicate, creamy, lily-like flesh that Richard Rivière once never wearied of caressing and clutching, just as she loved his body of firm, dry leather, and she felt her skin closing over those

69

words, and those words calmly, meticulously beginning to wreak their damage.

She had looked towards the window, she had seen the big chestnut tree on the square, and suddenly her hand began to itch, because, almost distracted by the memory, she could picture herself rubbing its ribbed trunk with that hand, and even now, it seemed, Richard Rivière taking that hand in his own and raising it to his lips.

Dimly, that gesture reminded her of another. Had she not, one long-ago day, pressed the servant's hand to her mouth? Had she not tried, not to soften her mother's sorrow, but to save herself from the pain and the knowledge of her own cruelty? And had that gesture saved her? Oh, now she didn't know.

Now she was staring emptily into the chestnut's leafy boughs, and, feeling Richard Rivière's rough lips on her hand, she thought it was the trunk itself kissing her palm, the whole tree trying to redeem itself after for some reason inflicting on her a sadness she would never escape – but now she'd forgotten what it was, or even if there was anything to remember, and so she tentatively turned her eyes towards Richard Rivière and saw he was about to speak again, suspecting she hadn't heard, which was true and false at the same time, because now she could feel a way being cleared inside her for a monstrous pain, but she had no idea where it was coming from, and with sluggish surprise she mused that the old chestnut tree patiently burrowing its roots under the asphalt on the square, if it really was that tree trying to redeem itself by exhaling a dry breath onto her hand, was in no position to torture her, that pitiful rubbish-ringed tree, and her so tall and pale in her sky-blue dress, her dainty-heeled sandals, oh, she would already have fled this room if she were not inexplicably being held back by one hand.

"I'm not sure you understand what I said," Richard Rivière was telling her in his steadily patient voice, insistent but detached, as if conscientiously discharging a duty he knew would be difficult, "I'm going away, I don't want to live here anymore, with you, which doesn't mean I've stopped loving you, you'll always be my . . ."

A siren began to shriek, but Richard Rivière's lips went on moving, his hand gently squeezing Clarisse's, and his lack of reaction surprised her until she realised the awful noise was coming from her own head.

At the same moment, a fierce wave of nausea made her moan aloud.

No doubt thinking she was about to collapse, Richard Rivière took her in his arms. She could see his anxious eyes, his moving lips, but not a sound could be heard through the wail in her ears, and she shook her head, vaguely ashamed to be making a scene.

But she felt so ill, so terribly ill that her embarrassment ebbed, pushed back by a grief full of nausea, disgust and unbounded horror, which now flooded through her, making her limbs twitch, vainly trying to throw open her breast so it could get out, but her firm, solid flesh had closed over that pain like the house's walls over Richard Rivière's irrevocable words, and nothing, she thought, would ever dislodge it.

She rubbed her face against his shirt, inhaled the fresh, childlike smell she knew so well, thinking "So that's what was coming to me," with an astonishment beyond measure.

No less immense was her disbelief that nothing showed in the mirror just a few hours later. A slight lostness in her eyes might tell the servant that something was troubling her daughter when she next went to see her, but what that torment might be she would never guess.

Clarisse Rivière found no comfort in this. For the first time in her life she wished she could confide in Malinka's mother, tell her not of her joy but her sorrow, and see that sorrow's reflection on the servant's face, so like her own.

When she called her daughter Ladivine in Germany the next day, she would tell her of Richard Rivière's decision in a halting but calm, steady voice, and Ladivine's palpable sadness would come as a balm to her, but then she would realise Richard Rivière had already told her, and, suddenly embarrassed, she would say nothing of her desperate need for consolation.

"I'm fine," she would murmur in response to Ladivine's question. "Yes, yes, I'm fine."

She would later admit to herself that, against all reason, she was hoping Ladivine might rush straight to Langon, try to talk her father out of going away, press her to her young, vigorous, supple breast, and then everything would be just as it was, Richard Rivière would once again climb into his four-wheel drive every morning to go off and sell cars, carefree as ever, quietly, humbly, but visibly proud of his success, while she set off on foot, her jaunty heels clacking smartly over the paving stones, for the pizzeria where she now oversaw the waiting staff, and maybe Ladivine would move home again, watch over them, open her father's eyes to the reality of their love.

Because they were in love, weren't they? Clarisse Rivière, at least, felt an unmingled passion for her husband, unquestioning and uncritical.

But no such thing was happening.

The memory of the way it actually was came roaring back at her whenever she let herself drift into that daydream, or in the earliest hours of the morning, and she returned to reality with tears streaming down her cheeks.

Richard Rivière was still there beside her, cordial, watchful and distantly polite in a way that stung her cruelly. He was packing up his things, and Clarisse lent a hand, though she could see he didn't like it, that it embarrassed him and, strangely, angered him.

She studied him when he turned his back, his tan nape, his hair, still thick and dark, the way his shoulder muscles bulged beneath his T-shirt when he lifted a box, then forgot to look away when he glanced furtively in her direction, catching her on the brink of tears, lost in thought, drained and hopeless.

He came to her reluctantly, gave her a distant embrace, as if taking care to avoid any gesture that might give Clarisse the idea his decision was anything other than irrevocable.

She felt that distance, and she clung to his neck, immediately thinking, Soon I won't be able to do this anymore, and panic knotted her stomach. She bent double, silent, breathless with grief.

Richard Rivière's body was as familiar as her own, and she thought she knew his face more intimately than hers, more than Clarisse Rivière's narrow, delicate face, once a certain Malinka's, which she always looked at askance in the mirror, uncertain and ill at ease, weary of that reflection.

She had never stopped studying Richard Rivière's face, in repeated but serene wonderment, no longer sure if it was handsome or not, little caring, knowing it had aged and surely changed, but seeing it in the eternal present of her love and devotion.

How, she wondered, distraught and unbelieving, how would she ever do without that face? She might have gouged out her own eyes, had she not realised that Richard Rivière's face would be just as absent to her blind.

"Where will you live?" she asked dully.

He paused for a very brief moment.

"In Annecy. I've found a place there."

"That's a long way from here," she murmured, shocked.

"Yes, it is," he said simply, with a half-shrug.

Then – out of discretion, she thought, perhaps to conceal any eagerness or anticipation in his eyes as he spoke the name Annecy – he gently turned away.

They made love one last time the night before he left, and Richard Rivière, considerate and giving as always, seemed to her almost too attentive, hurtfully so, as if trying to soothe or appease her, to ward off an anger that she thus began to feel, almost reflexively, no such thought ever having entered her mind before, immersed as she was in shame and despair.

But no righteous anger could she feel. Were Richard Rivière's reasons for leaving the house not perfectly valid, whatever they might be? Who was she to judge? Had she not made of the servant's life a bitter bread?

She pressed hard against her husband's body, bit his neck. He flinched, but he didn't object. She hadn't realised she was weeping, and her tears flowed between their two conjoined breasts, mingling with their sweat, equally salty, washing away any temptation or attempt to be angry, and leaving her, as for a few seconds longer she clung to that man who was at the same time herself, her husband and her son, horribly barren and sad.

When Richard Rivière's four-wheel drive turned the corner and its silvery gleam disappeared, the August sun no longer illuminating the chestnut tree, dry, ignored and alone on the asphalted square, Clarisse Rivière took a few hurried, uncertain steps down the pavement, as if she had remembered that she was supposed to follow him and feared she might lose sight of the car.

Suddenly she stopped, her legs tangling, and she nearly fell over.

She let out a hoarse moan, sternly crossed her arms to steady herself, and then, as she was approaching the front door of the house, she caught sight of a big red-brown dog, emaciated and ungainly, in the sunlight's almost unbearable blaze.

It was sidling towards her, watching her with one eye, its ugly head half turned away. Her vision dimmed in terror.

"No, absolutely not, not yet!" she shouted at the dog.

She began to run, raced into the house, slammed the door and pushed the bolt, turning the key in the lock.

Then she changed her mind, tremblingly opened the door, and offered herself to the wilting heat, putting on a brave smile but feeling her mouth and chin quivering. What did she care now, what could she care about anything now? What could possibly deserve her fear now?

The dog had gone on its way. She saw it turn the corner, it too, she told herself she'd been stupid and cowardly, and felt by turns freezing cold and devoured by a burning flame.

Had she not made of the servant's life a bitter bread?

She thought she'd been fatally wounded, and had only to wait for her time to come, settling into that wait with the visible detachment and resignation she was so skilled at displaying.

Through the fog of her deep indifference to everything said around her, and even potentially said to her face, she sensed that people saw her as a humiliated woman.

Her daughter Ladivine, who telephoned often, and her co-workers at the restaurant, and Richard Rivière himself, who dutifully called once a month and wired her money she never spent, they were all doing their best, discreetly, affectionately, sometimes with openly expressed concern, to rescue her from her humiliation.

But she had never felt any such thing. Nor was she humiliated that people thought her humiliated, only vaguely surprised.

Richard Rivière's leaving had filled her with shame, because it told her she'd failed in her attempt to offer all the love and generosity a human being might need, and more.

For, she thought, no-one could weary of such a gift if it was properly given, they'd know nothing of it, and it would filter invisibly into the tight weave of their lives.

And yet Richard Rivière had grown sick of it, and he'd run away, that was her failure, and that was what filled her with shame, but not humiliation.

She did not blame her husband, who'd done what he thought he had to, she blamed herself, and she felt ridiculous, pointless, heartless. She'd made of the servant's life a bitter bread and in the end nothing had made up for that, though in her vanity she was convinced all this time that it had.

She paid less attention to her appearance, her dress, and the clothes she wore were not as perfectly, rigorously clean as they once were. Her feet were yellowed and dry in her sandals.

She was aware of this negligence, and sometimes it gave her a grim satisfaction, for she thought of her body as an old dog that could never be punished enough for having, say, devoured a little child.

She settled into a long wait for death, exhausted by grief and loathing for everything around her, insensitive to everything else, frozen, and even the birth of Annika and then Daniel, whom she went to see several times in Berlin, little touched her, however hard she tried, as she took them in her arms, to revive the emotion she'd felt on embracing her own baby.

She knew her indifference and desperate attempts to conceal it gave her a slightly hunted, fearful look. She didn't know what to say, what to talk about, kept her mouth shut.

When Richard Rivière called, she could scarcely summon the strength to murmur a response to his "hello", and tears sprang to her eyes, trickled down her face and neck as she listened to his falsely cheerful chatter, against an indecipherable background of other lively, spirited voices that made her think that he lived his life amid unending revelry.

That didn't hurt her. She noted it without interest, but the sound of Richard Rivière's voice brought her ever fresh torments. Her fingers convulsively clutched the receiver, she could not catch her breath, could not listen, lost in dread of the moment when he would hang up and she'd be alone again in her house, the house that knew everything and never came to her rescue.

"Please, please, come back to the house," she would say, or think she was saying, since Richard Rivière never answered, and it was likely she had not said a word, though she couldn't help thinking the house must have heard her and swallowed her plea in its walls.

Nor, certainly, did she say "I love you so", but the words rolled around and resounded in her aching skull, making such a din that Richard Rivière could only have heard them, had he not striven so insistently to fill up the moment with his own harmless, light-hearted words.

He did come back to the house, though, just once.

Not, she thought dejectedly, and perhaps because for a few minutes she'd been foolish enough to think that it was, to surrender to her love and her sorrow, to rescue her from her quiet agony.

He was coming back to the house because his father had died in Toulouse, and so they drove off to the funeral together in Richard Rivière's four-wheel drive.

Three years had gone by since his leaving. Clarisse Rivière found him more handsome than before, a little more filled out, and dressed with a very studied elegance, like a prosperous, fastidious, slightly anxious man.

She threw herself against him as soon as she opened the door, and she found a certain taste for life tentatively coming back to her, slightly dimming her grief and bewilderment. She could feel his discomfort at having her in his arms. She did not care. She held him close, so happy to be seeing him again, nestling her face against his neck, thinking he might be uncomfortable because in his mysterious Annecy existence there was another woman who held him like this, but not caring, lost in her joy at rediscovering Richard Rivière's smell.

If he'd fled what she had given him so generously, that alone was worth thinking about. What he'd fled to didn't interest her.

Richard Rivière's mother looked at them with an almost hostile face. She seemed not so much stricken as infuriated by her husband's death, or rather, Clarisse realised uneasily, by its circumstances.

Without pleasure they drank a warm, syrupy *vin cuit* in the little flat where Richard Rivière was raised, above the stationery shop that the parents had still been running only the month before, when they had made the decision to retire. The mother had gone off for a mineral cure in the mountains while the father took inventory.

"The shop was locked up, the blind was down, and your father had the dog with him, that horrible dog," the mother said accusingly.

Richard Rivière swirled the sweet wine in his glass, looking around him in boredom and distaste.

"Not that same dog you brought to our house?" whispered Clarisse, with a nervous titter.

The mother almost roared in irritation. She tried to catch Richard Rivière's eye, but he very visibly refused. She seemed bent on rebuking him, and, unable to express her outrage in a shared glance, furiously shook her head. Clarisse remembered him telling her, one day long before, that his parents habitually blamed him for their every concern and sorrow.

"No, of course not, a different dog, the first one died ten years ago at least. But it was the same breed, and they looked so much alike you forgot it wasn't that other one. Not to mention that your father gave it the same name."

She began to sob, dry-eyed, her broad face contorted and creased.

"I never wanted a dog, myself," she whimpered, "and neither did your father, but he was convinced he didn't have a choice."

When the mother got home from her cure two weeks later, she found the father lying in the back room of the shop, his neck and part of his face ripped away. The dog was standing close by, and it growled viciously on catching sight of her.

"They told me your father probably died of a heart attack, and then the dog went after him because it was starving. But I know that's not it. What I think is that your father, who was in perfect health, was just doing his work, minding his own business, and that dog lunged at his throat and killed him on purpose."

Richard Rivière shrugged in a brusque gesture of scornful anger. He banged his glass of *vin cuit* down on the coffee table. A few drops jumped out and spattered on the varnished wood.

"Why would you think a thing like that?" he shouted. "Have you ever heard of a dog ripping its master's throat out for no reason?"

"I never said for no reason," the mother spat back. "You hear me, son? I never said for no reason. It wanted vengeance for something, that's what I think."

She leaned forward until her face almost touched Richard Rivière's, so he couldn't turn away.

"Do you have nothing to feel guilty about? Are you absolutely certain your life is in order?" she whispered, with such fury in her face that Clarisse saw him close his eyes in anguish.

"My life isn't hurting anyone," he murmured stoutly.

"I hope not, for your sake," the mother hissed, "because your father ended up paying for something or someone, and he was the most virtuous man there ever was. So, yes, I dearly hope you'll take care to live a life no-one will ever curse you for."

Surprised, almost insulted, Clarisse Rivière caught him glancing uncomfortably in her direction, not so much suspicious as wary and fearful.

She gave him the non-answer of an opaque, amiable gaze, but her slighted heart began to bleed again, protesting. Tears stung her eyes.

Can you really not understand, she silently murmured, that I will never call down the slightest hardship on you, nor anyone's wrath, because above all else I love you and will always see you as my husband, and you never once hurt me before the irreparable catastrophe that your leaving was for me, and even about that I've never felt any malice, only a grief that will never fade, which I don't hold you responsible for, because it was me you wanted to be free of, not the house that hears everything, which means it's my fault, can you really not see that, and believe that if anyone ever wishes sorrow on you it will never, ever be me?

"What happened to the dog?" she hurried to say.

"They put it to sleep, of course," said the mother, whose fat face suddenly seemed to drip with exhaustion and sadness.

In a disgusted voice, but as if she thought it her duty, she added:

"But it will come back, I know it will, that one or another, exactly the same, with the same name, and it will attack anyone who deserves it."

Only a few long-time customers and two or three neighbours came to the funeral, for the Rivière parents had never sought to make friends in their life, wholly occupied with each other and their shop.

Clarisse held Richard's arm, her fingers lightly caressing the fine wool of his elegant overcoat, which he'd picked out without her in a city she knew nothing of.

The bell of despair was tolling in the distance, nonetheless. She could just make out its muffled ringing from a future in which Richard Rivière's return to absence, once he'd driven her home and gone on his way, did not yet seem a certainty.

After all, it was her, Clarisse Rivière, who was standing close at his side by the grave, it was her that he suddenly looked down at with his moved, loving gaze, his tanned, full face marked with hollows and wrinkles but to her still the same as the shy young face she had first beheld in Le Rainbow, some twenty-five years before.

Did she not have every reason to ignore the grim thud of that all-too-familiar bell as she huddled against him in the biting wind and he patted her back with one hand as if to say, "Don't worry, everything will be fine"?

Maybe that baleful bell hadn't noticed all this, its every ring counting off the dreary, dark days of loneliness past and future – Richard Rivière's fingers brushed her hand, he turned his face to hers, no longer intimidated, no longer young or smooth but, she thought, as overflowing with inexpressible love as the face looking up at her when she came to take his order, long ago, at Le Rainbow.

Over and over her memory would replay those moments in the cemetery, the brief hour of perfect accord and loving harmony that had let her hold the reverberations of despair at a distance, almost inaudible.

She was convinced that she'd felt and understood that moment accurately, hadn't made too much of it. Her imagination hadn't run away with her, she was of course happy to see Richard Rivière again on the morning of his arrival, but she hadn't been hoping for anything.

He took her home, and their conversation in the four-wheel drive was untroubled, though she noted his refusal to talk about his father and the dog when she offered a thought on the subject and saw him grow silent, his lips suddenly grey and pressed tight.

He pulled up to the house and didn't want to come in. He hugged her, climbed back into the car, waved a final farewell, and Clarisse Rivière had a powerful feeling, so horrible and absolute that it was almost an icy relief, that she would never see him again.

Now it had been years, after Richard Rivière went away, since Clarisse's heels had clattered boldly and efficiently over the tiles of the pizzeria, where she oversaw a staff of four and still waited tables herself.

Not that her heels were never heard striking that hard floor, but the noise was now inadvertent, indifferent, with no resonance of contentment and innocent pride.

Sometimes, not realising it, she dragged her feet. Then, a moment later, the horrible shuffling sound snapped her out of it, reminded her of the need for some semblance of dignity, and she made what felt like a heroic effort to walk properly.

Everything meant boredom and weariness, except perhaps for her visits to the servant, when, as she sat in her bronze velvet armchair listening to her mother's morose chatter, she forgot that she was Clarisse Rivière, or couldn't recall who that Clarisse Rivière was, that woman whose husband had left her for Annecy, whom everyone thought humiliated but who was only ashamed of her own failure.

The pizzeria's manager had planned a party at the restaurant, and invited Clarisse with such insistence that she felt obliged to accept, despite her deep dislike of gatherings, high spirits and pleasantries.

She bought a violet jersey dress that clung to her slender frame and hung down to her ankles, with pumps to match. She didn't care about being pretty and nicely dressed. She only wanted to honour the sincere kindness of the man who'd invited her, who'd urged her to come, hoping it might lift her spirits.

When she got home, some three hours later, Freddy Moliger was with her.

She stopped on the square in front of her house and pressed her back to the chestnut tree, listening, with an almost violent attentiveness and concentration that surprised even her, to the detailed, meandering, alternately lyrical and chillingly raw tale of a life of grim poverty that wreck of a man was recounting.

Clarisse Rivière felt the fog parting inside her, the thick, dully buzzing cloud that kept her safely walled off from the rest of the world and filled her gaze with the gently frightened, languishing look that, she knew, made people see her as a woman untouched by guile. She felt it as a searing pain, a razor-sharp blade slicing cleanly into her mind, draining away all that now had no reason to be there, to linger there.

It happened the moment Freddy Moliger came towards her, with his doleful face, his unsteady, ravaged body, unwholesomely thin.

She felt it, that sudden feeling of exposure, a sense that no sheltering torpor now stood between her and this lost man!

Alarmed, surprised at herself, she immediately thought: He has to be told that my name is Malinka. This left her shaken and grateful, like a vision that might mean her salvation, though at a great price.

Every word Freddy Moliger spoke touched the vulnerable spot in her new sensitivity, her at long last unveiled ability to feel, and, she thought, it was as if her mother, the servant, had sent her this messenger to strip her bare, and perhaps, if she received him as she should, to free her.

His manner was open and plain, with a shy person's bluntness and awkward, joyless humour. Sometimes he looked at her full on, his gaze a dull blue beneath his pale brown eyelids, and sometimes he looked at her sidelong, as if suspecting she might be trying to deceive him with an unjustifiable good will, watching for Clarisse's duplicity to show. He spoke quickly and abundantly in a tangle of words, perhaps hoping this torrent would drown the grossest of the many grammatical errors he made, having of his own language only a vague notion, resentful and suspicious, because that very language looked down on him and laid traps for him, purely to expose his ineptitude.

Her forearms crossed behind her back, she caressed the trunk of the chestnut tree and thought the time hadn't yet come to go inside the house, its hostile walls heavy with words that never should have been spoken, with those countless cries of "Clarisse!"

"My name is Malinka," she whispered.

And then she was afraid, so deep was her emotion, afraid what had happened when Richard Rivière told her he was leaving might now happen again: waves of nausea, a horrible shrieking in her ears. Because she felt shocked in much the same way, not freed, as she had been foolish enough to believe, but terrified at what might become of her if she resolved to be Malinka again.

And now it was done, now she had said it, and she couldn't take it back.

"Malinka? They told me your name was Clarisse."

He nodded back towards the restaurant.

"My name is Malinka, that's my real name," she said, louder, her voice now steady.

And she felt as though she was forever turning away from the few people she was close to, her daughter Ladivine, her former husband, two or three acquaintances in the city, and towards Freddy Moliger's rough company, where no imposture would ever again make of her a comfortably deluded woman.

Malinka had never married, never had a child or a boyfriend. No-one remembered her but her mother.

Everything Freddy Moliger told her, with an urgency she read not as egocentrism but as a fierce resolve to show himself in all his destitution so anyone making the unlikely choice to take an interest in him wouldn't be disturbed or disappointed when bits of his past life came out, everything he told her in his slightly high-pitched, grating, disagreeable voice, every detail resonated in her with an excessive, exhausting intensity – even more powerful than if she'd lived through it all herself, and because she now felt as though she were carrying her heart outside of her body, unadorned and quivering and blood-soaked from the sacrifice of her disguises.

For the first time she felt a kinship.

She had of course desperately loved Richard Rivière, passionately loved Ladivine and the servant; she had given herself entirely and imperiously to her daughter and husband, but had she ever felt a kinship with them? Oh, no, she didn't think so, not as she did with Freddy Moliger.

She had no desire to devote herself to this strange man, and she would never love him as she still loved Richard Rivière. That made no difference. She found no real pleasure in this relationship, no fulfilment, but it tormented her in a way she'd never known, through no fault of Freddy Moliger's. She couldn't think of him without the servant's face appearing to her, enigmatic, unchanged, unavoidable.

Quietly accusing, too, and she didn't shy away, she took what was coming to her.

Was it too late to try to make of the servant's life less bitter a bread?

Freddy Moliger told her he had grown up with his younger brother Christopher in suburban Bordeaux, between a hard-drinking mother and a father whose mildest display of bad temper was emptying his children's satchels out their eleventh-floor window and then threatening to toss them both after their school things. Eventually they were taken from their parents and entrusted to their grandmother, a fairly benign woman, although Malinka immediately saw that Freddy Moliger was skipping over many occasions when the grandmother took out her chronic rage on the two boys with a broomstick or chopping board. He spoke of those objects in a light-hearted, almost affectionate tone, like emblems of a comical eccentricity in that woman who looked after them until he was twelve and his brother ten, and then died. Of what, Freddy Moliger never knew. He'd simply come home from school one day and found her dead on the floor of the kitchen, her heavy body stuck between the chairs and the table. The brothers were returned to their parents, who'd had two other children in the meantime. But their father couldn't stand having them around, as Freddy Moliger put it with a sort of stoical understanding, and as if that too were merely a quirk of his father's odd character, nothing that could be judged.

This, Malinka observed, was how Freddy Moliger always described the brutal or senseless acts by which adults had made of his childhood a torment: without rancour or reproach, no different from certain trivial events, certain minutiae he also occasionally brought up, their telling sometimes seeming to Malinka devoid of purpose or sense. Blows and cruel words, screaming and hostility were as much a part of the everyday world as the discomfort of rain on a bare head, as the fleeting itch of a mosquito bite, and none of those had anything to do with morality. Which is why, if Moliger's father or mother suddenly took a closed fist to Freddy's head or chest, there was no question of faulting them, any more than you could rail at the forces of nature.

Once again removed from their parents, the two brothers were placed first with one family, in the country, and then, now separated, with a second, because, Freddy Moliger calmly explained, they'd begun acting up. They were reunited at the junior high school, escaped together, stole two bottles of wine and a bag of crisps from the supermarket, then hid under a bridge, eating, drinking, drowsing, until it came time to get back on the school bus. They were unhappy in their foster homes, both because they were apart and because the families didn't like them and secretly mistreated them. Or so at least Malinka translated Freddy Moliger's account, because he never used fraught words, he simply described situations, answering, when she cried "They hated you, you were miserable!" that he didn't know, that it was possible, vaguely put out, she sensed, at hearing her explain with abstractions something she had not known or experienced.

He then came to the foster families' defence, saying "You know, my brother and I were pretty hard to handle" in an objective tone that condemned neither the adults' cruelty and thoughtlessness nor the children's unstable behaviour.

She came to sense that, in Freddy Moliger's eyes, any interpretation on her part was a sign of his own deficiency, that she was only restating what he'd just said, and only because he didn't know how to tell a story or make himself understood. This left him sullen and irritable. She noticed, and took to listening in silence.

She looked at his pallid, droop-cornered eyes, his mottled, pock-marked face, his coarse yellow hair, like a patch of grass burned by pesticide, she looked at him and thought to herself that it wasn't easy to love and want to touch such a damaged face, she told herself that and at the same time she knew she would manage, without forcing or feigning it, not out of generosity or kindness but because the time would come when she'd want to, unstoppably, once she'd learned how to know him, Freddy Moliger, in all his strangeness.

Then she would want to caress and protect his poor face.

It would not give her the sensual pleasure she felt on stroking Richard Rivière's handsome, healthy face, but she would learn to like it all the same, even without pleasure.

Nothing about Freddy Moliger was pleasant, but very soon Malinka couldn't imagine doing without the feeling of her own nature being revealed, which only Freddy Moliger's face and stories could bring her.

Not that he offered it, not that it was anything like a gift. But, though he didn't know it, he was showing her the way into her own secrets. Oh, it wasn't pretty, and sometimes she thought she'd never find peace again, but she wouldn't have traded that pain for all the serenity of the life she lived before, when Richard Rivière was still with her.

Freddy Moliger was there, sitting on a chair in the kitchen with a cup of milky coffee she'd made him. She stood leaning against the sink and saw him enjoying that coffee, adding some sugar, a little more milk, exacting and sullen at the same time, feigning disdain, as if afraid that any sign it was good would summon someone to snatch away the cup, to punish him for enjoying himself when he didn't deserve to.

Now, in bits and pieces, he was telling her that the police had come to arrest him and his brother. Though younger than he, Christopher put up an arrogant and defiant front while he himself trembled in terror, to such a degree that the police ended up letting them go, he said, so clearly finding all this coherent that she didn't dare ask him to explain. So they left the police station, and Christopher wanted to go and play by the railway line. They were in no hurry to get back to their foster homes, especially Freddy, whose family beat him, whereas Christopher never let anyone lay a hand on him. And then, as he was crossing the tracks, Christopher was crushed by a train. Freddy ran away as fast as his legs could carry him, he ran through the farm fields and into the little woods where there wasn't even a path, not going for help but because he was half out of his head, half out of his head, he said again in his piercing but still unemotional voice.

He took a sip of coffee and held the liquid in his mouth for a few seconds, lips thrust out. His eyes reddened. Malinka turned towards the sink, rinsed a glass.

A few years after that Freddy Moliger was in prison again, briefly, because he hadn't actually done anything wrong, but he was too young, and prison messed him up, he said coldly, as if stating a general rule. Then he got married and his wife had a baby, a girl, but she met another man and disappeared one day out of the blue, taking the baby with her, meaning that Freddy Moliger never really knew the child, so to speak, which still pained him to this day. He once tried to see his daughter, when she was little, but she lived far away with her mother and the guy, and Freddy Moliger couldn't afford the trip. And he had a feeling the mother was trying to turn the child against him, so he would leave them in peace, so they would be rid of Freddy Moliger.

That's how it was. He had also forgotten the name of the village where Christopher was buried, and that too saddened him deeply, he would have liked to put flowers on the grave now and then. But as always the problem was money, because cars and trains were expensive. Not to mention, he concluded with a terse little laugh, that he would have to remember the name of that damn village. He'd recently asked his mother, but she couldn't remember it either, assuming she ever knew. With all this he began to drink pretty heavily, and that's where he stood now, but his life was no worse than before. He thought things were looking up for him. Once in a while he did some work for a local farmer, in the vineyards, or picking vegetables in the summertime. He shared a flat with two or three friends, and in the end everything was fine, except that on a sheet with his signature at the bottom he'd written that he wanted to be buried alongside his brother and didn't know where the grave was, and that got to him.

He was thirty-four years old, he told her, and he knew he looked fifty but didn't care. He had a slight limp, the result of a fierce thrashing by his father twenty-five years before, and that didn't bother him either, it never got in his way or stopped him doing what he had to.

Here he snickered, as if he'd cracked a good joke. And all at once Malinka realised that he had to struggle constantly against howling rage, and that, if she herself had always refrained from judging others' acts because she was guilty of a perpetual, on-going crime against the servant, what kept Freddy Moliger from accusing anyone was rooted less in personal, spontaneous stoicism than in the fear of seeing his anger's terrible face come to life.

She took him to meet the servant just two days after they met.

"Do you want to come with me to my mother's?" she'd asked him, holding her breath.

"Of course," he said, surprised, happy.

She had not yet taken Freddy Moliger's face in her hands, and she was surprised to see a stranger's face when she looked at him. She was no less surprised by the importance that face had taken on in her life, that stranger's face she had to work to remember when he was not around.

And yet she wanted him to see the servant, and she wanted her to be introduced to someone by Malinka for the first time before she touched and caressed his skin.

In her eagerness to give her mother the gift that was Freddy Moliger, and to hear him call her Malinka in front of the servant as if no Clarisse Rivière had ever existed, she ignored the Tuesday rule, just this once, and took the train to Bordeaux on a Sunday, with Freddy Moliger at her side.

Malinka's mother opened the door suspiciously. Tufts of hair stuck straight out of her tight chignon, the zip of her jeans was only halfway up.

When she was expecting her daughter, she always came to the door impeccably dressed, not a hair out of place, thought Malinka in a sudden wave of sadness.

The servant gave Freddy Moliger a silent, unblinking stare.

"This is Freddy," said Malinka.

He embraced the servant as naturally as could be.

"Your daughter looks just like you, madame," he said, in a voice even more strident than usual.

The servant's face didn't trouble him at all, and Malinka was so grateful that she impulsively caressed his cheek. Freddy Moliger gave her a pleased smile.

He stepped into the room and exclaimed over the curios decorating her shelves, a thousand porcelain trinkets, mostly animals, cherubs, or shepherdesses, which Malinka's mother spent hours arranging and rearranging, their placement governed by secret affinities.

The servant stepped towards him cautiously, as she would a slightly dangerous dog. But her eyes shone with pleasure when she began telling Freddy Moliger the source of each object, and why she preferred this one to that, and he urged her on with lively questions.

Freddy Moliger was dressed in a pale green short-sleeved shirt and beige twill trousers. He'd plastered back his dead-grass hair, and when he wasn't speaking his washed-out eyes also seemed dead, so dead that the effort he seemed to expend to come back to life when he next spoke gave his most ordinary sentences a heroic, unhoped-for, even final quality, which, Malinka observed, commanded attention and a slightly anxious respect.

Everything about him expressed an artless, loyal good will towards the servant, and a sincere interest in the story behind every trinket, in all their special features.

Next he admired the décor and the furniture of the servant's flat, the unlikely jumble that somehow created a strange and sophisticated whole, not that she was trying for any such effect.

Then he suggested they go out to lunch, if they'd be so kind as to invite him.

He was exceptionally cheerful. He wasn't charming, thought Malinka, not the least bit appealing, with his high voice, his large pores, his straw-like hair, but so boisterous were his high spirits, between two bouts of sepulchral blankness, when he simply stood listening, motionless, all taste for life seeming to drain unimpeded from his thin, tortured body, so abundant were his high spirits and so stirring their repeated, miraculous return that Malinka found herself irresistibly driven to look into that plain face and study it, disorientated and moved, her hands jittering restlessly.

The servant gave a girlish cry:

"Oh yes, let's go out to eat!"

She glanced anxiously at Malinka, as if dreading her veto.

"Good idea," said Malinka, not far from tears.

How would she ever make of the servant's life less bitter a bread?

When, at afternoon's end, they said goodbye to the servant and started back to the station, she thanked Freddy Moliger for his thoughtfulness towards her mother. He seemed taken aback to be thanked for behaving, he said shrugging, as he always did.

He stiffened a little. Malinka half-felt the wing of an indistinct fear graze her cheek.

Then he shook his head, and his face went back to its usual expression, harmless and stagnant, like an animal bled dry in the gentle darkness of its sleep.

"It was no work at all," he said amiably. "Your mother's so nice."

She stopped, breathless. To her own surprise, she had to clutch Freddy Moliger's arm to keep from sinking to her knees on the pavement.

"If you only knew the pain I've caused her," she murmured. "Do you think that can ever be made up for? Do you?"

But he hadn't heard, unless he was pretending. As they passed by a bench where two neighbourhood women sat chatting, women Malinka knew by sight, having crossed paths with them many times, she gave them a nod, and he snorted.

"You say hello to that dirt?" he asked, loud enough to be heard. "Don't you think we've got too many of those people around here? I'll tell you what I think: they make me sick."

He stalked onward, caught up in a rage that covered his cheeks with red blotches.

Stunned, Malinka scurried mindlessly after him. When she caught up he gave her a smile, his serenity and good cheer suddenly restored, and she could feel herself burying the memory of that moment in a place where she wouldn't easily find it again, because the whole thing was simply incomprehensible.

She wanted to remember only Freddy Moliger's kindness to the servant, who'd greeted him just as Malinka had hoped: as the emissary of an ardent wish to repent.

*

Before long she suggested that Freddy Moliger move in with her, and he appeared the next day carrying everything he owned in a bag.

That evening they made love for the first time.

Although she felt tense, grown unused to pleasure and the search for it, and too lost in thought, she serenely took stock of herself and found she was at ease, found that Freddy Moliger's body caused her no aversion or sadness, and that at the same time she had no fear of disappointing him, or of being disappointed, whereas, she remembered, her immense, undiminishable love for Richard Rivière never slipped free of her self-imposed duty to live up to his expectations, her furious, consuming desire for self-sacrifice, without which she felt guilty and wicked.

She sensed that Freddy Moliger expected nothing he couldn't readily give.

When he first saw her trim, long-limbed body, its slender bones invisible beneath her solid flesh, he let out a polite and admiring little cry, but his eyes were indifferent, and Malinka understood that he'd neither hoped nor feared she would have a beautiful body.

Nothing was a problem, nothing wasn't good enough, and it never occurred to him to think of his body as attractive or not. He was what he was, without bluff or boast, like a plant, like a stone, and beautiful or ugly his body didn't belong to him, and wasn't his responsibility.

He was neither an attentive nor a selfish lover, but full of a strangely neutral, almost austere gentleness, and Malinka felt free and at peace. She was still lost in thought, but she was also serene, because Freddy Moliger's presence never challenged her to prove anything at all, no more the goodness of her soul than the perfection of her body, and because she wasn't lying to him.

Not that Richard Rivière had ever asked anything of her. But the fact that she'd become entangled in the snare of an endless striving to please did nothing to dispel the muted fear, which she felt even in their happiest days, that the most necessary discipline might be beyond her, and that only that discipline could make the thought of the servant, the bitter bread of her life, tolerable to her.

Nor did Freddy Moliger ask her to tell him about herself.

For the first few days after he moved in she could see his gaze drifting over the photos that ornamented the walls and the shelves, of Ladivine, of Marko Berger, of the children, or of Richard Rivière, and no interest or curiosity ever shone in his eyes.

She tried, in a casual, affectionate voice, to bring up her daughter Ladivine. He turned and walked out of the room, with a rudeness that wasn't like him. Whatever was closest to her, like all talk of emotion, seemed to plunge him into an impatience he objectively recognised, as if it were someone else feeling it, and he walked off as if to get hold of himself, such that Malinka came to see in those abrupt, maddening disappearances a sign of diplomacy rather than boorishness.

She stopped trying to tell him about her daughter and grandchildren, and about her emotions generally.

She sometimes thought, without resentment, that Richard Rivière and Ladivine must have longed terribly to hear what she was feeling or thinking, that towards them she'd always been tender and distant, giddy with an inexpressible love and yet hard to love, and here she was finally finding her voice and Freddy Moliger did not want to hear.

She knew Richard Rivière and Ladivine probably thought her an extremely simple woman.

Didn't she sometimes embarrass them, in their sparse social life, with her anxious, smiling silence, her frozen face, lips always slightly parted, her pleasant, wary, stubborn way of never saying anything even the slightest bit personal?

Oh yes, surely, they had resigned themselves to thinking her slightly witless.

Was she? She didn't know.

She only knew that her mind was now forever pondering thoughts that filled her with a calm, comforting passion, and that she owed this to Freddy Moliger, to the way he'd come to her that evening in the pizzeria, with his dead, desolate face, his limping form, and that, painfully, in a devastating glimpse of the inevitable, she'd abruptly realised they might rescue each other.

Now he lived in her house, and his company never disturbed her.

He moved through the house quietly, like a wild animal, she sometimes thought, whose way was to leave only the most discreet trail.

He cooked and cleaned energetically and efficiently, telling her over and over of everything that had happened in his life, the brutal parents, the brother killed by the train, the daughter he never saw, his impassive, reedy voice wanting nothing, accusing no-one.

And, though she'd heard these same stories before, never varying, their details always precise and identical, as if, almost bored, he were recounting the story of the same old movie over and over, she went on listening with an understanding and a friendship that drove her whole being towards him, and she suffered for him, since he showed no sign of suffering, and in this way hoped to displace the rage she now realised was trying to burrow into Freddy Moliger's heart.

Every new telling of those stories was as painful to hear as the first, perhaps more. Each time she felt Freddy Moliger's irremediable solitude all the more poignantly.

If, she thought, she could relieve him of the anger pointlessly besieging him, which he wore himself out trying to hold back, if she could do that by enduring his tales of woe, by trying to picture his woes so completely that they could only leave her weeping and wailing inside, then maybe they wouldn't weigh so heavily in Freddy Moliger's mind, and he would find peace and solace.

Give it all to me, let me shoulder the burden of your miseries, she silently begged him, because I know how to deal with them. And so she listened, never flinching at even the most harrowing moments, and she filled herself with his sorrow till she choked, so he would be free of it, he who after his brother's death had spent his life struggling on alone.

At night, in the bed she'd shared with Richard Rivière for more than twenty-five years, she took this other man in her arms, and then it was she who found peace and solace, who felt freed and delivered of all obligation.

She was simply herself, Malinka, in all the innocence of her ephemeral, precarious presence on this earth.

She was never humble with him. She could be authoritarian, firm, though never hard, and her voice was always gentle.

Freddy Moliger's habits and ways did not irritate or surprise her, except when he weakened before the onslaughts of his anger and sullenly let it submerge him, becoming a different man, at once exultant and despairing and almost greedily eager to get some good out of it, to vanish into it until he was absolved of all responsibility.

She glimpsed this most painfully in the course of a visit her daughter Ladivine would soon pay her.

"If it's all the same to you, please don't call me by my first name in front of my daughter," she said to Freddy Moliger in an uneasy voice.

He puffed out his cheeks and let out a little sigh of indifference.

It wasn't seeming to hide things from her daughter that embarrassed her, it was the thought that she wasn't yet ready to reveal to Ladivine that her name was Malinka.

I'll do that, she vowed, the day I introduce the servant to her. Because, she felt certain, that day would come.

Already she brought Freddy Moliger along whenever she visited her mother, and he thought of those visits as a perfectly natural thing and obviously enjoyed them, and very often Malinka sat silent and attentive in her velvet armchair as the servant and Freddy cooked the meal in the little kitchen, and she heard the quiet hum of their voices sometimes interrupted by Freddy Moliger's piercing laugh or the servant's playfully outraged protests when he tried to take on more than she wanted.

But with Ladivine she felt so intimidated, so self-conscious!

Had her daughter not had every possible reason, over the past twenty years, to find her stupid and pitiable, lost, inaccessible?

On the phone, she had no choice but to answer Ladivine's troubled but remarkably precise, probing questions, her startled concern all too clear, as if, thought Clarisse Rivière, she was convinced her mother could only have taken up with some shady and untrustworthy man, and she had a duty to come and investigate.

How surprising it was that her mother was with a man other than her father!

She would never have said so, but it was shocking as well, Clarisse Rivière could hear it in her incredulous voice and her flood of mundane questions, as if to prevent her mother from talking to her of love or carnal desire.

"Does this man have a trade, does he have money?" Ladivine had asked almost at once.

"He works here and there, when he finds something."

"But do you give him money? Does he ask you?"

Clarisse Rivière felt sad for the both of them, for Ladivine who thought she had to interrogate her like this, and for herself who didn't dare tell her, however gently, that it was none of her business.

"Yes, sometimes. When he needs it. I have more money than he does, it's no problem."

Ladivine went quiet, less so she could think all this over than so she could come up with a new line of attack – for that was how Clarisse Rivière saw these questions, in spite of herself, knowing there was nothing but solicitude behind them, and yet for the first time in her life she did not feel guilty towards Ladivine or Richard Rivière, or eternally obliged to them.

But she'd trained them to treat her like a foolish woman, ever indebted, elusive, easily taken in, and so she could hardly blame Ladivine for feeling concerned, or for talking to her like a child.

"Papa . . . Richard once told me you don't cash the cheques he sends you," Ladivine began, uncomfortable.

Clarisse Rivière hurried to come to her rescue:

"That used to be true, but not since a couple of weeks ago."

"Now that this man . . ."

"Freddy Moliger," she very quietly broke in.

"Now that this Moliger's with you?"

"Yes. We're living it up, you know," she added with a forced little laugh.

But on the other end of the line Ladivine wasn't laughing.

After another silence, she asked Clarisse Rivière's permission to come and see her, to come down to Langon, as she said.

Freddy Moliger greeted this as he did every piece of news involving Malinka's family life, with that amalgam of boredom and feigned arrogance thinly plastered over his displeasure, rage very visibly thrashing and growling below it.

"You're fond of my mother, aren't you?" asked Malinka, anxiously. "So why not my daughter?"

"Your mother's a pitiful nobody, and that's why I like her, and she feels the same about me," he said gruffly.

She remembered those words when Ladivine walked through the door and she saw her daughter's hesitant eyes turn towards Freddy Moliger, then immediately dart in alarm towards a corner of the room, then another, and then finally come back, veiled, slightly fixed, uncordial, to Freddy Moliger's shoulder or neck, her lips forcing themselves into a more or less polite smile.

And Clarisse Rivière thought of what he'd said and suddenly saw the truth in it. She blushed in pity and sadness.

She tried to look at Freddy Moliger through Ladivine's eyes, she saw his skinny alcoholic legs, his bony, slightly misshapen hips, his fleshy red face, his bad teeth, she saw the apathetic but untrusting and secretive expression on his averted face, she saw his straw-like hair, still wet where he'd parted it.

Ladivine could see nothing beyond that physical misery, she could see none of the ravaged kinship that bound her, Clarisse Rivière, to Freddy Moliger, could know nothing of the salutary impoverishment denuding her heart ever since she'd learned, for one thing, to suffer for Freddy Moliger, and, for another, to caress that damaged body with pleasure and tenderness, and find it soft beneath her fingers.

Ladivine could know nothing of this, very likely refused even to imagine it, and looking through her eyes Clarisse Rivière could only understand.

And she pitied her daughter for having to tolerate this, the presence of such a man in the house where her parents once lived in harmony.

But she felt a far sharper pity for Freddy Moliger, who couldn't escape the anxious, troubled stare of Malinka's daughter, having realised even before she laid eyes on him that he would be neither loved nor appreciated, just as he'd sensed before the servant laid eyes on him that she would be fond of him, that she would have no choice but to be fond of him, in her own misery.

Clarisse Rivière sat down on the blue couch, and, though feeling an infinite sadness, brightly asked Freddy Moliger to bring them a beer.

"And maybe a little something to nibble on, dear?"

Was she trying to show Ladivine how docile Freddy Moliger was?

She then realised that she was afraid they might somehow prevent her from keeping this man by her side, on the pretext, say, that he had an unhealthy hold over her. But that was absurd, she told herself, suddenly reassured. No-one had the power to forbid her anything, nor try to protect her against her will.

Ladivine took her to the Galeries Lafayette in Bordeaux, and all the way there Clarisse Rivière silently refused to speak of Freddy Moliger, just as she refused to let Ladivine buy her an outfit for her birthday.

She thought it would be a betrayal to accept a gift from someone who'd taken so strong a dislike to Freddy Moliger.

Because Ladivine clearly loathed him, with an unreasoning, frightened, irreparable loathing that left Clarisse Rivière as uncomfortable as some vile obscenity. In the eyes of her daughter who knew her so little, he could only be a creep who'd wormed his way into her life solely to take advantage of the naive woman that, for Ladivine, through her own fault, she would always be.

She glanced sidelong at her daughter's preoccupied face as Ladivine somewhat roughly pulled a yellow gingham dress from its hanger, held it up to her firm, opulent body, and looked at her questioningly. For a second, in the tiny contraction of her mouth, in her one raised eyebrow, Clarisse Rivière saw the little girl she'd raised and pampered, she recognised her child and lost her nerve: how could she ever confess to her daughter that she was Malinka, and that a certain servant was leading her solitary, bitter, forever ruined life just a few streets away?

Several days after Ladivine left, she got a beige cardigan with little mother of pearl buttons in the post.

Freddy Moliger was standing nearby as she opened the package, found the gift, and, an anxious intuition running through her, answered reluctantly when Freddy Moliger asked where it came from.

"It's from my daughter, for my birthday."

"It's your birthday and I didn't even know it!"

He was speaking in his high-pitched, grating voice, unsteady and heated.

"Birthdays don't mean anything," she said, trying to put on a smile.

"Well, they must mean something to your daughter, and to you too, since you're happy with your present! Isn't that right, aren't you happy?"

She shrugged, folded the cardigan, hid it under the tissue paper.

"So why didn't you tell me it was your birthday? What, I'm not worthy of giving you a present? Only your daughter knows how to pick out something you'll like?"

She turned to face him and immediately realised she'd made a mistake, because she felt the fear that had flickered on in her gaze.

But she didn't know until that moment that she'd realised something very important about Freddy Moliger, didn't know that she'd realised it from the start, which was that, as with a dog, you had to be careful not to let him see your fear.

But at the same time she felt what she'd felt with her daughter a few days before: in the glint of boyish anger in Freddy Moliger's eyes, in his puffed-out cheeks, she saw, she recognised her child – or rather the child he once was, but at that moment it felt as if he were hers.

A great tenderness flooded through her.

She took the cardigan back out of its package, quickly slipped it on over her dress, and ran off for her camera.

While Freddy Moliger was framing the picture on the machine's little screen, his composure returning as quickly as his rage had erupted, she wondered if he could still see the fear in her eyes, if he could perhaps even see, should that fear now have vanished, the shadow of the fear that she knew would come back.

CLARISSE RIVIÈRE FELT HERSELF FLOATING BACK AND FORTH on a warm, thick swell, whose density stilled any move she might try to make. She didn't want to move anyway, because it would hurt, it would hurt terribly, she knew, if she made any attempt to change her position. She couldn't remember if she was sitting or standing, lying or crouching, outdoors or at home, but it didn't much matter. She had to place her faith in the mindless but confident perseverance of the heavy, dense tide now carrying her off, and when she spotted the edge of the dark, overgrown forest, its treetops towering and black against the black sky, her only thought was "I've never been in a deep forest", but she put up no resistance, certain that there she would be just where she was meant to be.

SLOW AND PRECISE, LADIVINE SYLLA LIFTED EACH FIGURINE, caressed it with her chamois, gazed at it meditatively for a few seconds, then put it back where it was, or, if she'd chosen to move it to a different shelf, set it aside in a shoebox.

She liked to imagine the boldest ones' eagerness at the prospect of changing places, and the fears of the shyer ones, the very young shepherdesses, the newly weaned lambs, the dolphins and kittens, which didn't like to be disturbed. To them she carefully explained in a half-whisper that like it or not things had to be shaken up now and then so every member of her little world would know all the others.

She herself couldn't feel at peace if she sensed a disharmony in her trinkets' society, and certain rainy Sundays, when a grey daylight filled her ground-floor flat, seeming to make the room even darker, she blamed her melancholy on the tension turning her figurines against one another because she hadn't paired them up properly.

Her mind at peace, her hair carefully pulled back, she threw a cream linen jacket over her shoulders, took her shopping trolley from its place by the door, and went out.

It was a sunny Saturday in May. The narrow pavements shone, freshly cleaned, and the cramped, dingy street had the pure, comforting smell of a springtime morning.

Ladivine Sylla began to review what she would need from the

105

market to make the nice lunch she had planned for the following Tuesday, when Malinka and that Freddy Moliger would be coming.

She could only think of him as "that Freddy Moliger", and even this, even this distant and circumspect way of naming him stirred her so violently that she went weak at the knees.

She didn't dare think of him simply as "Freddy", though that familiarity would have more precisely expressed the affection and gratitude she felt for that man, because she feared the depth of her own emotion, she feared that, should she ever happen to murmur "Malinka and Freddy", she'd have to sit down on the pavement, trembling uncontrollably.

"That Freddy Moliger" let her hold her excitement at bay.

She walked towards the market at her unhurried pace, pulling her squeaking trolley along, and with mingled pleasure and astonishment remembered Freddy Moliger's thin face, his off-blue eyes, like stagnant water, so empty and dull when words weren't enlivening them, and the fact that her present happiness, her fondest wish, had taken the desolate form of that stranger intrigued her endlessly. That was simply how it was, there was nothing more to understand.

That man was rescuing them both from their curse, her, Ladivine Sylla, and her daughter Malinka, the only real creature she loved in this world – how hard it was to have only her daughter to love!

Malinka had brought her that Freddy Moliger, and he'd settled into Ladivine Sylla's life and thoughts with miraculous ease and inevitability, and she immediately realised he would free them from the spell.

What matter that he seemed such a sad case! Was that not the very sign of an envoy's power, the perfect humility of his appearance?

She wanted to cook a leg of lamb with Soissons beans, and haricot-vert bundles bound up with strips of bacon. She'd forgotten to ask when he last came if he liked his meat rare or well done, but she could get around that, she thought, by putting the lamb in the oven only when they got there, even if it meant waiting a while with a glass of wine and some finger foods. She was already, delightedly, imagining whipping up puff-pastry canapés with Roquefort or anchovies and mini-tartlets with onion jam.

That Freddy Moliger was always hungry, she'd noticed, almost gluttonous, he ate quickly, preoccupied and contemptuous, as if scorning his own appetite, but, thought Ladivine Sylla indulgently, isn't that how those who weren't well fed as children always wanted to seem, people used to having badly cooked, meagre helpings slammed down before them, with even less love than for a dog?

She entered the Marché des Capucins and made for the butcher's stand she considered the best, even if, because its meat was expensive, she almost never shopped there. But for that Freddy Moliger she wanted only the finest and tenderest.

As for her daughter Malinka, she ate everything in the same way, without to-do, without interest or awareness, and she was happy with everything because food meant nothing to her.

Oh, her daughter Malinka! How heartbreaking, yes, that Ladivine Sylla had never found anyone else to love!

She'd long been convinced that Malinka kept her out of her life because she was ashamed of her, Ladivine Sylla, who couldn't be other than what she was. Then, as the years went by, she came to believe that they were both entangled in the coils of a shared spell, bonds that Malinka could no more loosen than she could, that they were both being punished with the same cruelty, the same injustice, and this helped her bear her bitter existence and cast off all ill will towards Malinka, whom she loved since then with a purified heart, a comforted heart.

And Malinka had brought her that Freddy Moliger, and now displayed a new face, shimmering with hopefulness, and her clear, quiet gaze, now unafraid to meet her mother's, told her she had accepted, with joy in her heart, this new order: the introduction of Ladivine Sylla.

Suddenly it was all nearly too much for her.

She'd often tried to picture the life Malinka was leading. Once she thought she saw faint brown patches on her daughter's cheeks, as if she were pregnant, and then she disappeared for several weeks.

How she used to dream of meeting that child, and how she feared it as well! He or she would be over thirty by now, and Ladivine Sylla was an insignificant woman whose appearance, whose status, whose uninspired conversation might very well, she had no doubt, come as a disappointment.

At the activities centre where she went several times a week to play draughts or knit in the company of other women of the neighbourhood, she generally sat silent, imprisoned in the shameful emptiness of her life, listening distantly as her neighbours talked of their children and grandchildren, of their husbands, living or dead, asking no questions so none would be asked of her.

Who could claim to know Ladivine Sylla? There was nothing to discover in her, there was too little to her.

She bought a two-kilo leg of lamb, a pound of haricots verts, some apricots for a tart. The shopkeepers knew her and greeted her amiably, despite her reserve, her habit of answering their banter with nothing more than a nod, and their observations on the fine weather with a thin smile. But that Saturday she was open, almost cordial. Little by little, her daughter Malinka was acknowledging her!

Leaving the market, she decided to make a detour down a street parallel to her own, where she could enjoy the sunshine.

She was passing by a newsstand when the front page of *Sud-Ouest* caught her attention after a few seconds' delay, making her retrace her steps, still pulling her trolley, and then, her legs suddenly weak, her arms limp, as if her limbs had understood before her head, she stared hard at a photograph of a beautiful, serious Malinka, her face slightly sad and uneasy, narrow and delicate like her own and framed by locks that fell in light waves over her slender shoulders, looking into the lens, at the photographer, anxious to please.

That attractive fifty-four-year-old woman was her daughter Malinka. No question about it, that was her.

Ladivine Sylla tried feebly to reach for the newspaper, but her arm refused to move. She clutched the handle of her trolley with both hands and bent down to read the headline: *Woman stabbed in her home in Langon.*

She stood up with a little cry and, still clasping the handle, scurried off down the sunlit pavement, in the perfumed air rich with anticipations and promises. She realised she was crying out as she lurched along, but her voice was muffled, hoarse, low, and no-one paid her any attention.

THE DOG WAS THERE, ON THE OTHER SIDE OF THE STREET, it was there for her now, waiting for Ladivine Rivière to emerge squinting from the dimness of the hotel and stand for a few seconds on the potholed pavement, in the blazing late-morning light, as she did every day, undecided, happy and deeply calm, until some chance happening, a child's cry, a flight of pigeons, oh even a fly on her cheek, led her to set off to the right or the left.

Never straight ahead, because that's where the dog was, because it was watching her.

She had no doubt that the dog came for her now, after first coming, perhaps, perhaps, for Marko or the children.

But she so hated the idea of Daniel and Annika being monitored, guarded, or looked after by that dog, the idea that they might need any such protection or oversight, and that the dog might have known it, she so hated that idea that she'd pushed it aside in disgust, and the very notion came to strike her as absurd.

Not because it was, but because even thinking of it was troubling, repellent and hurtful.

The children needed only the vigilance, the deep, anxious love that she gave them, she and Marko, and the big brown dog that in this unknown land had decided to serve as her consort or sentinel had that right alone, for her alone – certainly not the right to take responsibility for her children.

But suppose Marko might have liked to have that dog looking after him?

Still, she was by no means sure that the dog meant her well, she never approached it, never waved at it, never even met its gaze.

Marko could nonetheless have liked that animal's discreet solicitude, unmistakable or uncertain. It seemed like this trip was bringing them nothing but trouble, he'd complained once again at breakfast, defeated and confused.

If he could believe that some citizen of this strange country had found it natural to express his devotion by temporarily inhabiting the flesh and the skin of a huge scrawny dog, its mission to follow Marko Berger's every step, if he could believe such a thing as she did, trust in it as she did, he would have found infinite consolation.

But Marko could imagine no such thing.

And so she'd given up thinking the dog might be coming for Marko as well.

It came for her alone. And so, too, she never spoke of the dog around Marko.

He wouldn't have mocked her, no, would have shown none of the coldness – the irritated scowl, the condescending pursed lips, the shrugged shoulders – that, for example, his father would have.

He would have looked at her closely, his brow furrowed and slightly concerned, gauging her seriousness, and then, once convinced that she wasn't joking, he would have laid out all the ways in which such a thing was impossible.

But she never said it was possible, never claimed it was conceivable.

It simply seemed to her that it happened, and happened like this: every morning, when she came out of the hotel and waited for her eyes to adjust to the dazzling light, the big brown dog was watching her from the opposite pavement.

She set off with no goal in mind, one way or the other, striding firmly over the dusty, uneven asphalt, joy in her heart.

And the dog followed, always keeping the street's width between them, and it was from the corner of her eye, her upper body slightly turned, that she saw and tracked it as it weaved its way, disdainful and faithful, through the crowds, the men selling swimming costumes and caps, the women with their displays of fruits and vegetables on a tarpaulin spread over the pavement.

Often it lost sight of her, when a bus passed by or a red light stranded a long line of cars.

And with that she slowed down a little, she couldn't help it, not that she was afraid she might unintentionally leave it behind, but because the anxiety she imagined invading its canine heart saddened her own.

This was their first time away from Europe as a family, and after three days they couldn't help feeling that, by an infuriating irony of fate, their troubles were multiplying in direct proportion to the care they'd put into planning their stay, as if in this country earnestness were a thing to be punished, and quiet enthusiasm, simplicity and worthiness generally.

They had spent the previous summers at Marko's parents' in Lüneburg and at a campsite on the Baltic, and it seemed to them a reasonable way of going on holiday, perfectly suited to the sort of family they were, and neither ever regretted aloud that it was so dull, over time almost exhaustingly dull, so this summer could have gone by in just the same way, between the elder Bergers' home, where it was tacitly forbidden to go without slippers, to speak loudly, and to get up after eight (and them, Marko and her, thinking themselves responsible for the children's obedience to these rules even when they were very small, and struggling to keep them from making noise and always to show them at their very best to the two old people they wanted on their side at all costs, not quite knowing why, maybe because they were plain, simple folk, and their judgement of people and situations seemed grounded in some primal, luminous, indisputable truth, when in fact it was often nothing more than a hodgepodge of hoary received ideas, she now thought with some animosity, pat opinions unthinkingly, unfeelingly parroted), and the campsite at Warnemünde, where the camper van they traditionally rented was in a way their second home, they liked to tell the children, whose happiness at going on holiday was heightened still further by the illusion that they were rich enough to own a summer house, even if she and Marko soon spent the days looking forward to evening, awaiting the aperitif hour, and then dinner, with the slight tension, the feigned, electric insouciance caused by those long hours of forced idleness on the windswept beach, and the crowds, the need to keep constant watch over the children, the feeling of absurdity that regularly ran through them when they caught themselves longing for the end of the holidays and the return to Berlin and to work and the coming of autumn, when in fact they wanted no such thing, they wanted only an escape from the inertia and emptiness of Warnemünde.

And there they found themselves drinking to excess.

Early in the afternoon, when the children were napping in the camper and they themselves were sitting under the canvas awning, inattentively reading, often glancing up at the threatening skies (and what to do if it rains, if there's no going to the beach?), their thoughts turned to alcohol, to the type of wine they would happily uncork when the day came to an end, and not infrequently, especially if the grey clouds appeared and the cold little wind of Warnemünde came up, one of them went off for a bottle and two glasses, on the pretext of acquainting themselves with a new vintage.

Back home in Berlin, they remembered Warnemünde with bewildered shame and faint terror.

They discussed it, and agreed that they'd drunk more than was sensible.

They scarcely recognised themselves when they thought of the people they'd turned into in Warnemünde.

Because could they be sure now that they would have been able to make the proper decisions had something serious befallen one of the children, that they had been in any state, even before evening, to keep a vigilant eye on the children in Warnemünde?

Was it not by sheer luck, rather than attention to their responsibilities, that they hadn't had to drive Annika or Daniel to the emergency room in Rostock, and if they had, would it not have been immediately apparent to all that they were drunk? That they were, both of them, unable to care for their children and deserved only one thing, in Warnemünde at least: the immediate removal of their children on whom they nonetheless so desperately doted?

What had happened in Warnemünde?

It would have been nice to think that the spirit of the place had exerted some force on their souls and secretly estranged them from their own nature, but she and Marko prided themselves on their unflinching realism.

And even if their memory of Warnemünde was vague and gap-riddled, even if it sometimes seemed they never left that windy, dull-white beach, or perhaps precisely because blurred images were all they remembered of Warnemünde, they confessed to themselves that they'd spent their time tippling not because the spirit of the Baltic had refashioned their nature but out of weakness, out of boredom and laziness.

And this left them shocked, unhappy, concerned.

The thought that the children were now big enough to see a connection between what they might learn about alcoholism on television or at school and their parents' behaviour in Warnemünde deeply demoralised them.

Because all year long she and Marko strove to be ideal parents.

But the alcohol had clouded their memory, and now they could not completely recall what they'd said and done in Warnemünde, and the nature of their possible excesses in front of the children.

They fought back the urge to question them.

Nothing could be more foolish, they told themselves, nothing more inept, than forcing the children to remember upsetting details or even, if they'd noticed nothing, filling their heads with the idea that their parents had not been quite themselves in Warnemünde and were now feeling guilty about it.

They observed the children closely, watching for the word, the gesture that would reveal a discomfort around their parents.

But the children seemed to harbour no unspoken thoughts on the subject of Warnemünde.

Eventually she and Marko forgot their concerns, forgot to reflect on the dissipations of Warnemünde, and the year went by, not without happy moments or sound reasons for joy, and when the summer holidays came back they innocently set off for Lüneburg and Warnemünde once again, and what happened to them there, what seemed inevitably to recur as soon as they found themselves in the dull, windy idleness of Warnemünde, came as a surprise, and they were angry with themselves for being surprised, for having been cowardly enough to drape themselves in their innocence and succumb once again to surprise.

That, their Warnemünde dissolution, happened three years in a row.

And so they'd decided to spend their holiday far from Europe, far from Lüneburg and Warnemünde, from Marko's parents and the camper where the howling night wind often woke them with a start.

"They're not going to be happy," Marko had said, referring to Lüneburg.

Although he was smiling his little sly smile and raising his eyebrows, adopting a comical air, she sensed and understood his fear, because she felt it too.

She put her arms around him, whispered that she could call his parents herself, if he liked, to let them know that they wouldn't be coming to Lüneburg this year, but she was hoping he'd say no, so fearful was she of Marko's parents and their opinion of her.

He was in her arms, trembling and tall, abandoned, hesitant.

And no doubt he understood the fear that, like him, she felt.

"We'll send them a letter," he said, his confidence restored, pulling away and, she sensed, getting a grip on himself in every way.

Her written German was weak, so he took on the task, and she saw the slump in his back as he sat there, his broad back, usually so straight and so strong, now as if awaiting its punishment, consenting to the well-deserved reprimand that would surely be meted out by his disappointed parents, to whom, he observed in melancholy surprise, he hadn't written since his childhood and his few stays at summer camp.

They went off to post the letter together at the Nestorstrasse post office.

The queue seemed to be made up entirely of women just like Marko's mother, with their brave, tired faces, their drab padded jackets, grey locks emerging from under their knitted hats.

It was so easy, she thought, to pity old age and fault the hardhearted son, but did they know the price that had been paid, in sorrows and miseries, for that necessary hardening?

Because she felt her own body taking on Marko's anxiousness, his unease, of which only complete absolution from his parents could relieve him.

After a few days, they answered:

Dear son,

You will not be surprised to learn that we were startled by your letter, and deeply hurt, perhaps more deeply than you can imagine. We prefer to think that, had you foreseen the depth of our displeasure, you would not only never have written that letter, but you would have abandoned your plans for this trip, which in any case we are certain is not within your means, financially, and will force you to ask for a loan from your bank. As you know, we are resolutely against all indebtedness for leisure purposes; we raised you according to those principles, and the fact that you can discard them so easily, on the pretext that the two of you are "a little tired" of your very simple, restful, inexpensive holidays at Lüneburg as at Warnemünde, that is a thing we cannot understand. But this is not what matters most. We want to speak to you less of our anger or hurt, or our concerns, than of the deep, unanticipated emotions that followed that anger. Thanks to your cruel letter, we have come to understand the reasons for the strange disenchantment that came over us after each of your visits, which we attributed, wrongly, to the feeling of emptiness that settles into a house with the departure of its youngest and noisiest occupants. That truth, which we have now finally seen, forces us to concede that your letter has at least that to be said for it. For without that letter, without the deep relief that followed and drowned out our anger, we might never have understood why such a wound always opened in us after you had come to stay at the house, why it seemed that nothing had taken place even though everything had gone well, why, in short, we felt more alone, more melancholy, and more insignificant after enjoying your presence than in all the long months we had gone without seeing you. It was because we were hoping for a communion, and that communion never came. We were hoping for an outpouring of heartfelt words, and we never heard them. Of what sort, exactly? you will ask. But we do not know. We only know, and we have just realised, that the falsity of those relations, or at least their incompleteness, their superficiality, plunged us into a disheartenment that your departure revealed or aggravated. We so longed for something more – but what? Confessions, effusions? Possibly, but what else? We have always sensed, in your wife as in yourself, a dread of displeasing us on the most trivial matters, a quickness to agree with us about everything, which aborted any hope of a fulfilling conversation, and left us feeling like ogres or boors. We sensed that you adamantly refused to open your heart, even a little, lest we seize the occasion to upbraid you for something or other. Your wariness, your deep reserve, your excessive, hurtful politeness quite naturally influenced your children's view of us, and our relationship with them too became cautious and stiff. Why should that be? We who find empty socialising so intolerable that we have stopped seeing some of our friends whose sincerity proved less absolute than ours, how did it come to be that our own son's visits were so marked by awkwardness and unspoken disappointment? With summer approaching we felt an anxiety and a sadness coming over us, though we were unsure how to interpret it. Then your letter arrived, and our first reaction, angry and hurt, was nothing more than the predictable reflex of two mistreated parents. When, later, we found ourselves forced to admit that we were in the end relieved not to be seeing you, we were at first frightened and ashamed, then thought it over and arrived at the reflections we have just shared with you. So, you will perhaps ask, what am I to conclude, do they want us to come all the same, now that we know the situation, and perhaps work to improve it, or would they genuinely prefer not to see us, never to see us again? What am I to feel, how am I to act (you will perhaps be wondering), in response to so many contradictory statements? How to answer you, dear son? We ourselves cannot say. Do as you think you must, you and your wife, and above all do not abandon your plans for that senseless trip simply for fear of displeasing us. If you do, let it be because you think it best to avoid it. Should you choose to go all the same, do not concern yourself with our judgement, even if, as you surely understand, that judgement is severe and unsparing. And should it turn out that you cancel that trip because all things considered you want nothing so much as to come to Lüneburg, because the thought of forgoing Lüneburg would make you simply too sad, know that we will welcome you without reservation. We could even, if you find it easier, pretend that nothing had happened, that we had never written this letter, that you had no idea how hungry we are for unsimulated emotions. In short, you are free.

Your parents.

Marko read the letter, then handed it to her without a word, and she deciphered it slowly and laboriously, astonished to hear such language from people she'd feared precisely for their rudimentary minds, their limited vocabulary, which often led them to express themselves in a blunt and, for her who was used to more urbane ways, disconcerting manner.

She looked up, not knowing what to think, surprised, wanting to ask Marko to translate some of the sentences.

But his glance stopped her, and made her blush with a pity beyond words.

Never, in her husband's pale eyes, had she seen such bewilderment, such grief.

For the first time she glimpsed the child he once was, sensitive, no doubt easily hurt, few signs of whom could be seen in the confident, slightly aloof man he'd become, who appealed to her precisely because he so rarely allowed himself to be troubled.

She reached out to touch his cheek. But that would have been a mistake, would have humiliated him and brought no consolation.

She pushed the letter aside, turned away, and although they always talked about everything, neither would ever again speak of the letter from Lüneburg, nor of Marko's parents, whose names they would soon utter only when the children now and then posed some question concerning them.

Though they said nothing of it, it was clear that they would never again call Marko's parents to see what was new, that they would not, that June, go to the Karstadt store to buy a birthday present for Marko's mother.

It seemed to her, but she couldn't discuss it with Marko, that by writing "You are free" the elder Bergers had in effect delivered them of the impossibility of being angry.

She was angry with them for the pain they had caused Marko, and she was certain that Marko was equally angry and perhaps even outraged at his parents, whose decisions, until this question of their holidays came up, he had always obeyed, whose wishes he'd respected even when his own were very different, as when they had obliged him to find a trade and give up on a veterinary degree, which to his parents' mind took too long to achieve and offered no guarantees.

From the tension in his face, the new hardness in his gaze, she sensed the sharpness and durability of his anger, but she also sensed that he was not unhappy to be feeling and cultivating this newfound right to hate his parents, that it made him seem bigger in his own eyes, and bound him more tightly to his own will, heretofore often feeble because subjugated to his parents', which was implacable, enigmatic and savage.

His voice became firmer, there was a hint of aggression in his humour, and even that she understood and respected.

The dog followed her to the vast walled lot set aside for the tourist market, wedged between the beach and the road.

There, as if finding such a place beneath its dignity, it sat down by the entrance and watched her, from the greatest possible distance.

It knew, she thought, that she would have to come through this same gate to start back for the hotel.

Were there some other way out, the dog would surely have stayed close by her heels.

It knew she would come through this same gate again, she thought. And it would be there, sitting in the dust, in the heat, its long tongue hanging out and its chest heaving, and the watchful look in its black eye would give her no clue, convinced though she was that its vigilance was intended for her alone, by which to decide if it was spying on her or protecting her, if she should flee it or revel in its care.

That didn't concern her. The question was moot for her now.

Because even were the dog spying on her, its watchfulness made her feel safe, not so much in the streets – perfectly sedate, as it happens – of this big, unfamiliar city, but more broadly, safe from sorrow or unhappiness, failure or ruin.

She walked through the market stands with her new stride, at once lazy and confident, loose and firm, looking at everything and knowing she'd buy nothing because she and Marko now had to avoid all unnecessary expense, but not wanting anything anyway, neither fabric nor pottery nor metal bangles, simply happy as she thought she'd never been before (because anxiety had always subtly spoiled her most joyful moments, the birth of her children or the completion of her degree), feeling her healthy, familiar, faithful body move freely through the warmth, her thoughts wandering this way and that, unencumbered, weighed down by no worry, no incomprehension.

She could, if she wanted to, or if the miracle of this new outlook had not come to pass, easily find something to torment herself with, she knew that.

But it was as if, rather than deposit her in another land, the plane had delivered her to a universe apart, where she could finally feel the happiness of being herself free of existence's gravitational pull.

Is this what death is like? she wondered. Could she have died and not remembered?

But what she was feeling bore all the hallmarks of life at its fullest, particularly her awareness of her warm, rounded body, lightly dressed in pale linen, which she guided through the stands, she thought, smiling to herself, simply for the pleasure of enjoying its perfect mechanics.

She stopped at a straw hut that sold mango juice.

She put her elbows on the counter, ordered a drink, and the young brown-skinned woman who puréed the pieces of mango, added water, and poured the nectar into a glass was not a stranger, though this was the first time she'd seen her.

She recognised the woman's very motions, her precise way of peeling the fruit and then pulling the flesh from the stone – she'd seen all that before, exactly the same, no less than the high, smooth forehead, the little dark mouth, the cheek slashed by a thick scar, the faded red T-shirt and the pointed cones of her breasts underneath.

Down to the tiniest moment, she'd experienced all this before, though she'd never been to this market – how she raised the glass to her lips and saw that the rim wasn't clean, saw the lingering trace of other lips, slightly sticky, perhaps crusted with sugar, and how she deliberately placed her own lips on that residue and found no distaste in her untroubled heart.

In what dream had she as it were made a date with this woman and this glass and this thick juice, whose sweetness in her throat was exactly what she'd already known, though she'd never before drunk the juice of a freshly-puréed mango?

With a frivolous little laugh that she did her best to make re-assuring, she asked:

"Have you seen me before?"

"Where? Here?"

"Here or somewhere else."

The woman looked at her, slowly shook her head, then at once turned away, as if dreading another idiotic question and embar-rassed in advance for them both.

"Well, I've seen you before, but I can't recall when."

And with good reason, she thought, if it was in one of those dreams that seem so perfectly real you wake up convinced that you really did travel somewhere, that there are no such things as oneiric visions, only realities you assume to be dreams, even though you see yourself with no age, and the seasons have no tang.

Suddenly eager to strike up a friendship, to confide in this woman and rouse her curiosity, she nearly added:

You were wearing this same pale red T-shirt, and I could see the shape of your breasts underneath it. I drank this same mango juice, which you served me in just the same way. Isn't that incredible?

I have a husband and two children, a girl and a boy, and I went out this morning and left them sleeping at the hotel. We have troubles, but in a way we're very lucky too.

Instead, she only gave her an insistent smile.

And the woman was still stubbornly looking down, refusing that dubious alliance.

"I have to be going now," said Ladivine, "but I'll be back, and I'll bring my husband and children with me."

Didn't that last sentence sound more like a threat than a promise?

Again she laughed her deliberately superficial little laugh, but she sensed at once that this triviality was no less out of place than that longing for a connection founded in a wondrous hallucination, on the incarnation of shadows she alone had perceived.

Reluctantly, she walked away, and now her enchantment was dimmed by the feeling she'd done something wrong, shown a lack of discretion.

It would soon be eleven o'clock. The market was gradually emptying out, the hubbub receding in the thick heat.

She realised there was no point in trying to make anyone understand the strangeness of what she was feeling, or the vastness and harmoniousness of her joy, or how natural she found it to see her anxious life dissolving here in the big brown dog's watchful gaze.

And it wasn't because she was on holiday. How misplaced that word seemed, given the rash of mishaps they'd endured since their arrival, and if they compared these past three days to their weeks-long holidays in Warnemünde and Lüneburg, they clearly should have been sorry they hadn't gone once more to Warnemünde, sorry they'd so dreaded the tedium of Warnemünde that they dared to believe there was another way.

But not for anything in the world would she have wanted to be waking up in the Warnemünde camper van at this moment, and she was sure Marko felt the same, even if for now he seemed unable to find any palpable pleasure in their holiday here, perhaps, she told herself, because no-one had seen fit to lodge his or her conscious-ness in the skin of a dog and become Marko Berger's guardian.

She smiled as she walked, a vague and ingenuous smile.

She never doubted that Marko would rather be suffering here than stewing in his discomfort and anxiousness at his parents', and even that he would sooner die here than surrender to Lüneburg and lay at his parents' feet the weapons he'd just discovered he had.

He was so angry with Lüneburg for making him spineless and vulnerable.

But he'd granted himself the freedom to change. He woke every morning energised by a new sense of himself, able to make decisions, whether weighty or trivial, undaunted by Lüneburg's judgement, and even defying it.

Would his humiliated parents' distraught faces never rise up before him, hurt and uncomprehending, Ladivine worried, would pity not one day end up crushing his attempts at liberation, his necessary initiation into hard-heartedness?

Having realised that they could not safely return, summer after summer, to the creeping misery of Warnemünde or the restless stupor of Lüneburg, they had still had no idea where to spend their holiday – as they put it, out of habit, knowing perfectly well that what they needed was nothing less than an escape from a quagmire.

They would not necessarily have to go far away to find that new lucidity.

It only had to be someplace utterly apart from the world of Lüneburg.

The ideal, thought Ladivine, would almost be to make sure that the elder Bergers had never heard or spoken the name of the country they'd call home for three weeks, would almost be for that country not to appear on the illuminated globe in Marko's parents' living room.

Every year she set aside three thousand euros from her French-teacher salary, while Marko, who repaired watches and alarm clocks in the timepiece department at the Karstadt on Wilmersdorfer Strasse, managed to save up two thousand, and though that sum was more than enough to rent the camper van and buy low-end wine at the Warnemünde minimarket, they soon discovered it wouldn't go far for a family of four holidaying in any spot unknown to the elder Bergers and to Lüneburg in general.

Night after night, they put the children to bed and sat down at the computer to compare not only the prices of flights and hotels the world over but also the hundreds of comments posted by Internet-wise travellers, because more than anything Marko feared that their trip, that mighty step towards emancipation, might turn into just one more example of the horrible ways the most gullible and least well-heeled tourists could be fleeced, and yet, far from reassuring him with their potential preventative effect, these testimonials only further inflamed his anxiety and suspicion, sometimes pushing him to the brink of despair.

How, he asked Ladivine with a sort of dour satisfaction, when so many experienced people, far savvier than they, fell for the same old scams (and here he made as if to tap at the screen, to point out yet another grim, edifying tale), how could the two of them, who'd travelled so little, who had never even been on an aeroplane, hope to escape fraud and deception?

"Just listen to this," he would say.

And, although she was sitting there beside him, eyes fixed on the screen like his own, he read out the monotonous tales of swindles endured by strangers of whom an uncomfortable Ladivine would have preferred to know nothing.

What did they have to do with these people, she thought, who sought only ordinary amusement from their holidays abroad?

What did they care that the B. family thought they'd booked a room in a four-star Majorca hotel and ended up in a cubbyhole looking onto a malodorous airshaft? Or that the F.s, having paid for a full-board week's stay in Djerba, found themselves shelling out for breakfasts and bus excursions?

She longed to reach out and turn Marko's anxious face towards her own – that sharp-featured face she so loved, inevitably summoning up memories, faint or vivid depending on the circumstances (and sometimes only stirring up a very gentle melancholy in her heart), of the handsome Teddy Ted, the thin-cheeked, yellow-haired cowboy who in her childhood had inspired a love so passionate that she had to force herself to forget, lest she sink helplessly into despair, that he was only a character in a comic strip – and remind him that their goal with this trip was not relaxation or entertainment or an introduction to some new sport.

Let some unscrupulous hotelier put them in a windowless room; their wish for a more clear-eyed existence would come true all the same – and maybe even more fully?

"Oh, this stuff doesn't matter that much," she would say, cautiously.

He said nothing, his thin lips frozen in a cheerless smile.

This fierce determination not to be hoodwinked, now Marko's obsession, was heightened by his resentment of Lüneburg, and, imagining his parents darkly exulting on learning that they'd had a dreary time in a disappointing and venal land, its charms long since faded, he raced frantically from site to site, unwilling to place his faith in any, pretending to linger over an offer only to observe, in a sudden paroxysm of spite, that the prices were well beyond their means.

Towards midnight they would go to bed, their eyes weary, their minds dulled. Marko's cheeks were so hollow that Ladivine could clearly see the outline of his jawbone.

To convince themselves that their spirit was positive all the same, they'd picked out a few possible destinations, a handful of packages that the next day they saw as the preposterous or suspect things that they were, to which their exhaustion had nearly blinded them.

How could they ever reconcile the choice of a "Tour of the Magical Maghreb – bargain casbahs – Berber feasts – colourful folklore" with the only ambition that could justify such a trip, which was precisely to take them away from banality, from bleakness and inertia?

Not to mention, said Marko, that his parents probably found that very same sort of flyer in their letter box, and while there was little danger of bumping into the elder Bergers in the streets of Agadir, since they never left their own part of Germany, there were Lüneburg neighbours, people Marko had known since childhood, who might well, like them, end up at the Hôtel Igoudar, chosen for further consideration the night before because of its discounted rooms.

He spoke with an exaggerated composure, an only faintly sarcastic detachment. His arms hung at his sides, hands slightly raised, palms up, resigned. But Ladivine saw the lids of his blue eyes twitching.

Unthinking, she blurted out:

"I'll call Richard and ask what he thinks."

"Richard?" said Marko after a pause. "That's a good idea, give him a call."

And from his relief Ladivine, slightly taken aback, realised the depth of Marko's admiration for Richard Rivière, even though he'd never met him and knew of him, Ladivine's father, only what Ladivine happened to tell him, tentative, reticent and terrified.

But it isn't Richard that fascinates him, she thought, it's Richard's tragedy, it's what Richard's been through.

And what about me, she then wondered, wasn't my loss even more terrible than Richard's?

She felt herself growing heavy and numb, she felt her heart go cold, as it always did when she thought of her parents, and she was grateful to the part of her mind that controlled her emotions for protecting her in this way, because with her faculties alert and her heart afire she could never have withstood the incomprehension and grief.

And yet "I'll call Richard," she'd said, and those words had come to her spontaneously and for a very simple reason, which was that Richard Rivière had done some travelling, of course, but above all that he was the most sensible man she'd ever known, who, without to-do or any real desire to triumph, always calmly and quietly turned out to be right.

She'd never described him to Marko in exactly those terms, not wanting him to think she was boasting of her father, and yet the portrait she'd painted of Richard Rivière over the years, through her hesitations and reticences, in her terror and sadness, had firmly planted in Marko a fascination with Richard Rivière, whom he hadn't met before the tragedy and of whom, afterwards, Ladivine always told him, in the breathless, gasping voice that took hold of her when the talk turned to her parents, "You'll see him after the trial, we'll all breathe easier then", though she found those words unconvincing even as she spoke them, seeing no logical connection between the trial and the long-delayed meeting of her father and her husband, and sensing that Marko knew it and could have easily, gently disputed what she was saying, held back only by his good manners.

And what was, in the early days of their marriage and then the birth of the children, an odd and slightly embarrassing situation – since even the elder Bergers, indifferent to everything about Ladivine, had expressed their surprise that neither their son nor the children knew Richard Rivière – gradually took on the almost sacred status of just how it is.

Clarisse Rivière, Ladivine's mother, had come to Berlin for the wedding, and lived long enough to see the birth of Annika and then Daniel, but not, thought Ladivine with an aching, mournful relief, to be loved by them, meaning that the children felt no pain at suddenly never seeing her again, and had even completely forgotten that she once held them in her delicate arms, delighting in their smell, their satiny skin.

Clarisse Rivière and Marko hit it off at once. They smiled at each other profusely, and sometimes, in the evening, when fatigue put a pinched look on their faces, their smiles turned slightly excessive and fanatical, so deeply did they fear some misunderstanding, one of them thinking the other bored or annoyed for some mysterious reason.

As for Richard Rivière's absence from the wedding, while Ladivine apologised on his behalf to Marko, to their friends, to the elder Bergers, citing her father's many responsibilities as an import car dealer, she knew, just as Clarisse Rivière cruelly knew, that Richard Rivière would have postponed any meeting to be at Ladivine's wedding, were it not for his insurmountable fear of a face-to-face meeting with Clarisse, his ex-wife, who'd kept the name Rivière, his name, fiercely, militantly insisting that she had every right.

The mere thought of seeing her again made him quake, and Ladivine and Clarisse knew it, felt it.

Not that there was any real danger of an incident.

But, thought Ladivine, was he not far less afraid of a scene than of the naked, devouring, silent sorrow he would surely see in the eyes of that woman he'd left so long ago, who refused to give up the name Rivière, his name, keeping and displaying it like the emblem

130

of her distress, like the one miserable treasure she'd been allowed to hold on to?

Clarisse Rivière had never complained, would never cause any trouble. Clarisse Rivière had never reproached her husband or anyone else for leaving her, for going away, had in fact helped Richard Rivière pack up his things, intent as always on sparing herself no labour, no fatigue, if her labour and fatigue could be of some use to someone.

She did all she could to make leaving easy for Richard Rivière, with the same discreet, tireless solicitude she drew on to help people out at the restaurant, far beyond what her duties required and on her own time, people who never even thought of expressing their gratitude, since she'd convinced them that for her nothing was ever a burden.

But, Ladivine sensed, Richard Rivière was not taken in by those simple ways.

Beneath her unquestioning helpfulness, he could see the wrenching sacrifice Clarisse Rivière was making for the sake of his freedom, the need for freedom he'd evoked to justify his leaving her, and whatever disregard or disdain it might earn her she did all this as if she didn't even see the sacrifice, as if she expected no reward, whether thanks or vague shame on the part of the person obliged to her, absolutely not.

She would have been shocked and mortified had anyone suspected she hoped for such things.

Confronted with that accusation, thought her daughter Ladivine, she would have stammered, wide-eyed, one open hand rubbing the air as if to erase what had just been said:

"No need for . . . Oh, no, no, it's . . . I'm just helping out."

"Really," she would have added, forcing out a little chuckle to show that she wasn't a complicated person, that there was nothing behind anything she did or said, no meaning other than what was obvious and outright.

Was that true? wondered Ladivine.

It was, no question, she told herself after every visit from Clarisse Rivière, whose big, bulging, murky-water-coloured eyes seemed to grow even cloudier when she heard talk of ambiguous acts, perverse behaviour, cunning lies.

A vague, lost smile would come over her, like the smile that parted her hesitant lips when someone spoke to her in a foreign tongue, her damp eyes seeming about to well over with the anxious tears always set off in her by a failure to understand, whether the German language or other people's behaviour, but the tears never flowed, and her smile took root and bloomed on Clarisse Rivière's delicate, mobile, scarcely wrinkled face like an ephemeral flower of innocence.

She accepted her ignorance and pulled away, seeming to hear nothing more, making an offering of her smile, of her devoted, generous presence, just as she did when the day came for Richard Rivière to leave their house in Langon, and leave her as well, Clarisse Rivière, his wife of more than twenty-five years, helping him seal the boxes of tools, clothes and dishes he would be taking to his new home, even carrying some of those boxes downstairs, though they weighed nearly as much as she did, taking care not to bump anything, not to hurt anything, because whatever Clarisse Rivière undertook she undertook with care and conscientiousness.

Did it make Richard Rivière angry, Ladivine wondered, to see his frail, abandoned wife working so hard to make his leaving easy?

Far more likely, she supposed, he simply shot her a look of helpless exasperation and turned away, thinking he would never again have to endure Clarisse Rivière's excessive kindliness, and that naive, impalpable, shocking devotion he'd come to find so unbearable, and

132

Clarisse Rivière's preposterous ways, the comically baffled or belea-guered look that sometimes appeared in her huge eyes, the hurried trot of a walk, neck thrust out like a turtle's, making quick work of her rare attempts at elegance and concealing the strange beauty of her long, sinuous, agile body, unknown even to her.

Richard Rivière must often have found his wife ridiculous, thought Ladivine, must have been ashamed of her in public and even more deeply ashamed for seeing her that way, but very likely Clarisse Rivière never suspected it, she who knew nothing of ridi-cule, who never mocked anyone, not because she was virtuous but because she was innocent, and whom some, Ladivine knew, just as Richard Rivière must have known, thought a fool because she lacked the capacity to see malice.

"I'll call Richard," Ladivine said, then, her heart quailing, her hands suddenly damp, and she was so relieved to hear the phone ring and ring fruitlessly in the house (or flat?) outside Annecy, where her father lived, where she'd never been, that her legs trembled and her forehead went cold, like someone miraculously saved from some deadly menace.

The second day Richard Rivière answered, and his severe, pre-occupied voice turned gentle, surprised, and loving when he realised it was Ladivine.

"Is that you, my girl? How are you, darling?"

And Ladivine was struck dumb, though she had no reason to suspect any disaffection on her father's part, since it was she and she alone, she thought, who had decided they couldn't see each other until the trial, and Richard Rivière had complained at the time, writing her long e-mails to tell her he missed her, that her resolution was unjust.

And it was, and Ladivine knew it.

But the mere thought of seeing Richard Rivière before Clarisse Rivière had been restored to her place of quiet, pure respectability (by the grace of a severe prison sentence? and suppose that's not how it turned out?) set off a long shiver of almost loathing resentment towards Richard Rivière, and left her heaving and breathless, like an animal driven too hard.

It was cruel, it was unjust, and she knew it.

Because what had happened was in no way his fault, because there was nothing to blame but the very thing Richard Rivière had tried to escape, Clarisse Rivière's inability to grasp the concept of malevolence.

But Ladivine could not help thinking that horror and vileness would never have entered their lives had Richard Rivière not left Clarisse, had he sacrificed his hunger for a new life to the need to protect Clarisse Rivière.

By leaving her, he'd handed her over to savagery, which she didn't know how to see.

She was defenceless, he'd left her that way, alone and naked and no doubt already drunk with the need to give of herself as soon as Richard Rivière's car turned the corner.

"Hello? Are you there? Ladivine, sweetie?"

"Yes, I'm here."

She was gasping for breath, clutching the receiver, trying to hold back the wave of anger threatening to submerge her, as always when she pictured Clarisse Rivière abandoned on the house's front step while Richard Rivière's four-wheel drive (was it already the Mercedes M-Class then?) sped away, filled with suitcases and boxes, gleaming dimly in the pale sunlight of that wintery Sunday, then vanished at the corner, bound for a brand-new existence that Clarisse Rivière would never be part of.

Oh, but Ladivine understood how he'd come to find life with Clarisse more than he could bear, she understood it the moment he told her, slightly sheepish but also visibly proud of himself for daring to take such a step, that he was planning to leave the house, she understood it, yes, and in a way gave him her blessing.

Was that why she so resented him now?

Because she'd wished him happiness, and had never said any such thing to Clarisse Rivière, because she might thereby have brought sorrow crashing down onto Clarisse Rivière's poor head?

She'd wished the wrong person happiness – was that why she couldn't forgive Richard Rivière?

Hearing him confide in her with that mixture of pride and embarrassment, she thought he needed her support, her assurance that she would not judge him, and she gave it to him, her heart pounding, bleeding, she gave it to him not as the daughter stunned and shocked by that man once so perfectly stable and faithful in his well-ordered life, but as the twenty-eight-year-old adult that she was, tolerant and capable of understanding the hunger for adventure (he talked like that now, that dwindling man, that weary, diffident man whose one extravagance was his passion for four-wheel drives!) that might come over a father who'd irreproachably acquitted himself of his every duty and wanted to devote the last phase of his life to himself alone.

Would she not have done better to rush straight to Clarisse Rivière, drag her out of her deserted house, bring her back to Berlin and look after her until her vast, rudderless goodness found others to take on?

She had not. It never even occurred to her.

And that, she thought, is why her anger at Richard Rivière was misplaced.

"We're looking for somewhere to go on our next holiday," she said in a stolid, almost blank voice. "Somewhere south. Do you . . . do you have any suggestions?"

He let a moment of surprised silence go by. He was expecting me to talk about the trial, she told herself, he was thinking we'd finally talk about that damned trial, and all I want to talk about is our holiday.

But when he spoke, it was in the gentle, light-hearted, warm, infinitely fatherly voice that Richard Rivière always used with his daughter Ladivine, which, a little more than ten years before, had led her, almost forced her, to absolve him (was leaving Clarisse Rivière a misdeed, a crime, a mistake? or was it nothing of the sort?).

Because she was powerless to resist the love in her father's voice, for her and her alone, because she was powerless to snap herself out of that enchantment and consider how to go about rescuing Clarisse Rivière, because she preferred to think he was the one who needed support.

Oh, for that she would never, ever forgive herself.

He fell silent. He let out a loud sigh, and Ladivine sensed that he wanted to bring up the trial.

A twinge of panic set her trembling again, and she was desperately looking for an excuse to hang up when she heard, behind him, distant, piercing, beguiling, a woman's voice calling out.

"That's Clarisse," he whispered, "but don't worry, she'll never be Clarisse Rivière. Talk to you soon, sweetie."

Ladivine just caught the echo of a fluting, cascading laugh, then Richard Rivière abruptly hung up, as if given away.

She picked up her bag and walked out into the warm, golden May street, the yellow-walled Droysenstrasse, their home since Annika's birth eight years before, almost running in the shade of the lime trees whose dripping sap left the pavement sticky beneath her sandals.

The cloying smell of the fallen, crushed lime flowers rose up from

the pavement, stronger than the scent of the clusters still hanging –
cloyingly sweet, too, she thought as she raced along, was the odour
of Clarisse Rivière's spilled blood, or perhaps rank and overpowering in her tidy house, but why, she thought, feeling her own blood
throbbing in her temples, why did the honeyed perfume of light,
frothy, yellow-white lime flowers always remind her of what she had
not seen but had a thousand times imagined, her mother's blood
brutally, abundantly spilled in the living room of her Langon house,
untouched until then by anything violent or out of place?

A whimper escaped her as she walked under the railway bridge.

Not because of the roar of the train racing by overhead, but
because she couldn't inhale Doysenstrasse's Maytime scent, richly
perfumed with lime flowers, without immediately thinking she was
once again smelling Clarisse Rivière's blood, the innocent but pun-
gent, stifling blood of her mother who didn't know how to shield
herself from malignancy, made suddenly strange and unknowable
by her blood spattering the couch, the floor, the curtain – so much
blood in so slight, so discreetly fleshly a body!

And smelling Clarisse Rivière's blood in the air, mingling with
Charlottenburg's springtime perfumes, the Langon calamity slowly
flooding the faraway, unsullied heart of Berlin, left her quivering in
terror – because then what escape could there be?

"The trial will heal us," Richard Rivière had told her one day.

But would the trial stem the tide of blood, stop it befouling the
quiet streets of western Berlin where she and Marko had chosen to
live, prudently distancing themselves from both Lüneburg's virtuous
judgements and Langon's silent, irreparable sadness?

She, Ladivine, Clarisse Rivière's daughter, had chosen to turn
away from that sadness rather than shoulder her share, and the worst
had then happened.

Tears clouded her vision.

But now the smell was gone, the smell of lime blossom and blood, replaced by the faint odour of stale cooking oil borne on the breeze to Stuttgarter Platz, when the weather was fair, from the chip stall on Kaiser-Friedrich Strasse.

She wiped her eyes with her bare arm, skirted the little park where she no longer took Daniel and Annika to play.

How many long, even tedious hours had she spent there, on this bench or that, and yet, and although she felt no desire to relive those days of stiff limbs and backaches, the sight of children at play in that same sandbox always brought an ache to her heart.

That's all over now, melancholy's insinuating voice whispered in her ear, they'll never be little again, that's over for you.

But, she objected, half aloud, I don't miss it.

All the same, she looked away from the bustling toddlers in the park, and the spectre of her carefree, happy, irreproachable self (no-one having yet shed Clarisse Rivière's blood) sitting on a bench watching over her children and letting her thoughts drift unafraid, like the two mild, dreamy-looking women she saw there, whose mothers' blood no-one had spilled in the tranquillity of a provincial house.

Yes, it hurt her to look at them.

That was over for her, the simple life she led in those days, and her children's first years would forever meld in her memory with the time when Clarisse Rivière was still alive, even if she silently disapproved of what her mother was doing with that life, even if any mention of her mother's life filled her with apprehension and unease.

Oh, but she had never secretly wished for an end to that life, only to the way Clarisse Rivière was living it since her husband left, a way not so much chosen as fallen prey to.

And now that the children were too big to take to the park, it was as if they'd been banished from the enchanted wood by Clarisse

Rivière's death itself, as though the awful wave of blood had driven them out, her and the children, stranding them, forever guilty and stained, in the flower-and-blood-scented street.

She stopped by the park's entrance, laid her hand on the gate.

Her palm knew the feel of the flaking paint, the warmth of the slightly sticky metal, for she'd so often pushed that gate open, sometimes limply cursing the hot sun or the sameness of those afternoons.

She adjusted the strap on her sandal.

My heel's so dry, she thought, that's no good for summery shoes.

And again her eyes filled with tears.

She'd had the very same thought about Clarisse Rivière when she last came to visit in Berlin, when Ladivine, walking behind, spotted her callused heels, incongruously revealed by elegant sandals with multiple gilded straps.

She was unsettled and moved by that sight, like the unveiling of something slightly sad in her mother's private existence, but it also irritated her a little, the contrast between those delicate shoes and those yellowed, cracked heels seeming to show once again that Clarisse Rivière could never do anything right.

She hadn't exactly thought: "If you're going to parade around in such flashy, probably expensive sandals, you should learn to take care of your feet."

She didn't have it in her to express such a thought, so sharply phrased, not even to herself.

Sympathy and shamefaced devotion often tamped down her bursts of annoyance with Clarisse Rivière.

But she couldn't help seeing her mother's rough heels, and now, as she pulled up her own sandal strap, she recalled the many times she'd been infuriated by some display of Clarisse Rivière's careless or absurdly trusting nature, when, confident of her judgement, her reason, she'd taken cover behind disapproval, forbidding herself to

139

see that no fault could be found with Clarisse Rivière, that she could only be watched over, because, like a cat, like a bird, Clarisse Rivière lacked all discernment.

Had she been willing to see that, Clarisse Rivière would no doubt still be alive, she told herself. Had she only been willing.

She went on past the park, started down the pavement overlooked by the tracks of the S-Bahn.

Stuttgarter Platz's pick-up bars were still closed at this slow, vacant afternoon hour, but a woman was heading into the Panky, a woman Ladivine knew, having regularly crossed paths with her for years, and she gave her a wave, and that woman was more or less Clarisse Rivière's age when she died, and her body was similarly long-limbed, taut, compact, but her hard, jaded, impassive face, the set of her lips, not bitter but tired and scornful, were nothing like Clarisse Rivière's, who'd kept her full, gentle features, almost untouched by time, well into middle age.

The woman's only reply was a quick twitch of the lips, making a rudimentary "hello", while an almost irritated and untrusting look crossed her face, as if, though long used to seeing Ladivine around the neighbourhood, she suspected her of unspoken judgements and didn't think her greeting sincere.

Does she think I'm only saying hello because I know she works in that bar and don't want her to get the idea I look down on her? Ladivine asked herself.

But I say hello to everyone I run into around here. Although, oh . . .

She also knew that by raising one hand in the sunshine and waving it at that ageing woman's coldly disenchanted face, that woman who, Ladivine had learned, got the evening off to a start at the Panky by dancing on a table (in gold sandals, her cracked, grey heels showing beneath the thin straps?), she knew she was greeting an image of herself, Ladivine Rivière as she could easily have become.

For her upbringing by Richard and Clarisse Rivière had done nothing to protect her from a life of that kind.

They had raised their only child Ladivine in accordance with a neutral morality, or unstable, or infinitely relative.

That was their outlook on life, so utterly unjudgemental that Ladivine learned as a child to find it deeply indecent to express a firm opinion on anything at all, or simply to think it, even if you would never speak it aloud, to consider the only honourable attitude an unwavering tolerance for every aspect of the private life and public behaviour of all those around us.

Never could Ladivine, caught up in girlish ardour and sometimes forgetting the house rules, rage against some act perpetrated on the playground without Richard Rivière or Clarisse Rivière, so alike in this way that she could rarely remember which had spoken, asking benignly, almost smilingly reproachful: "But, little girl, who are you to judge?"

Very unkind things were sometimes done in that crowd of children, words were sometimes spoken with the clear intention of causing damage or hurting feelings, and sometimes those acts or words were Ladivine's, and she told her parents of them without hiding their source, and although she knew how they saw things she was always a little surprised, confused, at the way they shrugged their shoulders and vaguely ascribed these things she found so appalling to the unchanging nature of the human race, to the necessarily legitimate reasons (necessarily because all of them were) motivating this or that person or even their own daughter, Ladivine, who shouldn't try to be perfect.

Richard Rivière and Clarisse Rivière never forgave: they never saw any wrong.

Especially Clarisse Rivière, blind to all misdeed, committing none herself.

Once in her teens, Ladivine stopped telling them what went on at school, knowing it would bring her no guidance, no lessons in right and wrong, and instinctively fearing, as she laboured to establish the precepts of her personal morality, that in her parents' infinite indulgence she might lose her way forever.

Then, when she started secondary school, with her sexual awakening and her wonderment at the purity of her fresh, young body, with the fascinated discovery that a pretty girl's fresh, young body is a most precious currency, she gradually forgot the unbending principles of propriety and frugality that her ardent, virtuous pre-pubescence had convinced her were necessary.

She soon made a name for herself, in the little world of Langon's middle class, as a sort of well-bred call-girl, driven on Saturday evenings to a restaurant and a hotel in Bordeaux by divorced shopkeepers or unmarried bank clerks, who dropped her off at her door Sunday morning in their white or gunmetal-grey people carriers, sometimes one or two child seats in the back.

They honked goodbye as they drove off, and, her key in the lock, she turned around to blow them a kiss.

She did not lie to her parents. She did not tell them she was babysitting or spending the night at a friend's.

She said: "I'm going out with a guy I know."

She showed them the money she got, and while she sometimes saw Richard Rivière's alert, cheerful eye briefly dimmed by a faint veil of discomfort and hesitation, Clarisse Rivière never showed that she found anything untoward about someone paying her daughter to go to bed with him.

And her daughter Ladivine was convinced that Clarisse Rivière sincerely saw no harm in it, that she was incapable of judging such a thing, because that was how it was, and whatever was had to be accepted.

Clarisse Rivière's eyes widened in admiring surprise at the fifty-franc notes Ladivine casually pulled from her little purse, as if Ladivine had won them in the lottery or found them on the pavement, not that she pretended to believe this, but because to her mind it was much the same – if her daughter Ladivine was earning some pocket money and seemed to enjoy her work, little matter that it was by prostituting her fresh, young body, the body of a beautiful, vigorous girl.

And Ladivine did enjoy her work, on the whole.

But she could not shake off a dark unease when she caught sight of a loving young couple, boys and girls her age pressed close together, as if seeking to erase the tiniest gap between their two bodies, and, surprised and unsettled, reflected that they were doing all this for free, and her disquiet expressed itself at home in sudden bursts of unfocused hostility stoically endured by Richard and Clarisse Rivière, who were unused to conflict, who neither enjoyed it nor knew how to quell it.

Had she found the words, Ladivine would have screamed at them:

"I never wanted this, I never wanted my first time to be with a paying customer! That's not what I wanted at all!"

Also holding her back was the slightly desperate devotion she felt for her parents, fervent but worn and exhausted, which compelled her to protect them from her own attacks.

Would Clarisse Rivière not have answered, with her tremulous, hesitant little smile:

"But you said they were just guys, a girl can have sex with all kinds of guys nowadays, isn't that right?"

She almost never spent the money. She stuffed the notes into an old pair of tights and shoved it under her bed, nothing more.

Besides, Richard and Clarisse Rivière gave her money, and unquestioningly bought her anything she might need.

And yet she went on making appointments with her regulars, meeting them at their place after her parents bought her a scooter, spending nights in suburban houses not unlike her own, with their beige plaster exteriors and roofs of interlocking tiles, in beds exactly like her parents', the same model finished in light or dark laminate, and her bare feet trod the same shining, hard floor tiles as at home, white or grey, and the various rooms all looked alike, the little kitchen off the entrance with its fibreboard cabinets, the living/ dining room with its puffy leather couch, its oversized armchairs, its giant TV screen, then the passage to the bedrooms with their square windows veiled by sheer curtains, their orange or yellow imitation colour-wash wallpaper.

Never, with those men she knew well, who treated her respectfully, often even thoughtfully, did she have any contact of the sort she saw among the girls and boys in her high school, never did she feel the urge to press herself urgently to them, and neither did they.

She shared their beds with no particular pleasure, but no disgust either.

Riding home on her scooter in the dark or the first light of morning, weary, tired of life, and humiliated by the very absurdity of that sadness, since nothing was forcing her to do what she did, she thought furiously of Richard and Clarisse Rivière peacefully asleep in their bed, hating them fiercely, briefly, for the absolute freedom they'd given her, and the high opinion they would always have of her.

The Panky's heavy steel door opened to let in the woman just as Ladivine walked by.

And the darkness inside, thick with the odour of old cigarettes, stale beer and filthy carpeting, seemed to take hold of the woman and snatch her away from the sunny world of the street, where the smell of chips, now stronger, seemed the very essence of innocent freedom.

Ladivine unconsciously picked up her pace, anxious to put the grimy façade of the Panky behind her, and the Blue Hot further on, presided over with icy indifference by women who could have been her, Ladivine Rivière, since her parents had never cautioned her against anything, and would have treated her to their blind, cheerful visits and unconditional love had she ended up turning tricks in one of these very bars.

She crossed Kaiser-Friedrich Strasse, feeling the sun-baked asphalt stick to the soles of her sandals.

Her chest was heavy with a sudden flood of affection.

How, in spite of everything, how she loved the life she had made for herself in Berlin, how afraid she was, sometimes, of losing it, out of carelessness, or failure to remember what could have been!

She realised that Germany had rescued her from Langon, and that Marko, Annika, Daniel, even the fearsome Bergers of Lüneburg, with their implacable morality, had extricated her from the flat, dull-witted stupor that Richard and Clarisse Rivière were letting her founder in.

And so she could look on the sooty façades of certain Kaiserstrasse buildings, still pockmarked with bullet holes, in the winter she could endure the long weeks of grey skies and cold, the dirty snow, she could even find a melancholy pleasure in the feeling of exile and aloneness when she happened onto an image of the eternal, radiant French countryside on television (and saw herself and her parents pedalling down a sunlit road lined with acacias or plane trees), she could look on the irremediable ugliness of neighbourhoods cheaply rebuilt fifty years earlier and in spite of it all feel deeply grateful to be living there, beneath that leaden sky, in that architectural chaos, that absence of sweetness and harmony, she who came from a region where a gentle clemency suffuses all things.

Although, although . . . Deeply ashamed, she remembered their Warnemünde lapses.

Wasn't it the summer after Clarisse Rivière died that all that started up?

She turned onto Wilmersdorfer Strasse, headed for Karstadt.

Still no crowd in the pedestrian street, which in two or three hours would fill with a parade of families whom Ladivine, remembering Langon's one-street business district, always thought oddly provincial in their serene, ambling gait – but now a man had locked eyes with her, and now, as a game, she was returning his stare, a quiet smile on her lips, and the man's typically German air, she mused, her mood brightening, made that little advance all the more special.

Because people rarely made passes in the streets of Berlin, more rarely even than in Langon, where it was largely the same people crossing paths, day in and day out.

Their elbows brushed and she looked away, her lips very slightly pinched, signalling that the game was over.

She immediately confessed to herself, with unusual candour – her habit was to sidestep upsetting thoughts, or shove them away with a violent mental thrust – she confessed to herself, then, as she turned towards Karstadt's front door, that she was exceedingly grateful to men such as this, genteel, not the womanising type, who paid her the homage of an interested and even relishing glance, who met her own surprised or playful gaze with the look of a wistful and elegant "Why not?"

Once a shapely young girl, though not so tall, not so slender as Clarisse Rivière (how she used to envy her mother's fine bones, willowy figure and slim legs, she who seemed stuck to the ground by a more powerful gravity, thanks to the ungainliness of her slightly thick ankles and short calves), she had become a woman of some heft, with a round, full face that made her eyes, mouth and nose seem almost incongruously delicate, as if out of proportion.

That was less apparent, she thought, when she was young, since she was thinner, and her face narrower.

But now that she'd done some living, as Clarisse Rivière sweetly put it, and filled out a bit, her little mouth and nose looked as though they'd been stolen from some other woman and glued onto her broad face as a joke.

Oh no, she took no pride in her physique, even as she looked on such questions with a scornful detachment, a disdain unfeigned even if belatedly acquired, at the cost of great struggles against long-standing, naive dreams of breathtaking beauty, or simply of piquant, Parisian charm – she would have loved to be a mere slip of a girl, here in Berlin, as svelte as she was distinguished, refined and sporty, her glamorous French accent the ideal finishing touch.

Which is why, though resigned to being just barely pretty, to being a very ordinary woman whose careful attention to her clothes, to the cut and colour of her hair, shoulder-length, warm-brown and wavy, compensated respectably for her homeliness, she was still moved and surprised when, like that man, someone caressed her face with a gaze full of a longing to know her, to touch her.

But she accepted that there was nothing special about her, she accepted it now, without heartache.

When, long ago, she stripped off her clothes before the men who were paying her, she always took care to conceal the parts of her body she found unlovely – her ankles, her knees, even her stomach, which she thought bulged more than it should.

At the time she saw those physical flaws as something like moral failings, and thought she could only be despised for not being magnificent.

She felt no shame today at those imperfections.

She even learned to show them off, when summer came, like inventive, slightly quirky accessories she'd chosen precisely for their novelty, and if her knees, which she'd always found pudgy, showed beneath the hem of the dress she was wearing that afternoon, a dark pink cotton swing dress with two big buttons fastening the straps, it was to suggest that she was as happy with those knees as she was with her curving, golden shoulders, that her shoulders complemented her knees in a harmony both subtle and bold, that this was just how it was supposed to be, that she wasn't, for instance, supposed to be graced with the shapely, light, dimpled knees of Clarisse Rivière.

And so she made her way through the streets, not particularly tall but standing very straight, poised on her stout legs, mutely proclaiming: Am I not, all in all, a fine-looking woman?

She pushed open Karstadt's glass door and headed straight for the timepiece department.

She immediately spotted Marko's tall silhouette. With nothing to do at this hour, he'd risen from the uncomfortable chair where he spent most of his day, repairing watches or, more often, changing their batteries, and now, on his feet behind the counter, he was staring into space, hands in his pockets, with his usual gentle and serious air, which made him seem lost in profound meditation when he was only daydreaming, not a thought in his head.

She kept her eyes on him as she walked forward, surprised to feel how much she loved him.

Sometimes she feared she was emotionally cold or numbed, and excessively hardened.

But she had only to glimpse Marko or the children in their own distinctive pose, or even simply remember that pose, to feel her love for them throbbing inside her, though she now knew such emotions were not without danger, too easily leading her into similarly fond memories of Clarisse Rivière (that way she had of sticking her lower lip out so far that it almost completely covered the other when she had to read something complicated!).

And thinking of Clarisse Rivière was a very hard thing for her.

She could, fleetingly, imagine the scene of the murder and Clarisse Rivière's blood, or perhaps the lawyers and the upcoming trial, but remembering the eloquent details of Clarisse Rivière's personality drowned her in sorrow.

Now that she'd lost him, the memory of Richard Rivière was scarcely less painful.

Would he, she wondered, say that of his daughter Ladivine, that he'd lost her?

She had no answer. She only knew that she'd forever distanced herself from Richard Rivière not because he'd gone off to embark on a mysterious new life but because, left to her own devices and the hostile world through both of their faults, Clarisse Rivière had been bled dry in her own living room, her throat slashed like a poor quivering rabbit.

And Ladivine knew she and her father were guilty, but Richard Rivière had shown by his behaviour that he did not see it the same way.

Because he could speak of the events and the trial with no hitch in his voice and no faltering in his gaze, because he could complain of the slow workings of justice and curse the accused, he could think of that man, speak his name, if only with horror and loathing.

Healthily, he could feel horror and loathing, he could say "that monster", as thousands of readers all across the country must surely have done when Clarisse Rivière's story, and photographs of her face, her smiling, gullible face, open, modest and charming, had appeared in the papers, with Richard Rivière's aid, for, raging, distraught, he'd handed over those photos of the wife he'd abandoned, the woman he'd offered up to be preyed on.

He could, in those same papers, proclaim his desire for vengeance.

His desire to see the monster spend the rest of his life behind bars.

149

He could be effusive and sincere, sometimes he could even feel the tears coming afresh to his eyes when a reporter asked what he'd felt on hearing the awful news.

This was what convinced Ladivine that Richard Rivière thought himself blameless, that no other possibility ever entered his mind, since he was clearly neither pretending nor lying nor exaggerating when he did these things.

He was himself, sensitive and open, a touch calculating, but never cynically.

Whereas Ladivine couldn't bring herself to speak Clarisse Rivière's name, or the man's, or the month and the day it all happened.

Whenever she thought of the months of the year, the days of the week, a blur blotted out the month and day she could no longer speak of.

And if her eye lit on the name Clarisse in a book or an article, her breath came quicker, and she moaned silently to herself.

As for the man, he inspired in her a sacred terror.

She'd once dreamt she was kneeling before him, or before a vague form that was unmistakably him, offering her throat to be slashed.

She could not vent her rage at that man, could not picture him or imagine any real life he might lead, could call down no curse on him.

She could only tremble in terror and incomprehension.

By that act, by the murder of Clarisse Rivière, that man had entered Ladivine's life and emotions, he'd taken root, and she could only submit to it, like, she sometimes told herself, an unwanted pregnancy discovered too late to abort.

Sometimes she felt that man's violent spirit kicking inside her, leaving her nauseous and faint.

Whereas, she sensed, Richard Rivière could think of it all like some horrible news story that curiously just happened to involve him.

And when he was not thinking about it, it did not upset him. His life went on.

How she resented that, how easily he'd got off!

She waved to snap Marko out of his daydream before she reached his counter.

She didn't like to surprise him at work. Caught idling, even without a customer in sight, he couldn't hold back an expression of childish shame, as if fearing he'd misbehaved, and that pained her, and made her vaguely indignant.

The fact that this wasn't Marko's place, that he was talented and hardworking and perhaps brilliant enough to get through the veterinary studies he once wanted to pursue was, for as long as she'd known him, so obvious that it tormented her to see him trapped behind a counter in a department store, with his gentle, penetrating gaze and too few occasions to make use of his intelligence.

But that he had, on top of that, acquired the reflexes of a humble employee, wary of a dressing-down from his boss, and even afraid of him, though at home he mocked that unpleasant man's dull-wittedness and pretention, that tormented Ladivine with pity for Marko and anger at the elder Bergers, who'd dissuaded their son from going on with his studies, wanting to see him settled and independent as quickly as possible.

Marko never complained. He was both too proud and too naturally discreet to dare speak of his situation as anything but a privilege, and even a blessing, having as he did a job not far from home, and a job at which, he claimed, though she didn't believe him, he was almost never bored.

Oh, no, how could she believe such a thing?

And was he right, she often wondered, to give in like this, to adapt so readily to something so unsuited to him, was it wisdom or weakness, admirable humility or mere passivity?

She didn't know. She was sure of one thing only: whether he admitted it or not, working at Karstadt was a sacrifice Marko had made, and how great a sacrifice she alone knew.

He spotted her, surprised.

She'd put on a broad smile to reassure him, so he wouldn't think something important or terrible had happened, since it was unlike her to come to see him at the store.

Relieved, he smiled back at her, with the shy smile that always gave him a touching, childlike air.

She loved everything that made Marko who he was, a German she'd known for some ten years, who'd become her husband and the father of her children, for all time and to her great surprise, so utterly did Germany and its people seem, back in her native Gironde, to belong to a distant and exotic world, inspiring too much indifference to leave room for prejudice, but at the same time so foreign that no-one would ever imagine living there without a dismissive little snort.

And yet this was how it was, she'd bound her existence to that of a German – and the very word still rang in her perplexed ear with the slightly quaint charm of a mystery into which she'd never been initiated.

She loved Marko, and he was German – what did that mean, and wasn't it odd!

How that word separated him from her, however delightfully!

She'd long noted certain habits of his, rooted in his upbringing, different from hers, she knew their tastes in food did not always concur, not having loved the same dishes as children – but above all she felt everything that was unknowable in Marko's heart, in the depths of his enigmatic, simple self, which sometimes surfaced in a glance whose intention she couldn't decipher, and she sensed, moved, that what it expressed was, more than anything, that he was German.

Privately, she called that the Secret of Marko, though she knew he had no idea he was inhabited by a secret, and couldn't possibly care less about being German.

And yet he was – how odd!

She leaned over the counter and gave him a quick hug.

He patted her back, a little embarrassed, his pale eyes looking around to be sure no-one had seen. Then he pushed up his heavy-framed glasses.

He was a thin man, tall and bony, who always stood with his weight on one leg, arms crossed and hips forward, in a vaguely feminine pose.

He had a bass voice, and belonged to the Karstadt staff choir.

"I talked to Richard, he told me where we should go."

Marko's faintly anxious face brightened at once, not so much, perhaps, because he was happy and relieved to see the matter of their destination decided as because he was thrilled at this confirmation of his long-held, ecstatically favourable opinion of Richard Rivière's almost superhuman sagacity.

And all at once he looked so young, his healthy light chestnut forelock sweeping untamed over his thick lenses, his flat torso beneath his short-sleeved shirt, even, she thought, the way his long waist plunged into his slightly drooping jeans, like a flower's strong, endless stem bowed ever so slightly against the lip of the vase, still so youthful in his obliviousness to his own gangly charm that it pained Ladivine's heart and suddenly, though their ages were the same, made her feel much older, she who had always worried so about her appearance.

She whispered the name of the country Richard Rivière had suggested.

"He has friends there, apparently. People he sold a car to."

"We'd never have thought of that," Marko cried, "but . . . Oh yes, it's perfect!"

But would he not have applauded any suggestion made by Richard Rivière, that man he'd never met?

His notion of Richard Rivière's tragedy, the murder of his ex-wife, was vastly inflated, Ladivine realised uncomfortably, and Richard Rivière felt nothing with the searing intensity Marko imagined, Richard Rivière was in no way the heroic, shattered man dreamt up with a certain self-indulgence and perhaps a long unmet need for someone to admire by a Marko who himself had been deeply shocked by Clarisse Rivière's death.

The blood rushed to Marko's thin face. Dreamily, leaning against the counter on one hip, he studied the cheap jewellery displayed across the aisle, and, not looking at Ladivine, murmured:

"Who knows? Maybe we'll decide to stay?"

A noncommittal snicker escaped her, slightly cross and disapproving, and she immediately chided herself.

Because she'd noted that habit of hers. She was quick to silence any thought of flight with a sarcastic remark, a prosaic appeal to reason, and yet she hated that attitude, which she thought an envious person's reflex.

She glanced at her watch.

Marko was smiling into space, eyelids quivering.

Ladivine very clearly felt herself walking away from the counter, leaving the store and emerging into the sunlit street, because it was well past time she was on her way.

And yet she was still there, one arm resting on Marko's counter, her legs, whose stoutness and damp nudity she could feel beneath her dress, seemingly unable to do as she asked.

Not knowing what she was about to say, she stammered:

"Yes . . . maybe we'll stay . . ."

And she felt as if she were placing a terrible curse on herself.

And what about Marko? What would become of him, so ill-equipped to protect himself?

And the children?

Who would come running to protect them, and how to be sure they wouldn't wander off, alone and unthinking, on paths unknown to their parents?

Was it really a good idea to listen to Richard Rivière?

He'd already shown that he could unwittingly sow desolation all around him, yes, even as he doled out nothing but love and tenderness – yes, Ladivine knew, he went on making long, frequent phone calls to Clarisse Rivière after he went away, so that even though he'd left her no-one could accuse him of abandoning her, certainly not, and had in fact enveloped her from afar in a solicitude that, Clarisse Rivière told Ladivine with pitiful pride, few long-gone spouses ever displayed, yes, to be sure, that's how Richard Rivière was, generous with his attentions and overflowing with love, none of which had prevented him from delivering his wife into the hands of brutality, of blind, fatal chance.

Suppose that with this advice Richard Rivière was doing misery's bidding?

Suppose that deep down what Richard Rivière wanted was to keep her away from the trial?

But one thing at least was beyond question, which was that she herself wanted nothing more than to be kept away from the trial, and Richard Rivière must have seen it.

With great effort and a faint suction-pad sound, she unstuck her legs.

Now she was walking up Wilmersdorfer Strasse towards Otto-Suhr-Allee, only vaguely glancing at the bazaars, their cheap wares cheerily spilling out onto the pavement.

Oh look, Jenny's Eis has closed down.

Storewide discounts at Heimwerker.

The water rippling over the huge, polished stone balls recently installed as an ornament for the pedestrian street, a sort of Zen fountain, sluiced towards her feet with its flotsam of cigarette butts and beer-can tabs.

She knew every shop, every sign, and nearly every one was connected to some moment of her life in this neighbourhood, from when she'd recently met Marko and they used to come for a kebab or a box of Asian noodles that they ate on a Pestalozzistrasse bench, to the time she'd gone into that pharmacy on the corner and asked for a pregnancy test, to that December when she took the children to watch the Christmas market being set up and drink not-very-good hot wine or cream punch and eat grilled sausages, and that graceless Wilmersdorfer Strasse with its provincial air and its reminders of Langon was so dear to her heart that, though Marko had often found less expensive apartments in livelier neighbourhoods of Berlin, she'd always refused to move away from Charlottenburg.

Dear old Charlottenburg – her attachment to the place had at least something to do with the charming name and the equally enchanting and desirable figure of Sophie Charlotte in her château, her oval face, pale complexion and abundant hair reminding her of Clarisse Rivière.

But didn't every woman who died too young remind her of Clarisse Rivière?

Every woman who died tragically, leaving behind a little crowd of inconsolable, eternally guilty people, and wasn't Clarisse Rivière herself, in her own humble way, a lonely queen in her oversized house?

Dear old Charlottenburg, unfashionable, sleepy – how she loved it!

Even the awful, morbid Rathaus she was now nearing, where she taught French four times a week, even that grim edifice, with its blackened walls, its outsize, graceless proportions, its overblown majesty, ridiculous but intimidating, even that ugly town hall whose dark green, too high-ceilinged corridors, she couldn't help thinking, had seen their share of terrified, unknowingly doomed people pass through, she'd learned to love even that, to feel at home even there.

She climbed to the top floor, walked towards the room used for French classes, a brown door, sea-green walls.

A few of her students were already waiting inside.

Knowing the answer, she asked:

"Who let you in?"

"Madame Sargent," one answered.

She looked at her watch to make sure she wasn't late – oh, two minutes at most.

Sargent, the other French teacher, a native of Caen, always watched for Ladivine's students and unlocked the door for them early, not so they wouldn't have to stand in the corridor but simply, thought Ladivine, to plant the idea in their heads that Ladivine Rivière was never on time.

Why on earth did Sargent not like her? Ladivine wondered, troubled.

It could not be rivalry.

Ladivine's students were in their first year of French, Sargent's in their second and third.

But Sargent did not like her, and subtly strove to undermine her. Why should that be?

Ladivine couldn't understand it.

To her shame, she also recalled that when she first came to the Volkshochschule, a few years before, she did all she could to ingratiate herself to Sargent, who had been teaching there for years and intimidated her with her authority, her severe poise, her adamant slenderness.

Sargent answered her every attempt to charm with a deflating brusqueness, the thought of which still made Ladivine's cheeks burn in humiliation.

She began taking worksheets and a collection of pencils from her bag.

Her students, some fifteen adults of all ages, looked on in silence.

Suddenly Sargent was there, on the other side of the desk.

Still peering into the depths of her bag, searching for the copy of *Les vacances du petit Nicolas* she was sure she'd brought with her, Ladivine recognised the smell of Sargent's clothes before she was aware of her presence – a nauseating blend of mildew and expensive perfume, as if every morning Sargent extracted her very chic person from a crypt.

"Ladivine . . . This is your mother, isn't it?"

"My . . . my mother?"

She looked up at Sargent's thin, excited, eager face, finding it deeply repellent.

A dull-white foam clung to the corners of Sargent's mouth. The wings of her nose shone beneath her thick, orange-tinted make-up.

Sargent was staring at her with fascinated yearning, and Ladivine half thought she was fighting off the urge to clasp the back of her head and pull her face to her crotch.

"It's this week's *Le Point*, have you read it?"

In her hands was a magazine open to a photograph and a long article.

She tried to thrust it into Ladivine's face, but Ladivine stopped her with one raised, bent arm, her movement so unintentionally violent that the magazine flew from Sargent's startled hands and fell to the floor by the table, open onto Clarisse Rivière's gentle, slightly frightened, hesitant face, her white cotton collar chastely and tidily poking out of the beige cardigan she'd got for her last birthday.

Oh yes, she herself, Ladivine, had picked out that fine-knit sweater at Karstadt, then posted it to Clarisse Rivière for her fifty-fourth birthday.

Who took the picture? she wondered, her head spinning. Was it Clarisse Rivière's killer himself?

Ladivine never saw her mother in that cardigan, since she died four or five days after she got it.

Had she put it on for him so he could take her picture, and because she thought it looked nice on her?

Had she told him, "My daughter sent me this cardigan from Berlin for my birthday"?

Sargent stiffly bent down and picked up the magazine, while Ladivine, sitting perfectly still, feeling the sudden scowl on her face, vowed not to apologise.

Sargent tapped on the crumpled page.

"It says here the trial's starting soon. Your poor mother. I had no idea. They mention you too, the victim's daughter."

Ladivine felt herself blushing. Sweat was flowing from beneath her bare arms, dampening her pink dress.

Her students didn't yet understand French well enough to follow Sargent's words, but Ladivine felt dishonoured before them.

Because who but a thoughtless daughter and a blameworthy family deserved to be exposed in the sordid true-crime pages for all the world to see?

"I suppose you'll have to go," Sargent went on in her breathy, lachrymose voice. "To the trial. Don't worry, I'll take your students."

"No, no," said Ladivine briskly. "This is none of your business. I'm not going."

She'd spoken angrily in spite of herself, her raised voice sending a ripple of unease, she realised, through her intrigued, watchful students.

To her great surprise, Sargent backed away, vaguely raising two conciliatory hands to Ladivine and giving her a glance unmistakably tinged with almost fearful respect, which, superimposed on her excitement but not concealing it, gave her the dewy-eyed air of a woman in love.

At the same time, she displayed the magazine once again.

And Ladivine looked deep into Clarisse Rivière's astonished eyes, achingly contemplating the little white rounded collar, the cardigan buttoned up to the top, picturing the knife plunging into the fine skin over her jawbone, just under her ear.

Gripped by a sudden nausea, she caught herself with one hand on the table, then fainted at Sargent's feet.

She never doubted that the dog would follow her when she came out of the market and started serenely back for the hotel, and so it did, that big, emaciated, grave-eyed brown dog, and she took care not to walk too quickly, because she thought it must be hungry and thirsty, though she had yet to see it display any need to eat or drink, urinate or defecate.

The dog seemed to be bound to her, committed to protecting or tracking her, body and soul.

Whom or what should she thank or curse for this she did not know.

But never once, from the start, had she felt the slightest fear or unease, though she realised early on that the dog was following her every step and she knew nothing of its intentions.

She abandoned herself, perhaps more thoroughly than she should, she told herself now and then, to the trust it inspired in her.

But she was tired of wariness, tired of expecting the worst, of fearing the future on her children's behalf, of fearing, on her children's behalf, life itself.

Sometimes she wished that by some miracle they could already be old, so she could stop being afraid for them, so she could be sure they'd get by in one way or another.

Now such thoughts never came to her. Was it the dog, was it the place?

And yet they'd got off to such a rough start in this country so warmly recommended by Richard Rivière, as if Ladivine's vanished father had resolved to counter Marko's admiration with a cold, sardonic, definitive rebuttal, or as if, she told herself, contemplatively and without rancour, her father had to grasp at and make use of anything that might keep Ladivine from the trial.

Was he secretly hoping she'd never come home?

Not, for there was no question he loved her, because of some unimaginable catastrophe, but on the contrary because she'd found such happiness and serenity here that she would gratefully make herself a prisoner of the place?

Was it him, Richard Rivière, who had cloaked himself in the skin of that dog, was that him trying to hold her spellbound?

But I'm not set on going to the trial, not in the least, I'm not sure I can bear it, and shouldn't he know that?

Keeping her head down, she slunk into the Plaza's air-conditioned lobby and hurried to the lifts.

She preferred not to be seen by the staff or the manager, who sometimes stood at the front desk and looked at her, she thought, with a mix of irritation and contempt.

Everyone in the hotel knew the Berger family had lost their bags at the airport. Ladivine sensed that this misadventure had earned them no sympathy, that it aroused only stern disapproval, untrusting and disdainful, particularly in the manager, so obsequious with the other guests, either, she thought, because he suspected her and Marko of hoping to get out of paying the bill with the claim that they'd lost everything or because he took them for a couple of ninnies who didn't know enough to keep an eye on their things.

161

She silently entered the room, immediately enveloped by stifling warmth and a musty smell.

She pressed a button by the door to start up the clamorous air conditioner, and it was as if she'd set off the alarm clock – Marko springing up in the bed, startled, exhausted (what new sources of fatigue had he gone to find in sleep's depths?), the children recoiling in their cots, two rusty, squeaking old things hastily assembled by an employee in one corner of the room the night they arrived, when they found no sign of the promised second king-size bed (so they were no different from the disgruntled tourists whose recriminations Marko had so ravenously absorbed from the Internet, so they too would soon be venting their spleen on the travel sites, so they were, oh, neither more nor less than a couple of suckers who can be counted on not to stand up for themselves even when they know they've been had?).

She came in, lively and fresh, still jubilant from her morning outing.

How could they lie there macerating in their night-time sweat, sticky with heat and troubled sleep?

"It's 11.30 already," she cried in her vivacious voice.

Actually, they'd all woken somewhere around seven, stifling and sweating in the room's hellish humidity.

The air conditioner made such a racket that on the first night they'd decided to make do without it. But it was hard to fall asleep in the heat, and they all woke up early.

They waited for eight o'clock to come and then went down to breakfast, after which Ladivine went out while Marko and the children headed back up to bed, not so much, thought Ladivine, to sleep as to fill up a daunting expanse of vacant time.

Because that, incredibly, was what was happening: it seemed Marko would rather pretend to be resting than leave the hotel, even though the hotel turned out to be far less pleasant and comfortable than they'd been led to believe by a host of photos and comments.

And – Ladivine wasn't quite sure, so dimly did she remember her phone call with Richard Rivière – it might have been her father himself who'd recommended the Plaza.

But the room was small and cramped, and the window couldn't be opened, guests being expected to endure the air conditioner's horrible din.

A once pale green carpet, now dull grey and mottled with stains, covered the floor even in the bathroom, where it stank from spattering water.

And what else? Ladivine was reluctant to list all the hotel's many deficiencies, finding in that mentality something small-minded and subtly demeaning.

But she couldn't completely shake off the feeling of dereliction, of ambient, vainly concealed filth that the Plaza had given her from the first day – nothing specific to complain of, she told herself, only an atmosphere of decrepitude, exacerbated or ineptly camouflaged by sordid half-measures.

And that, among other things, was what surprised her about Marko's insistence on going back to the room after breakfast, as if the disasters that greeted their arrival had convinced him there were still graver troubles to be feared if he ventured out onto the street, as if, disheartened, he'd decided to take no chances and hole up in the hotel until the time came to leave – but, she wondered, who or what was he afraid of?

And who would take note of his efforts, and so spare him any further unpleasantness?

She didn't dare tell herself outright, but she was disappointed by Marko's cowardice, and hadn't expected him to give up so easily on making the absolute most of this trip, as, she thought, she was already doing.

She had the dog to help her, of course. But if no dog was bothering to cling to Marko's heels, wasn't that his fault?

Coming into the room to find him sitting up with that lost, weary look, she almost told him of the dog, as an encouragement to bring about that same phenomenon for himself, that blessing or that calamity, she wasn't sure which, but in any case that antidote to anxiety and suspicion.

But she didn't. Was she afraid Marko might divert the big brown dog's attentions to himself?

I can't tell him in front of the children.

Was she afraid she might be jealous of Marko, should the dog choose a new master or prey?

The children mustn't know, for the moment.

She'd never even spoken to them of the trial, she'd never found the strength to tell them, even in the most cursory way, how their grandmother died.

Where to seek the words to tell such a thing, and didn't it sometimes seem wiser to forgo having children, and so not run the risk of one day having to tell them of such horrors?

Daniel and Annika seemed downhearted that morning, though when they saw her they did their best to put on a childish enthusiasm – exactly as if they were playing at being children, simply for politeness' sake, and so as not to worry their parents.

They carefully climbed out of their squeaking beds, dressed only in their underwear, and Ladivine knelt down before them and put one arm around each.

"Are we going to the pool?" asked Daniel.

"Oh yes, the pool!" cried Annika, with what struck Ladivine as affected enthusiasm.

"How about a walk first?" said Ladivine in her gentlest, most reassuring voice.

Daniel energetically shook his head. A pall of anxiety veiled Annika's pale eyes.

"They're afraid to go out," murmured Marko, rubbing his cheeks with a weary hand.

"Oh, so you're afraid to go out, are you?"

She'd adopted a mocking, affectionate tone, choosing to pretend she couldn't understand their trepidations.

But suddenly she found herself feeling defeated, almost conquered by an absurd, humiliating, unwarranted panic at the thought that their holiday was only beginning and that, if this kept up, the failure would be so pathetic that she and Marko would never recover.

She was equally disturbed that Marko had just spoken in German. It was their custom to speak French at home, and Marko forgot it only in moments of deep distress.

"And just what is there to be so afraid of outside?" she asked in her artificially playful and teasing voice, wishing at once that she hadn't, since the question might give a shape and a solidity to what must not be allowed to exist.

Daniel shrugged, unsure what to say. Annika compressed her delicate, thin little face into a horrible grimace. Daniel let out a small cry and covered his eyes.

Unrecognisable, Annika was clenching her fists to go with the hideous face she was making, and suddenly Ladivine was alarmed.

"Stop it," she said, a little sharply.

She grasped her daughter's hands, forced her fingers apart.

Tears were streaming from Annika's closed eyelids. She began to shake her head back and forth with a desperate violence.

Terrified by her contorted face, Daniel turned away.

"Come on now, stop it," said Ladivine, "that's not funny."

"She can't, she's stuck!"

Marko jumped up from the bed, bounded towards Annika.

He was in his underwear, he was thin and lanky, neutral and perfect, an exemplary image, for Ladivine, of a masculine body in its prime, in all its vigorous health and unconscious grace.

He squatted down beside Annika and began gently massaging the girl's distorted face, now wet with tears.

"There, there, my beauty," he was murmuring, "everything's going to be alright, Daddy will give you your face back."

And he forced his lips into a reassuring smile. Little by little Annika calmed down, her features freed themselves from their horrible expression.

Ladivine went to the hermetically sealed window.

She glanced out and saw that the dog was downstairs, not far from the entrance, lying in the ragged shadow of a dusty palm tree.

It looked up at her with its big, placid eye.

And she found her serenity flooding back, she who had lost all confidence on entering this room.

The children were splashing around in the deserted little pool behind the hotel, jumping and frolicking in a water so heavily chlorinated that it seemed to give off a sort of vapour.

At first, Ladivine had taken that dull white mist for a mirage.

She and Marko were stretched out on chaises longues, the smell of bleach coming to them in waves.

Sunglasses hiding their eyes, they lay motionless, sour and still.

Two days before, on discovering the mediocrity of the pool, they'd made a vow not to so much as sit on the edge and dabble their feet in the water, deciding as one that it would be humiliating to seem to find this little bean-shaped basin good enough after all.

It struck Ladivine that they were displaying their anger and disappointment in a way all too like them, muted and indecipherable.

She told herself they should have gone straight to the manager and complained of the scandalous difference between the pool's photos on the website and the pool as it actually was.

"It's all in the focal length," Marko had spat out, bitter and resigned.

It was this same pool on the website, but photographed at night, lit from within, and shot from above, from one of the rooms, making it appear fairly substantial and concealing its surroundings, missing tiles, battered dustbins, dirty concrete.

No-one ever seemed to use it but Annika and Daniel.

"All that chlorine can't be good for them," murmured Ladivine, groggy with heat.

Marko grunted in agreement.

But what could they do? If they forbade them to use the pool, how to entertain two children sick with fear at the idea of leaving the hotel?

Why not let them stay till it gets dark, that would be nice, she caught herself thinking.

How exasperated she was by the children's incuriosity! But weren't they simply taking their cue from Marko?

She turned her head to look at him, his mouth closed tight, his face tense behind his sunglasses, lying stiffly on his deck chair, like a prisoner on the rack, accepting his fate.

She reached out, took his hand, and found it cold as ice. She wanted to tell him, "Nothing's ruined, nothing so terrible has happened that suddenly we . . ."

But so grey, so stricken had she seen Marko's face two days earlier, when after more than two hours' wait at the airport they realised that they wouldn't be retrieving their bags, that their bags had in all probability been stolen from the carrousel before their passports were stamped, that they would have to go and fill out a stack of useless papers and draw up a pointless list of their two suitcases' contents, now gone forever.

It was just clothes, after all, she'd immediately told herself, but it seemed like some vital part of Marko's self was being excised, or his oldest, most ardent expectations betrayed.

She'd seen his harmonious face crumble, no longer held together by a certain optimistic and light-hearted vigour.

The cracks in his face went deep, the bones as if shattered with a hammer, and two days later he still had that same face, here by the pool where the children were bathing, tense, tortured and haggard.

She'd felt deeply defeated herself. It had been a long trip, with a stopover in Amsterdam because flying non-stop cost far more, and Daniel was whining and snivelling when they got off the plane, so much so that Ladivine wondered if he was ill.

Then that fruitless wait at the baggage claim, the hours of irritation and fatigue when they'd so long looked forward to this moment, and having to deal with grumbling, indifferent employees whose bizarre English neither of them could understand, and that demeaning sense of ridiculousness she tried to fight off, all the while holding a whimpering Daniel whose thirty kilos gave her sharp pains in the back – nothing was forcing us to put ourselves through this, why did we ever get ourselves into this, and at such enormous expense too, stupid, stupid.

As she was putting her lips to Daniel's hot, damp little cheek for a kiss, he raised his arm and slapped her.

Oh, nothing one couldn't pretend not to notice, perhaps only a hungry and exhausted child's erratic, unintentional gesture.

And yet, and yet.

She was sure Daniel knew just what he was doing – him, the gentlest, most loving little boy there ever was.

But she pretended not to have felt it, even as tears of surprise and dismay sprang up in her eyes.

When they finally reached the hotel, very late at night, with no other luggage than Ladivine's bag, they were too tired to dwell on their disappointment at the shabbiness of the room and the inadequacy of their reception, the children's beds having been forgotten.

For dinner they shared the half-box of butter cookies in Ladivine's bag, then they waited forever for the close-mouthed man in slippers and a stained T-shirt who'd been assigned to bring in the folding beds, a task he performed with a sullen, resentful, proud air, as if, Ladivine thought, he'd been punished or reprimanded on their account.

Marko watched him unfold the beds, blankly, like a feeble old man.

Much to Ladivine's surprise, he made no move to help as the worker wrestled with the recalcitrant, rusting metal.

Because it was Marko's habit, founded in discomfort and guilt, always to step forward and lend a hand, sometimes even to prevent any act whose aim was to serve him.

Marko could not stand to see people working for him.

But now he sat motionless on the bed, watching the man toil away, his gaze distant and vaguely empty.

In the doorway, Ladivine pressed a few coins into the worker's hand. He jiggled them in his open palm, sorted through them with his index finger, then dropped them wordlessly into his pocket.

She felt a surge of anger, though so brief that she couldn't grasp its cause.

She was so rarely angry.

Like Clarisse Rivière, who was incapable of anger.

Clarisse Rivière had helped out the man who would end up murdering her, she'd given him money, sometimes large sums, sometimes just a note or two for the shopping.

Did her killer display that same disdainful sneer as he dropped the money into his pocket? Did he look down on Clarisse Rivière for her generosity?

And why should she, Ladivine, Clarisse Rivière's only child, have to hear such a person's explanations and rationales?

Why should she have to hear every detail of what he'd done to that woman, Clarisse Rivière, who was once Ladivine's mother?

"The trial will heal us," Richard Rivière had said.

Ladivine came back into the room, exhausted, briefly furious again.

"Here we are," she said tersely to Marko.

Then, more gently:

"Here we are at last."

Was it the sun pouring into the room at dawn, was it a few hours of sleep, which restores everything to its proper proportions, was it simply the daytime, which, unlike night, makes every drama more modest, Ladivine didn't know – but when they walked out of the hotel the next morning, after a copious, serviceable breakfast, she sensed that Marko and the children had recovered a little of their enthusiasm, and it was even becoming imaginable to think of the loss of their luggage as a piquant detail in the story they'd one day tell of their stay.

It later seemed to Ladivine that the dog wasn't there for this first stroll.

She would never know for sure. It might have appeared without her knowing, it might even still have had the face and the look of a human being she would have no reason to distinguish from the rest of the crowd.

But she would always like to think it was looking after her from the very first day.

They got on a bus that would stop near the supermarket, where, they'd been told at the hotel, they could buy clothes.

Ladivine was deeply disturbed by Marko's fragile air when her eye landed on him in the bus and she realised she was seeing him, from a few metres away, as he appeared to strangers – a slender, pale man with a slightly lost look, a deeply temperate and vulnerable man whom any violence would find trusting and defenceless.

Annika and Daniel stood on either side of him, clutching his pockets.

But how, thought Ladivine, her heart aching, how could such a man ever hope to protect two little children from even the mildest aggression, and what about him fuelled their illusion that such a father could be their rampart?

Really, what was it, about that impressionable, over-sentimental man?

Oh, she loved them all three, but not without torment.

Sometimes she yearned to run far away from them, to know nothing more, ever again, of their existence and so shed all responsibility for them, those three who so completely depended on her, so fragile where she was strong and hard.

But not so strong or so hard that she could shoulder such a heavy burden of love and demands – and yet that's just what she did, so clearly she could, and it was in part thanks to her that her husband and children had so far led a happy life in which love and its demands were never questioned, in which love and its needs fell on their heads like a gentle spring rain, life-giving, always welcome.

She never doubted that she was loved back, by husband and

children alike. She had no grounds to complain about any of them, no, she had nothing but perfectly justified contentment and pride.

So . . . ? she wondered as she stood in the bus, clutching the aged, grimy, cracked leather handles, smelling the slightly fetid but comfortably familiar odour rising up from her exposed armpit, under the cotton of her T-shirt, unchanged for two days.

So why should she feel so weary, so beset, why this feeling of not being up to the task when she looked on those three trusting, beloved faces, which, even when as now they were not turned her way, seemed to be forever searching her face for lessons, advice, displays of tenderness and guarantees for the future?

She was ashamed, telling herself that this man and these children demanded nothing they did not have every right to expect, that she gave them nothing but what it was only right that she give them, and that, this being how family life was, it was her duty to submit without fear or pointless regret, because after all nothing had forced her to marry or procreate.

Yes, she was sometimes ashamed of her fear and exhaustion, which she had in a sense chosen – and among all the countless possible sources of fear and exhaustion, were that lovable man and those delightful children not the least onerous?

She knew all that. But there were times when she wanted nothing more than to slip away, not so much disappear as withdraw, though without causing anyone the slightest twinge of grief.

Little Daniel was looking at her, slightly anxious.

Resetting her face, adopting the benevolently confident, light-hearted expression that comforted the children as nothing else could, she gave Daniel a wink. The boy's features relaxed, reminding her how deeply Clarisse Rivière had loved that child, not more than Annika (Clarisse Rivière's heart was too simple and too just to have a favourite), but more serenely, because passionate love for a little boy reminded her of nothing, whereas, she one day confided to Ladivine, her joy and exhilaration at Ladivine's birth were so powerful that she couldn't keep them within endurable limits and, as she put it, she came under a depression.

Thirty years later, she still reproached herself for having, in the first weeks of Ladivine's life, shown her melancholy's unsettling face.

And Ladivine, gazing on Daniel's pretty, loving face, felt a stab of unquellable sorrow – never again would Clarisse Rivière stanch her remorse against that child's cool, silken neck. Worse, Daniel might have crossed her mind as she poured out her blood in her silent, deserted house, she might even have tried to cry out her grand-children's names, in a gargle of blood and phlegm, and realised she would never see them again.

Why should that woman's only child, Ladivine Rivière, run the risk of hearing her mother's killer describe her last minutes?

Why should she have to endure that, on top of everything she'd already endured?

"The trial will heal us," Richard Rivière had said.

But the only thing that could heal her, Ladivine, was protection from the horrific details.

Nor did she want to learn of that man's difficult childhood, of what, as Richard Rivière had told her, shocked and almost moved in spite of himself by so many failures and miseries, had irresistibly driven him, as they would no doubt say at the trial, to bullying and murder.

She wanted to know none of that, convinced that her sorrow would be even deeper and without end, because she might con-ceivably pity the murderer were she shown that he was a victimised child.

How not to feel sorrow and pity for all tormented children who turned into lost men?

After he'd hurt her so deeply and unendingly, she had no desire to compound her pain by imagining some part of his.

Whatever he might claim or imagine, Richard Rivière was already healed. But she, Clarisse Rivière's daughter . . .

The bus braked abruptly. Ladivine's shoulder bumped the chest of a heavily perspiring woman.

Between her breasts, half-covered in bright blue cloth, grew a few tightly curled, longish hairs, glued down by sweat.

Ladivine mumbled an apology.

Very tall and offhand, the woman looked at her closely, then smiled and said, in that brusque, rasping English Marko and Ladivine could scarcely understand without exceptional efforts of concentration:

"Wasn't that a beautiful wedding? Splendid party, don't you think?"

"Excuse me?" Ladivine said after a pause.

She too was smiling, full of good will, her brow very slightly knitted.

"A beautiful wedding," the woman said again. "Lots of money, but it was nice, well worth it. Pretty dress you had on, where did you buy it?"

Ladivine shrugged. She let her gaze drift past the woman, still smiling her polite, uninvolved smile.

The woman turned her back, and Ladivine sensed she'd been rude.

Her face turned red and hot, and she tumbled into a panicked despair, as always when she thought she'd hurt someone without knowing how or why.

What she would not have done in Berlin or Langon she did without a second thought in this packed, sweltering bus, full of people with calm, wide faces that she longed to see turn her way in friendship. She gently clasped the woman's elbow and said:

"Forgive me, you're right, it was a beautiful wedding. That dress, you know, I think I bought it in France."

Swept along by an inspiration that at the time she thought must be sound, she added, her voice a little too eager even to her own ear:

"You're talking about that yellow gingham dress, with the balloon sleeves and the wide belt that tied at the back? Yes, yes, that's right, I bought it in Bordeaux, at the Galeries Lafayette."

Then she remembered that dress was among the things that had disappeared with the luggage. But little matter – if this hairy-breasted woman had seen her at a wedding, wearing a memorable dress, that was the only one it could be, the yellow gingham dress from Bordeaux, the nicest she owned, the most flattering to her complexion, and the one she would certainly have chosen for a cer-emony of that sort.

"Oh, in France. So I won't find one here," the woman said simply.

And from her tone it almost seemed Ladivine herself had brought up this inane subject.

The supermarket was new, empty and frigid, standing alone in a stretch of wasteland where a few blocks of flats seemed to have burst from the red earth through sheer force of will.

They showed no sign of being lived in, nor of work in progress – no tarpaulins, no piles of breeze blocks, no machinery of any sort. Bits of rubbish, bottles, beer cans, torn cardboard boxes dotted the uneven ground, rutted, hard and dry.

Ladivine noted that the four of them were the only ones getting off the bus, and that nothing marked the stop but a blue plastic barrel, toppled by the wind from the bus as it drove away.

Marko set it upright, his hands now red with dust.

To Ladivine's great relief, the children were finding fun in this shopping trip beneath the fierce morning sun, in this deserted, sin-ister neighbourhood not yet shaded by any trace of greenery.

175

They ran off down the faint path to the supermarket, all glass and blue glinting metal, and soon their legs were red and their sandals dirty and all at once Ladivine's heart swelled with joy. Her children were happy, they were running in the dirt!

She thought nothing else mattered at this moment, she thought life was easy, straightforward and good.

She took Marko's hand, and he squeezed hers back, smiling.

"So that woman in the bus knew you?"

"She thought she recognised me; she was confusing me with somebody else," Ladivine hurried to answer, suddenly uncomfortable but not knowing why.

Marko gave a little laugh and let go of her hand.

"Well, you're right, you don't have to tell me," he cried, amused or pretending to be.

Then:

"I've seen several women who look like you since we came here."

He pointed with one finger at a figure in pale blue, just emerged from the supermarket and heading towards a block of flats, pulling a cart behind her.

A voluminous cotton drape hid her body and hair. Ladivine could scarcely see her face from that distance.

Annika and Daniel were waiting patiently at the supermarket's front door.

There was a dog standing guard, a large, muscular dog, chained to a ring sunk into the ground. It looked at them with its big, black, gentle eyes, and Ladivine was stunned to see herself in those dark pupils.

She was tempted to let them swallow her up and never come out again, imprisoned, untouchable.

How could Marko think she looked like a woman whose face he couldn't see?

No, she had the eyes and the gaze of that dog scrutinising the customers, and had Marko more closely studied the animal's manner he would have reached out to pet it, perhaps moved by something he did not at first recognise but which he would soon see was Ladivine's soul.

Later, she would be unable to say with any certainty that the dog at the supermarket and the dog unfailingly waiting outside the hotel were the same.

It was possible, it was probable. But she would never be sure.

Given the prices charged at the supermarket – the only one of its kind in the city, they'd been proudly assured at the hotel – there was no question of reconstituting the whole family's summer wardrobe. Ladivine picked out a pair of shorts, two T-shirts, a cap and a swimming costume for each of the children, and for herself a beige linen skirt with a matching blouse. The absurdly high prices gnawed at her.

She and Marko had budgeted twelve hundred euros in spending money for their three weeks in this place, and already these clothes had cost them almost three hundred.

She joined Marko as he was emerging from a dressing room, the menswear department's sole customer.

She stifled an anxious little laugh.

"What have you found there, darling?"

He examined himself in the mirror, pleased at what he was seeing. His face had a closed, aggressive, brazen look she hadn't seen before, and which immediately troubled her.

Not that it wasn't attractive, but only in the manner of a masculine type she found slightly frightening, crude and confident in a way that nothing seemed to justify.

He was wearing an outfit composed of a long pink tunic with purple floral motifs and a pair of trousers that came down just to the very top of his athletic shoes.

"Perfect for the climate," he said. "And it suits me, don't you think?"

She could only concur, at first reticent, almost hostile (like, she wondered, a dog baring its fangs because it doesn't recognise its master?), and then fascinated, the longer she looked at him, by Marko's undeniable beauty, his height, slender neck and well-defined shoulders seeming to have found in that curiously feminine get-up just what they needed to show themselves to their fullest advantage.

Never before had she seen Marko admire his own image, or take even the most meagre interest in his reflection.

And here he was finding in that mirror a man who surprised and delighted him, and he made no attempt to hide his naive pleasure at realising he was that man — why should that bother her?

Was she afraid that, like Richard Rivière who in the prime of his life realised that nothing, neither law nor morality, obligated him to go on living alongside a woman for whom he would always feel a deep tenderness but whose peculiarities wearied and bored him, a Marko suddenly aware of his beauty could only end up abandoning her, Ladivine Rivière, stained forever by her mother's blood pouring out in a provincial suburban house, streaming into the Berlin apartment, spattering their neighbourhood's pavements, sullying even the springtime sky?

But Richard Rivière and Marko Berger had nothing in common, save, perhaps, their love for her, Ladivine.

As for the obscenity of that murder, as for Ladivine's feeling that, as that woman's daughter, she'd been diminished, disgraced by the event's squalid horror, she was sure no such thought would ever cross Marko's mind.

Why should a new confidence suddenly make him want to abandon her?

"Yes, it's perfect for you," she said softly.

Leaving the store, she stopped before the chained dog.

Marko and the children had passed by without seeming to notice it, and now they were walking on to the bus stop, cheerful and happy in their new clothes, as proud as if they'd put on a remarkable performance in some contest, earning unhoped-for honours and discovering unexpected but incontrovertible reasons to be pleased with themselves.

The dog raised its big, matted head towards her.

Fearing vermin, she stayed her outstretched hand.

She looked deep into the quietly doleful, quietly imploring gaze, and that docile animal's humanity and unconditional goodness filled her eyes with tears, she yearned to be it, and realised that this would come naturally and in its own time, not, as it had for Clarisse Rivière adrift on a life that had lost all direction and coherence, at the detestable whim of a man bent on avenging who knows what wretched childhood.

No animal had stared into Clarisse Rivière's dying eyes with its friendly, compassionate gaze.

She might perhaps have glimpsed the crazed eyes of the man she'd taken in, the man she'd rescued, who killed her not like a dog but like the vacant woman she'd become after Richard Rivière went away, easily manipulated and perhaps, perhaps, in her own way, begging for the knife, the attack, begging to lose herself and be done with it.

It was a long wait for the bus by the blue plastic barrel in the blazing sun.

Even though Daniel and Annika had their new long-visored caps shading them, one red, the other green, Marko worried aloud that they might be in danger of sunstroke.

Ladivine felt the same fear, but she was irritated with Marko for mentioning it in front of the children. Daniel awoke from a daydream and immediately began to whine, while Annika groaned that she was dreadfully hot and it was too much to bear.

Ladivine then noticed that Marko seemed in a bad way. His scarlet face was dripping with sweat, his glasses had slipped almost to the end of his nose, and he seemed too exhausted to push them back up.

She herself had never felt better, her mind clear and alert. Her cheeks were scarcely damp.

But she wondered how they would fill up the many days to come in this country with nothing to see, and the tediousness of holidays, shot through with impatience, regret, almost despair, appeared to her in all its bleak truth, even more worrying here, where they were on their own to come up with activities and distractions, than in Warnemünde, where the boredom was familiar, orderly, mapped out in advance.

She and Marko had thought that, once free of Lüneburg and Warnemünde, they would have only to be – but that was impossible with the children, they also had to do, and how could Marko, more sensitive than she to the rigours of the climate, to the little ordeals each day holds for a tourist, be expected to find in this holiday something preferable to inexpensive, trouble-free boredom on a windy Warnemünde beach?

His new outfit, his delighted discovery of his own comeliness, none of that seemed like enough, she reflected, to convince him he was something other at heart than the man with the crushed ambitions who sold watches at the Wilmersdorfer Strasse Karstadt.

How she dreamed, sometimes, of being alone in the world! No weight on her back, no family or parents at all!

Obligated nonetheless to protect them all from a potentially jealous fate, she took a step towards Daniel, enfolded him in her arms, kissed his damp forehead, then turned and hugged Annika, who stiffened a little, with all the proud impassivity of her eight years.

This battle between love for her children and fevered longing for aloneness had been going on in her only since Clarisse Rivière's murder — why should that be?

They climbed aboard a packed bus and rode back into town. A thick fog dimmed the sunlight, the air now grey but still every bit as stifling.

They ate slices of pizza standing up across from the bus stop, then set out to tour the neighbourhood, entrusting their route to the recommendations, at once enthusiastic and vague, of the one guidebook to this city they'd found in Berlin, which as it turned out described, and seemed to know, nothing of what they saw before them, detailing only what clearly no longer existed, or never had, evoking both an ambience of decadent prosperity and a quaintly carefree indigence when they could see only a very contemporary poverty, all plastic and sheet metal, surmounted by satellite dishes, and an apathy almost wholly without spirit, smiles or hope, which seemed to leave Marko gloomier on every corner, not so much, she told herself, because he'd naively conjured up an illusory image of a city that was in reality cold, unmysterious, threadbare, as because, an insignificant intruder in this hard, closed place, he was wondering why he'd come here, how he'd ever hoped he might find himself encountering a different, more complete man who would nonetheless, fantastically, be him, Marko Berger.

Or rather, she thought, studying Marko's cringing face, the face of the man she so loved, whom she couldn't stand to see frightened or sad, because such narcissistic hopes seemed obscene in these destitute streets.

Because no-one had murdered Marko's mother in her Lüneburg house, no-one had punctured his mother's body to set her blood

181

flowing to distant Charlottenburg, forever reddening the pavement's paving stones, the blooms on the lindens.

Whereas she, Ladivine Rivière, had earned the right to want anything at all – hadn't she? she thought, feeling her face going dry in the dusty, baking heat.

Given all she had been through, what self-centred wish of hers could ever be thought indecent? She could only be pitied, for the rest of her life.

Your poor mother, people said to her, afterwards, in Langon.

Oh yes, poor, poor Clarisse Rivière, and poor Ladivine, having to deal with all that.

Which is why she felt no inhibition, but rather a savage, cheerless joy as she walked through the ramshackle streets of a city she was hoping would let her forget, let her stop caring.

Clarisse Rivière's blood hadn't flowed this far.

"Look," Annika suddenly said, touching her arm. "Look!" she shouted to Marko and Daniel, who were walking ahead, the child now perched on his father's shoulders.

On a folding chair sat a woman wearing the yellow gingham dress Ladivine had bought in Bordeaux.

Before her, on an enormous piece of cloth spread out on the pavement, were all their clothes, carefully folded and laid out in an elegant tonal array.

Marko turned around and came back. He seemed to be clasping Daniel's calves not so much to support the child as to keep himself from collapsing.

He stared dully at his T-shirts, his old jeans, his blue-and-red striped bathing suit.

The woman had lowered the magazine she was reading, and now she eyed them expectantly, a stern look on her face. The yellow dress's bodice hung slightly loose over her skinny chest.

"That was mine, and so was that, and that," said Annika, pointing at her things, her delicate, pale face intent as she catalogued her former possessions, but at the same time detached, almost unsurprised, accepting that the clothes on display were hers no more.

"Something interest you?" the woman asked haughtily.

Marko let out a low laugh. He shook his head, chuckling in silence.

That dress didn't really fit me anyway, thought Ladivine.

She then spotted a pair of white trousers and a long-sleeved navy-blue blouse that she knew she hadn't brought with her, but which were beyond all doubt hers.

For example, she recognised a very faint yellowed spot on the front panel of the pants, caused, she remembered, by spattering bleach.

But she knew she'd left those two garments in her chest of drawers in Berlin, the trousers because they showed dirt, the blouse because it was corduroy, and unsuitably warm.

She felt her cheeks and brow redden in embarrassment, in perplexity, and also, oddly even to her, in fear, in the fear that Marko or Annika might observe that she'd never placed those trousers and that blouse into her suitcase – but how would they know?

And why did she feel guilty about all this? Was it because, unable to explain it, she nonetheless found it neither surprising nor frightening?

Marko had stopped laughing.

But the corners of his mouth were still turned up in a taunting smile.

"Lovely dress you've got on!" he threw out at the woman, in his slightly posh, supercilious English.

She answered simply:

"Thank you. I sewed it myself."

"Did you? My wife here has one just like it. She bought it in France."

He began to chuckle again, now menacingly, thought Ladivine in alarm.

She turned to walk away, hoping Marko would follow. But he held his ground before the display, vigorously tugging at Daniel's calves, the one then the other, like the teats of a cow.

Numb with heat and exhaustion, the child winced but didn't complain.

"Those French are always copying us," said the woman, in that tone of austere rectitude that inspired in Ladivine only a fervent urge to nod along.

"Isn't that dress a little big for you?" said Marko, starting in again.

"Stop it!" cried Ladivine. "What do you want from her, anyway?"

He gave her a surprised, reproachful, deeply suspicious glance.

"Somebody stole our things, didn't they? Don't you think we should go to the police?"

"Certainly not!"

Doing her best to stay calm, she added:

"There's no point, we'd be wasting our time. You know they won't do anything."

"That one shouldn't be here," said Annika, pointing at the navy-blue blouse. "You left it at home."

"No, no, you're mistaken, I brought it," Ladivine hurried to answer.

And this, she realised, was her first lie to her child, a lie with no perceptible reason, not to protect her from some hard truth but only to separate herself from the family she nonetheless so loved, from that husband and those children she couldn't or wouldn't let into her new life.

"You left it at home," Annika muttered stubbornly.

Ladivine shook her head, determined to deny it to the end, and silently saddened by that.

The one thing she refused to let herself do was exploit her motherly authority and order the little girl to say no more about the blouse.

She could only, her heart bleeding, accept Annika's bewildered insistence and cling to her lie for as long as it took.

A sudden exhaustion seemed to descend over Marko. Righting Daniel before the child could slide off his shoulders, he grumbled:

"Alright, then, let's get back to the hotel."

The children spent the afternoon and early evening in the pool, visibly relieved not to have to go out again.

Now and then a few other guests paddled around them, fat old people with quivering, pale flesh and a disgruntled air, sometimes casting quick, wary glances at the children, pre-emptively irked.

At the edge of the pool, the palm trees had died. Their dry, pale brown leaves hung limp against the grey trunks.

She reached out and took Marko's hand, finding it cold as ice. She wanted to tell him, "Nothing's . . ."

But he spoke before her, and, not moving his head, lying stiff on the chaise longue, asked in a distant voice, thickened by the heat:

"That blue blouse, the day before yesterday . . . It's so warm . . . Really, you brought that?"

"Of course I did."

She could feel herself blushing.

"Otherwise it would be impossible," she murmured, protected by her huge sunglasses, whose lenses almost covered her cheeks.

"Yes," said Marko, "otherwise it would be impossible, that's just what was bothering me."

He squeezed her hand, and she realised the depth of his relief. He sat up, opened the guidebook, and said, more confidently:

"There's only one thing to see here, the National Museum. It's supposed to be interesting."

Marko's skin had turned precisely the colour of his golden-chestnut hair, luxuriant, wavy, untamed, the locks snaking over his thin, rippling neck. She couldn't help reaching out to touch it. He bowed his head and gently kissed her fingers.

Fleetingly, foolishly, she prayed that she and Marko wouldn't be parted, knowing it was unlikely, and certainly not a thing she should be wanting despite all the pain it would cause her.

What was Marko Berger's place now?

What was his role here, if it turned out she could do without love and tenderness?

That, even more than sex, must have been what Clarisse Rivière couldn't live without when she was abandoned at fifty, but love hadn't worked out for her.

Their imagination running low, the children had started to quarrel. Marko stood up and called them out of the water. They shrieked in pain when their feet touched the burning hot paving tiles.

Their faces were red, overheated, their bodies pale and wrinkled and redolent of chlorine.

They looked distinctly unwell, Ladivine abruptly realised, though they had been the picture of health in Berlin.

When, thirty minutes later, the four of them emerged from the hotel to start for the National Museum, the big brown dog across the street rose to its feet, its back a bristling arch.

Watching it from the corner of her eye, Ladivine was sure she heard it growl.

Suddenly she was afraid it might charge across the street and lunge at Marko's throat, or the children's, unwilling, perhaps, to see her in the company of people it wasn't responsible for. And what did that dog care that she had a husband and children, if it was not meant to bind its fate to theirs?

Their plan was to walk to the museum by the corniche road, but instead she herded Daniel and Annika towards a taxi parked before the hotel, waved Marko in with them, and then, after a moment's hesitation and a glance at the dog, already sick at heart to be hurting and angering it this way, Ladivine too disappeared into the car.

"It's just too hot to walk, don't you think?" she said to Marko, slightly breathless and still trembling to think of the dog biting the children or their father to get them out of the way.

And, saying nothing to Marko about the dog, knowing she never would, and not simply because he might not believe her (he'd believe she was sincere, but would set out to show her she was mistaken, to prove that it was impossible to be guarded or spied on by an anonymous dog in the vastness of a poor, foreign city), she already felt accountable for any rash acts the dog might commit, that dog for which she'd broken her tacit accord with Marko never to keep secrets, a rule that Marko had always obeyed, she was sure, because he was a deeply virtuous and conscientious man, even a little vain about his virtue, as had she, she thought, until now, or rather until Clarisse Rivière's death, whose horror and pointlessness had stranded her, Ladivine, her only daughter, on shores of unspeakable shame.

Before the National Museum's severe, modern façade, a very young man seemed to be waiting for them.

No sooner were they out of the taxi than he came running, lively and good-humoured, friendly as no-one had ever been in this city, which, Ladivine would later reflect, explained why they trusted him at once, something they never would have done at home with an intrusive, slick, ingratiating young man such as this, but that's how it was, they felt fragile and alone in this place where their mere presence seemed a sound reason to treat them with indifference, even suspicion or cold hostility, and not being used to such things they found it hard to adapt, wanting deep down to be liked, to be recognised and admired as the good people they rightly thought they were.

And the welcoming, intelligently obliging but in no way obsequious look on that boy's face found them disarmed, eager for human warmth.

He was of average height, muscular, dressed in a pair of jeans cut off at the knees and a long NBA jersey.

His hair was cropped very short, and a little gold ring set with gemstones adorned his right ear.

Oddly, thought Ladivine, he was barefoot, for all the care he took with his appearance, his delicate, hairless, adolescent feet were dirty grey and peppered with scars.

He extended a firm hand first to her, then to Marko, looking at them both with sparkling dark eyes.

Smiling an indefinable little smile, he examined Marko's new outfit, his tunic and trousers.

Next he shook Annika's hand with a slight, playful bow, and then Daniel's.

"I'm Wellington," he said in his languid accent, "as you might already know."

Ladivine let out a little laugh.

"Why no, how could we?"

He laughed along with her, as if delighting in her repartee.

"Come with me, I'll show you around the museum."

"We don't need a guide," she exclaimed, just as Marko was avidly accepting.

She raised one hand to take back what she'd said, and she saw Marko's relief, his eagerness to let himself be taken in hand and entertained by a spirit of congeniality.

The boy started off with the children, and she held Marko back, whispering:

"We'll have to give him money, you know."

"Yes, I suppose so."

Suddenly he turned anxious again, and a little lost:

"How much?"

"I don't know, we'll see."

Annika and Daniel were usually reserved children, not difficult or capricious but private and hard to charm. And yet they were already laughing with Wellington when their parents caught up with them in the entrance, and, Ladivine observed with a tiny premonitory twinge in her heart, particularly Annika, usually so restrained and aloof, who was looking up at the boy with a gaze of complete, almost love-struck trust, pushing up her hair and clasping it to the back of her head with one hand.

Suddenly this eight-year-old was a ravishing little girl.

"Now, you pick up the tickets, and I'll wait for you here," said Wellington in his unctuous voice.

Past the ticket-checkers, he led them into a deserted first gallery, where huge canvases very realistically depicted various massacres – here a squadron of soldiers armed with bayonets skewering wild-eyed rioters, here three men slicing intently into the belly of a living woman pathetically endeavouring with blood-soaked hands to protect the foetus contained in that belly, there a man in an elegant suit bearing an expression of boundless disgust as he whipped the back, now a hash of flesh and blood, of an adolescent boy who must have been his servant, as the scene was set in a book-lined drawing room.

Enchanted, Wellington undertook to describe each painting as if they were blind; that's right, thought Ladivine, mystified, exactly as if they couldn't see or understand what they were looking at, as if they needed Wellington's words to help them grasp the very obvious horror of each scene.

Not understanding English, Annika and Daniel merely stared at the paintings with a dumbstruck, fascinated gaze.

In the next room, the gore and sensationalism far surpassed Ladivine's grimmest fears.

She reflexively covered Daniel's eyes with one hand, but the boy wrenched himself away, and, standing immovably in the middle of the room, turned his gaze in every direction as quick as he could, greedily, as Wellington's fine, velvety voice gaily recounted the events of each canvas.

"Here they're torturing two poor old people who tried to escape, they were locked up in that cage you can see in the background, and you can tell from the broken door that they managed to escape, but look, the overseers have caught up with them, and now they're pulling out their toenails with red-hot tongs, looks like they're having a good time, it's fun, they're laughing. In this next one there's a burning house. Who's that trapped in the flames on the second floor? Two women and their babies, and these people down here, the masters, they're all safe and sound now, they won't even look their way, they're thinking about their own children, who've all been rescued. Yes, that's just how it is."

Marko's lips were pinched, his jaw taut and aggrieved.

"Is he trying to make us feel guilty or something?" he whispered in Ladivine's ear.

But in fact the toxin of guilt seemed to have attacked him already, she observed, saddened and anxious, knowing she herself was secretly protected.

And in any case, Wellington rarely looked her way.

Cool and watchful, gently severe, he kept his eyes trained on Marko's face, as if wanting to be sure that his words were getting through, and especially that Marko made no attempt to fight them off.

And so highly developed was Marko's moral conscience, so long-standing and deep-rooted his acknowledgement of the most horrific crimes and his compliance with a duty to be above all reproach, that he never tried to evade Wellington's gaze but rather latched onto it, as if demanding to be told of the most unthinkable tortures, again and again, so that he might feel for his forebears the shame they themselves never felt.

Ladivine was appalled. She told herself she should snap Marko out of that ridiculous trance and drag them all to the exit.

But the possibility that Wellington might be gravely insulted, the thought of so soon losing the sort of friendship he was offering them, stripped her of her courage.

She herself, with the dog at her side, with that big all-knowing beast to rely on, felt more than a little indifferent about Wellington's friendship.

But she understood that Marko and the children might feel they'd abruptly been rescued from self-consciousness, boredom and fear, thanks to a boy who made his home in this country and had chosen them as the beneficiaries of a very real and undeniable thoughtfulness.

He knew what he was doing, she observed.

The way he casually raised one hand in front of Daniel, urging the child to do the same, then slapped his palm with a wink; the courtly, understated, but winsome voice he used with Annika, visibly respectful of her femininity; the mild, intelligent glances he cast at her, Ladivine: that was all typical of a clever but not cunning boy, perceptive and perhaps, she told herself, perhaps even sincere.

But could he not see what an aggressive thing it was to be showing them such paintings?

The third room was all carnage, with similar victims (my ancestors, said Wellington proudly), and the very same torturers. Marko was ashen.

He nonetheless forced himself to study each painting, and suddenly Ladivine had had enough, finding this childish.

He didn't have to work so hard at flattering the boy – or did he?

Was it actually necessary?

But weren't those paintings just trash?

"Alright, let's go now," she said firmly.

She took Marko's arm and ordered the children to follow, noticing that they waited to see Wellington's reaction before they obeyed.

Gracious, charming, he turned on his heels and made for the exit himself, the children trotting gaily along at his side.

"All those horrible things," Ladivine whispered into Marko's ear, "it's too much, don't you think? Are you sure this is the museum they recommend in the guide?"

"Yes," answered Marko, in a halting, confused voice. "But the paintings they talk about aren't anything like this. I can't understand it!"

Lowering his voice, he added, urgent and anxious:

"How much do we give him?"

"Two euros' worth," said Ladivine.

She was exasperated by the fear she sensed oozing from Marko's every pore, the fear of not living up to expectations, of not being generous enough, grateful enough, deserving enough of their approval.

There was a time when she loved that torment of Marko's, that excessive conscientiousness.

Lately she often thought it misplaced, faintly ridiculous.

How she missed the innocence of Clarisse Rivière!

*

Wellington knocked three times on the very low door of a cinder-block house with a red sheet-metal roof.

Suddenly it was dark. One blink and it's night-time, thought Ladivine, and just a few seconds ago the sun was so blinding.

Equally strange, to her mind, was the fact that they'd become Wellington's guests, even if at the time it had seemed perfectly natural to be following him out to this distant neighbourhood.

Ladivine had simply assumed that Wellington had nowhere special to go, and was thus sticking with them, falling in with their vague plan to watch the sun set over the sea (how silly, she would later tell herself, amused, since the sun didn't set here, but literally vanished), but now here they were standing before Wellington's house, as he told them, at precisely the early-evening hour assigned to dinner in this rigid country.

Winding, narrow, the dirt street ran through an unbroken succession of shabby little bare-cement huts, old bicycles chained up at the front with gigantic locks.

The prospect of an evening at Wellington's filled Daniel and Annika with delight.

And indulging one's children's delights, reflected Ladivine, often led to imprudence. For were it just she and Marko, she told herself, she would never have accepted this invitation to a stranger's house in a remote district of a city she didn't know.

Were it only the two of them, she would have run the risk of offending Wellington, and they would have gone back to the hotel without for one moment worrying about maintaining and even cultivating an unwholesome friendship with that teenaged boy.

As they stood waiting to be let in, a feeling of being watched from behind forced Ladivine to turn around.

She made out a pair of dark eyes glinting in the night, a few metres further on, down a little hill from the street.

The dog had found her.

Sitting very straight, ears pricked up, watchful but calm, it stared at her with its neutral gaze, perhaps waiting, she then thought, perhaps waiting for some sign from her, no, not even that, a breath, a thought, and with that it would come to take her away to some mysterious place with no name.

She shivered and quickly turned around again.

Before the closed door, Wellington was losing patience.

He began to pound on it with his fists, bellowing, and when it finally opened, he bitterly upbraided the girl at the door in a language that Ladivine thought something like English stripped of all gentleness, only the harshest sounds left.

He introduced the girl as his sister, then thoroughly and categorically denounced her, as if to excuse the long delay, along with the girl herself, since, plagued as she was by so many deficiencies, she could certainly be slow to react as well.

The girl let him talk, limply scratching her arm.

She smiled into space, neither friendly nor hostile, simply detached, absent.

To her we don't even exist, thought Ladivine, she wouldn't care if we died right here on the spot, or ran away, or collapsed in the street.

This disturbed and upset her.

Because she herself cared deeply about that girl's existence the moment she saw her face, her existence and almost her happiness, for which, had it been possible, she would gladly have given some small part of herself: time, a little money, thought, or emotion.

Wellington ushered them down a passage dimly lit by a single naked bulb, then across a pitch-black courtyard and into a vast room where a small crowd had just sat down to dinner.

Apart from a long table of dark green plastic and matching chairs, the room was bare.

Every plate was laden with chunks of sweet potato and lamb in sauce, lit by a fly-specked fluorescent tube unevenly diffusing a flickering, greenish light.

Intimidated, Annika and Daniel retreated to the darkest corner of the room. But Wellington went and gently led them back, talking to them in a soothing voice, as though to a couple of skittish kittens.

Marko circled the table, shaking everyone's hand, slim and charming in his pink suit, his face sallow in the fluorescent light, and Ladivine admired his confidence, his casual, easy manner.

Nonetheless, she chose not to imitate him, thinking there was no need to go to such lengths. She simply glanced around the table and threw out a collective hello.

Wellington disappeared, then immediately returned with more chairs, and everyone slid aside to make room, silent but with a good will Ladivine found reassuring.

She'd blamed her discomfort and guardedness on her reluctance to intrude, but from the intensity of her relief she realised she'd been fearing a trap, and her tablemates' mute civility allowed her to put that suspicion aside.

But she was unhappy with Marko for never even considering the possibility that Wellington was luring them into an ambush, for so readily trusting in a friendliness that back in Europe would have put a sceptical, embarrassed smile on his face.

Why, here, could he be so easily convinced that a young stranger had taken a sincere liking to them?

It was immature and unworthy of him, Ladivine told herself crossly.

But she had to concede that their hosts seemed determined to prove Marko right, and to persuade her that he was guilty of neither credulity nor blindness, that he had shown only the soundest of judgement.

Some ten adults of various ages were sitting around the table. Ladivine saw them all quietly trying to put the new guests at ease, even Wellington's sister, whom Ladivine first found so coldly dismissive and who was now keeping a discreet eye on the platefuls of tasty lamb stew she'd efficiently served, ready, Ladivine guessed, to leap up as soon as they were empty and bring out a second helping.

Sitting across from Ladivine, an old woman nodded and smiled each time their eyes met.

A man who might have been Wellington's father cut the lamb shanks into little pieces on Daniel's plate, having seen the boy's difficulties with his dull knife.

That handsome, thin-faced man was dressed in a light green short-sleeved shirt. Ladivine couldn't take her eyes off it, her head swimming slightly.

Hadn't Marko packed that shirt for this trip, with the tone-on-tone crest on the breast pocket?

She hoped neither Marko nor Annika would notice, as if, once again, her own responsibility was caught up in something repugnant, something deeply ignoble.

To avoid drawing their attention to that shirt, she resolutely looked away from the man, whose chest, more filled out than Marko's, strained the buttons every time he inhaled.

Now she was feeling more at ease.

Her dining companions didn't talk much, but those who did now and then break the silence did so in careful English, articulating carefully, looking now at Marko, now at Ladivine, making themselves easily understood.

Marko was always quick to answer. He praised the food, which was excellent, he offered his warmest thanks.

And Ladivine knew he meant it, because she herself was gripped by an unexpected euphoria in this atmosphere of slightly austere but placid, reassuring conviviality, from which all threat of tasteless jokes or complicated humour seemed to have been banished.

It struck her that Clarisse Rivière would have enjoyed this sort of company, she who, on meeting new people, always worried she might not be able to follow their conversation. Clarisse Rivière was too modest, too self-effacing to fear being mocked, and when she was, and when she realised it, she heartily joined in the laughter.

But clever wordplay made her uncomfortable. She could neither enjoy it nor laugh at it, and she never knew how to answer.

"What did you think of the wedding?" asked the friendly old lady across from Ladivine, misinterpreting the sudden panic on Ladivine's face and repeating the question still more slowly and clearly.

Ladivine cast an anxious glance Marko's way. He was talking with Wellington and no doubt hadn't heard. On the other hand, she caught Annika giving her a questioning stare, having almost certainly grasped the word "wedding".

She leaned as far across the table as she could, her face almost touching the old lady's, and hurriedly whispered:

"It was a beautiful ceremony, everything was lovely."

Cheeks burning, she prayed the old lady would leave it at that.

Marko would never understand her lying like this, her pretending to have taken part in festivities she knew nothing of, and he would find such behaviour good cause for reproach and concern – but if somewhere in this city there was a woman so like her that the one could be confused with the other, what could Ladivine do but accept that confusion? Nothing could seem more suspicious than denying you'd been in a place where people are certain they saw you.

Best just to play along, so no-one will be embarrassed or think you odd or suspect.

So thought Ladivine, though she was not sure she could explain this to Marko or Annika.

And to herself she confessed that she found a certain pleasure in being taken for another, for a woman invited to a memorable wedding in this enigmatic city, that somehow it flattered her.

"We weren't there," the old woman resumed, "but I heard there was money involved, lots of money. They must have thought we weren't good enough to be invited, even though we're more or less cousins, on the bride's side."

She seemed to be waiting for some sort of acquiescence, which Ladivine accorded her with a nod.

"What was the meal like? Were there several fish dishes?"

Ladivine gave her a quick "There were", but, far from discouraging the old lady, her laconic answers only inflamed her curiosity, as if Ladivine were coyly withholding the choicest details.

"How was the fish cooked? And what did they serve with it? What about the wine? What was the wine like?"

"It was a very good Graves, and they had monkfish à l'américaine and shark in green sauce and one more I don't know the name of, it was grilled, in big boneless pieces."

She spoke very quickly and quietly, hoping that Marko, if he heard her, wouldn't be able to follow her words.

"What about the bride's gown?" the old lady asked eagerly.

"The gown . . . it must have been ivory faille satin, with a lace bodice and a big ribbon for the belt."

"Was it long?"

"Very long, several metres of fabric at least."

"And what about you, what were you wearing?"

"A yellow gingham dress, with balloon sleeves."

And then, unsure just what was urging her on, perhaps vanity, perhaps a desire to please the old lady, perhaps simply a lifelong fondness for telling tales, Ladivine found herself recounting the whole wedding as if she'd been there, now unconcerned that Marko or Annika might hear.

A mischievous "I'll show you" was ringing defiance's merry little bells in her head.

And little by little the entire table fell into a listening silence as she described the ceremony in lavish detail, not knowing where it was coming from, not wanting to.

She told of the church's simple decorations, the slightly shrill organ, which played "Ave Maria", and the bride's slightly belated entrance (no doubt because of a traffic jam, since everyone had come by car) on the arm of her father, who was dressed all in grey, from his panama hat to his cotton lisle socks, which showed when he sat down in the front row.

She also described the profusion of lilies and white gladioli, recalling as she spoke that it was at Clarisse Rivière's funeral that she'd seen those flowers, losing her way a little, downing a gulp of water, eyes lowered, smiling a smile that she knew must seem forced, then struggling to start up again in the expectant silence, to recapture the pleasure still making her heart pound, struggling to push aside the memory of Clarisse Rivière's funeral and the abundance of luxurious flowers ordered by Richard Rivière, greatly outnumbering the attendees and saturating the little Église de la Libération in Langon with their horribly cloying and sensual perfumes.

No-one had come to the Mass, then the cemetery, but a handful of Clarisse Rivière's co-workers, two or three neighbours and Richard Rivière's aged mother, confused and whimpering, who was living out her life in a retirement home near Toulouse and begged, disoriented, to be taken back as quickly as possible, seeing in all this a ploy to get her out of that place, which she hadn't left for over fifteen years, not even to run an errand, convinced that someone was after her room and her things. As for Clarisse Rivière's side, she was an only child, her parents long dead, and no cousin, no aunt or uncle had taken the trouble to come.

And so, Ladivine thought at the time, frozen in sorrow, it was as if Clarisse Rivière had secretly deserved her degrading death, despite everything Richard Rivière had done, surrounding the altar with that heap of intoxicating flowers, in his attempt to honour her.

And how it comforted him, clearly, to find a knot of reporters awaiting their chance to interview him and Ladivine outside the church, for where she'd managed to choke out only two or three flat, rehearsed sentences, he'd held forth at length, fervidly, mingling in one single vindictive rage Clarisse Rivière's murderer, some second cousin who hadn't even apologised for not coming to the funeral, and his own distraught mother, who, clutching his arm, regularly broke in to ask when they would finally take her back home.

He angrily jerked his arm, as if to shake her off, but she seemed to have concentrated all the vigilance and strength she had left in her fingers, and her whole body, wispy, friable, weightless, lurched in time with her son's furious twitches.

May guilt clutch him exactly like that for as long as he lives, Ladivine wished at the time, may it burrow its hooked head into his consciousness and never be dislodged, inaccessible as a tick in the middle of his back.

Oh, she loved her father all the same, she loved him with infuriated tenderness and dismay, yes, but what, if not love, was the warm delectation that swelled her breast when she thought of Richard Rivière?

She was still going on about the wonderful wedding, almost not hearing herself, the words pouring from her mouth in gilded torrents, sparkling with a thousand evocative gleams in the sparsely furnished, dark room. The old woman stared at her with a fascinated, vaguely hurt gaze.

Suddenly she heard Wellington snort. She paused and coolly turned towards him.

"We don't care about those people," Wellington growled. "You know where they get their money from? You know that, I imagine?"

"Not exactly," answered Ladivine, as, she thought, a tension very slowly began to take shape, something coming her way, not yet outright hostility, but a stiffening, as if she'd abruptly fallen from favour.

"Well, you should have done some digging, maybe then you wouldn't be here telling us all this. What gives you the right to think we give a damn about those people?" asked Wellington aggressively.

"Let her talk," the old woman implored. "I love hearing about weddings."

"We've got to be going," said Marko firmly. "The children are tired."

"Let her talk," the old woman sobbed.

And from the others' complete disregard for that woman, Ladivine realised it may have been a serious mistake to rely on this old crone's presumed influence, of which as it turned out she had none, as she wandered into fabrication.

She was counting on the sway of a crazy old lady to lend her credibility!

And yet she'd spoken so well, with so many vivid details, she could so clearly see what she'd described that she almost found herself doubting she'd invented it.

Marko had risen to his feet, imitated at once by the children, their trepidation returning in the frosty, suddenly inhospitable atmosphere.

Ladivine knew she should stand up in turn, but a leaden inertia kept her in her chair.

And, although not quite sure what she'd done wrong, she wanted to make amends.

The old woman's still-hungry gaze latched onto hers.

"How was the dance? Did they hire an orchestra, or what? Was there waltzing, or just salsa?"

"It was the famous orchestra of the Grand Hotel Regent's," Ladivine murmured. "They played a little of everything, but especially rock. They had that clarinettist everyone's talking about, Tom Evert."

"Ladivine, we're going!" Marko cried angrily.

"We're going, Mummy!" Annika frantically echoed.

Daniel began to sniffle. Ladivine slowly stood up, in a fog.

This time Marko dispensed with the handshakes. He merely addressed a vague wave to the silent assembly. Accusing, their huge shadows loomed on the dull blue wall.

Someone moved beneath the fluorescent light, his shadow surged, and Marko's eyelids began to flutter, which meant, Ladivine knew, that he was afraid.

She took Daniel's hand and, to her faint disgust, found it clammy.

She was crushed that the evening was ending this way, the children witnessing their parents' failure to make themselves loved, their cowardice.

Although she knew it was unfair, she was angry with Marko, both for so quickly and with such manifest gratitude accepting Wellington's invitation and for refusing the role she herself had consented to play for the pleasure of their hosts.

Because, had Marko only seconded and supported her, had he chimed in with a few details of his own (but what did he know of that wedding? was it not clear that she enjoyed an awareness of things he knew nothing of?), then Wellington would have kept his opinions on that family's fortune to himself, thought Ladivine, and nothing would remain of this whole turn of events but the memory of a remarkable gift for fitting in. But no: here they were fleeing, ashamed and afraid, what had perhaps opened its doors to them as a model household.

She thought Marko had failed her terribly, that he'd lacked faith in her and was now dragging them into his own disgrace, infecting them with his craven terror. Hot and damp, Daniel's poor hand attested to that, as did Annika's eyes, open wide in ugly apprehension, whereas the two children had entered this room with joyful hearts, open and cordial, and ready to give of themselves without stinting.

Wellington's sister sullenly showed them out, scuffing her soles on the concrete floor.

Obliged to open the door and lock it behind them, she had no choice but to accompany them to the threshold, but there, to chase them out into the street, she waved one arm in a sweeping gesture of contempt that eloquently expressed her real opinion of them, Ladivine noted sadly.

Then she viciously slammed the door, they heard the key turn in the lock, and Annika dissolved into tears. Ladivine thought she could so precisely feel what the little girl was feeling that she might easily weep along with her!

This rejection, this abandonment to the darkness and its possible dangers, no-one even trying to make sure they could find their way back to the hotel or successfully hail a taxi, all this proved that their lives were as nothing to their hosts, nor their safety, nor every last one of their emotions.

"Treated like dogs," Marko mumbled, with a slightly unconvincing snicker.

He shot her a quick, accusing glance.

"Why did you have to tell them all that, all those lies?"

"I wasn't lying," protested Ladivine, shocked that he'd spoken the word in front of the children.

She smoothed Annika's hair, gently pressed her close, feeling the sob-racked little chest against her stomach.

"You weren't lying, Mummy?" asked Daniel.

"Of course not. It's something else," she said firmly.

She started off down the dark, empty street at a falsely decisive pace, having no idea of the way back to the hotel. The ground was sandy and shifting. She felt tiny pebbles in her sandals.

She heard Marko and the children following after her. Reassured but still vaguely angry, she did not look back.

For reasons she didn't understand, her resentment, disappointment and irritation at Marko had begun to spread to the children as well, though with somewhat less virulence.

But what fault could she find with them, what fault could anyone find with such young children that wasn't largely one's own doing?

All the same, she could feel them blindly siding with Marko, and she blamed them for her own inability to win them over, wishing they could believe unconditionally in her prescience.

But they did not, no more than Marko did.

From a rustling in the dark, the air discreetly shifting on the other side of the street, she knew that the dog was close by, no need to seek out the dim yellow gleam of its eyes in the night.

It wouldn't let her go astray, she thought, and if it was now by her side, that could only mean the hotel was this way.

They were back in their room far sooner than Ladivine expected, from which she concluded that Wellington's neighbourhood could not be more than a few hundred metres from the Plaza, that it was perhaps that very district's winding streets and metal roofs they saw gleaming in the east each morning from their window.

Who knows, with binoculars, Wellington might well be able to spy on them from his house.

In any case, they were virtually neighbours, she breezily observed to Marko, determined to make peace, taking him in her arms as the children crawled into bed, but to her surprise he heaved an irritable sigh and wearily informed her that he'd had more than enough of her mystifications, that Wellington's house was by the corniche, and thus a long way from the hotel, as evidenced by the lateness of the hour and the children's exhaustion, not to mention his own, for unlike some people he couldn't retreat into grandiosity and imposture and weirdness to take his mind off fatigue and sore muscles.

"I don't want to fight," Ladivine said in shock.

And tears rolled down her cheeks, her first since the death of Clarisse Rivière. Shaken, Marko put his arms around her.

She laid her forehead on his shoulder and smelled the strange, musky odour of his new tunic, the cotton stiffened by some unknown substance, something slightly oily.

"We all need some sleep," Marko whispered.

His hair had picked up his new clothes' strong smell, imbuing his whole person with a harshness that wasn't his, as if he'd put on a disguise in a crude ploy to survive.

One or two hours later, she wasn't sure, a violent noise woke her, and she thought the air conditioner must be malfunctioning.

At the same moment she realised Marko wasn't beside her, and she saw shadows lurching and heaving on the tiny balcony.

She glanced at the children, both sound asleep.

The air conditioning was working in its usual way, with its loud thrum that always made you wonder, before you drifted off, how sleep could possibly escape it, and its sudden, unpredictable shutdowns that like it or not left you lying awake waiting for it to start up again, your ear vigilant, your heart pounding and raging.

She sat up, put her feet on the carpet.

Now she could make out Marko's form, which seemed to be grappling with another, shorter and slighter.

Marko's back hit the glass door's metal frame, again making the noise that had roused her.

She stood up, took a few steps forward, hiccupping in terror. What was she supposed to do? Call the front desk, ask for help?

She felt as lost as a child with no experience of the world.

She pictured herself picking up the phone and saying "Help!" in a muffled shout, but even as those images took shape in her mind she was moving towards the balcony, pulling aside the sheer curtains, stammering, "Marko?"

He was wearing only his underwear, and the other one was in jeans and a T-shirt, barefoot like Marko.

She'd recognised him a few seconds before, but she hesitated to utter his name.

Even given the circumstances, wasn't she relieved to see Wellington before her, and not, as she'd vaguely feared from her bed, the big brown dog standing on its back legs? And Marko throttling that big brown dog as it panted in the dark?

Which would she have come running to rescue?

But no, it was only Wellington, thank God, she thought (not exactly a thought, more a sequence of sensations, first terror, then relief), and he seemed to be yielding to Marko's calm, silent violence as he bent Wellington's back over the railing.

Wellington rasped in pain.

And then, calm and silent, as if he knew just what he was doing, thought Ladivine dumbstruck, as if he'd been awaiting this moment to grasp at long last what his strength was for, the unforeseen strength of a thin, gangly, peaceable man, the strength of an urbanite finally unleashed, Marko clasped Wellington's legs and flipped him over the railing.

They heard the adolescent's surprised moan, then the thud of his body landing six floors below.

A stunned "oh!" escaped Ladivine, as if she couldn't believe that this sound, like a heavy bundle falling onto hard ground, had been caused by Marko's act, by his calm, silent, inflexible will, as if there were no conceivable link between the surprise revelation of Marko's calm, silent violence and a teenaged boy's body dropping onto a concrete terrace.

She leaned out, hoping to catch sight of Wellington, a string of singsong, almost light-hearted sentences running through her muddled mind – He's about to get up and run off into the night, should we call him a taxi, we'll stop by tomorrow and apologise, what on earth for – but she had only enough time to make out a still, dark shape on the pale grey pavement before Marko jerked her back inside.

He locked the balcony door, drew the curtain.

Then he went to the children, studied their sleeping faces in turn, almost suspiciously, Ladivine thought.

He wants to be sure they're asleep, but what would he do if they weren't?

His breath was loud and wild. Then he began to pant like a dog.

Little by little his face relaxed as he looked at the children.

The cold, quiet, self-assured fury that had clenched it and hardened it was now fading away.

He mechanically pulled the sheet up to cover Daniel's shoulders, wandered aimlessly around the room for a moment.

Ladivine gently lay down again. She was trembling so hard that the bed creaked.

Marko turned on the water in the bathroom, then came back and lay down in turn, his hair and cheeks still wet.

"Marko, Marko," murmured Ladivine, surprised at her own anguish-choked voice.

He took her hand, pressed it to his breast. He whispered:

"He was here to harm us, I'm sure of it. Rob us, kill us, who knows, maybe both?"

"But how . . . how could he have climbed onto the balcony?"

"I don't know. Maybe he went through the next room. If I hadn't woken up in time . . ."

He began to sob, like a dog, Ladivine thought again, in stifled yelps.

She pressed up against him and stroked his thin back, his delicate, hard shoulders, herself feeling fluid and limp, her boundaries erased, her body a liquid flesh spreading freely.

For the first time since they landed in this country, since she noticed the big dog before the hotel, she felt her fate bound up with Marko's and the children's just as it was before, no indecipherable exception now covering her, protecting her.

The thing in this place that didn't like Marko, or Daniel or Annika, the thing determined to mortally test them, had tonight turned to her, abruptly wiping out any complicity between this land and her privileged self.

At this she felt more resentment than fear. She sensed that a vast undertaking would now have to be started anew, that she would now discover the true difficulty of that task, whereas before it had all happened without her even realising.

When she saw that Marko had gone back to sleep, she pulled away to a cool spot on the mattress.

Suddenly she was disgusted by the touch of Marko's skin, the warm odour of his breath.

Wasn't it like sharing a bed with Clarisse Rivière's killer, inhaling the air expelled with his every tranquil breath, caressing his faintly pulsating skin?

Perhaps Wellington's firm young skin was still moist and warm, she told herself, but Clarisse Rivière's was most certainly now half-eaten by vermin.

And as for breath, oh the air Marko and that man were inhaling swelled with the air neither Wellington nor Ladivine's mother could any longer breathe.

She shook Marko awake by one shoulder.

"What if he's not dead?" she whispered. "We have to call an ambulance. He might still be breathing."

"That's impossible, did you see how far down it was?"

His voice was flat and irritable.

"I don't want to save that guy's life," he went on. "I don't want any problems because of someone who came here to harm my children. I don't want to hear another word about him, you understand, I don't care if he's dying or dead down there."

He choked up on those words, and Ladivine realised that the thought of the boy slowly expiring on the concrete weighed on him all the same.

"He could have been coming to warn us, to save us . . ." she murmured miserably.

"Save us? From what?"

"That's just it, we don't know. Maybe he was the only one who did . . ."

She thought she could feel him shrugging in the dark.

"People around here," he said after a moment, "well, you've seen how they are. If we call an ambulance, if we tell them what happened . . . they could kill us, you know that. Darling, I'm so tired."

He drew closer, but she gingerly pushed him away, her mind still on Clarisse Rivière's killer, who was very likely asleep at this moment, his moist, warm skin faintly pulsating, his breath tranquil and gentle, his nostrils and mouth blithely inhaling and exhaling the air he'd robbed Ladivine's mother of forever.

So, she reflected, shivering in dismay, Marko had to disgust her for the first time in their lives, she had to feel this tormented revulsion at his pulsing, living skin for her to dare turn her mind to the man who'd killed Clarisse Rivière in the Langon house three years before, her cautious, frightened mind, which until tonight fled that man's very name, and which now, beside a Marko whose skin had been sullied, whose breath was corrupted, consented to remember it.

The man who killed Clarisse Rivière was named Freddy Moliger. She repeated that name to herself until it stopped hurting.

Because until now any hint of a similar string of syllables had left her breathless, and tortured her brain like a searing migraine.

And now, next to a sleeping, untouchable Marko, she could let her lips form Freddy Moliger's name, let it reverberate in her head like a grimly tolling bell, sombre as the knell that rang in the modest church on the Carrefour de Libération, amid the noise of the passing cars, on the day of Clarisse Rivière's funeral.

She lay quiet and still, taking care not to touch Marko's skin, her fingers mechanically smoothing the sheet over her stomach as Freddy Moliger's name slowly sounded its lugubrious, clear tones in her head.

Now and then she heard the children turning over, Daniel moaning in his sleep.

And suddenly it was as if she was hearing them from far, far away, because Freddy Moliger's name was deafening her, pure, potent, unstoppable.

Had Daniel or Annika cried out to her at that moment, she would not have found the strength to let their voices silence the pounding syllables of Freddy Moliger's name, any more than her children's voices, no matter how pleading, could stop their mother's heart beating if her hour hadn't come.

Her hand moved to her cheek, wiped it dry, then touched her lips. Yes, those were tears, she observed, in detached surprise.

She'd been weeping without knowing it, but was it for young Wellington or Clarisse Rivière, or was it for Marko, whom she knew she could no longer love as ardently and innocently as before, whom she even knew she might never love again?

Now she could hear a dog barking.

She forced Freddy Moliger's name to mute its deafening drone so she could think back on that big brown dog, and she smiled in the darkness as she recognised its bark, not that she'd ever heard it bark since it began watching over her, but because, as she understood it, whether in her own dream or someone else's she'd appeared in, she had met that dog long before they came to this country, just as she had met the woman who sold mango juice in the market, and that earlier big brown dog had barked, and she'd learned its voice, and so she could recognise it now.

The next morning, sitting at their usual breakfast table by the terrace windows, they noticed a long, dark stain where Wellington's body had landed.

They said nothing about it, and not because of the children, thought Ladivine.

No, they would never speak of Wellington again, never again speak of that awful struggle on the balcony and the revelation of Marko's calm, deadly resolve.

She saw him glance once at the terrace and quickly turn away, with something hard, aggressive and unyielding about his chin, as if he were even now fiercely proclaiming his innocence, like a guilty man determined never to confess.

He ate more than usual, he even stuffed himself with buttered rolls while she pretended to eat so as to arouse no suspicions in Annika, whose watchful eyes darted from her to Marko and sometimes lit on the terrace just where the concrete was stained, Ladivine noticed, nausea rising up inside her.

"I had a dream about Wellington last night," said Annika in an overly casual voice.

Oh, you're lying, thought Ladivine, her heart gripped by pity and understanding, you're lying because you think it might bring you an answer.

"He was looking for us to invite us to a wedding," Annika went on, "and he said I was the bride, and we didn't even know."

Daniel giggled.

"Don't you think we've heard quite enough about weddings lately?" said Marko slowly and coldly, a tone he took with the children only in rare, extreme situations, when one of them had done something reckless, had endangered his or her safety out of heedlessness or a desire for attention.

And although he immediately tempered that severity with a wry smile, butter and crumbs stuck to his lips, Annika wasn't fooled, and, suddenly turning very red, tears pooling in her eyes, she heard Marko's words as they were intended, as a threat.

She gave Ladivine a pleading, questioning look, and her mother's only answer was a meaningless little shrug.

She looked down at her plate, her index finger tapping at a smear of jam.

Ladivine knew she and Marko had just lost everything that was absolute and unwavering in Annika's trust, she knew Annika now believed or knew her parents to be capable not only of foolishness, which her mature, indulgent mind would eventually have accepted, but above all of cruelty towards her, she who was nonetheless, as surely she'd never doubted, a deeply loved child.

Feeling the sudden tension in the air, Daniel began to sulk very visibly.

"We ought to leave today, and go and see your father's friends," said Marko.

He'd tried to put on a casual smile, and the gentleness and warmth had returned to his voice, but the lower half of his face was still frozen in a savage, inept, belligerent denial, the very mark, thought Ladivine, of the killer.

She heaved a long sigh. She gripped the edge of the table to keep her hands still.

On the phone, she was remembering, Richard Rivière had spoken of a couple he knew who'd moved to this country long before, and she'd briefly mentioned them to Marko, half hoping Richard Rivière would forget to give her their phone number and address.

But he didn't, and a few days later she got an e-mail with complete contact information for her father's old friends.

However put off by the idea of meeting anyone from Richard Rivière's new social circle, people Clarisse Rivière had not met, did not have the right to meet, people who, if they'd heard anything of her at all, must have pictured only the worn, humiliating image of a tiresome wife abandoned in middle age, however powerful her sense that she was betraying Clarisse Rivière, whose slender body, whose kindly face, whose whole fervent, timid, generous person Richard Rivière's friends would never know, she nonetheless conscientiously copied down the address and put the slip of paper in her wallet, vaguely, superstitiously fearing that if she didn't they would end up in desperate need of help from those very people, an expatriate French couple of whose history with Richard Rivière she knew nothing, and who she thought, without knowing just why, would have turned up their noses at Clarisse Rivière like the others, not being the type to like or understand her, and Ladivine pre-emptively

213

held this against them, just as she felt a baseless but profound anger towards her father, who allowed himself to be friends with likely disparagers of Clarisse Rivière's strange mind and boundless simplicity.

And so Marko's suggestion found her unwilling, irascible, almost venomous.

"You really think it's a good idea to look like we're running away?" she hissed.

"I believe it would be prudent to leave as soon as we can," said Marko, unruffled.

Not long after, taking the children to the pool, they saw two workers washing away the dark patch left by Wellington's body.

Ladivine could not hold back an image of the boy's stomach bursting open as he hit the ground, his healthy young entrails spilling onto the concrete, through Marko's fault and her own, because, weak-willed, unable to bear the solitude of the foreigner, they'd let themselves be talked into accepting the boy's company for a tour of the National Museum.

Would Wellington's death be the subject of the museum's next acquisition, Ladivine wondered, and would it show a sadistically grinning Marko ripping the intestines from Wellingon's living flesh with his bare hands, would it show the woman in nightclothes, half hidden behind a pillar, feasting her eyes, would it go so far as to show the already dissolute children laughing in drooling delight?

Oh, the only thing to think was that Wellington had come back to harm them, maybe make off with Daniel and demand a ransom.

Only that intuition, only that certainty could have turned Marko violent, he who'd never raised a hand to a living soul, never screamed in anyone's face.

The only thing to think was that Wellington had come back to harm them.

Evidently there were no witnesses to Clarisse Rivière's murder in her Langon house, but, Ladivine now wondered as she sat at the pool's edge with her calves in the warm water, if there had been, if some face peering in through the living room window had seen Freddy Moliger's crime, had watched Clarisse Rivière's blood pouring out onto the floor, soaking the sofa and the needlepoint cushions, would that face then have turned away, would that person have gone home to dinner and then to bed thinking that in any case there was nothing more to be done for Clarisse Rivière, that she was in all likelihood dead, as Ladivine had let Marko convince her that Wellington could not possibly still be alive on the terrace?

What would she feel, Clarisse Rivière's only child, on learning such a thing, on learning that someone had witnessed her mother's last moments and not tried to save her?

She would curse him, that's what, she would want him to die in the same abject aloneness.

Annika and Daniel waded sullenly in the pool, looking bored.

A similarly opaque and unhappy expression marked the faces of the few old people who came to bathe there each morning, who never answered Ladivine's timid greeting, pretending not to have noticed her.

Successive sunburns had left their fat shoulders stippled.

Fate seemed to have condemned them to spend an infernal eternity in the confines of the hotel and the pool, submerging their weary, pale, fragile flesh in the murky water, then laboriously pulling themselves out again, in an endless, absurd cycle, evidently thinking the hotel's other guests and employees responsible for their torment, and thus never answering their hellos.

Ladivine was ashamed to be with them. She found them ugly in a way that worried her just a little.

When the heat grew too much to bear she called Daniel and Annika out of the water, and they gratefully hurried to obey, as if, for them too, swimming was now an element of some ritual torture.

Slightly dazed, painfully aware of her own haggard appearance, Ladivine caught sight of Marko coming towards her through the glimmering light, dressed in his pink tunic, whose radiant colour bathed him in a rosy glow.

She realised he'd gone off without her noticing, and now he was back, crossing the terrace, enveloped in the bleeding aura of his deed, giving himself away, thought Ladivine, drunk with anguish, as surely as if he'd cried out, "It was I who killed Wellington, that sweet boy, so full of life, who opened his door to us!" – now his athletic shoes were trampling the still-damp spot where Wellington had laid in repose, now he was coming to her with his head high and a bright, pleased look on his face, an impatient, excited little smile at the corners of his mouth, as if chafing to report wonderful news.

Annika saw him too, and she ran towards her father, forgetting that she usually thought such impetuous effusions unworthy of her age.

Did that vulnerable little girl believe she needed forgiveness for something? Ladivine wondered. Did she, in the tortuous ways of her childish logic, believe she was guilty of thinking, or perhaps vaguely seeing, that something terrible had happened with Wellington?

She pressed herself to Marko, her arms encircling his waist, in a demonstration of tenderness utterly unlike the reserved child she usually was.

As if it were she who'd done something wrong, thought Ladivine.

And she wanted to run to Marko, rip him from the child's arms, horrified to think of Annika lingering one moment longer in that apotheosis of guilt, to think of that guilt impregnating and infecting her while perhaps Marko was delivered of it forever, not that he'd planned or wanted anything of the sort.

But she stayed where she was.

A misgiving raced through her mind: Maybe I'm the one who's infecting her? Maybe she's picking up that guilt and remorse from me?

She walked slowly and heavily towards Marko, holding Daniel's hand, the boy scratching her palm with his nails, like a little trapped rodent.

"Let go, Mummy, let go!" he was whining.

Will we be ordered to give up Daniel as a replacement for Wellington, will we have to sacrifice Daniel to be washed clean of Wellington's murder?

When her bare feet touched the damp concrete just cleansed of Wellington's blood, her legs – her big, fat, solid, earthy legs, their flesh dense and firm – buckled beneath her. She fell to her knees on the concrete, and Daniel, now freed, sped off to join Marko and Annika.

Marko hurried to her side and helped her up, his arm no longer trembling.

He held her close, and his tunic's strong, tallowy smell, Marko's manly new smell, filled her nostrils till it choked her.

"We're leaving," he said triumphantly. "I reserved a car, it'll be here in thirty minutes. We're going to spend the rest of our stay with your father's friends."

"We have to call them first," she protested weakly.

"Out of the question. We'll show up, and they'll have to take us in. Suppose we called and they said it was impossible, what would we do? We've got to back them into a corner, there's no other way."

"We're leaving, we're leaving!" cried Annika in a burst of wild joy.

She began leaping about, stamping on the damp spot, her big, limpid, blue eyes almost popping out.

Ladivine was troubled to see that the little girl's shorts had slipped down, her bottom partly exposed.

More disturbingly still, the fiercely modest Annika didn't seem to care, and Marko himself was watching the child's frenzied capers on the concrete with an amused, light-hearted, happy eye.

Then a bitter taste filled her mouth.

How could the big brown dog ever follow her into the bush, where Richard Rivière's friends lived? How could the car not leave it far behind, and even if it did manage to follow her trail, wouldn't it come to her dangerously depleted?

Now she was certain she didn't want to leave, not the city nor the hotel, and she wouldn't care if she was doomed to be imprisoned there forever, and she would blame no-one but herself and her perfectly lucid choices, and would thus resist the temptation to go to the trial and harangue the judges: Will the time come to judge Marko Berger, the murderer of a minor named Wellington, and myself, here before you, I who made no attempt to rescue that poor boy?

Caringly, Marko took Ladivine's arm as Annika spun around and around on the slowly drying stain.

She was pivoting on one foot and propelling herself with the other, her arms arched around her hips.

Ladivine was convinced her bare feet were absorbing the damp of the concrete, soaking up everything that had spilled there.

"We have a very talented daughter," said Marko. "She should start dance lessons when we get home."

Couldn't he see that Annika was dancing with Wellington's death, that Wellington's death had invited her to dance and now she couldn't push it away?

Marko had a dreamy smile on his face. He was already thinking of going home, of Berlin, of the life quietly waiting for them there, ready to be put on again like a freshly cleaned and pressed garment.

She wished she could tell him that nothing was waiting for them to come home anymore, that their whole life, and their real life, was here, that they would never escape it, except with their death.

Or was Marko right about himself and the children, and she alone, Ladivine Rivière, had no life to go back to in Berlin, because she'd brought it with her, at its most essential, to this place?

She reflexively reached out to take Daniel's hand and start up to their room, but the boy recoiled in something not far from terror.

"I can walk by myself!" he shrieked.

"Annika, we're going," said Marko, in a clear, firm voice.

The girl stopped spinning at once. She collapsed on the ground and lay prostrate, waiting, thought Ladivine, to recover her spirits and drive Wellington's away.

The four-wheel drive Marko had rented was already outside the hotel when they came down with the purse that was their only luggage.

Ladivine paid the bill, avoiding the clerk's gaze, but as she turned to leave her eyes met the manager's, standing in the lobby with his back to the light.

She thought she saw deep revulsion curling that usually distant, inexpressive man's lips.

She nodded at him, as any departing guest would have done, and she felt as if her huge, heavy head was about to tumble off onto the carpet.

Making no reply, he stepped to one side and disappeared into the shadows.

She wanted to scream at him, "What of Wellington?"

Nothing came out but a sob that might well have passed for a sneeze. Marko and the children were already settled into the car, waiting.

She didn't have to look around to find the big brown dog, across the street as always.

It was sitting up very straight on its haunches, its front legs proud and firm, the rust-coloured fur on its belly showing between them.

She held the dog's gaze and gestured apologetically towards the four-wheel drive – but wouldn't the dog know full well she had no wish to leave?

Wouldn't it know, couldn't it decipher her sentiments better than she herself, and didn't it inhabit Ladivine Rivière's skin more intimately than she herself, who sometimes felt she'd become nothing more than Clarisse Rivière's bereaved daughter?

Marko gave a quick honk. She steeled herself and climbed in beside him, stunned at the coolness of the air-conditioned cabin, its appealing scent of new leather and jasmine air-freshener.

"This must have cost a lot of money," she murmured, just to say something, caring little now for their financial condition.

"It's not cheap," said Marko, "but there's no way around it, we can't get there without a four-wheel drive. When you don't have a choice, you just go along, right?"

She sensed Marko's body quivering with a merry, childlike, vaguely malign excitement, not, as anyone else might have thought, because he was relishing the prospect of driving such a vehicle but because, Ladivine noted uneasily, his body, his face, even his hair, everything about him seemed different, more intense and more glowing, cruel, strong and fiery, as well as – strangely, given his usual sweetness and seriousness – far more gleeful, a hard, gemlike glee without cheer or merriment.

That fierce ardour filled the car with something cynical, and, Ladivine thought, something sensual.

How stifling it was, how disturbing!

She was sure Marko would laugh out loud if she spoke Wellington's name, a new laugh, aggressive and sarcastic.

And the children? Would they laugh along with him?

Oh yes, they would, they were following Marko's lead now, and who could blame them, since she herself was so uncertain, inspired so little confidence, since Wellington's mere name made her tremble and gasp?

She could hardly expect the children to take trembling anxiety's side, to embrace foolishness and pointless shame.

In all sincerity, she couldn't even want them to.

On the GPS's instructions, Marko drove down a narrow, pot-holed road through endless suburbs.

Low blocks of bare-cement flats succeeded the little dirt houses roofed with mismatched sheets of corrugated tin, in front of which slim-hipped women with diminutive breasts underneath oversized T-shirts disapprovingly watched the four-wheel drive go by.

Sometimes the wheels sprayed little pebbles at the houses, built close by the road.

With this Marko would slow down, just as Ladivine was about to ask him to, then little by little he'd speed up again, his features relaxing, as if he feared that some peril might pounce on them if he drove any slower.

He cast Ladivine glances whose tenderness she could plainly see, as well as their longing to draw her into the sphere of licence and vitality forming around his new, unbridled nature, but she turned away, looked out of the window, her heart heavy with resentment.

But suppose Wellington had come back to harm them?

Wasn't that the most likely thing?

Had she not in fact sensed the boy's hatred, his feigned friend-ship mere groundwork for carefully calculated misdeeds?

Marko was seeking out the children's attention as well, wiggling his fingers at them or smiling broadly towards the back seat in the rear-view mirror.

It seemed to Ladivine that, without being aware of it, by his

221

emanations alone, he was stirring up an odd frenzy in the children, especially Annika, an excitement at once teasing and frustrated, denied a conclusion that Marko's provocative manner seemed to promise.

Daniel squirmed in his seatbelt, giggling as if he'd been tickled, something questioning and faintly anxious in his piercing voice, his baby voice, which he'd playfully reverted to.

Annika was screaming with laughter as she might scream in pain, spurred on by the goad of a scandalous sexual appeal that she couldn't understand but perceived all the same.

This was what Marko was bringing about, this was how far he was willing to go to absolve himself – drawing the children into his miserable, guilty conscience, then corrupting them with their desperately delighted consent.

Or was it she, Ladivine Rivière, who was looking at all this with an unwholesome eye?

She closed her eyes, hunched forward in her seat.

She often feared, having once been that teenaged girl who slept with the uncomplicated men of her little city for money, and unable ever since to look back on those days without a shudder of dismay, almost disbelief, that she wouldn't be able to keep a cool head with her children when the subject of their bodies came up, that she might betray her unease by a stiffness they would interpret as an odd prudishness, that she might find it hard to make clear what was perfectly acceptable and what to steer clear of, and so she'd always found Marko's casualness and simplicity about sex reassuring, and she'd always counted on him to fill in the children when the time came.

But what she felt in that car, that indecent, toxic, hopeless excitement, could not be good for the children, she thought, and she knew the old Marko would never have allowed it, could never even have imagined behaving in a way that might encourage it.

Or was she imagining things?

Oh no, she could feel it, as plainly as she could smell Marko's tunic's harsh, oily scent.

He'd decided to turn Daniel and Annika into hard, perpetually inflamed creatures, either, she thought, because he couldn't bear to be alone in his wickedness or because he believed they might find protection in that debasement.

And here she felt Marko had betrayed her, Marko whose uprightness and modesty and even, yes, whose cowardice she loved more than anything, not because she might somehow turn it to her advantage but because she thought it meant he would never hurt anyone, and he never had, gentle and good as Clarisse Rivière, until (at her urging?) he one day resolved to tell Lüneburg that he would rather never set foot there again.

Ladivine had met him after two aimless years at the University of Bordeaux, which, on a whim and a friend of a friend's vague promise of lodging, she'd left for Berlin, with no great enthusiasm, under the illusion that time and life would go by more quickly if she moved on, stupidly, because she had no plans, no hopes, because at twenty-one she felt tired and worn, and she saw Marko at the watch counter of the Hermannplatz Karstadt, where he'd recently found work, and realised that a young man like him, with his long hair, his big glasses, his delicate, kindly, calm, endlessly patient face would never feel the need to hurt anyone at all, that there was a kind of glory about him that he didn't work at and didn't believe in, though that word would have made him laugh, as he was a practical man, and this serene scepticism was an element of his grace, since he had no knowledge of that grace, since he had no access to it.

She came back to the Hermannplatz Karstadt every day, and every day she pretended she was trying to decide on a watch to give Richard Rivière, who hadn't yet left Clarisse Rivière behind in their Langon house.

Eventually she invited Marko for a cup of coffee over his midday break, a step that, by his own admission, he would never have dared take, and the next day she moved her things into Marko's room.

He was living in a shared flat on the Mehringdamm, and his little room at the end of the passage served as their marital home for two years, while Ladivine earned her diploma as a French teacher.

And that mannerly young man, resigned to the sameness of life and the docile abandonment of his ambitions, submitting without rancour, placidly accepting the way of things, requested a transfer to the Karstadt on Wilmersdorfer Strasse when they decided to leave the little room in Kreuzberg for the Charlottenburg apartment.

And so their life had gone by, thought Ladivine in the four-wheel drive, a good life, easy and serene, made perfectly happy, for a time, by the birth of the children.

Sometimes back then she woke late at night, not to find Marko locked in battle on the balcony, not to flee the torrent of blood pouring in from Langon, carrying Clarisse Rivière's silent cries, but simply for the immeasurable joy of gazing on Marko, Daniel and Annika's sleeping faces, one by one, it was the anticipation of that matchless joy that pulled her from her slumbers, that made her get up and walk soundlessly through the apartment, her blood throbbing in her neck, not her mother's blood but her own, neatly contained in vessels that no loser would ever set out to slash with a knife.

And it was Marko's face that she looked at the longest, sometimes drowsing, then waking again with a start, but never slipping out of that ecstatic, surprised, almost incredulous meditation on a man who meant far more to her than her own life, who inspired in her an inextinguishable gratitude, whose discreet, childlike breath she greedily inhaled from his nuzzling mouth, trying to solve the mystery of Marko's love for her, he who in his clarity seemed so much more honourable than she.

Nothing could possibly be more disturbing, she thought in the four-wheel drive, than the hard flame now burning in Marko, with which he was trying to consume Daniel and Annika.

Such a man would never again make her long to inhale his breath, she wouldn't even want him to love her.

But was she not the cause of all this? Was it not her idea to call Richard Rivière and ask for advice, knowing that Marko would take anything her father said as an absolute truth?

And suppose, thought Ladivine in the four-wheel drive, suppose Marko wanted to be a little like Richard Rivière, suppose he was striving to attain what he saw as Richard Rivière's marvellous force, his charming authority, the perfect certitude of his word?

Wasn't she to blame for that too?

Without trying to, had she not, in the first years of her life with Marko, spoken of Richard Rivière in such terms that Marko could only feel crushed by the weight of his own insignificance?

On various plausible pretexts, Richard Rivière had never bothered to come and meet either the children or Marko, thereby, in her husband's eyes, heightening his prestige, which, troublingly, grew more powerful still with the murder of Clarisse Rivière.

But instead of keeping quiet, shouldn't Ladivine then have convinced Marko that Clarisse Rivière would still be alive had Richard Rivière stayed and looked after her, had he not so completely and so coldly abandoned her, like a wife he'd come to despise years before?

And that couldn't be, could it?

One thing that often irritated Ladivine was that Marko never seemed to appreciate the full splendour of Clarisse Rivière's innocence.

Yes, he treated her with the same kindness and thoughtfulness he offered everyone, but that was just it, he never showed, through a special, exceptional attitude, that he was aware of that ragged, dismantled woman's unique grandeur, never showed that he had every reason to respect her far more than he did Richard Rivière, whom he admired childishly, without knowing him.

Oh yes, that had often infuriated Ladivine.

But, she thought in the four-wheel-drive, wasn't that her fault? How to know?

Hadn't she too treated Clarisse Rivière with condescension, hadn't she hidden her tortured love under a mask of off-handedness and even, sometimes, effrontery?

How could Marko have suspected her burning desire to see Clarisse Rivière rescued and loved when she expressed it so badly, so obliquely?

He was just as casual, just as amiably distant, polite and unforthcoming with Clarisse Rivière as she was, and what could he be accused of, thought Clarisse Rivière in the four-wheel drive, except refusing to understand that he was much like Clarisse Rivière, in the special sort of drab saintliness that they shared?

But now Marko was dazzling, now he radiated a glorious, wicked flame.

Unusually, the children hadn't yet drifted off to sleep.

Even Daniel was squirming, his eyes wide open and slightly bulging.

Ladivine thought him rapt in an unfocused pleasure that the mere presence of Marko's body, of his flesh as if on fire beneath his pink tunic, was pretending to offer him, then suddenly snatching it away, refusing any possibility of fulfilment.

Now and then Daniel snickered, understanding nothing but, thought Ladivine, putting on the forced cynicism of a teenager who suspects some hidden meaning and doesn't want to seem clueless. He snickered with a horrible knowing smirk, thought Ladivine, frightened.

The GPS's silken commands landed in that electric silence like sly insinuations.

Marko was driving a little too fast on the now-deserted road, freshly asphalted, past fields of banana trees.

An amused little smile floated on his lips, ready to burst into full bloom at the slightest provocation.

How handsome he was, how appealing, how, clearly, he wished Ladivine would come over to his side and delight with him in this new, untrammelled, superior, brutal way of being!

She remembered that Marko always needed her approval, express or implicit, in everything he did.

Never, she was sure, had he tried to exclude her from something in which he found happiness or satisfaction, as she had with that big brown dog, and she had even wondered if he was capable of any pleasure at all, of any kind, except insofar as Ladivine consented.

Those days were gone. With all her being, with all her flesh, she could feel Marko breaking free of everything that bound his gratification to Ladivine's approval.

No less clearly, she saw the desire he still nonetheless felt, not desperate or cunning but simply companionable, to include her in his new enchantment.

A wave of regretful, anguished nausea swept over her.

She looked at him, that bewitching man, she remembered the deep tenderness she once felt for him, she recalled that he was the father of her children and could be hers again if she liked. She wanted to whisper "Marko, my love." She reached out to touch his shoulder.

But just then he turned towards her, and in his eyes she thought she saw a gleam she'd never seen before, something she didn't want to get close to for anything in the world, not even with love's help – a joyous, arrogant rejection of decency and rectitude, of fear and compunction.

The smile on Marko's lips came to life, and it was his usual handsome smile, loving and slightly tremulous, put on to tempt her.

But in his eyes was there anything other than cold calculation?

Ladivine sensed a distance between that smile and himself, as if his wicked spirit had remembered that smile and realised its power to placate her, the deployment of his new omnipotence having failed to sway her.

Soon, she wondered, would he have even that smile to draw on?

Because his smile was hovering at the very edges of his lips, a faraway, uncertain memory of what even now was no more, while his gaze, turned inward, was fixed on another goal, a secret goal – oh no, not even secret, Marko's new desires radiated from his whole body, the car thrummed with those waves, forbidding the children to take refuge in sleep.

Surprised by the sound of her own voice, Ladivine shouted:

"Wellington!"

Then she huddled on the edge of her seat, as far from Marko as possible.

Sullenly, he pretended to focus on the road ahead, roaring recklessly past overloaded old lorries and rusting, old-fashioned little cars whose drivers sometimes sent a vigorous gesture of hostility Marko's way.

"I want to see him again," Daniel whined.

"We'll never see Wellington again," said Annika, in a grave, superior voice.

"Why not?"

"Because Daddy says so."

Never, in the old days, would that little girl have announced that something involving the whole family wouldn't come to pass simply on Marko's orders, Ladivine thought.

"From now on, it's forbidden to speak Wellington's name," said Marko, calmly.

Annika burst into a painful, sharp, prolonged laugh, which seemed to brighten Marko's gloomy heart.

To keep her company and express his approval, he began to laugh too, his fists pounding little blows on the steering wheel.

After two monotonous hours on the perfectly straight road, flanked by endless banana and sweet-potato plantations, Marko turned onto a yellow dirt road that soon entered the forest.

Ladivine had stopped looking back to see if Daniel and Annika were finally asleep – the atmosphere individually embracing each child was arousing enough that she could feel them holding themselves at the ready, unsure what they were waiting for but maniacally attentive to their father's every move, his every word or sigh, anything that might give them a lead to follow, give them a place in the wake of his dazzling vigour.

Were they afraid they might fall from Marko's favour if they slept, and so find themselves back in Ladivine's camp, where a tedious remorse about Wellington was accompanied by an utter inability to bring him back?

Wellington!

Why shouldn't the children have concluded that their father could produce the boy whenever he pleased, and that if he didn't want to he must have had very good reasons, whereas, manifestly, Ladivine could only cry Wellington's name in subdued, pointless sorrow, unable even to speak of him, to summon up his image with amusing words and anecdotes?

Wellington!

Why, for that matter, shouldn't the children rather be forbidden to speak that name than hear it heartlessly cried into their mystified ears by their frightened, opaque, uncommunicative mother?

The poor little things must have feared that Ladivine would take over their minds if they slept, then drag them away from Marko's wondrous influence, spirit them away from that radiant force.

She turned around in her seat and caressed Daniel's bare thigh, squeezed Annika's calf, trying to smile reassuringly.

The children's flesh felt hard, clenched. They refused to meet her gaze, and she realised she was being a nuisance, but what did she care, if she didn't want to lose them?

Because, she thought, could she still see in them her beloved children if they turned into depraved little monsters?

Wellington!

She longed to tell them the boy was dead, and that she and Marko, for all their pretentions to excellent parenting, were, with this refusal to speak of what they'd done to Wellington, lying to them.

But it was too late, she couldn't talk to her children now, and her children didn't want to hear, she could tell by their averted eyes, the way their limbs tensed beneath her fingers.

Suddenly a broad clearing appeared down the road, opening up in the forest.

"We're there," said Marko.

Ladivine felt a shared astonishment briefly reuniting her with Marko, for what they now saw was nothing like even the vaguest image they'd conjured up of Richard Rivière's friends, whom Ladivine, not quite knowing why, had pictured as a couple of grizzled drifters temporarily stranded by a lack of funds or a need for rest, but the dozens of clearly brand-new four-wheel drives, white, black, or grey, parked in the clearing beneath sheet-metal roofs, and the big pink house, which reminded Ladivine of certain villas in Langon, revealed the presence, deep in this forest, of prosperous car dealers, and why not, thought Ladivine with a stab of ill will, since that's what Richard Rivière had become once he left Clarisse Rivière (as if Clarisse Rivière had somehow been keeping him down), having gone from assistant manager in Langon, at the Alfa Romeo dealership he'd been hired to just out of high school, to the head of a Jeep dealership in the Haute-Savoie, and Ladivine always wondered how he'd settled on that area, having, to the best of her knowledge (which is to say from what Clarisse Rivière told her), never spent any time there before going off to make it, perhaps forever, his home.

Oh yes, she'd thought on being told by her father that he now lived in Annecy, Richard Rivière had been quietly plotting his Haute-Savoie escape for some time – because how to believe that he'd rushed straight from Langon to Annecy with no plan in mind, no prospects, no idea even what the city was like?

A couple emerged from the house and stood looking in their direction, hands shading their eyes.

But why, the insidious little voice of common sense whispered in Ladivine's ear, why should Richard Rivière have revealed to his daughter that he wanted to leave Clarisse Rivière and make a fresh start in Annecy?

So she would try to talk him out of it?

And on what grounds would she have sought to persuade him to go on wasting away with Clarisse Rivière?

He did the one thing he could do, not uncaringly, and no reasonable person could blame him for failing to foresee that his wife would end up drowning in her own blood because he wasn't there beside her, because he wasn't there to keep her from foolishness – to keep her from being herself, that is, to keep her from being the slightly dim Clarisse Rivière.

The sunlight that made the sheet-metal roofs sparkle poured

down on the couple's two identically unmoving heads, as if to designate them for veneration.

The woman's wrists and throat glimmered, laden with gold.

She took a languid step forward, very consciously offering her adorned body to their gaze, and Ladivine felt a small shock on realising that this diminutive figure in spike heels, capris and a little sailor shirt was in fact an old woman, whose long hair, dyed deep black, seemed to wrap her gaunt, tanned, heavily made-up face like a scarf.

She was neither smiling nor looking at her expectantly, but only waiting, infinitely patient and docile in her certainty of being admired, and she raised her chin a little, boldly exposing her wrinkled face, slightly smoothed over by the make-up, to the stark sunlight.

"I'm Richard Rivière's daughter," said Ladivine, after nodding a hello.

She couldn't help adding, so as to say something, for she was intimidated by the woman's imperial aloofness:

"His only child, Ladivine."

"Yes, I know, he said you'd be coming," the woman answered, ever so slightly bored, as if she found the obligation to speak pointless when one had only to show oneself, exhibit oneself.

"Oh, he told you?"

"Yes, a few weeks ago, on the phone."

She realised that Richard Rivière must have talked to his friends as soon as she'd hung up, and although she could have considered that diligence a sign of his eagerness to help out, it irritated her.

Because there was little chance that either she or Marko would ever have felt the urge to rent a car and drive out to these strangers' property were it not for "the Wellington thing", as she privately called what had happened, and did it not seem that, from his mysterious Haute-Savoie lair, Richard Rivière had foreseen the events that would bring them to this place, and so was it not in his power, a power he'd left unused, to say or do something to forestall those events?

Shouldn't he have put her on guard, he who claimed to know this country?

And said to her: Beware of courtly teenagers who accost you at the front door of the National Museum? Beware of the violence nestled in your heart, waiting to be roused when you meet a young man with impenetrable schemes, beware of the sympathy you might begin to feel for your own extraordinary misdeeds, your new-found longing to let go and plunge endlessly into senselessness?

Marko and the children had now joined her before the woman with the cold, serene face, not so much covered with make-up as carved from it.

Marko held out his hand, and with a weary resignation she gave him her own.

Oh, how he'd changed, how he wanted it to be seen, thought Ladivine.

Because Marko had climbed out of the car and, smiling, his back ramrod straight, had materialised in front of that woman.

The old Marko would have thought it enough simply to be there.

He glowed with pride and confidence in his pink tunic, the huge purple flowers ornamenting the front like the insignia of some ignoble order.

Ladivine was beginning to loathe that outfit.

She felt Marko's hunger to present himself to this stranger in all his new magnificence, she sensed his pleasure that this woman had never seen him before, she saw his brazen manner, the full depth of his emancipation.

And was he not now even handsomer, far, than before?

He took the children by the shoulders to herd them before him, adorning himself with their presence, she thought.

The woman gave them a thoroughly indifferent glance, then looked again, interested, almost intrigued, and the curiosity that neither Marko's nor Ladivine's face had sparked in her jaded eye was now roused by Daniel and Annika's two ardent little faces, a hint of a smile even taking shape on her crimson lips, and she looked again at Marko, now realising, now knowing what she would find on his face, thought Ladivine, and then back at the children, all the while smiling as if she'd seen something surprising and glorious, something important and wonderful, and finally she looked at Marko with her real eyes, now shining and quick, cynical, hungry, which said to him: I've seen your children's lost, avid faces, and I know what manner of man you are, because we're the same, you and I.

Marko let out a charmed little laugh. Annika feverishly echoed him.

The woman briefly caressed each child on the cheek and cried out:

"Your children are adorable."

Which, though no surprise now for Ladivine, nonetheless displeased her, for to her mind Daniel and Annika looked anything but adorable at the moment.

She herself, had she just met them, would immediately have been wary of such children.

Would she not go so far as to think: These children are guilty? These children have done wrong, or believe they've done wrong, because some unnameable misdeed has been placed on their shoulders, and their sense of their own wickedness is ruining their faces and incomprehension is pinching their little noses, twisting their mouths into a detestable rictus?

"They're very tired, they're not quite themselves," she said curtly.

"They look fine to me," the woman decreed, not even bothering to glance Ladivine's way.

"We're not tired," said Annika.

The children clung to Marko, rubbed their hair against his noisome tunic.

He tenderly pressed them to him.

There was something desperate, thought Ladivine, her heart bleeding, in the way they clutched at their father's body, as if that contact alone could enlighten them on everything that was strange and different inside them, but that enlightenment never came.

Marko was embracing them with the same love and gentleness he'd always shown his children.

But perhaps they could sense that he himself no longer needed to feel and receive love, that he could now do without love, that he was strong enough for that, even as, kindness being a habit with him, he went on making the loving gestures they were used to.

Oh, come to me, she thought, my love for you is healthy and pure and I won't force you to bear the burden of any crime.

But her thick legs, her legs like two very straight tree trunks, with no taper at the ankle, which she'd taught herself to display proudly as if fashions had changed and long, slender legs were now a curse, not a blessing, her massive legs wouldn't let her move, wouldn't let her run to her children, and her tongue, too, had turned sluggish and fat in her mouth, from which no sound emerged.

She could clearly see herself reaching out and pulling the children from Marko's maleficent embrace, but her arms still hung limp at her sides, her fingers only feebly clenched against her linen skirt, sweat-stained and rumpled from the trip.

It was clear that Richard Rivière, Ladivine's father, had, since leaving Langon years before, led a professional life as busy as it was prosperous, a life of which Ladivine had known little, and neither, surely,

235

had Clarisse Rivière, notwithstanding the money she got from him every month, as Ladivine was aware, a sizeable sum that she never touched.

It was not long before her death that she'd told Ladivine of her refusal to make use of that money, with the stubborn, childish, patient air she sometimes had when she'd made a resolution she couldn't or didn't want to explain but would never go back on, though she was perfectly willing, as if to make up for her hard-headedness, to repeat tirelessly, always in the same affable voice, the simple words that expressed her decision.

She did just that when Ladivine finally voiced her surprise at everything Clarisse Rivière, her lonely, ageing mother, seemed to be giving Freddy Moliger, since Ladivine had to limit herself to the subject of gifts, oh even there blushing at her own indiscretion, and there was no question of broaching the principal subject of her fear and dismay, the sexual passion Clarisse Rivière seemed to feel for that vile man, Freddy Moliger, that loser no doubt picked up off the bar he collapsed onto each night in some Langon hostelry that stayed open past midnight.

Arming herself with a stubborn but amiable expression, Clarisse Rivière assured her that she liked making Freddy Moliger happy, just as she told her she never withdrew a euro from the money Richard Rivière wired to her account, and did not want to.

Ladivine realised that her mother didn't dare ask Richard Rivière to stop sending that money, that she wouldn't know how to go about it without seeming aggressive or sentimental or absurdly contrary, and Richard Rivière obviously would have said no, and she would have had to come up with reasons, and so it was easier to say nothing.

But Ladivine knew that, deep in her modest, thick-skinned, battered but unresentful heart, Clarisse Rivière thought it cruelly inconsiderate to be helped out by standing order.

She would have liked to get a letter each time, and the fact that a cheque was enclosed wouldn't have bothered her in the least, on the contrary.

Richard Rivière thought he had only to direct his bank to wire a fixed amount on a fixed date, and then he could forget it, and that, Ladivine sensed, was what hurt Clarisse Rivière, his seeing to it that he would never have to think about her again, even just once a month.

That was why money was tight for Clarisse Rivière even before she met Freddy Moliger, she would gladly have taken Richard Rivière's money but she couldn't agree to receiving it in this way, or ask to be treated more thoughtfully, and this intransigence might have seemed an expression of wounded pride out of character for that unassuming woman, but it wasn't that, Ladivine knew, because no-one was less proud than Clarisse Rivière, less aware of her dignity, it wasn't that, it was rather the sign of a pain that still hurt, mute and incurable, the pain that had taken Clarisse Rivière by the throat when her husband walked out of the house and she realised that she too was now out of his life, Richard Rivière's mysterious new life, as irreversibly as her reflection disappearing from the rear-view mirror when he turned the corner.

"Your father seems to be doing pretty well," was all she had said to Ladivine of Richard Rivière's business, and Ladivine didn't ask for details, almost certain her mother knew nothing more and not wanting to make her confess that ignorance aloud, Clarisse Rivière who for twenty-five years of married life had listened each evening as Richard Rivière told of the cars he'd sold or not sold, the models he particularly loved or found sadly lacking in style or finish, or design, as he liked to say.

Neither Clarisse Rivière nor Ladivine quite knew how Richard Rivière was making all that money in Annecy, and so Ladivine felt vaguely uncomfortable, almost fraudulent, as if she'd stolen her identity as his daughter, when with a broad sweep of her skinny arm the Cagnac woman showed her the fleet of four-wheel drives, saying she hardly needed to explain whom they had to thank for all this, she and Cagnac, and after a moment Ladivine realised she meant Richard Rivière.

Her husband Cagnac was a tanned, lean man with swept-back grey hair and wearing espadrilles adorned with an intricate little knot.

The Cagnac woman introduced Marko and the children to him first, with a fervour that Cagnac must have seen as a sign, thought Ladivine, for a gleam of curiosity, of devout interest, immediately flickered on in his pond-water eyes.

Marko gave him a warm greeting, so casual that he might simply have been arriving at some gathering of friends.

Did he see, Ladivine wondered, the anticipation he aroused in these strangers, full of desire and pious respect, did he see that they'd pegged him as one of them?

When at last Cagnac turned to Ladivine, his wife having left her to introduce herself, the particular gleam in his eyes dimmed, that brief flame of longing and deference giving way to a slightly chilly politeness that was however immediately warmed by the words "I'm Richard Rivière's daughter."

Cagnac let out a cry of delight.

For a second time he clasped Ladivine's hand, having first shaken it somewhat stiffly, and held it for a moment in his, as if to fill himself with some substance peculiar to the Rivières, or to attempt, through his daughter's flesh, to recapture Richard Rivière's real presence.

"We owe him so much, you know," he said with emotion. "And your father's often told us about you, very often."

"Is that so?" asked Ladivine, sceptical but thrilled in spite of herself.

Though, she wondered, why should she think Richard Rivière never spoke of her to his friends?

She'd never doubted his affection for her, his only daughter, even when he proved little interested in having her come to Annecy, or in meeting Marko and the children.

And when she thought of Richard Rivière, she told herself love did not have to mean wanting to know all about a person's life and companions, did not have to mean needing to be with or talk to that person, because this, she believed, was how her father loved, with a love both abstract and unwavering, vague and absolute, incurious and unlimited.

He loved her, she told herself, and that was all there was to it.

And so she'd learned to make do without the usual displays of fatherly love, and the fact that Richard Rivière asked her for news of Daniel and Annika, and often sent them presents as costly as they were inappropriate, but never thought it only natural to want to meet them one day, never even seemed to believe that that was another thing he could do, she accepted all that, since this was how Richard Rivière loved.

"He's very proud of you," Cagnac went on.

He cocked his head, narrowed his eyes.

"But you're not how I pictured you. Completely different. And yet he described you so often, it's strange."

She could feel her breath coming heavier, hotter, her scalp prickling.

She scratched her head with a sort of fury, hoping Cagnac would say nothing more.

"We thought you'd be thin and light-haired," said the Cagnac woman in her cold, jaded voice.

"That's how my mother is, I mean was," Ladivine murmured.

239

"He never mentioned your mother."

"Well, they were divorced," she said, with a disagreeable sense of defending herself.

"He never told us he'd been married, not to mention divorced. He only talked about you, his daughter, and actually we had the idea you were Clarisse's daughter."

"Well, yes, that's right, my mother's name was Clarisse," said Ladivine with a forced little laugh, feeling the blood drain from her cheeks and her lips, her mouth at once horribly dry.

"We must not be talking about the same Clarisse. Anyway, it doesn't matter. What do you say we sit down to lunch?"

Cagnac must have been afraid he'd said too much, thought Ladivine, relieved, and so neglected his duty to be discreet where his friend Richard Rivière was concerned.

And although she had no desire to go on talking of Clarisse Rivière, although she was in fact delighted at this change of subject, she was astounded to find words crossing her lips, immediately wishing she could cram them back down her throat.

"My mother was murdered in her house in Langon," she said hurriedly. "The trial will be starting soon."

"Let's go and eat, since you're here," said the Cagnac woman. "We'll make do with whatever's on hand."

Had she not heard her?

Marko and the children were looking away, towards the gleaming cars, at once uneasy and distant, thought Ladivine, as if unconcerned by all this but nonetheless embarrassed for her, Ladivine, who couldn't seem to get into the spirit of things.

She'd never spoken so plainly of what happened to Clarisse Rivière in front of Daniel and Annika.

And yet there was no dismay in their faces, in their eyes, still fixed on the shining four-wheel drives, nothing troubled or tense.

The Cagnacs were heading towards the house with Marko close behind, one hand on each child's shoulder.

"The real Clarisse Rivière must not be forgotten!" Ladivine sobbed aloud. "Who will remember her if not us? After all, she was . . . she was a very good woman!"

Marko turned around and gave her a cautious smile.

He's trying to shut me up. Well, it won't be that easy.

In two furious strides, she was beside him.

She then realised that a strap on her sandal had broken, where the delicate leather bands crossed.

She squatted down as Marko and the children went inside, and now she was alone on the gravel path, in the heavy, scorching silence, now with tears in her eyes she was remembering Clarisse Rivière's gold sandals and yellowed, callused heels and the shame they made her feel for her mother, because they made her seem like an unrefined woman doing her sad best to dress up.

Were her own heels not also dry and cracked, in the dust of that path?

And her legs, whose brown hairs were beginning to grow back, her doughy legs, what leap could they make to propel her away from the Cagnac house in case of danger?

Far, far in the distance, she thought she heard a dog bark.

The strap was beyond a quick fix. She'd have to clench her toes to hold the sandal in place as she walked.

"This was all his idea, our opening a dealership in the forest," Cagnac was explaining. "We came out to this country with him two or three years ago, and he told us it was only his second visit, but he led us straight here, as if he'd been thinking of it for some time, and he said, 'This is where you should build,' and he dealt with leasing the land, all the paperwork, he found an architect for the house, all in just a few days. We trusted him, but still, he seemed so sure of himself that it scared us a little, we were half convinced he was going to swindle us in some way or other. I said to him, 'Richard, what's the scam?' If that had angered him, then we'd have dropped the whole thing then and there and never seen him again, but he hardly even blinked, he just smiled his friendly smile and told us it wasn't his way to deceive his friends. And we went back to Annecy, and that's where we sealed the deal. He sends us practically new cars, almost never driven, and then we sell them here, and you know what, it's going well, there's a real demand."

Cagnac smugly clicked his tongue against his palate.

A table had been laid in the vast marble-tiled dining room, and two servants were standing against the wall waiting to serve lunch, two boys dressed in white short-sleeved shirts and black slacks, hands clasped over their belts.

They'd brought out a special wine for the aperitif, yellow and strong, shipped in by the Cagnacs from the Haute-Savoie. Unbidden, the Cagnac woman poured a little into each glass, Daniel's excepted.

Ladivine snatched up Annika's glass, spilling a few drops on the table.

"She's not old enough to be drinking wine," she said, not looking at the Cagnac woman.

She was so angry she could have smashed the glass on the ground.

Even more swiftly, Annika took back the glass and swallowed the wine in one gulp.

She banged it down on the table, wiped her lips with one hand, and gave a little laugh, pretending she'd played a prank on her mother.

But there was no laughter in her eyes, only a coldness and a despair that wrenched Ladivine's heart.

Marko broke into a half-amused, half-irritated grimace, as he often did when the children wouldn't go to bed and insisted on acting up.

"Really, Annika," he said, ruffling her hair.

"A little good wine never killed anyone," Cagnac said jovially.

The servants next brought out an array of dishes, all of them, Ladivine noted, exceptionally heavy: pork cutlets covered with melted cheese, potatoes sautéed in goose fat, salad drenched in walnut oil, and for dessert thick crêpes stuffed with chocolate cream.

The children ate greedily, and far more than Ladivine would have thought possible, they who usually ate like birds, as she liked to say.

She herself was struggling to fend off revulsion. She ate a little piece of meat, a potato, then pushed away her almost untouched plate.

The Cagnacs ate energetically, saying nothing, the better to concentrate on their pleasure. Now and then they let out satisfied little grunts.

Ladivine saw them eyeing Marko and the children, as if to be sure they too were enjoying the food, clearly willing, she thought, to do whatever it took, perhaps have still other dishes brought out from the kitchen, so vital did they seem to find it that Marko be like them in every way.

She looked at them, lowly and sorrowful, impotent, unhappy, and she felt the awful bond between the Cagnacs and her children and husband growing ever stronger thanks to the repellent meal they were sharing.

How can you like such food? she wondered.

Although she wasn't eating, she was the only one sweating. Her hair stuck to her forehead, lay clammily against her neck.

Marko was serenely stuffing himself.

We know what you did to Wellington – and what about the Cagnacs, what's their crime?

What vile act is illuminating their faces with that hard, white, triumphant light, so intense that they don't want to be alone in it?

Which is why, seeing Marko and the children giving off that same radiant glow, perhaps still a bit dim and flickering, they're drawing them close to expose them to the full light of wickedness.

Oh, it must wear them down, having to endure that incandescence day after day with no company but each other.

And she thought: Well, not me, I won't be a part of it, my darkness keeps me . . . Not me, I won't . . .

She wasn't far from feeling a genuine hatred for Richard Rivière.

Because were it not for his advice they would not now be at the Cagnacs', ensnared in their vile web, they wouldn't even be in this country.

No, not the country, she wasn't sorry to be in this country, and she never would be – not for anything, come what may.

She'd made a very dear friend in the big brown dog. She'd never had such a friend.

Where they shouldn't have come was the heart of this forest, it was the Cagnacs', it was into this forest that Richard Rivière never should have sent them.

What was he after?

Above all, what did he want to come of his daughter Ladivine's meeting these immoral people, and what was he trying to tell her?

That here she was seeing everything he loved, everything he most prized?

That this world, so utterly alien to Clarisse Rivière's, hostile to that world on principle, was now his world, in his new Annecy existence, filled with a joy unknown in Langon?

Was he trying to show Ladivine, his one, precious daughter, just what sort of man he'd become?

Did he want his daughter Ladivine to be so charmed by the

Cagnacs that she would finally allow herself to choose Annecy over Langon, that her allegiance would finally desert Clarisse Rivière?

She'd remained ever faithful to Clarisse Rivière's spirit, which he might have seen as a condemnation of his running away from it, from Clarisse Rivière's intolerable innocence.

Well, thought Ladivine, snorting to herself, if the Cagnacs had been sent to this outpost for the purpose of enchanting her, if their mission was to deliver her into Annecy's loving, treacherous arms, then clearly Richard Rivière did not know his dear daughter so well.

Because nothing could possibly disgust her more than these old faces aglow with their crimes, these fatty foods, this sweet yellow wine.

And they were no more taken with her. It was Marko they wanted on their side, flanked by his children, ripe for the plucking.

She leapt up and hurried out, her nausea peaking.

Her broken sandal dragged over the tiles.

"No coffee?" asked one of the servants, coming back from the kitchen with a cup-laden platter.

Ladivine thought she heard something insolent and contemptuous in his voice, and she had the distinct impression that he was deliberately barring her way to the front door.

She sidestepped him, giving him a brusque bump with one shoulder, and walked out into the white-gravelled courtyard.

The heat hit her in the face, throat and arms, like so many blows aiming to knock her off her feet or drive her back into the air-conditioned hall.

But she held her ground, tottering, resolute, took a few uncertain steps forward, searching for a shady spot.

The forest started up close by on all sides, and yet no tree shaded the Cagnacs' property, not so much as a parasol sheltered the table and three metal chairs in the middle of the courtyard.

If the Cagnacs could tolerate this blast furnace, didn't that mean they were made of that same metal, which could burn but remain unchanged inside?

Suddenly emerging from the forest, a couple came walking towards Ladivine.

Young, handsome, both dressed in white cotton, they greeted her pleasantly as they passed, then changed their minds, as if struck by something they hadn't first seen, and walked back to face her.

"I'm sorry, we didn't recognise you," said the young woman, taking her in her arms.

Ladivine felt a pair of firm little breasts against her chest, a delicate ribcage, a heart full of sincere affection beating inside.

Perfumed with a renowned, high-priced scent, the woman's neck bore a dark down, like the cheek of a new-born.

The young man embraced her, maintaining a slight distance, respectfully, thought Ladivine, so his chest and her breasts wouldn't touch.

They smiled at her in such simple, obvious friendship that tears came to her eyes.

After a quick glance at Ladivine's feet, the young woman took a pair of sandals from the big leather purse she had over her shoulder.

"I brought these for the test drive, but here, take them, you need them more than I do."

She bent down and waited for Ladivine to hold out one foot, then the other, which she did, not even embarrassed.

Though her feet were wider than the young woman's, the sandals fitted wonderfully.

They were pretty, flat-heeled, made of natural leather.

In one quick, nimble move the young woman slipped Ladivine's old sandals into her bag, as if to put right a mistake or expunge a lapse in taste, then stood up again, pleased and pink-cheeked.

246

Just then Cagnac came out.

He hurried towards the young couple, his back slightly bowed, smiling obsequiously.

"So you know each other?" he couldn't help asking, more curious than he wanted to seem, Ladivine told herself.

"Why yes, she came to our wedding," said the young woman.

"Oh, I didn't know, I didn't know."

And the young woman gazed thoughtfully at Ladivine. Her large, dark, expertly made-up eyes closed halfway.

In a quiet, distant, melancholy voice she said:

"That yellow dress you had on, it was so pretty . . . I'd love to have one just like it."

"And I'd be so happy to give it to you, if only I still had it!" cried Ladivine.

At that moment she would have given her her very life.

While the young couple tried out the car Cagnac had brought them, slowly circling the grounds at the forest's edge, Ladivine went back inside, overcome by the heat.

The absurdly vast, high-ceilinged entrance hall, imitating a French château with its broad, flaring stone staircase, was empty but echoing with lively voices that Ladivine thought must be coming from the kitchen, and among them she thought she heard Wellington's, which she put down to the shock of her encounter with the newlyweds, still coursing through her trembling, drained body.

She could not, she told herself, have been at that wedding.

Who looked so like her that people might mistake them?

And why did she feel it would be an outrageous lie to deny she was there, why did she feel she wasn't lying at all when she confirmed that she'd gone to that wedding in a little yellow gingham dress

247

bought three years before at the Galeries Lafayette in Bordeaux?

Just three weeks ago she was laying it in her suitcase, fully aware that it was too dressy for a trip such as this and would surely go unworn, and even then she had yet to wear it.

Oh, Ladivine knew why, even if she'd tried hard to convince herself that she was only waiting for the proper occasion, because in its plainness it was a very elegant dress.

No, it wasn't that.

She'd never found the strength to put on that dress because she'd bought it during her last visit to Clarisse Rivière, with Clarisse Rivière at her side, and two weeks later Clarisse Rivière would be killed, not in a yellow gingham dress but in the beige Karstadt cardigan Ladivine had sent for her birthday, because Clarisse Rivière had gently but stubbornly refused to be given anything at the Galeries Lafayette in Bordeaux, even with her birthday so near, and even though a peeved Ladivine thought it would be only polite of her mother not to make such a fuss and simply accept a present that Ladivine would otherwise have to go out of her way to send from Berlin the next week.

But Clarisse Rivière wouldn't be moved, smiling in her vague, cautious, uninvolved way.

"No, thanks, I don't want anything," she would say each time Ladivine showed her some potentially suitable garment.

"But it's for your birthday, I want to give you something," Ladivine answered in mounting irritation.

I have to give you something, and it would make my life easier if I could just do it now – that's what she was thinking, slightly ashamed of herself, as she briskly slid the hangers along the rods, inspecting the clothes with a vexed and critical eye.

She was still angry from the day before, when she'd first met the man who was sleeping with Clarisse Rivière.

248

And, seeing Ladivine's deep disapproval of Freddy Moliger, her mother had turned distant and cold, as if her consenting to a gift might authorise Ladivine to speak of her horrified misgivings about that man.

But Ladivine had no intention of bringing up Moliger.

She found this whole affair so incongruous, so shocking, that she couldn't have spoken of it without disgust and dismay, and the last thing she wanted was to hurt Clarisse Rivière's feelings, even if she suspected her mother was not quite as happy as she claimed.

In truth, she would not have known how to begin.

She did not want to think about that man, about her mother's relations with him, and yet a quiet foreboding was forcing her to do just that.

And so she said nothing.

She'd taken Clarisse Rivière to the Galeries Lafayette in Bordeaux so together they could pick out her fifty-fourth birthday present, and now Clarisse Rivière was saying "no thanks" in her closed, quiet way, telling her there was nothing she wanted, now Clarisse Rivière was leaving Ladivine no choice but to face her own anger.

And Ladivine savagely shoved the hangers aside, one after another, confessing to herself that Clarisse Rivière's desires and motivations were completely beyond her, and that this angered and upset and even disappointed her.

And she also admitted that, given the way things were, she had no real wish to please Clarisse Rivière, that this would be a purely pro forma present, because her anger was heavy with spite and frustration, and Clarisse Rivière had seen it and was now gracefully, somewhat frostily choosing not to take part in that joyless game.

She was there, but she wasn't alone, because her lover was with her, even though he'd stayed behind in Langon.

Both felt his presence beside Clarisse Rivière, and both knew that man's existence was turning them against each other, or rather, since Clarisse Rivière wanted nothing more than to see Ladivine one day approve of Freddy Moliger, turning Ladivine against her mother, fuelling an anger born with her first glimpse of Moliger's sly, uncouth, stupidly cunning face, his way of sizing her up as he held out one clammy, evasive hand.

Ladivine couldn't say a word about Freddy Moliger, because the simple fact of his being there was unthinkable, his being there between them, with his snickering half-smile, his perpetually furious, outraged, wary face.

It's degrading to criticise someone like that, she was thinking.

It was simply unacceptable that she and her mother were having to deal with Moliger.

How, then, could she possibly imagine Clarisse Rivière offering him the vulnerability of her naked body, her undisguised, trusting face, perhaps her words of love?

That idea, those images, were more than Ladivine could bear.

Not because they involved Clarisse Rivière, her mother, but because they involved Freddy Moliger, whose mere hand repulsed her, his big, cagy, shiftless hand.

She gave up the search for Clarisse Rivière's present and, resetting her sights, began looking for something for herself, so this trip to Bordeaux wouldn't be for nothing.

It was then that she came onto the yellow gingham dress. She held the hanger up to her chin and clasped the dress to her chest.

Very nice, she read in Clarisse Rivière's admiring eyes.

And indeed, were she invited to a wedding at this time of year, that was exactly the dress she would choose.

There was nothing she'd be more likely to wear than her yellow gingham dress, despite the abhorrence it caused her ever since Clarisse Rivière's death.

Far from Langon, far from Berlin, in this land where her mother had never been, where nothing evoked her memory, she would certainly have found the courage to put on the yellow dress.

Who had done it for her? What woman, like her in every way, had worn that dress to the wedding?

Not the woman they'd seen at the market, who, even in that very dress, looked nothing like Ladivine. She must have got hold of it after the wedding, legally or otherwise.

Who, then, had boldly appeared in the yellow gingham dress from the Bordeaux Galeries Lafayette, bought by Ladivine out of anger and spite because Clarisse Rivière would not accept a gift offered with implacable bad blood, just as she silently refused to chase off the invisible but palpable presence of her lover, that Freddy Moliger she'd been seeing for several months, to whom she herself gave presents that were never spurned, whom she'd brought home, into her lonely, respectable house, where no blood had yet been spilled?

Ladivine could have worn that dress to a wedding, but even here, would she have found the courage?

And should she feel offended or grateful that someone had shown a daring that was perhaps beyond her, and that a stranger whose face people confused with her own had gone to that glamorous wedding to dazzle an admiring crowd with a yellow gingham dress that Ladivine had never put on, no more than Clarisse Rivière, to whom Ladivine had given not that dress but a beige cardigan later bought at Karstadt, after the anger and spite had subsided, but not the worry, nor the profound sense of disgrace?

Should she feel rescued or deceived? Should she feel humiliated or chosen?

Oh, she didn't know, and perhaps she never would.

She climbed the broad staircase to the rooms the Cagnac woman had shown them before lunch.

The soles of her new sandals were neither slippery nor stiff, she thought she'd never worn any so comfortable.

Her legs felt slenderer, sprightlier, and her feet seemed to spring off each tread as if the young bride had also given her a little of her vitality, her high hopes.

On the second floor, in two rooms separated by a sliding door, Marko and the children were asleep, each in a generous, white-sheeted bed.

What was there to do after such a meal but sleep? she thought, apprehensive.

She took off her sandals and gently lay down beside Marko.

She closed her eyes, knowing she wouldn't sleep, and when Wellington's voice resounded in the corridor she first thought she was dreaming, having drifted off without knowing it.

But then she heard it again, a young voice, slightly sneering, speaking, in his peculiar English, words that Ladivine couldn't make out from the bedroom.

Another boy answered, and they both began to laugh.

Lying hushed and stiff, Ladivine concentrated so hard on that voice that her head spun.

"Wellington, Wellington," she murmured, sweat suddenly pouring down her face.

A still doubting joy, a still hesitant hope kept her pinned to the bed, perhaps waiting for some unambiguous sign, perhaps afraid that rushing into the corridor might shatter any chance that it really was Wellington.

At last she carefully got out of bed, opened the door, and there, at the top of the stairs, leaning on the banister, Wellington and another boy were chatting — one of the boys, she mechanically observed, who'd served them at lunch.

She saw Wellington in profile, speaking in his languid voice, head tilted back, ever ready to laugh at his own jokes.

He was resting his weight on one leg, and his very young man's bony hips showed under the light fabric of his Bermuda shorts.

She silently closed the door and hurried to Marko, so excited that she stumbled on the polished wooden floor, suddenly unsure how to put one foot in front of the other.

"Wellington, Wellington," she murmured, her breast swelling with overpowering rapture.

She shook Marko's shoulder.

He opened his eyes, immediately breaking into a smile, and reached out for her.

"Marko, Wellington's here, I've just seen him. He's alive! He's out in the passage . . . Oh, darling, what a relief . . ."

He frowned, perplexed, lost, and his arms fell back to the mattress.

"What Wellington? Who are you talking about?"

"You know! The boy you . . . who went over the railing . . ."

She broke off, realising Marko was only asking in hopes of a moment to choke back his fear.

For, beyond confusion, it was a blend of terror and deep disillusionment she saw pouring from Marko's eyes, his suddenly ashen face, his trembling lips.

Rather than sit up on the bed, he burrowed under the covers.

She felt as if her body was slowly contracting.

"What's the matter, Marko? Aren't you happy? Aren't you relieved, at least?" she whispered slowly.

"I was happy he was dead, you can't imagine how happy! I don't want to see him, I don't want to hear about him!"

He was almost shouting. Tears of rage burst from his eyes.

Then the anger faded, and there was only bewilderment, disappointment, helplessness, very like the helplessness, thought Ladivine, that had gripped Marko's face and made her afraid for him when they first landed in this country.

He turned his head to one side on the pillow. His cheeks were quivering like an old man's.

"We've got to go back to the Plaza, I don't want him alive here in front of me," he whispered. "This damn holiday, it's like it's never going to end!"

To Ladivine, too, their stay seemed to be stretching out endlessly before them, like their very existence to come, but she was shocked to find Marko so anguished, when she herself felt only joy at the thought of it.

When Ladivine once again stepped out onto the gravelled patio, her feet so cosily and perfectly adapted to the new sandals that she could feel them throbbing with an eagerness to walk, a four-wheel drive pulled to a stop just in front of her, the young bride at the wheel.

It was gigantic, with a belligerent snout and dazzling silver trim.

She lowered the window and shouted to Ladivine to climb in beside her.

In the back seat, her husband and Cagnac were talking like a couple of new friends, animated and effusive.

Ladivine hoisted herself onto the seat of buttery, enveloping leather.

"What do you think, lady? I'm leaning towards this one, myself," said the young woman with a wink.

"But it's the most expensive one," said the husband, feigning torment.

Cagnac chortled, merry and obsequious.

"Isn't it comfortable!" murmured Ladivine, reclining her seat.

The young woman turned towards the forest.

But, rather than follow one of the many lanes vanishing into the massive trees, she gently veered away and began skirting the forest's edge, as Ladivine had seen her do before.

Then a strange, aching regret wrung her heart.

To erase it, she turned halfway around and asked Cagnac:

"That boy who works for you, Wellington . . . Has he been here long?"

"Wellington, Wellington," said Cagnac, searching his memory. "Oh, yes, that young one. We have him out now and then, when we need him, two or three weeks at a time, and then he goes back. Fine boy," he added, dreamily.

"And when did he come this time?"

"Oh, I'm not sure . . . Maybe last night."

Cagnac sat up straighter and, avoiding Ladivine's eye, adopted the impatient, somewhat pinched air of one who finds this subject unsuitable in the fragile, momentous midst of a test drive, of a deal in the making.

He turned to the husband and threw out a few flattering words on the young woman's skill at avoiding the branches that sometimes blocked their way, fallen from the trees of the forest.

The husband smiled contentedly.

"So," the young woman asked Ladivine, "what do you think?"

"Of the car? Very nice, very comfortable," said Ladivine eagerly, guessing that her new friend, or her old friend, perhaps her lifelong friend, had her heart set on it.

She didn't say that the bright, beckoning voices of the forest were calling her, and that beneath them she also heard a throaty, muted summons that scorned those happy little cries, a summons Ladivine would not escape.

You can listen to that happiness, the summoner said, if it helps you, but you won't get away.

What was Clarisse Rivière doing in the forest?

Clarisse Rivière had never commanded anyone to do anything – or had she?

After her last visit, when Clarisse Rivière introduced Freddy Moliger to her daughter, who immediately conceived the most unpleasant impression of that man, she could nonetheless only concede that Moliger seemed to hold no power over Clarisse Rivière, whereas Ladivine had thought it likely or even certain that he had her mother firmly under his thumb, unable to imagine any cause but coercion and contamination for the shocking new life Clarisse Rivière had chosen.

She had in fact almost exploded at her father on the phone, having called him two or three times solely to tell him what Clarisse Rivière was doing with her life, and express her concern, and hear, she hoped, Richard Rivière's concern echoing back.

But instead, almost silent, uncomfortable, as if he thought it was no longer his place to know of such things, he simply said in a hesitant voice that Clarisse Rivière might finally have learned how to be happy, and those trite words threw Ladivine into the icy waters of barely repressed rage, which came back to her a few months later when he called to tell her of Clarisse Rivière's death.

"You see, you see!" she cried. "If only you'd shown a little concern too!"

"But, my little girl, what would that have changed?" he'd answered, very quietly, distraught, tears in his voice.

Ladivine thought he was trying to dodge his responsibility, that this was hardly the real question.

No-one, she thought, could in good faith deny that shared, unhidden concern might have a protective force, and that Clarisse Rivière might have lived her new, strange, thorny life more carefully had she felt the shared concern of a daughter who loved her and an ex-husband who didn't hate her and was worried about her.

Or would she have behaved more foolishly still?

Or would she have decided that at her age she had no reason to think her freedom in any way limited or complicated by the ground-less anxieties of two people she loved who had, each in their own way, turned away from her?

In any case, when Ladivine met her mother's lover, her mother twice asked a favour of Moliger, and to Ladivine's almost outraged surprise he obeyed her at once.

"Go and get us some beers, would you?" Clarisse Rivière asked in a firm, confident voice as she dropped onto the blue couch, not yet soaked with her gushing blood. And then, a few minutes later:

"Maybe a little something to nibble on with these beers?"

And Moliger hurried off for a bag of crisps from the kitchen, docile, solicitous, but always with something both derisive and furious about him, as if he had to make up for his evident pleasure in obeying with a look that expressed just the opposite, concealing that pleasure from anyone who might find it laughable.

What was Clarisse Rivière doing deep in this foreign forest?

And why did it seem, oh yes why, wondered Ladivine, that Clarisse Rivière was calling to her in her true voice, her dark, solemn, trusting voice, that the naive, sunny songs also winging their way from deep inside the forest were meant only to attract her to what would otherwise fill her with terror?

But nothing that involved Clarisse Rivière could ever frighten her, far from it.

She had not heard her mother's whimpers or screams as her blood drained away, as she weakened with each passing second, and any unspoken appeals Clarisse Rivière might have made after Ladivine's father left she'd refused to hear, in self-defence and embarrassment.

And so, if Clarisse Rivière was now calling her in her true voice, her dark, solemn, trusting voice, she would come running with all the fervour of her uneasy conscience, her remorse-choked affection.

When Marko came down to dinner that evening, Ladivine's first thought was that her husband had been handed a death sentence.

Neither Marko nor the children had left their rooms all afternoon, and Ladivine, feeling uncomfortable for the Cagnacs, had tried to keep their hosts company, though she saw she was disturbing them as they dealt with the four-wheel drive's sale to the young couple, typing up papers, a purchase contract, flattering and fussing over them to make sure, Ladivine realised, that they didn't get any ideas about backing out.

Doing her best to seem carefree, she drifted from room to room on the ground floor, where the Cagnacs had a large office decorated with automotive posters, and everywhere she went she furtively looked around, trying to see Wellington.

Should she come face to face with the boy, she told herself, she'd have to beg his forgiveness, however real or serious or otherwise the thing she and Marko had done to him.

Yes, she told herself, humbling herself before Wellington was no sacrifice at all, and no apology on her part could erase all the terrible things Marko had thought about the boy, and the appalling happiness he found in his certainty that he'd destroyed him.

Wouldn't she simply be trying to show him her joy that he was alive?

Not that she could seriously hope to find Marko relieved, for the moment, to see Wellington on his feet and evidently unhurt.

But when, with the children beside him, he entered the dining room where Ladivine and the Cagnacs were waiting, he had the face of a man condemned.

Wordlessly, with a wan smile, he pulled out his chair and slid into it.

And Ladivine didn't need to study the Cagnacs to know that those two, that inflexible man and woman, had just dropped the blade onto Marko's neck, moved more by disgust than by cruelty.

Gone was the Cagnac woman's avid pleasure on discovering Marko's beautiful, glorious face just that morning.

She impatiently tore at her bread, and her lean, flat, clenched person radiated such coldness, such hostility, that Ladivine thought she saw Marko shiver.

She'd never seen him so low, so wretched and uncertain.

Although angry with him for that, although mortally angry, she felt a violent, painful pity.

Yes, Wellington! she wanted to shout in Marko's face. Be happy for him, and for us, instead of dragging the children into your defeat!

Because with one glance at Annika and Daniel she'd seen everything.

Their poor little bewildered faces, anguished and empty, no longer turned to their father but downcast over their wringing hands, bore witness to a disaster that was already total, and as if already past, beyond all repair.

Just that morning, Ladivine thought in dismay, the children were ready to go over to Marko's radiant, cruel side, and now his fall had left them as devastated as if they'd learned he was dead.

How furious she was!

Could she not fill them with delight at Wellington's return?

But what had they known of Wellington?

"Something wrong, kids?" asked Cagnac grumpily.

Annika and Daniel didn't look up. Ladivine wasn't sure they'd even heard.

"They must be tired," Marko whispered.

The Cagnac woman let out a snide, almost contemptuous guffaw.

259

She shot Marko a look that would be the last she bestowed on him, thought Ladivine, a look heavy with disdain, disappointment, almost torment.

The Cagnac woman could not be wrong.

If Marko were simply tired or ill, she would never have treated him this way.

She could see he was no longer the man she'd met a few hours before, and if she didn't yet know the reason for his fall (because how could she know about Wellington?), the mere fact that he could let himself slump into melancholy and terror showed quite clearly that he had, in a sense, fooled her — her, the incorruptible Cagnac woman. Wellington, Wellington, Ladivine repeated to herself, in a quiet, singing little voice.

The Cagnac woman called out:

"Wellington!"

She yawned wide, like a wild animal, showing her teeth, her bluish tongue.

Wellington hurried in with a salad bowl full of brawn in vinaigrette.

He set it on the table, stirred the chopped snout to coat it with the dressing, and his gestures were at once expert and slightly perfunctory, as if, however it may seem, he was only playing a role that he could abandon whenever he pleased.

Yes, Ladivine told herself, this was the Wellington they'd met at the National Museum, the young man with the long, slender limbs, the protruding hips, the resourceful, independent, clever, very faintly arrogant manner.

She found herself studying his walk as he circled the table to pour a taste of wine into Cagnac's glass.

Was he limping?

Perhaps he was dragging one foot a little, or was he just side-stepping a chair leg?

She did not yet dare try to catch his eye to learn, from the way he looked back at her, whether she and Marko were guilty of something.

But what would the neutrality of that discreet, professional gaze ever say?

Sitting clenched in his chair, an anguished grimace on his lips, eyes half closed, Marko was beyond even pretending to be simply a tired guest, and in any case the Cagnacs had lost all interest in him.

And when Wellington approached to fill his glass, Marko pressed his fists to his closed eyes and began to moan quietly.

"I can't take this anymore, I can't take it," he stammered.

Wellington broke into a suave, knowing smile.

He nimbly stepped away from Marko and walked out of the room, as if he'd got what he came for and now had only to disappear.

"I want to go home!" cried Daniel.

"Papa, papa!" howled Annika, eyes wide with terror.

"I can't take it anymore, I can't take it . . ."

"This is intolerable!" cried the Cagnac woman.

She hammered at the table top with the handle of her knife. Annika stood up and awkwardly put her arms around Marko's shoulders as he repeated, at once leaden and fervid, perhaps drunk on his own surrender:

"I can't take it anymore, I can't take it . . ."

Later that evening, with Marko and the children up in their rooms and the Cagnacs closed away in their office on the pretext of urgent work to be done, Ladivine went out and walked towards the forest in the gathering darkness.

A deep calm slowed her thoughts, freed her footsteps of any imaginary burden.

Never hesitating, and although the forest's edge was already dark, and remembering, too, that she was not a brave woman, she started down a narrow path.

Her first thought was that she was entering the domain of a silence so full and so thick that it hurt her ears like a deafening roar, and she almost gave up, almost turned back.

But then she made out the gentle, secret, insinuating appeal she'd heard from the newlyweds' four-wheel drive, that dark sigh, like a heavy beast dying or in labour, calling Clarisse Rivière to her mind just as clearly as if her mother's face had suddenly appeared on the half-moon above her.

That afternoon's happy, sprightly little voices had gone silent.

There remained only that fearsome plaint, that breath exhaled by a breast at once anguished and resigned, but resolute, quietly unyielding in its determination to convince her.

Ladivine walked onward, with no fear in her gait.

The path snaked through the tall trees with their alien perfumes, through the thorny bushes, the big blood-red flowers bursting out on their stout stems, sprouting like mushrooms from the roots.

How far was she supposed to go? she wondered, half-aloud, simply curious, as if to someone responsible for guiding her, someone who might conceivably answer.

Growing tired, she sat down at the foot of a tree and pressed her back to the smooth, warm trunk.

Behind her she heard footsteps lightly treading the leaves and twigs.

Guessing who it was coming to join her, if not why, but her faith was blind, she didn't turn her head as it came to her side and lay down against her legs.

It stank of humus, sweat and exertion.

Once that smell would have bothered her, but knowing how far it had come to find her, and what fidelity, what courage lay behind it, she inhaled it with pleasure and gratitude.

Her eyes closing, she lay on her side, one arm under her head, the other draped over her friend, as she did in the bed she shared with Marko.

The night was warm and peaceful, stirred only by Clarisse Rivière's unrelenting sigh.

And Ladivine felt herself falling asleep, violently aware that she was sinking, tumbling into a world she might well find unpleasant or paralysingly frightening.

She tried to break free, struggling to open her eyes, but it was as if a will more powerful and assured than her own was holding her back, and forbidding her to make a sound, to voice an objection.

She felt herself suffocating, stifled by a light, implacable hand.

She wanted to struggle, but her legs wouldn't answer her frantic commands, as if lethargy were winning out over panic even though panic was obviously right.

Now she could clearly see the new-paved road, glistening from recent rainfall, that she was being forced to follow by this will that wasn't her own, and she knew she didn't want to go that way, not yet, and would have to struggle against her soul, not her body, which had no part in all this.

But she'd never been trained in that sort of combat, lacked the weapons, the spirit.

And that smooth new road was pulling her along, and she felt herself giving in, surrendering in anguish, weeping without tears for Marko and the children, who she knew would not be waiting at the end of that road, which had been laid out for her alone.

And then off to one side, she caught sight of a path – a mere fleeting glimpse from the corner of her eye – she wasn't meant to see it but did.

She threw herself towards it, dealing a terrible blow to her soul.

And her lost, hurting soul, not yet relieved, heard the path's little pebbles crunch under the soles of her wonderful sandals, which were as one with her feet.

And with this she could open her eyes, stretch her limbs.

Now she was hearing all sorts of sounds, from Clarisse Rivière's growling moans to the insects' tiny cheeps, from Clarisse Rivière's howls to faint creaks from the branches far overhead.

It was still dark, but the darkness was sharply detailed, alive with tiny forms, clearly outlined.

Ladivine turned her head.

She saw her own face beside her – the curve of a full, damp cheek, a mass of strong-smelling brown hair, the scents familiar but sharper.

She stood up and began to trot through the forest, and then, her breast swelling with pleasure, to run on her strong, slender legs.

She thought she could go on and on running this way, without respite or fatigue.

She emerged from the forest just as day was breaking.

In front of the Cagnacs' house, Marko, Daniel and Annika were climbing into the rental car.

Once the four-wheel drive had started up and gone on its way through the clearing, Ladivine set off running again.

Joyful and proud that she'd found them and could thus place them under her care, she let out little cries she alone could hear, immediately swept off by the rushing wind.

◘

THE DOG WAS THERE, ON THE OTHER SIDE OF THE STREET, it was there for her now, waiting for her to come out of the building each morning and head off to school, accompanied by her father and the invariably whining Daniel.

Annika looked deep into the dog's black eyes, unafraid. I know who you are, she thought, and the dog stared back with an austere, steady tenderness that Annika found infuriating. It seemed to be saying that it would always be watching over her, and perhaps over them, should Marko and Daniel one day take note of its presence, but Annika felt no need to be protected, and she was offended that the dog had presumed to make of itself her guardian.

She slipped her hand into her father's, trying to infuse in him some of her overflowing strength and rebelliousness.

She didn't dare admit it, but she was also afraid Marko would end up spotting the dog, and she delicately squeezed his hand and spoke any words that came to mind to keep Marko's attention on her, his daughter Annika, who, though only eight, thought herself seasoned enough to accept calmly that her mother had chosen to look after them from inside the skin of a dog on the Droysenstrasse's icy pavement, whereas her father, she thought, her poor distraught father, should he ever realise such a thing, could never accept it without even more grief than he already felt.

Annika was unhappy with her mother for choosing this way of leaving them.

It was November. The pavements were covered with packed, frozen snow, the dog's fur was thin and sparse on its flanks.

Nevertheless, Annika was sure nothing and no-one had forced her mother to live with them in this distant, uncomfortable way, that she'd willingly chosen to shelter herself in the skin of a dog, which, though it did little to protect her from the cold, suited her better than the skin of a woman. That was how it was, Annika knew.

She saw no sorrow in the dog's eyes, only a serene, stern resolve.

The dead must have that kind of face, she thought.

Annika was a sturdy girl, and nothing she'd realised about her mother kept her from succeeding in school or proving unfailingly happy and calm before her father, who, for his part, had to be protected from certain difficult truths.

Which is why, when they set off for her school, she refused to cross the street outside the building, so they wouldn't come face to face with the dog. Because if her father's eyes met the dog's, might he not recognise them, even in spite of himself, and in spite of his little capacity for believing in such things?

Since their return from holiday, three months before, Marko was spending all his free time on the Internet, and he explained to Daniel and Annika that wherever their mother may be she would some-day appear, one way or another, in the Web's inescapable universe, either in person or through someone with news of her. No-one could vanish completely and forever these days, their father assured them in his weary voice.

Her father's sadness and fatigue pained Annika's heart.

But she thought he was better off thinking their mother adrift in the wide world than withdrawn into the skin of a dog, guarding her truncated, lost, unhappy family from the Droysenstrasse pavement. He was better off this way, he who suffered so.

He tried to put on a good face with the children, but his sadness never left him, and Annika preferred him disconsolate to falsely light-hearted.

He was the nicest, most thoughtful father she knew, and the best-looking too, she thought, with his lush hair, tousled because he paid it no attention, and his tanned face and pale eyes and carelessness about his appearance, like some magnificent animal with no notion that anyone might think it beautiful, and no understanding of people's admiring stares.

Often Annika was angry with Daniel, who, rather than shield their father as she did, continually nagged at him with his whining and whims, and tried to pull him away from the computer, to which Marko consented with an infallible patience and a gentleness so wistful and sad that Annika would later take Daniel aside to lecture and shame him – why try to take their father away from the one thing he thought brought him nearer their mother, that endless, painstaking search through the wilds of cyberspace?

He was in touch now with people all over the world, always asking this single question: Have you seen Ladivine?

And those strangers, he told them, put all their ingenuity and good will into the search for Ladivine Rivière, or, if they could do nothing else, into the attempt to console Marko Berger, which made Marko's pain a little easier to bear, he added, wanting to be honest, but with a certain reluctance, Annika sensed, since his children could do nothing to unburden him of his grief, even a little.

How furious Annika was at their mother!

Every morning she stared at the dog with all the rage she could muster, then ignored it as it kept pace with them on the opposite pavement.

And in the afternoon, when their father escaped from Karstadt for thirty minutes to pick them up from school and hurry them back to the apartment, where they would stay on their own until his workday was done, the dog was still there, shivering, eternal, faithful to its charge and perfectly indifferent to Annika's withering stare.

Young though she was, and aware of her youth, of her ignorance, she believed she understood that their mother had tired of them, the children, their energy and their needs, their inevitable, daily company, their moods and their chatter. She herself, Annika, often wearied of Daniel. She felt largely responsible for her brother, and she found the burden heavy and oppressive.

But she couldn't forgive their mother for leaving Marko in such distress and despair.

Some freezing mornings, when they had to set off for school in the dark and the leaden sky foretold yet another grey day, Daniel would stamp his feet on the front step, find some pretext for refusing to go on. Bundled up stiff in his snowsuit, he would shriek:

"I want Mummy!"

Seeing Marko's defeated face, and feeling herself at the end of her tether, she wanted to cry out:

"Let's bring that dog with us, let's take it home!"

But she held back, out of pity and love for her father.

THE MAN WAS TAKING HIS TIME LOOKING OVER THE CAR, and Richard Rivière saw the elegant drape of his navy-blue overcoat, unbuttoned and gracefully rippling as he circled the vehicle, bent down to inspect the wheel rims, then lithely stood up again, his body visibly honed by regular exercise.

The coat must be cashmere, he thought, and the dark grey pinstripe suit a silk and wool blend. On his feet Richard Rivière had noted, with a fervid curiosity he knew well, and which always filled him with self-disgust, a pair of polished, point-toed ankle boots.

And when the man first squatted down Richard Rivière was astonished to see he was wearing raspberry-red socks.

Astonishment gave way to envious loathing, and that too was an emotion he knew well, always depressed and disappointed to be feeling it, him, Richard Rivière, who aspired to be a sensible and thoughtful man, noble in his sentiments.

Why, then, could he not help feeling jealous and frustrated when a well-dressed man had the breezy audacity to display some accessory – gaudy socks or a comical tie – that Richard Rivière would never dare buy, lest he give himself away as what he thought he was in others' eyes, a parvenu with odd and dubious tastes?

He was not unaware that such encounters with tall, thin, chic men also inspired in him, along with envy, an immediate, baseless respect, slightly craven and limp.

How stupid, and how pitiful!

He put on an aloof and superior air, checked his watch. He glanced at the ground-floor windows of his apartment building and was relieved to see no sign of movement behind the sheer curtains. He would rather Trevor not see him trying to sell the four-wheel drive to a man of this sort, exactly the type Trevor made a great show of mocking, with their tailored suits and their gym-room physiques.

"OK, it's a deal," said the man, striding athletically towards him, his young, tanned face friendly and, Richard Rivière fleetingly thought, almost fawning.

"You'll take it?" he asked, surprised.

Collecting himself, he added:

"You won't be sorry."

The man inside Richard Rivière who forever strove to decipher a customer's uncertainties or unspoken misgivings thought he could make out an anxious little twinge behind the smile, a touch too unwavering, and the gaze, a touch too ostentatiously frank, in this man whose elegance was perhaps also, in the end, just a little too impeccable, he thought, every detail as if carefully weighed for its charismatic effect.

But why must those intuitions always be silenced by the Richard Rivière who was intimidated by wealth or its appearance, and anxious to sell what he had, to be rid of it, like some ill-gotten gain?

As the free, severe, impotent part of him whispered that question in his ear, he glanced again at the ground floor of his building and saw the kitchen window ajar.

That meant Trevor was up, eating his breakfast, perhaps observing his stepfather's obsequious charade from his chair, with that awful little smirk he'd developed, full of smug, listless irony. Trevor's implacable judgements meant nothing to Richard Rivière, but he did not like being spied on, did not like feeding the young man's mindless censoriousness at his expense.

He turned his back to the window, irritated, and grimaced a smile at his customer, who was explaining that he was planning to give the car to his wife as a present. Yes, yes, let's get this over with, he thought.

His eye lit on the man's white cotton shirt, darkened by two little sweat stains on either side of the purple polka-dot tie. A few drops of sweat, too, he observed, between the upper lip and the nose, so short and straight that it must have been artificial, surgically reshaped.

Richard Rivière felt preoccupied, out of sorts, he didn't know why.

He'd forgotten about Trevor. He'd almost forgotten that an over-dressed stranger was on the verge of buying a Grand Cherokee for forty-seven thousand euros without haggling, nearly five thousand more than he'd paid for it at the Jeep dealership.

Come on, let's get this over with, he was thinking, depressed, his mind elsewhere, but fixated in spite of himself on such trivialities as the beads of sweat glinting on the man's suntanned skin or the way he stuck out his lower lip after every sentence to blow at the lock of hair draping his brow. The lock fluttered up, and Richard Rivière saw the pale skin, fragile and tender, at his hairline.

He would later realise that the wide-awake Richard Rivière inside him had tried to sound the alarm. Wasn't this man clearly nervous, though a skilled enough actor to give himself away only by a sudden sweat in the chilly air of this autumn morning?

He would also realise, later, that he had refused to understand out of sadness and weariness, perhaps even that he had understood but wouldn't accept it, because sadness had suddenly got the better of him.

He looked past the man's shoulders at the mountain, still covered with snow, and the bright, frozen sky beyond.

Nine years he'd been living in Annecy, and he'd never got used to the mountains. They left him cold, wary, vaguely hostile, because he enjoyed none of the pleasures they seemed to offer, and he found them unfriendly, stupid and portentous in the way they loomed over the city.

He had never wanted to learn how to ski, he did not like the atmosphere of the resorts, the pointlessness of such arduous exertions.

Sometimes he woke with a start in the night, shivering as if shaken by a huge icy hand, and then he got up, went to the window, and found the mountain looking at him in the dull grey darkness.

The idea that it would always be there, when he got up and when he lay down and long after he was dead, immovably there and watching, discouraged him.

He lay down again with the disagreeable feeling that he wasn't his own master, that at any moment the mountain could blow a cold breath down his neck.

It could feel his dislike, and it scorned him, that was what he was thinking, and he had no-one to tell of it.

"I'd like to be paid by bank transfer," he heard himself announcing, his voice almost hostile.

"Of course," the man answered warmly.

Richard Rivière took a contract from his briefcase and handed it to the man, who sat down behind the wheel of the car to look over it.

He stayed outside, shivering, suddenly unable to rejoice at having so effortlessly made a sale that would bring him a tidy profit. What would he do now, what desire would enliven the days to come?

For the past several months, ever since he took out a loan to buy that four-wheel drive for resale, each new day dawned with that question, which he'd managed to turn into something exciting and even ennobling: Would this be the day that he sold the car?

Much of the pleasure he felt on waking each morning, much of the good cheer he displayed both at home and at work came from the idea of earning five thousand euros for doing virtually nothing. And now it was done, and he felt only a weary gloom, and now he dreaded the prospect of an existence stripped of that motivation.

And what, for that matter, would he do with the money? Nothing tempted him that he didn't already own, and what did he actually have? Nothing much, compared to what his colleagues or wife thought important.

Sometimes he thought he spent money only to justify his urge to make money, and he alone knew his enthusiasm was feigned, that his interest in clothes, and now even in cars, was an act, borrowed from a personality he scarcely remembered as his own, now alien to him, and unpleasant, too. Visits to the city's most lavish restaurants, multicourse menus, pricy wines he could not appreciate, every delight he felt obliged to indulge in left him bored or withdrawn.

Nothing in this world, he thought, quite met his desires, but what those desires were he couldn't say.

That reticence before everything that should have made him happy, everything he seemed to want from his work, from his cogitations and calculations, dated back to the year after he'd left Langon. Oh, he saw it now, even if he had denied it at first. He saw it.

He was sick, in a way, but his illness had no name, and wasn't easily described, even to himself. Was it nostalgia?

It was not what he once knew, what once was, that he missed; what he missed was what should have been, or could have been, had he only known how to go about it.

Because he missed not Clarisse Rivière but the woman Clarisse Rivière should or could have been, a woman he didn't know, a woman he couldn't so much as imagine, and that, he thought, was nobody's fault but his own.

Through the windscreen he saw the man sign his name at the bottom of the contract, where he himself had already signed. That was that.

The buyer got out of the car, displaying a broad expanse of raspberry socks and, just above them, two slender shins, orange-tanned and hairless like his face and his soft hands, every fingernail highlighted by a white pencil line under the tip.

There was something comical about such fastidious grooming, Richard Rivière thought to himself, and yet once again he felt inadequate before that younger, taller, fitter, better-looking man, he felt horribly heavy and worn and provincial.

At such times he always feared a resurgence of the faint south-western accent he'd struggled to disguise even when he lived in that part of France, as a precaution, on the theory that losing it couldn't possibly hurt and might one day prove useful, and because it made him secretly proud not to speak like his parents. But his accent had not gone away, he knew, he'd only tamed it, and emotion could always bring it back. He had particular difficulty saying *cette* rather than *c'te*, and so at work never referred to a car as *cette voiture*, sticking to the far less risky *ce véhicule*.

"You can pick it up as soon as the money's in my account," he said, casually kicking one foot towards the four-wheel drive.

"You'll have it the day after tomorrow," the man said.

He blew on his forelock, flashing a practised, perfect smile. How charming and slim he was in the blue mountain light! A master skier, obviously, able to cut pure, complex lines in the snow, like his signature's long, self-assured strokes.

Richard Rivière had planned to offer him a cup of coffee in the apartment if the deal went through, but now he didn't feel up to

274

it. Suppose Trevor appeared in his old pyjama bottoms, hangovers from his teenage years, and possibly bare-chested, his hair unkempt, suppose he spoke to the customer with that irritating way of giving a caustic turn to the most ordinary words, having already judged you too dull-witted to notice the sarcasm, or his contempt for you – between his exasperating stepson, whose every supercilious little manoeuvre he knew all too well, and this man who to his deep shame intimidated him, Richard Rivière had lost all confidence in his ability to stifle his accent.

What cruel joy Trevor had felt, one evening when they were celebrating his mother's birthday and Richard had drunk a full bottle of champagne, on hearing his stepfather wisecracking with a Toulouse accent! Weeks afterwards, Trevor was still forever shouting *Merci bieng!* and erupting into a mirthless laugh, hard and triumphant, as if he'd finally put his finger on the most contemptible thing about Richard Rivière.

The man drove off in the strange, battered little car he'd come out in – not his, he'd immediately made clear, but on loan from the garage while his own was being serviced.

Wasn't it odd, Richard Rivière mused, that a man so obsessed with his appearance should go putt-putting around in such a ridiculous car? Or was that merely the sign of an elegance too self-assured to care what others might think? If so, why was the man so bent on informing him that it wasn't his car? What did he care if Richard Rivière was surprised?

His inexplicable dejection faded, and for a few minutes, as he stood in the car park of his building, he congratulated himself on selling the four-wheel drive.

In the distance, the mountaintops were shrouded in clouds.

Now he could see only the pink and brown roofs of the old town below him, only the gentle, green slopes halfway up the mountains, like the hills between Langon and Malagar, where, some Sunday mornings, he used to go walking with his daughter Ladivine.

How much better he felt with the snow out of sight!

But that relief led his memory, suddenly roused and enlivened, to bring back old images of long drives with Clarisse Rivière, early in their marriage, leisurely jaunts through the vine-covered hills in their old Citroën 304, the top down, both smoking and talking, he thought at the time, in his happiness, in the bliss of a young man deeply in love, with a sweet, innocent frivolity – or his walks on those same roads with his serious, attentive, very young daughter, starting from just behind their house, and so exquisite sometimes was the feeling of the child's hand in his, of the forthright, benevolent sun, of the child's limpid, upturned gaze, that he would have wept with gratitude and trembled in terror had he not held himself back, lest he frighten the girl.

Such memories did him no good.

Colleagues his age, even his wife, however luckless with her children, seemed to love reminiscing about their days as young parents, when their joys were stronger and deeper than now, they said fatalistically, now that their job was essentially to resist as best they could those charmless children's demands for money or favours, and to fight off their own disappointment.

Richard Rivière was not at all disappointed at the young woman his little girl had become. In his eyes, she was an entirely successful adult.

And the two children she'd brought into the world, whose pictures she often sent him, those two little Germans he'd never seen, seemed two perfect little human beings themselves.

He had nothing to regret but his own agonising unease. Because he could no longer bear to see his daughter Ladivine, nor even to think about her for long.

He himself found this scandalous. What kind of father was he?

He wasn't much good in that way. He was no good at all, now, in that way.

But how could it be helped?

Every meeting with his daughter, every phone call, every day-dream about his child brought him back to the awful feeling that the three of them had lived a life deformed by something huge and unnameable, hovering over them but never taking shape or fading away, making of their life a hollow travesty of life.

It began four or five years after their wedding, and he was convinced it had nothing to do with the child or with him, but with Clarisse Rivière.

Sometimes those Langon years seemed so artificial that he wondered if that life was real, and not merely a dream he'd had, despite all the evidence to the contrary.

He'd been happy enough in those days, he knew, but he couldn't feel it, because the memory of that happiness was tainted by a sense of unreality, almost perversion, that blotted out all the rest when he thought about the life he once led.

Perhaps there was no ill intent behind that perversion. But if he believed that he'd unwittingly loved, lived with, procreated with a simulacrum, dimly sensing it and finding it deeply repellent, what did it change that that imaginary woman wasn't responsible for her state?

For so he thought. Still today, he held Clarisse Rivière blameless.

Whereas he, Richard Rivière, had let himself drift through that counterfeit life because he felt weak and helpless, and then in a way he'd woken up, and revulsion, a sort of horror, of fear, drove him far away, far from Clarisse Rivière.

He was ashamed that he had not gone to Ladivine's wedding, that he had never met his son-in-law or his grandchildren.

Less because he feared a face-to-face meeting with Clarisse Rivière, as Ladivine thought, than because at the time he was terrified of seeing his daughter. What was she made of, he couldn't help asking himself, this child born to Clarisse Rivière? Even more than her mother, Ladivine reminded him of the life they'd once led, and those memories left him deeply confused, unsure if he himself had actually lived or had only passed through an interminable dream, an insincere, fabricated dream.

He could bear only the memory of his child's first years, and the first years of his marriage with Clarisse Rivière. Nonetheless, such memories did him no good.

He tiptoed into the apartment, trying to determine which room Trevor was in — his bedroom, most likely, since he could hear computer noises through the door.

Relieved, he made for the kitchen, only to collide with the young man, who was lurking in the corridor. He started and cried out in angry surprise.

"What are you doing here?"

"Nothing. Meditating."

And Trevor let out a little laugh, but Richard Rivière scarcely noticed, so often did the boy snicker and cackle for no reason.

Putting on a thick south-western accent, Trevor asked, "So, you sell that heap?"

"Could be," Richard Rivière answered coldly, brushing Trevor aside with one hand.

Unintentionally, his fingers sank into the young man's limp, bulging belly through the T-shirt, and he gave him a taut, uncomfortable smile.

Trevor had gained so much weight since moving back that Richard Rivière couldn't help feeling embarrassed and sad for him, which he did his best to conceal, when his fingers inadvertently grazed the boy's flabby flesh, behind an awkward display of sympathy.

He felt no trace of affection for Trevor, only those waves of pained, morose pity at the sight of that young man of twenty-two imprisoned in his bloated body, he who, Richard Rivière remembered, was once a slim, agile teenager.

However dour and forced, that pity made him more patient with Trevor's crass ways.

He walked into the kitchen, and through the half-open window saw his four-by-four in the car park, and the spot where just a moment before he himself had been standing, contemplating the mountains half-hidden by clouds.

Now those clouds had cleared, and he saw the mountains' glistening peaks, the triumphant, seemingly indestructible sharpness of their snow-covered flanks.

He saw himself too, standing there in his expensive clothes, a fine-looking figure in every way and yet studying the dress and the manner of the man in the raspberry socks with an insecure, already defeated eye, and despite the relaxed, distant air he tried to put on at such times, that man must have known he was being looked at and envied, or worse yet, secretly idolised.

Disgusted with himself, Richard Rivière slammed the window shut. And since Trevor had followed him into the kitchen and he realised he wouldn't be having the quiet, solitary lunch he was hoping for, he lost his temper, and shouted:

"A hundred times your mother's asked you not to leave this window open! We've already had one burglary, she did tell you that, didn't she?"

"Probably shouldn't have bought a place on the ground floor, then," said Trevor with his eternal smirk, shifting his weight from one leg to the other as if making ready for a fistfight.

Richard Rivière sometimes told himself that with any other over-weight, jobless, lonely young man, stuck living with his mother and stepfather as Trevor was, he would see this derision and childish defiance as nothing more than the sad effect of a difficult situation, and if they just tried to give him a hand, even love him a little, show some interest and faith in him, then he would drop that tiresome insolence, that whole mechanism of aggression and immediate, unc-tuous denial Trevor had put in place on his return.

Richard Rivière knew all that, he knew a case study of such a young man would have filled him with almost unlimited under-standing and indulgence.

So why, he often asked himself, could he not give the real Trevor the gift of his sympathy and encouragement?

He chided himself for this when he was alone, vowing to change his attitude towards his stepson, even impatiently looking forward to seeing him again so he could put those good intentions into practice.

Then Trevor was there, ever the same, neither more nor less awful than he recalled, and a sort of cold stupor fell over Richard Rivière, a strange dismay at his inability to feel any emotion for the boy but squeamish pity before his misshapen young body.

The idea of devoting himself to Trevor's rescue, and especially of affecting warm feelings for the boy, suddenly struck him as prepos-terous and indecent.

Because it was obvious that Trevor didn't like him, and wanted no part of his support or solicitude, and even, for some mysterious reason, looked down on him.

That didn't shock Richard Rivière, didn't anger him, but it did make him wonder.

How could he have become the target of Trevor's disdain when he'd always taken pains to bare nothing of his inner self to his wife's difficult children? How could anyone despise him when they knew him as little as Trevor?

Deciding to act as though he were alone, he made himself an omelette without asking the young man if he wanted any. It pained him to feel rude, but Trevor always refused what he was offered.

Why was he standing there, watching him?

He sat down and began to eat, then glanced at the boy's face, unable to help it. He knew Trevor found it hard to stand up for too long, and yet he'd not moved since he had come into the kitchen and leaned against the wall by the door.

He was surprised to find the young man looking faintly ill at ease.

Again and again he ran his hand through his ratty, strawberry blond hair, and his pale little eyes, as if pushed deep into his abundant flesh, darted this way and that, avoiding Richard Rivière's. Below a pair of broad, bright-pink boxers that came down to mid-thigh, his legs were purplish and swollen.

"Well, sit down," Richard Rivière snapped.

He pushed away his empty plate. He was so on edge that he'd scarcely even realised he was eating.

And now the omelette was eaten, shovelled in without awareness or pleasure, and it was almost one o'clock, and he had to be at work in forty-five minutes.

Still, he'd sold the car. Why couldn't he be happy?

Trevor stood where he was, shrugged, and said, very hurriedly:

"So I saw on TV . . . that trial, you know, that trial, it's going to be starting soon. The lady who got killed . . . that was your wife?"

"You know it was, don't you?"

He was breathing quickly and heavily. Trevor's face went blurry, as if he were seeing it without his glasses.

He mechanically raised one hand to his eyes, feeling the lenses, suddenly tortured by the little pads pressed to the sides of his nose. He tore off his glasses, rubbed his eyes.

He was breathing heavily – pathetically, he couldn't help thinking. Was that why Trevor looked down on him? Because, at bottom, he was pathetic? But who was Trevor to judge, with his huge legs, his puffy little feet, his fat, spongy breasts?

"I think I do, yeah," Trevor was saying. "I mean, you never said anything, but . . . well, you know, I could guess."

"So why are you asking?" He sighed.

"Um, just to be sure."

For once, Richard Rivière couldn't help noticing, Trevor had neglected to mask his unease behind a sarcastic, moronic or arrogant front. His face bore an almost childlike expression of respectful, intimidated interest.

Rather than feel moved or simply indifferent, Richard found a savage rage burning inside him, because it was Clarisse Rivière's murder that had brought about this change in the boy. That's the one thing that excites him, he thought, feeling his own furious, savage excitement, but also suspecting that Trevor was not so much excited as shaken, and, in his dull way, frightened.

He went on breathing in noisy little gasps, rubbing the inflamed wings of his nose with his thumb and index finger, making the pain even worse. But so terrible was the gnawing hurt in his heart that this other pain was almost a relief.

He wanted to snuff out the boy, see him disappear from the kitchen, where he'd just spoiled his lunch, from the apartment, bought with a loan in his own name and no-one else's, and finally from his life, perpetually poisoned, he thought, by Trevor's presence.

There was nothing he wanted less than to talk about Clarisse Rivière with Trevor. The mere thought of it sickened him.

When Clarisse Rivière was murdered, three years before, Trevor was still living in Switzerland, and neither Richard Rivière nor Clarisse, Trevor's mother, ever told him what had happened, nor Clarisse's other two children, twin brothers in their thirties who drifted from city to city in the south of France, so rarely heard from that Richard Rivière was always stunned to remember that they existed.

Those few years together, temporarily free of Clarisse's three wearying children, were the one happy period of Richard Rivière's life in Annecy, and now he missed it bitterly, as if he'd been perfectly happy in those days.

He had not, but he never expected to be, never even hoped to be, and so that sedate existence with an agreeably ordinary woman seemed the best he could wish for, and he enjoyed what he thought of as his good fortune, the bland, restful, soothing pleasure of a half-hearted attachment, of a daily routine without turmoil or upheaval.

Then Trevor came back from Switzerland, where he'd failed to start up a modest computer repair business with two friends. That project had struck Richard Rivière as nebulous in the extreme from the start, and because he had serious doubts about Trevor's skills, given his uselessness when any little thing went awry with the family computer, he saw the young man's shamefaced, bitter return as simply one more in a logical series of very predictable defeats.

And among his own string of defeats, thought Richard Rivière, was Trevor's return.

He wasn't particularly surprised that he had to endure this ordeal, oh no. He might well be forced to go on living with Trevor for years to come, maybe till he died.

Sometimes he rebelled at that prospect, as now, wishing he could expunge the young man from his life. And yet secretly he had accepted it, as fitting punishment for everything he'd failed to grasp in the past, when Clarisse Rivière was alive.

Now and then he wondered if the sight of Trevor's decline, that ruined body, that panting breath, those endless jeers, was intended to test him: what would he do this time, faced with such obvious signs of distress? What would he fail to grasp now?

But he rejected that suspicion, wearily telling himself that he'd never promised to love or protect this young man. And hadn't he been punished enough as it is, accepting that his life had turned so unpleasant, accepting that it might never be any more serene or agreeable, accepting that he was irreparably guilty of betraying Clarisse Rivière?

That he accepted, yes, but he admitted it to no-one. He'd sensed that his daughter Ladivine blamed herself, and wanted him to do likewise. He refused. He thought he'd be taking the easy way out, seeking consolation for his shattered soul, if he gave in to the temptation of mutual despair and shared tears. He was bitterly sorry he couldn't give Ladivine that gift, an admission of guilt, but he thought it ignoble to give up any part of that guilt. It was his fault and he knew it, so why seek to lighten the punishment?

He wanted to be alone with his remorse, with his difficult days. He did not want to suffer less. He wanted what he deserved.

What poor Ladivine thought she had to feel guilty for was nothing.

He believed he'd told her that one day on the phone, unless he'd thought it but never said it, he no longer knew.

What could you possibly have done, so far away, with your children, your own life to lead? Could you have prevented your mother from seeing that guy, from spending time with anyone she pleased?

How he hoped he'd said that! He vowed to telephone her that evening and make sure, and ask how the holiday had gone, if she'd met the Cagnacs, if she'd had a little fun in that country he'd suggested.

He felt an odd hope stirring inside him, the hope that she might have something to tell him. Because he had made several visits to that country, though in the beginning he knew nothing about it, had never been told of it, ostensibly to look into the market for imported cars, but in truth cars were the last thing on his mind.

He did not know it, but he was awaiting a revelation, and that revelation never came, and only when he found that nothing had come, that he was as empty and unquiet as when he arrived, did he realise he'd been awaiting it.

He put on his glasses and smiled vaguely at Trevor, who was making his usual dish of pasta with cream and lardons, facing the stove, not looking at him. He stood up, put his plate and cutlery in the dishwasher.

He thought the kitchen looked dowdy, messy and sad, and yet he'd put more money into this one than any of the flat's four rooms.

He'd had it completely remodelled, with a slate floor and pale grey glass tiles on the walls. The built-in elements were finished in dark grey, the table was a glass plate with black metal legs.

In the early days, he and Clarisse found that kitchen so beautiful and so elegant that they scarcely dared use it, and frying was out of the question for months.

And yet here as usual was Trevor browning his lardons on high heat, spattering grease on the gleaming black hob and the little tiles around it.

All sorts of things that had no place in a kitchen cluttered the marble worktop and the corner bench, its pale-rose patterned chintz now dark with wear and heavily food-stained: DVD cases, flyers, a scarf, plastic bags carefully folded in four.

The fact that Clarisse or Trevor could go to the trouble of folding a plastic bag and then simply leave it on a chair or on top of the refrigerator, as if the very minimal act of folding it made it a pleasing sight, wearied Richard Rivière beyond measure.

He had an awful feeling that the irreparable loss of his kitchen's purity was a sign of his own life's disintegration.

He pictured the bathroom, which had also required much thought and tens of thousands of euros, and those months-long deliberations had plunged him into a state of happy beleaguerment that he didn't regret in the least.

Spending hours on the Internet comparing total immersion tubs, sinks carved from a single slab of sequoia, mysterious, subtle taps, he felt intensely aware of his being, of his tense, quivering body, of his mind working to judge, to eliminate, to select, with a glorious self-assurance and the faint, thrilling terror that he might be spending far too much money.

But little matter, he applied for loans and inevitably got them, because he made a good living.

And that feeling of being at once outside and fully inside himself, in his self's heady depths, now suddenly open and luminous but unburdened by care and remorse, by unease and difficult days – however ephemeral, that feeling was beyond price.

What did his magnificent turquoise faience-tiled bathroom look like now?

He knew all too well, and he bridled in advance at what would be waiting for him when, in a few moments, he finished his coffee and went off to brush his teeth, comb his hair: towels tossed haphazardly over the heated rails, wadded against the wall behind them, draped any which way in front, Trevor's toothbrush abandoned on the glass shelf, worn, dishevelled, ill-rinsed, and Trevor's clothes, which he never dropped into the Grand Hôtel laundry basket but always to one side of it, and the glass shower door that Trevor never wiped down, white with water stains.

It was beneath him to care so deeply about such trifles, Richard Rivière told himself. And yet . . .

Though he accepted the meticulous, unstoppable demolition of his life because he'd baulked at the strange labour of knowing Clarisse Rivière and because, in his cowardice, he'd let that woman he once so loved race unhindered towards her perdition, he could not bear the thought of Trevor, and to a lesser degree Clarisse, carelessly or wilfully befouling that existence's setting, for it could be painful and dark, but absolutely not dirty and disordered.

"Kind of weird that Mum's also named Clarisse, though, isn't it?"

Trevor's eyes were glued to his plate, his tone hurried and gruff.

"It's a common enough name, you know," Richard stammered.

Flustered, he gave up on making himself a cup of coffee. He left the kitchen with the disagreeable feeling that he was running away, and the suspicion that Trevor knew it.

No sooner was he outside than the mountain pounced on his back.

He forbade himself to look at it. Nonetheless, the image of that mountain sternly poised against the bright, blinding sky seemed to have fixed itself on his retina, because he could still see it now, even without raising his eyes, and he could feel its fearsome weight on his spine, its cold claws on the back of his neck, like a corpse latching onto him before he could shake free, before he could even think.

An aching homesickness for his native Gironde, a clement place without snowy slopes or skiers, put a lump in his throat, so fleetingly that he only had time to realise where it had come from.

His back hurt.

Stooping, he started out to the car park. He'd sold the four-wheel drive that morning – wasn't that good news?

He decided to pay off one of his loans, the one he'd used to replace the bedroom's squares of white carpet with Burmese hemp.

The carpet was only two years old at the time, but the traffic lanes had gone grey, and that daily reminder of his foolishness in choosing white for the floor so gnawed at Richard Rivière that, awakened one night by the mountain's insidious growl, he sat down at the computer and ordered twenty square metres of Burmese hemp.

He was much happier with it now, except that the hemp was so rough and the weave so coarse that he and Clarisse had to forgo the pleasure of going barefoot. He tried it at first, and his soles stung for two days.

"Monsieur Rivière, I want a word with you."

She had the fierce, despotic air of the pampered women who seemed to abound in this neighbourhood and this city, a thin, sun-tanned face beneath pale, fluffy hair.

She knows my name, he told himself, surprised. He had no idea of hers, though for the nine years he'd lived in that building they'd been neighbours.

He stopped by his car, eyebrows raised in an expression of inter-est, automatically switching on his businessman's smile. But she didn't even repay him with a tight smile of her own. Her lavishly ringed hand lashed the air before her face, telling him don't bother, the time for feigned conviviality was over. He couldn't recall the slightest disagreement with this woman.

The mountain was pressing on his spinal column with all its weight. Stifling a grimace, he leaned on the bonnet of his car.

"I've been wanting to see you for at least a week, Monsieur Rivière, but I never managed to run into you, and you're not here during the day, there's only that boy, not very friendly, may I say, not particularly well raised, if you understand me. In any case, this isn't about that."

She inhaled mightily, with a sort of refined disgust.

Through the yellowish fluff of her hair, like a very young child's, he could see the dull white skin of her scalp. Her face, her skeletal hands, everything else looked as if it had been seared.

"It's that four-wheel drive of yours, Monsieur Rivière. I believe you're allotted one single parking space, like the rest of us. Your vehicle's so wide that I can't get into my place when there's a car parked on the other side. It takes me four or five tries, and all that because you're encroaching. And then how am I supposed to get out without rubbing up against the car next door? I literally have to extricate myself. I want it out of there, Monsieur Rivière, right now."

To his astonishment, he saw tears in the eyes of this flinty, authoritarian woman.

But she went on staring at him, bristling and unyielding. It was he who turned away a little, rattled.

Could this be, that a tiny, unthinking act on his part had brought someone to the brink of tears?

Suddenly he was ashamed to have forced that woman to let him see her like this. He mumbled a few words of apology, then assured her the annoyance was temporary, since he'd sold the four-wheel drive.

"But you have to move it now, Monsieur Rivière, right now!"

"As a matter of fact, I was just on my way to work," he said, to put an end to this.

The dealership was located outside the city, on the Val d'Isère road, so heavily travelled by cars laden with luges and skis that a sort of bad taste lingered in Richard Rivière's mouth every evening.

It made him feel more exiled than ever, and different from his colleagues, not to mention from Clarisse, who'd been skiing since her earliest childhood, in a way that made him seem not just an outsider but a slightly lesser man.

He himself didn't care, but sometimes he thought it must be annoying and embarrassing for Clarisse, as if he were forcing her to put up with an infirmity he'd kept secret, something no-one could seriously consider a grave failing, perhaps even legitimate grounds for regular teasing, but nonetheless, admit it or not, one that might well end up undercutting the fragile foundations of a couple come together late in their lives.

"I so wish I could ski with you," Clarisse would sigh, melodramatically, to show she was joking.

And yet she did say it, he understood, because she couldn't hold in that regret, and if there was one realm in which he could never begin to rival her children's father, a real estate agent who in every other way wasn't much of a husband, whom Clarisse had left almost as soon as Trevor was born, it was knowing how to ski.

Sometimes, when she couldn't find anyone else, Clarisse invited her ex to go skiing with her. At this Richard Rivière felt only indifference.

He was simply unhappy for her, because he thought she must feel vaguely humiliated before her friends, before her ex, obliged to confess that she lived with a man who'd never strapped on a pair of skis in his life.

But she would say it without shame, he was sure, with that sweet, steadfast pride he so loved in her.

She was in the showroom, amid the cars, when he came in.

She was a saleswoman. She had a passion for her work, a way of ordering cars or dealing with sales contracts as if it were her calling, in return for which she asked neither salary nor thanks, but only the joy of knowing the customer was just as delighted as she was, and the other salespeople as well, for whom she was a staunch and sensitive colleague, never seeming to expect the same devotion from them, only wanting them to feel at home in her company, graciously making it clear that they could leave the heavy lifting to her, as well as the slightly exhausting late-afternoon displays of good cheer.

Less driven, Richard Rivière felt cynical next to her, slightly fraudulent, burned out.

He wasn't, he knew. He was methodical, prone to anxiousness, particularly since his move to Annecy, where he couldn't quite resign himself to the certainty that he'd never feel at home, where the fear of a mistake in figuring a customer's loan sometimes knotted his stomach, because what would then be questioned and judged, he thought, was not his competence but his very essence.

Clarisse came towards him with her broad, hearty smile, her warm, encouraging gaze, a reassuring sight for customers worried they might have blundered into a stupid misadventure when they walked through the dealership's door.

She was so helpful, so cordial, so naturally likeable that some of them hesitated to disappoint her by declining to commit to a purchase on the spot.

And sometimes, she'd noticed, not quite knowing why, they did their best to avoid her when they next came, to escape the barrage of an attentiveness so generous that it could be wearing, Richard Rivière had more than once thought, affectionately amused.

The showroom was empty so soon after lunch, only two salesmen chatting in one corner, hands in their pockets, swaying to and fro on their heels, their slacks' dark grey nylon stretched tight over their slightly ponderous rear ends.

Clarisse brushed his cheek with her lips. She wore high heels for work, making her face more or less level with his, small though she was.

As usual, he stared intently at her face, longer than he should in such everyday circumstances, a face he'd known for six or seven years.

And as always he hid his disappointment by murmuring whatever came to mind, always intended to please her in one way or another, for she must never know how let down he was, since it was in no way her fault.

"I sold the Cherokee, the guy didn't even bargain."

She raised one thumb in a victory sign.

She was plump, vital, her body an assemblage of firm curves. Her face was open and simple, unmysterious, but Richard Rivière was forever hoping another face might show behind it, a face he wouldn't know but would immediately recognise as the real face of Clarisse Rivière, not the one he'd been wed to for twenty-five years but the one he'd never managed to seek out and find, he thought, behind the impersonal, irreproachable, innocent woman he'd ended up leaving, too bored and frustrated to go on.

He knew what he was waiting for, that apparition on Clarisse's face, and he silently berated himself for his credulity and duplicity.

Because the face that she offered him, suspecting none of this, was nakedly trusting.

But he could not help himself, and he searched those features for some revelation: at long last, he desperately hoped, he would know who Clarisse Rivière had been.

The two women had nothing in common apart from their name, but the fact that this was the face of a Clarisse, that it was stamped and suffused with those very syllables, authorised him, quite logic-ally, he thought, by the rules of his own irrationality, not to lose hope that he might one day see Clarisse Rivière's real face showing through.

What that face would be he had no idea.

He knew only this: the sight of that face would instantly fill the great emptiness he had in him, amid a tangle of insipid material longings, petty terrors, annoyances.

He would feel less guilty, he would almost feel redeemed, if Clarisse Rivière's soul did him the mercy of showing him the face that he couldn't find before.

She would still be alive had he tried to reach her back then – but why had she striven so to stop him?

Why had she set out to make herself impossible to love, transformed herself into a figure without qualities, the image of a fleshless, evanescent, unbearable perfection?

From her intent, faintly questioning air, he sensed that Clarisse was saying something about Trevor.

He pretended to listen, nodded as a thought came to his mind and transfixed him with sorrow.

That Moliger, her killer, had he seen Clarisse Rivière's real face? Did he see it as he watched her die? Or before, when he lived with her?

"He'd be more likely to go if you took him," Clarisse was saying. "I think he's embarrassed to go to the doctor with his mother. That's the only reason he doesn't want to, I'm sure of it. And one of us has to be with him, you know how he is, he'll never tell us everything the doctor says if it makes him uncomfortable."

"A doctor?" he echoed.

"He's not in good health at all, not at all."

"He eats too much," he murmured, distant, bored.

"Oh, not that much, for his size and his age. Young people have to eat a lot, everybody knows that."

"He eats too much," he said again, now aware that he was annoying her but unwilling to promise to take Trevor anywhere. "Incidentally, I sold the Cherokee."

"I know, you just told me."

"Are you sure?"

"Of course I'm sure!"

Being an unaggressive, fundamentally generous woman, she chose to let the matter drop.

She gave a little laugh and patted his cheek, like a mother.

Her brown-dyed hair fell in waves around her full, opaque face, which was only itself, innocent and trustworthy.

And Richard Rivière was torn between the respect he owed that face and his yearning to see it fade away to reveal the other.

He spent the afternoon at his computer, studying the supply of available cars.

He regularly left his desk, when people came in and the salesmen were all busy, to keep the waiting customers company.

He offered them coffee, asked a few questions, affable, assiduous, informed, but his mind was not there, and without even knowing it he summoned up memories of the hundreds of times he had done this before, smile, ask questions, point the customer towards a sales-man, because he was thinking about none of that.

His thoughts jumped from subject to subject, freed of his control.

And, perhaps because he remembered resolving to call his daughter Ladivine, he thought of the Cagnacs, and an unpleasant feeling started to nag at him, something dark and jealous that he was not used to, that took him by surprise.

The Cagnacs were the only friends he'd made in Annecy.

They'd met at the dealership, five years before, and their Périgord roots had had far more to do with their pull on him than their quick, fuss-free decision to buy the most expensive car of the line.

The Cagnacs were in the restaurant business at the time, bored and wanting a change.

And Richard Rivière took them to that country he'd already visited alone several times.

He'd chosen it purely by chance, he told them sincerely, because at the time that's what he thought, as he was searching the Internet for a sunny holiday spot one night, and everything he found there enchanted him, and not a year had passed since that he didn't go back, and Clarisse never came with him, and never asked to.

And it occurred to him, since his friends the Cagnacs were looking for a new direction in life, to suggest that they open a dealership there.

He'd seen to getting them settled, doing far more than a new friendship demanded, with a zeal and a generosity that even left the Cagnacs a little wary.

But they soon realised he'd take no cut from their profits.

Richard Rivière knew he was too scrupulous, too honest, he had too much confidence in his own integrity, for their suspicions to last.

Saint-like, never seeking to defend or justify himself, his devotion never flagging, he held fast to the strange joy of setting the Cagnacs up in their business.

He visited them regularly, rejoicing in their success as if it were his own.

And yet, once he'd left them, once he was back on the plane to Annecy, he could not hold off a sense that the Cagnacs were not exactly letting him down, but neglecting some vital duty, which he couldn't define for sure, but which they should have grasped all the same, that they weren't repaying him for everything he'd done for them, and, in their disappointing insensitivity, did not know it.

What he wanted from them, he eventually confessed to himself, was an illumination.

About what? Oh, he didn't know, he didn't really want to know till the Cagnacs revealed all, both the subject of the illumination and the illumination itself.

But his friends' indifference to his obsession now gave rise to that touch of rancour when he thought of them.

He envied them, he wished he could live in the clearing at the end of the rugged road, in that beautiful, brand-new house, on the edge of the forest no-one ever ventured into.

He left the dealership an hour earlier than usual, claiming an important meeting.

The truth was that he wanted to call Ladivine without Clarisse around, not that she would have eavesdropped, not that she would have asked any questions about Ladivine's life, the two children, the German husband.

Such concern had her sons caused her, and still did cause her, so many reasons for sadness or melancholy had they given her that she seemed to have prudently opted to express no opinion and endanger no affection by any involvement in Richard Rivière's previous life.

She had thus learned of Clarisse Rivière's murder with the same fleeting horror, the same sombre, superficial sympathy she felt for any victim of the horrible things she read about in the papers.

She'd never met Ladivine, never spoke of wanting to, and not, he was sure, out of jealousy, because there was no-one less possessive than Clarisse.

She simply preferred, insofar as possible, to take no interest in the matter, to invest no sentimental capital in that relationship.

That was fine with Richard Rivière. Nevertheless, he did not like knowing she was in the next room when he talked with Ladivine.

She might call out to Trevor or laugh aloud at something funny on television, as she had last time, and Richard Rivière would be so unhappy that he'd want to slam down the phone.

Because it wasn't Clarisse Rivière laughing or calling out as he talked with their beloved daughter from their house in Langon, where they would have been happy, had he only found the way to let the real Clarisse Rivière appear, had he not, perhaps, frightened her off.

It was only Clarisse, a perfectly nice woman who didn't deserve to make him feel so disappointed.

Whom or what had he frightened away?

Before what mystery had he shown a lack of courage or depth?

He turned into his building's car park and found it impossible to park. The next car's tyres intruded so far into his slot that he would be trapped in his four-wheel drive, even if he did somehow insert it into such a cramped space.

He looked up at the windows, at once fearing and hoping he might see the bony face of the aged, baby-haired woman, no doubt watching for his return and now savouring her vengeance. Did he dare go up to her apartment, firmly ask her to please leave room for his car when she parked her own? A vague disgust held him back, a feeling that he couldn't take on such a trivial problem just before calling Ladivine. He drove out of the car park and down the street until he found a free space.

The mountain seemed to have eased its grip just a little, no longer pressing down on his back with all its terrible might, though his spine was still aching, and when he started towards the building he realised he was walking like an old man, shoulders hunched, head bowed.

Trevor wasn't there. He checked to be sure, opening the door to each room, even the little laundry at the far end of the kitchen, his weariness and heartache calmed by intense relief at being alone.

This was his home, picked out on his own and furnished to his own tastes, Clarisse and Trevor having moved in two years after he bought it, such that he always felt more as if he was putting them up than sharing the apartment with them.

But since moving back Trevor so rarely went out that Richard

Rivière could almost never come home without finding him there, and that got on his nerves.

He took off his business suit, put on a T-shirt and joggers, poured a glass of white wine.

He was so grateful to Trevor for not being there, as if the boy had done him an exceptionally kind favour, that he made a solemn vow to drive him to the doctor's, listen closely to what the doctor said, make it abundantly clear to Trevor, even ostentatiously clear if need be, that he cared.

He would help him lose weight, help him become once more the handsome, energetic boy he used to be – such would be his promise, as soon as Trevor came home.

As usual, his pleasure at being alone was slightly diminished by this vague, restless impatience to see Trevor again and make everything different, and the suspicion that everything would be just the same, the reality of Trevor's cold, mocking face yet again shattering the illusion that he could force the boy to let himself be loved.

Suddenly upset, he downed his wine in one go. Then he dialled his daughter Ladivine's number.

How long since he last called her? A year, a year and a half, more?

It was almost always on her initiative that they talked on the phone or met in a Paris café. "I'm coming down to see Mum," she would write to him now and then, in an e-mail telling of nothing more than the dismal or wonderfully mild weather they were having this year in Berlin.

I'll be in Paris myself, he would answer.

And Ladivine was convinced that he often had business in the capital, and he did nothing to suggest otherwise, though in truth he never set foot there save to see his daughter.

This was the only way they ever met. Leaving these reunions, he felt pathetic, unworthy.

He would gaze hungrily at the astonishing, adult, foreign face that was now Ladivine's, sometimes touched by the shadow of an expression that fleetingly summoned up the very distant, aching memory of a little girl now gone forever, and neither this young woman he vaguely resembled nor he himself as this surprising, autonomous person's father seemed in any way tangible.

They were the protagonists of a dream he was having in his Annecy bedroom, beneath the gaze of the hostile mountain, and when he woke his cheeks would be damp with tears because he would know none of this had existed, there'd never been a dark-eyed girl, he'd never had a child whose hand squeezed his own as they walked on the hill, behind a house by the vines.

He gazed hungrily at Ladivine's face, and it hurt him terribly: in a moment he'd wake up, the mountain would be snickering, he'd be lost and alone.

"Berger," said a little girl's serious voice.

"I'm sorry?" he said, caught off guard.

"*Sie sind bei der Familie Berger,*" she repeated, after a few seconds of silence.

He stammered:

"I'm sorry, I don't speak German. You must be, um . . ."

Unable to recall Ladivine's daughter's name, he let out an embarrassed little laugh. He didn't dare say who he was.

"*Ich verstehe kein französisch,*" she said curtly.

He heard the sound of a receiver being carelessly set down, then a brief conversation.

"Hello? This is Berger."

The accent, like the voice, was gentle and slightly sad.

"Hello, this is Richard Rivière, Ladivine's father."

"Oh."

The man seemed to come to life.

"Hello, hello, I'm very happy to . . . to hear you at last. It's not true, you know, what Annika said, she understands French, she speaks it very well."

"It's perfectly alright," Richard Rivière mumbled, since Berger seemed to be apologising for his daughter.

"It's just that she doesn't want to now."

Then he fell silent. Richard Rivière said nothing, unsure what to say, waiting for Berger to offer to put Ladivine on.

But a deep silence had settled in, peaceful, cosy, like the silence of a perfectly matched elderly couple, already well past the point where two people can pretend they find nothing odd in each other's muteness.

There was nothing to do, thought Richard Rivière, staring down the violet shadow-shrouded mountain through the kitchen window, but accept the awkwardness.

"How was your holiday?" he finally asked, feeling as if he'd come back from far, far away.

"Ladivine didn't come home with us."

"What do you mean? She stayed behind?"

"Yes," said Berger in a barely audible voice.

Richard Rivière himself didn't know if the cry that then burst from his lips was a cry of terror or joy or excitement, disbelief or eager affirmation of what he'd just learned. He understood only that concern had no part in it at all.

His legs went weak. He turned his back to the mountain, now fading into the darkness, and dropped onto a chair.

"But why?" he choked out.

"I don't know. She disappeared."

"Then how do you know she's still there?"

"I don't know anything," Berger slowly repeated, as if utterly drained. "That's what I think. That damned country swallowed her whole, you understand? You never should have suggested it."

"You met the Cagnacs?"

"Yes. That's where Ladivine disappeared, at their house."

"My God, oh my God!" cried Richard Rivière. "And they have no idea?"

"No. It wouldn't mean anything to them anyway. All they care about is selling their filthy cars."

Berger's tone was so desolate that Richard Rivière wanted to comfort him.

But, realising he'd forgotten this young man's name too, he dropped the idea.

The only name he could think of was Daniel, and he wasn't sure it had any connection to Ladivine's little family.

He fell silent again, pressing the telephone to his ear with all his strength as a hope full of terror and uncertainty rose up in him, and he found it at once exhilarating and shameful, because he couldn't be sure Ladivine had not freely chosen to bring him, Richard Rivière, who had so long sought his way in the dark, the possibility of an understanding.

But what if she never came back?

In truth, he thought no such thing. He had faith in the instinct that had led him to settle the Cagnacs in that clearing, to work for their success, to want them to stay there forever.

But if it was true that Ladivine could get at what for him had always stayed hidden, he couldn't be sure she was glad of that, that she hadn't felt forced or cajoled into it by her father's unspoken intentions.

What would she learn? What was there to learn? What was the place of Clarisse Rivière's will in all this?

"Are you still there?" Berger asked.

"Yes, yes," he whispered, starting, scarcely remembering who he was talking to.

"I've made a website, haveyouseenladivine.com. I've got a lot of responses, but so far nothing I can take seriously."

"It's no use. No-one will know."

He immediately regretted his blunt words, and, though impatient to hang up, added:

"Oh, maybe they will. We mustn't lose hope. Goodbye, Monsieur Berger."

"Call me Marko."

"Goodbye, Marko."

"Don't you want to talk to Daniel?" Berger almost shouted, desperate to keep him on the line. "He's not like Annika, he's willing to speak French."

But Richard Rivière was petrified at the thought of conversing with an unknown little boy.

"Goodbye, Marko," he said again, softly, and, as if to show Berger that the last thing he wanted was to be rude, he pressed the off button with a gentle, discreet finger.

Clarisse came home a few minutes later, with her slightly forced cheerfulness, her festive, overplayed, self-perpetuating enthusiasm, the work of Clarisse's good-hearted spirit, thought Richard Rivière, grateful even if he couldn't join in.

Because he could well imagine how hard it must be, after a long day at the dealership, to dig deep into oneself and draw out some semblance of joie de vivre just to keep everyone happy.

Clarisse had a special hatred of sullenness, of brooding silences heavy with vague resentments.

When the three of them were together she took care never to leave Trevor and Richard in the same room alone, fearing the emanations of spite and aversion she would feel spreading through the apartment, like toxic gas.

Sometimes Richard Rivière caught a helpless grimace on her still lips, when she turned away to open the refrigerator and, thinking no-one was watching, allowed her face to surrender to her real feelings, weariness, a longing to be alone, concern for Trevor and the two others, the twins she never heard from, who for all she knew might be dead or injured in a serious accident, no-one knowing whom to call.

Richard Rivière knew all that, felt indebted to Clarisse, because she was unbeatable, because she was never ashamed, because she always tried to do what was best.

He also knew he would never have dreamt of embarking on a love affair with this woman, his colleague since he first arrived in Annecy, were her name not Clarisse.

But that evening, in light of what Berger had told him, his irrational, enduring hope that Clarisse Rivière's marvellous face might one day show itself seemed pointless and sad.

Something much bigger had come to pass.

Since he had not been granted the power to do so himself, it was his daughter Ladivine who would travel through certain domains and return with a revelation that would finally bring peace to her tortured father.

How he loved her at that moment! How he wished those two could once again be together, Ladivine and Clarisse Rivière with her real face, and talk of him with the same love he felt for them!

He was a long way from Annecy, a long way from Clarisse and Trevor, at long last free of the mountain's baleful grip.

Through the window he looked at it, dark against the night sky, and his unburdened thoughts flew off far beyond it, his old foe frightened him no longer.

His one reunion with Clarisse Rivière, the day of his father's funeral, very nearly led him to abandon his life in Annecy, and the apartment he was outfitting with such anxious care, and Clarisse and the very young Trevor, who'd moved in just the year before, and his work, where he could do no wrong.

He had come close to giving all that up, and he trembled in retrospective terror all the way home.

Because the Clarisse Rivière he'd found waiting was in every way the one he'd realised he could not go on living with.

In her liquid gaze he saw only her usual abstraction, slightly heartless despite its show of deep kindliness, the same strange, ghostly presence that had troubled him more with each passing year.

She seemed to be there, with her delicate, sinuous body, her beautiful face, unlined, as if polished, satin-smooth, but her being was somewhere else, bound to something he couldn't understand, beyond his reach.

Clarisse Rivière was often awkward, shy beyond reason, unsure of herself – but that very diffidence had no depth to it.

Richard Rivière sometimes thought her a mere illusion of a human being, not wanting to be, perhaps not knowing she was – that he couldn't say.

But her actions that day were those of a love without rancour, entire and intact.

She threw herself into his arms, pressed against him with all her might.

He recognised the feel of the firm, serpentine body he once so loved.

And as he also recognised, unnerved, almost frightened, the emptiness in her vague and impersonal gaze, and something he could only call coldness, which made him stiffen in incomprehension and discomfort, he felt for the first time an overpowering desire to see the real Clarisse Rivière.

Because, he understood only now, this wasn't her.

He'd never seen or tried to see the real Clarisse Rivière, never realised or wanted to realise that he lived with her semblance alone.

And now it hit him, now he was ready to come back and live in Langon.

Might he also have heard, his ear now more acute, a muted appeal, a desperate plea from the very thing he didn't know?

But then they went to his mother's little flat in Toulouse, and that hateful old woman told them the repugnant story of the dog that supposedly devoured the elder Rivière, insinuating that it was all Richard's fault, like everything else that had gone wrong in the world since his birth.

It was always Richard's fault.

He felt wearied, sour, impatient, emotions he'd forgotten in Annecy.

Then, vaguely but with an aversion clear enough to keep him from going back to Clarisse Rivière, he remembered another dog, long, long before, when Ladivine was just a baby, he recalled Clarisse Rivière and his father very oddly coming together, against him in a way, he who at that moment lacked something, he didn't know what, that his father seemed to possess,.

Twenty-four hours after he'd shown the Cherokee to the man with the raspberry socks, Richard Rivière found the agreed-upon sum credited to his account.

He immediately called the buyer, invited him to come by that evening and pick up the car.

He paced lazily back and forth on the pavement as he waited, carefully studying his surroundings.

He felt watchful but calm, ready for anything.

No matter how Ladivine chose to reveal herself, he'd be prepared to accept her, and there was, he thought, nothing he could not now understand and say yes to.

The mountain was finally leaving him in peace.

He did not tell himself that he had beaten it, only that it had decided not to bother with him any longer, for there was a mightier force reigning over him now.

He was watching for his daughter's return, wherever she might be coming from.

In one way or another, she would be bringing Clarisse Rivière back to him.

He was surprised to feel so serene, so sure things would go his way.

He laughed to himself, thinking that should Ladivine send him some sign from the mountain, if it was there that she wanted to announce her presence, then he would go, he would climb, he would embrace those hated slopes. He would do even that.

A taxi stopped, and the man got out.

He was even more resplendent than two days before, though Richard Rivière noted something furtive in his gaze, then thought no more of it.

He did on the other hand look long and hard at the dark grey wool suit with pink pinstripes, the very pale pink shirt, the light grey tie and long, belted black coat, unbuttoned, hanging loose.

He gave Richard Rivière a brief, slightly clammy handshake, then quickly circled the car. Suddenly he stopped in the street, groaning in dismay.

"What's this? It's scratched!"

"Scratched?"

Richard Rivière came running to his side. The man pointed to a long scrape on the rear door.

"That wasn't there this morning," Richard stammered, reflexively looking around for someone who might be able to explain.

To his deep surprise, he felt tears welling up. He took off his glasses, looked around again, quickly wiped his eyes on his sleeve.

"Listen," he began, staring at an invisible point far beyond the man's face, and speaking in a professional tone that rang false to his own ears, "I can take it right now to the dealership where I work. It should be fixed by tomorrow."

"I can't stay in Annecy till tomorrow, there's no way! What have you got on you right now?"

"On me?"

"Give me whatever you can, I'll get it fixed myself."

Richard Rivière hurried, almost ran, back to his apartment and frantically rummaged under the bedroom closet's false bottom, where he kept a store of ready cash. He grabbed the bills, counted them quickly, clipped them together, and rushed out to the street.

"Will this do? . . . I have eight hundred and fifty euros."

The man gave him a taut, indignant smile.

Richard Rivière felt dishonoured, he didn't know what to do with the slightly trembling hand holding out the bills.

Finally the other man snatched them away and stuffed them into his overcoat pocket, grumbling.

He was as surprised as Clarisse to see Trevor so readily agree to be taken to the doctor, not that the boy had not met the proposal with his usual contempt, but Richard Rivière sensed that he no longer quite believed in the pertinence and the usefulness of his sarcasm, and fell back on it now only out of habit.

He shrugged, let out a resigned "Why not?"

And although, refusing to make any further concessions, he had dressed in the least flattering clothes his wardrobe had to offer, thereby expressing his disdain for the opinion of a doctor he'd never asked to see, Richard Rivière couldn't help feeling that Trevor had let down his guard, that he had in a sense tired of himself.

And so, taking note of that modest change, he refrained from commenting on the young man's grotesque get-up.

But it pained his heart.

He looked away when Trevor emerged from his room in a T-shirt that bulged over his belly and breasts, ornamented in large silvery letters with the English words I NEED A GIRL — CALL 0678986, and Hawaiian swimming trunks, and a sleeveless jeans jacket with a dirty fleece collar.

The thin black socks and beige tasselled loafers made his feet seem tiny beneath his gargantuan calves.

He looked like a mental case, Richard Rivière told himself, suddenly embarrassed by his own sympathy.

He couldn't help feeling sorry for Clarisse, who had done nothing, he thought, to deserve a son who looked like a pathetic madman.

But why did he suddenly find it so urgent to acquit himself of all his responsibilities, and more, to Clarisse and Trevor?

Who and what would be awaiting him if he left Annecy?

His certainty that Ladivine had gone off to demand explanations and would not fail to tell him what she'd found had little by little convinced him that Clarisse Rivière herself would be coming back to him, with her sinuous body, her face unchanged but the veil lifted from her gaze, her voice lively and musical — how flat was her old voice, how cautious, how droning!

And why should that be?

Why believe such a thing?

Clarisse Rivière would rise and return — but from among what dead, from amid what miracles?

To his dismay, he realised he could now conceive of no other solution, that his own wish to go on living was at stake.

308

If nothing happened, if Ladivine came back empty-handed, her heart cold, then nothing would ever matter to him again.

The mountain could pounce on his back, Trevor could grab him and have his way with him, he would put up no defence, he would lie back, close his eyes.

Had he not been awaiting just that for nine years, since he left the house in Langon?

And would he not be waiting still, in his empty Annecy existence, had Clarisse Rivière not been killed?

Because what explanation could he hope for, what real Clarisse could he hope to meet, if she were still living, withdrawn, hermetic, obscure, with that human wreck Moliger?

Trevor climbed into Clarisse's little car beside him, filling the closed, cramped space with his slightly musky odour, his loud breathing, his boredom.

And Richard Rivière realised he would feel guilty about Trevor if he went away, if he deserted Annecy without helping him somehow, unpleasant as Trevor was, and in spite of everything he'd put him through.

He remembered that Trevor had dropped the south-western accent after he brought up Moliger's trial, three days before.

"I have an idea for you," he said as he drove, staring straight ahead.

"Oh yeah?" Trevor said warily.

"After all, I did sell that four-wheel drive. I could help you get something going, a little software business. You could go back and study for a few months, get up to speed, and then the money from the car would be yours, to help you get started."

"You talk to Mum about this?"

"Not yet. But she'll be on board, and you know it."

Trevor acknowledged this with a grunt.

Glancing towards him, Richard Rivière found the young man serious, almost sombre, which he took to mean that he'd struck a nerve.

"Why would you do that?" Trevor asked in a hurried, clipped, gruff voice, as if he disapproved of the question but felt he had to ask so that everything would be clear.

Because I'm going away, and I want to leave you with a good memory of me, because I've never done anything more than the minimum for you, knowing you didn't like me, and so not much liking you either.

But he said no such thing.

Horrified to find himself blushing, he answered:

"After all this time, you're sort of my son, aren't you?"

Oh no, he wasn't, and he never would be.

How was it that even now he could not forget Trevor's many offences, or his own lack of love?

He felt only compassion and a need to do his duty, put his affairs in order and settle his debt, even if no-one but him thought he owed them anything, before he took off.

The vision of an abandoned Clarisse and Trevor tormented him.

He would simply say he was going back to Langon, back to the house, which was still up for sale.

Would Clarisse Rivière then come looking for him?

To take him where, into what frightful back ways?

In truth, he felt no fear, only burning desire and impatience.

Trevor grunted again, his forehead wrinkled, more sombre still. His left leg had started to twitch.

During their lunch hour that Monday, while eating in the kitchen with Clarisse, he got a call from the bank.

His bank manager informed him that to his deep regret the cheque he had deposited five days before had been refused as a forgery, and the credit to his account cancelled.

"There must be some mistake," said Richard Rivière. "I never deposited a cheque."

He smiled reassuringly at Clarisse as her brow furrowed in concern, but that smile was more for himself than for her, a dazzling forced smile that left his lips aching.

"A cheque for forty-seven thousand euros, deposited on the fourteenth of this month," the man replied, somewhat sharply. "It had your signature on the back, your account number."

"I don't understand."

He broke off and took a deep breath, all trace of his smile gone. Suddenly he found his own breath foul and repellent.

He turned his back to Clarisse and looked up at the mountain that had given up torturing him.

The midday sun was shining on the still-green slopes, suddenly reminding him of the landscape that came with an electric train he'd been given as a child, a little mountain covered in dark green felt overlooking a tiny chalet with doors and windows that opened.

How he had wished he could make himself small enough to get into that chalet and live there alone, undisturbed, far from his scolding parents, sheltered by that gentle springtime mountain!

"I sold a car privately, and the buyer paid by bank transfer, just as we'd arranged. I never deposited a cheque for that sale."

"You're absolutely certain it was a transfer?"

"I'm not, actually," Richard Rivière mumbled, trapped, now so worried that he could feel his strength draining away. "I saw the credit to my account, and since we'd agreed he'd be paying by transfer, I thought, obviously . . . And what about my signature, how could he have . . ."

"I assume you signed a contract. He must have copied it, it's not hard. I've heard of this happening before, you're not the first and you won't be the last," said the banker, as if to console Richard Rivière.

"What do I do now?"

He fleetingly remembered the desperation in Berger's last words on the telephone, his unspoken plea for Richard Rivière not to hang up just yet, hoping in vain for support or a few comforting words he could draw on when the phone call was over.

Now it was his turn to speak in that tone – oh God, oh God, he dully repeated to himself, and he saw the raspberry socks, the rippling overcoat, the lustrous, carefully styled brown hair.

The man had driven away in the four-wheel drive, gunning the engine, and Richard Rivière, standing on the pavement, had started to lift his hand in farewell, but his dishonoured, burning hand rose no higher than his shoulder.

And when the car turned the corner, the distant, indefinable memory of a similar scene flashed through his mind, disappearing before he could catch hold of it.

". . . file a complaint," the banker was saying, concluding a sentence that Richard Rivière hadn't listened to. "Goodbye, Monsieur Rivière."

Call me Richard, he wordlessly implored him, still pressing the phone to his ear after the other man had hung up.

He took the afternoon off to go to the police station, and when he walked into the apartment, hours later, so exhausted he thought he might faint in the hall, Trevor emerged from his room and announced that he had diabetes.

He'd just got the results of his blood tests via the Internet, and that's what was wrong with him, he blurted out, seeming at once anxious and strangely excited: type 2 diabetes.

FUCK YOU, YOU FUCKING FUCK, Richard Rivière read blankly on Trevor's green and black T-shirt.

Against a black background, the big green letters undulated like tall meadow grass on the boy's shifting flesh.

"Type 2 diabetes," Trevor repeated in a grave, pedantic voice.

FUCK YOU, YOU FUCKING FUCK.

Trevor bought these T-shirts with the money Clarisse earned.

Why did he seem so proud of himself for being ill? As if, forever failing tests, even the baccalauréat, twice, he could now tell himself he'd passed this one with flying colours?

Well aware of his cowardice, Richard Rivière realised this meant he could put off telling Trevor he'd lost the four-wheel drive money, thinking the lab results surely outweighed the swindle.

More than his own financial troubles, was it not the fear of letting Trevor down that had tied his stomach in knots as he waited in the police station?

Not to mention feeling like a pitiful failure, incapable of responding to Trevor's progress with anything but false promises, undone by his own idiocy.

Because this was all his fault, he never should have trusted that jittery, pushy, overdressed buyer.

And, sitting on a hard metal chair, head in his hands, he could think only of how to help Trevor make a new start all the same, relegating the money problems hanging over him to a future too uncertain to worry about.

He couldn't imagine how he might do it.

He owed the bank tens of thousands of euros as it was.

Well, he told himself, he'd just have to take out another loan.

So he'd be mired in debt – what did he care?

He laid an awkward hand on the boy's shoulder.

"We're going to get you the best possible care," he said stupidly.

A hint of a derisive smile grazed Trevor's lips, replaced at once by a thoughtful, diligent look.

"I've been reading up about it on the Internet. As a matter of fact I've got to get back to it now." And he lumbered quick as he could towards his room.

It seemed to Richard Rivière, who had almost never seen Trevor in the company of another person, that nothing had ever interested the boy like this diabetes business.

Clarisse burst into tears when Trevor told her the news.

He came running as soon as he heard the key in the lock, and, at once frightened and pleased with himself, beaming like a child who knows he has something big to divulge, he threw that word diabetes in her face, then took a demure half-step back, hands behind him.

Richard Rivière found them this way, Clarisse wiping her damp cheeks with one hand, Trevor shifting his weight from one leg to the other, basking, and what struck and saddened him was not only the helpless solitude, the ordinary, trivial sorrow of these two people of no particular note, but also that they seemed to expect nothing more from him, that, though not yet aware of it, they realised he no longer lived there, with them, if he ever had.

He wasn't worried that he had not yet heard from Ladivine.

A presage would have been nice, of course, even a simple hint that something was coming, and all day long, and at night in his dreams, he stood ready to open the way to any visit his daughter might pay him.

When he thought of her, he no longer pictured the young woman's face, now almost forgotten, but the guileless, quietly introspective face of the little girl. With numbing clarity, he remembered her hand in his as they went walking on the hill, even the feel of her skin, the mosquito bite on her thumb, his rough fingers absent-mindedly stroking it, which she liked.

Somewhere his beloved daughter, the child he once cherished, as he now remembered, was taking steps to flush out Clarisse Rivière – how grateful he was, and how aware that he had to welcome any form her reappearance might take!

He confessed to himself that he would rather Ladivine come back after the trial, the following month. The mere thought of it filled him with dread.

He couldn't help remembering that he had found a sort of escape from his grief, from the feeling of horror and then unreality that had filled him on learning of Clarisse Rivière's murder, in the many interviews he gave at the time, bewildered, faintly desperate, little understanding why anyone should ask his opinion of the murderer's personality, of that Freddy Moliger he knew nothing of, but offering it gladly, taking a strange pleasure in it, delighting in his role, his importance.

He'd read some of those interviews, and they made him ashamed.

Who on earth was that Richard Rivière, he'd wondered, competent, informed, speaking unguardedly of the depth of his pain?

Now he got up every morning with the trial on his mind, and he was horrified to think of his daughter Ladivine being there in person, and so he silently begged her to stay away, wherever she was hearing him from.

He'd hired a lawyer to represent them both, a certain Noroit, from Bordeaux, someone he felt comfortable with, finding nothing to intimidate him in that middle-aged man's dull, awkward appearance and plain polyester suits.

But if Ladivine were there with him, and if once again her presence gave him the painful impression that he could only have known her in his dreams, that her face meant nothing to him in real life, and that, no matter what he might think, he was therefore now dreaming, if that happened, as it always did, and he concluded that he would soon be waking up in his Annecy room, disoriented, desperately sad, how would he ever hold up till the end of the trial?

Wouldn't it be hard enough just to see Moliger, with that loser look he remembered from the photos, imagining that to this man, perhaps, Clarisse Rivière had shown her real face?

Because otherwise, he wondered, why would Clarisse Rivière have taken up with that creep?

It couldn't have been sex, he thought. He had the face of a drunkard, there was something repellent about him, something ignoble that he thought a sure cure for any sort of love.

She'd gone looking, he told himself, racked by a jealousy he'd never felt in his life, she'd gone looking for someone, anyone (preferably, perhaps, blind to what she was offering?) to reveal herself to.

Was that it? He wasn't sure of anything any longer.

All he knew was that he didn't want to see his daughter Ladivine in such circumstances.

He wanted to see her transformed, he thought, and enlightened about Clarisse Rivière, he wanted his heart to recognise her at once, without doubt or regret, never wondering if that woman was once the little girl whose hand he held, he wanted to see her and hear her say: I've brought Mama back to you.

He would not be afraid, he thought, of either one's new face.

LADIVINE SYLLA DRESSED AND GROOMED HERSELF WITH even more care than usual.

She oiled her hair, then pulled it back and bound it at her nape with an elastic band, tugging so vigorously that her scalp smarted, but she was long used to that, and scarcely noticed the pain.

Next she put on a tweed trouser suit she'd found for forty euros in a second-hand shop. She had chosen a dark red turtleneck to go with it, and her best pair of shoes, high-heeled ankle boots on which the trouser cuff broke ever so slightly, which she considered the height of elegance.

She went and said goodbye to her figurines, asking them to wish her luck. She clearly heard them answer, each in its own way, in its own distinctive voice.

"Luck with what?" asked the little gilded Buddha.

But she couldn't say, not quite knowing herself.

Luck one day entering her life suddenly seemed to her so absurd an idea that she nearly laughed out loud at herself. Did she even really want such a thing? Not likely. A stroke of luck now would be grounds for alarm, she thought, and it would feel like a punishment. What could be crueller than good things coming too late, when the worst possible thing had happened?

She went off to catch the tram on the quay, a thick, silty-smelling fog in the air. She did not quite know what she wanted for herself, but she knew exactly what she didn't, at any price: her words having some sort of influence.

The lawyer, that Bertin, had told her she had only to answer whatever she was asked with the utmost sincerity. She was not to try to work out what they wanted from her, nor even imagine they wanted anything in particular. In a sense, that was none of her business.

Ladivine Sylla did not believe a word of it, though she feigned absolute confidence in Bertin.

She was convinced there were things that he wanted her to say, and he'd called her as a witness in the hope or the certainty she would say them. That was his job. From what that Freddy Moliger had told him of Ladivine Sylla, Bertin thought her worth putting on the stand, and that was fine with her, Ladivine Sylla, but she wanted her words to carry no weight in anyone's mind, on one side or the other.

That was her only concern.

The rest, she told herself, she could handle. She'd long since stopped crying. Why should she break down there in front of all those people?

For two years she'd been buying figurines of young princes or damsels in tears, their necks bowed, their heads bent over their joined hands, and whenever she woke in the morning crushed by sadness she lined them up on the front row of her shelf, then sat down before them and stared at them for hours.

Finally she fell into the state she was seeking, between awareness and stupor, and the figurines seemed to be weeping for her, sharing in her pain, gazing on her with their suddenly living, damp, shining eyes.

In their porcelain pupils she saw her own dry, dead eyes reflected, and she felt better, and consoling words came to her lips, which she

318

murmured to her poor figurines, nearly reaching out to dry off their tear-streaked cheeks.

But no-one had ever come to console her, no-one had ever dried her tears with a tender hand, in those early days when she wept and wept for Malinka. That's how life was for her.

The one person she thought of when her need for solace grew so overpowering that her figurines' good wishes were no longer enough was that Freddy Moliger. Had she dared, she would surely have paid a call on that Moliger in his prison, and she had no doubt that her sorrow would have been lightened.

She got off the tram near the courthouse, walked with some difficulty in her high heels to the foot of the stone steps.

She felt tall, slender and very old, she thought her face must be like the face of her dear little Saxony porcelain shepherdess, smooth and old, thin, slightly vacant. Her scalp stung, which was good, because it made her feel alive, sharp, not dulled and lost, as she usually did since Malinka's death.

A dog was watching her from the other side of the street.

Afraid of cats and suspicious of dogs, Ladivine Sylla deliberately looked away, not wanting to attract it.

But she did once more glance its way. It was a big brown dog, scrawny and shivering in the damp air.

A memory of Malinka surfaced in her mind, the child's face looking up at Ladivine Sylla when she came home from work, in that tiny house at the far end of a courtyard, and herself trembling in gentle, grave astonishment when the girl's pale eyes met her own.

Where had she come from, that child with sand-coloured eyes and straight hair but a face so like her own? And that dog, where did it come from, its dark gaze inexplicably calling Malinka to mind?

She understood that it meant her no harm, and she briefly turned back towards it, breathless.

An old image of herself came to mind, as far as could be from the little shepherdess's cold face. She saw herself at a time when she was full of fury and hate, when her face was clenched around her pinched lips, her little quivering nose. Her anger at Malinka had become a rage at the spell that was gripping them both, and then even that had waned, replaced by a sad resignation.

But, in that angry time, she would sometimes wake in the morning and feel as if she'd been running all night. Her thigh muscles ached, her nostrils were red from breathing in drizzle or mist. Over what plains had she raced, over what meadows blew that wind whose grassy scent she thought she could still smell on the down of her arms? She longed to go back to that place where the wind had whistled in her ears, where the dry, packed ground had sustained her enchanted sprint, where the light, perfumed air had swept off her anger.

Because those mornings found her weary but freed of the impotent rage that was sapping her. Gradually it came back, but less virulent – exhausted from trying to maintain itself in those nocturnal sprints, of which Ladivine Sylla remembered nothing, except, now and then, a sensation of trickling warmth on her back, like flowing sweat on bare skin.

She turned away from the dog and started up the steps.

How old she'd become! Who would look after her when she was still frailer, who would lower her eyelids when she was dead, who would know she'd just died? Would Malinka? And that dog on the other pavement? What messenger would she have to announce her death? Who would care?

That Freddy Moliger might be sad. He alone would still sometimes think of her.

*

After a two-hour wait in a little room whose dingy corners and crannies Ladivine Sylla inspected with a critical eye, to pass the time (so experienced was she in removing all manner of stains that she could see just what the cleaning lady would have needed – bleach, the right sponge, thirty minutes more – to erase the shoeprints from the tile floor, the marks left by the chair backs on the painted wall), she was finally ushered into the courtroom.

She studied the ground at her feet, suddenly troubled by a pressure in her ears, as if she'd too quickly dived to a very great depth.

She made out a hum of voices and movements around her, and the room seemed enormous and packed. A roaring filled her ears, she staggered on her high heels. Someone caught her by the elbow and asked, she thought she made out, if she was alright.

"Yes, yes," she mumbled, embarrassed.

Nonetheless, the person kept a grip on her until she reached the stand, where Ladivine Sylla grasped the rail in relief.

Then she dared to look up, and found only friendly, attentive gazes.

She wondered if she should turn her head to look for that Freddy Moliger, then decided against it, vaguely afraid that this act might have the same force as speech, and remembering that she wanted nothing she said to have any meaning beyond what she hoped was the perfectly neutral sense of each word.

She gave them her name, as they'd asked. Then, when they asked her to verify that she was Clarisse Rivière's mother, and although she'd tried hard to get used to the name Malinka had chosen, an old pride flickered to life, and she couldn't help correcting:

"My daughter's name was Malinka."

The lawyer she'd met with, the one who introduced himself as Bertin, representing that Freddy Moliger, asked if she'd ever met his client.

"Yes," she answered.

He asked if she enjoyed that Freddy Moliger's company.

"Yes," she answered.

He asked if she'd even felt some affection for him.

"Yes," she answered.

He asked if her daughter Malinka seemed happy with that Freddy Moliger.

"Yes," she answered.

It took her a few seconds to grasp why her mind was desperately summoning up the image of her weeping figurines, and how they might help her now. Were they not called to suffer in her stead?

She swallowed, once again heard a dim, piercing plaint deep inside her ears.

Her figurines were meant to do the weeping, a frantic little voice was saying over and over in her head, so her own eyes would stay dry and no-one would know what she was going through. A thousand needles pricked her lower eyelids. She squeezed the rail with all her might, almost resigned, in her exhaustion, to let all her misery spill out.

But as it happened they had no further questions.

LADIVINE SYLLA REMEMBERED CATCHING A GLIMPSE OF THAT man's face as she turned on her heels to walk out of the courtroom.

The anguish she'd read on his features, the dumbstruck stare he fixed on her without seeming to see her, as if, through her skin and her flesh, through her old porcelain-shepherdess face, he was probing a mystery that brought him no joy, all that made her think, curious and apprehensive, that she'd be seeing him again.

And now he'd knocked at her door, now she'd offered him the velvet armchair that was Malinka's favourite, which she could no longer bring herself to use, now they were sitting face to face, without awkwardness, in no hurry to speak, knowing that what had to be said would be said, and perhaps, thought Ladivine Sylla, reflecting that there was no real need to say anything.

She needed only to know that he was Richard Rivière. Anything he might say to her of Malinka seemed beside the point now.

But she doubted, from his questioning, feverish air, bent forward in his chair and studying her, Ladivine Sylla, as if his searching gaze would eventually distract or wear down whatever it was in her that was refusing him, she doubted that he felt the same.

To put him at his ease, she'd sat down, their knees almost touching.

A pale winter light filtered into the cluttered little room. She offered him a cup of coffee, and he accepted reflexively, not even understanding what she was saying, she sensed, merely guessing that it was an offer of that kind.

And she could hear the water gurgling through the machine in her kitchen, she could hear it and look forward to the good coffee they'd soon be drinking, whereas Richard Rivière, absorbed in his quest or his wait, heard nothing, saw nothing, and never dropped that perfervid air, which she was almost tempted to mock, gently, so he would relax.

But no, that wouldn't relax him at all. He might, she told herself, even see it as an answer.

And then Ladivine Sylla was taken by surprise, whether because she was paying too close and too proud an attention to her burbling coffee maker or because she was having too much fun picturing the look on Richard Rivière's face if she began poking fun at him, and she heard the scratching at the door even as she realised it must have been going on for several seconds already.

She knew at once who it was. She jumped up, startling Richard Rivière.

"It's the dog," she whispered.

"The dog?"

He looked towards the door, lost. The scratching had stopped. The dog was patiently waiting, knowing it had been heard, thought Ladivine Sylla.

"You didn't see it in front of the courthouse?"

"No, I didn't see anything," Richard Rivière stammered.

Ladivine Sylla gently opened the door, and the big brown dog padded in on its thin, trembling legs.

She stroked the coarse fur between its small, upright ears, and the dog turned to look at her with its knowing eyes, its chaste eyes.

She felt a dizzying rush of happiness.

She was sure it had come here to tell them everything it knew, that it had endured many torments and exhaustions for no other purpose.

It was bringing Malinka's throbbing heart back to them, and maybe too, she thought in the ardour of her joy, the promise of a new light cast over each and every day.

MARIE NDIAYE was born in Pithiviers, France, in 1967 and studied linguistics at the Sorbonne. She started writing when she was twelve or thirteen years old and was only eighteen when her first work was published. She won the Prix Femina for *Rosie Carpe* in 2001, the Prix Goncourt in 2009 for *Three Strong Women*, and in 2015 she was awarded the Nelly Sachs Prize for outstanding literary contributions to the promotion of understanding between peoples, and the Gold Medal for the Arts from the Kennedy Center International Committee on the Arts. In 2007, after the election of Nicolas Sarkozy, NDiaye left France with her family to live in Berlin.

JORDAN STUMP is a professor of French at the University of Nebraska-Lincoln. He has translated many authors from the French including Marie Redonnet, Eric Chevillard, and Honoré de Balzac. His translation of *Jardin des Plantes* by Claude Simon won the 2001 French-American Foundation translation prize, and he was named a Chevalier de l'Ordre des Arts et des Lettres in 2006.